A *Swell* TO REMEMBER

E.R. JENSEN

Editing by Pam Elise Harris.

Copyedit/Proof reading by Madison Schutlz.

Cover photo and design by The Furious Fotog.

Interior images by Therena Carlin.

Interior Design by E.R. Jensen

Chapter 1: Kelsey

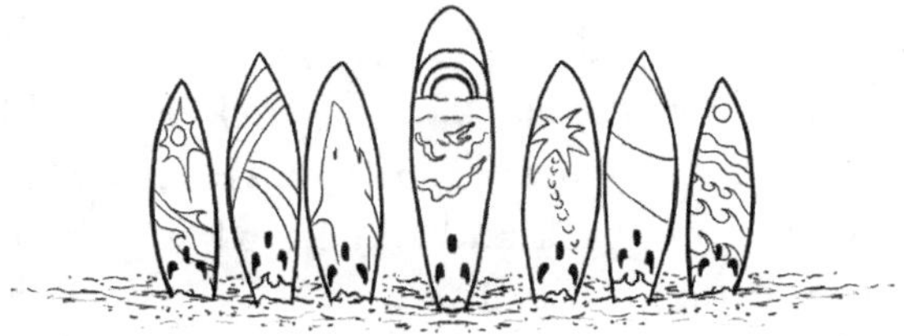

Saturday, September 7

I couldn't help but smile as I approached the charming and incredibly handsome red-haired Brit waiting for me at the small table in Toucan's, a bar the Santa Barbara locals favored. He had consumed my thoughts for the better part of the past forty-eight hours. Though we had initially agreed that it was *only* a weekend fling, nothing more than two people on vacation who would return to their lives and forget what happened, I wondered if there was anything I could do that would convince him to stay.

Feeling bold, I walked right up to him and gave him a kiss, then slid my hand into his and tugged. "Let's dance," I urged.

Conner chuckled and gave my hand a light squeeze, then followed me onto the dance floor. To my chagrin, before we had a chance to find an open spot, the song changed to a slow one. Deciding it would be the prime opportunity to chat, I placed my hands on his shoulders. Conner set his lightly on my waist, and we swayed slowly to the music.

"I'm sorry I disappeared this morning. I didn't want to get between you and whoever had showed up," I said.

"Don't worry about it," Conner replied. I opened my lips to say something, but he kissed me before I could. Shivers ran down my spine and I lost myself in the kiss; the words I had hoped to say vanished.

The band switched to a faster song, and I decided we'd have time later to talk. Right now I wanted to enjoy this evening with Conner, wherever it would lead.

I caught a glimpse of the clock on the back wall and had to do a double take when I saw it said one a.m. Conner ran his hands across the small of my back and I knew what I wanted to do. "Come home with me?" I asked.

"I'd love to," Conner replied and kissed me, pulling our bodies tighter together. His cock bumped against my thigh and a low hiss escaped my lips as my panties dampened.

We returned to the table so I could collect my purse and then I led the way out to my faded blue Prius.

Easing out of the parking lot, I was grateful that Toucan's was only a few minutes from Abuela's house.

The light turned yellow, and I stopped at the intersection opposite the gas station. It was far too late to assume that anyone else on the road would be thinking straight. The gas station's lights flickered. The signal turned green and I put my foot on the gas pedal. I was surprised when the engine made a loud noise but we didn't move. As I reached for my hazards, the car suddenly shot forward, then jerked to a stop. I growled under my breath.

Conner teased, "This might be a sign that you need a new car."

I stuck my tongue out at him. "I'm sure it's fine." He gave me a light kiss on the cheek.

We were almost through the intersection when out of the corner of my eye I saw a large truck barreling toward us. My whole body went rigid and I stomped on the gas pedal. "Go!" I whisper-shouted at my car. Except it wouldn't go any faster. My foot was to the floor and we were moving barely five miles per hour.

Terror flooded me. I laid my hand on my horn, praying the driver would notice I could not get out of the way. I didn't even have time to get out of the car.

Conner wrapped his arms around me—except they didn't feel like arms; they felt soft, like feathers—and then pain exploded through me.

Chapter 2: Kelsey

Thursday, September 5

Two days earlier

Closing my eyes and taking a deep breath, I listened to the soft beeping of the monitors and ran through the entire procedure in my mind, making sure I hadn't forgotten any critical steps. When I was done, I opened my eyes and stepped back from the patient. "That's a wrap," I said with a smile to the group of nurses and the anesthesiologist on my team for the appendectomy on Harry, an eleven-year-old boy. The procedure had been textbook. All that was left to do now was clean up and go talk to his parents.

Exiting the surgical suite, I tossed my white surgical gown in the trash. I washed my hands, then I grabbed the clipboard with the notes and headed toward the waiting room. Harry's parents were waiting nervously, and they both jumped out of their chairs when I walked through the doors.

"How is he?" Harry's mom asked. They had been up all night, from when Harry had woken them up around two a.m., through their lengthy ER wait, to the case being assigned to me. She had shadows under her eyes, and her auburn hair had mostly escaped from its braid.

I gave them a reassuring smile. "The surgery went well. He is in the recovery room. As soon as he wakes up, a nurse will come get you."

Harry's mom threw herself at me, and I hugged her awkwardly. "Thank you, Dr. Floras."

When she released me, I shook Harry's dad's hand. "You're welcome. They'll come for you soon," I said, then departed.

The appendectomy marked the last day of the first half of my pediatric surgical fellowship at Los Angeles Children's Hospital. After completing my surgical residency and board exam, I had applied and been accepted to the fellowship to become a pediatric surgeon, which required specialty training. Appendectomies were straightforward procedures whether they were in a child or an adult, and Dr. Pierce had allowed me to do those solo within the first month of my fellowship. However, many of our cases were complex, and quite a few I'd never even experienced in adults during my residency. As I learned the nuances of treating pediatric patients, Dr. Pierce began allowing me to do additional solo procedures.

I kept my steps measured until I was through the door and out of sight. Then, my pace quickened, and I couldn't help but grin. I was going home for three weeks. *Nothing but the ocean and my surfboard*, I promised myself.

My last stop before I could leave was the nurses' workstation—the bustling central hub for the pediatric surgery department. A large screen on the back wall had a list of patients and surgeries that would update as statuses changed. As many as six nurses could sit behind the counter at one time, though usually there were only two or three. It was the domain of Ronda Fitzpatrick, the charge nurse. Ronda had immigrated from Guatemala with her parents when she was five and had grown up in Los Angeles. Over my twelve months in the residency program, I had learned that her husband, Mr. Fitzpatrick, had recognized her love for helping people and had supported her education through nursing school. She was also fluent in Spanish and at times made me almost feel like I was home with Abuela. I leaned over the counter, offering my clipboard with the surgery protocol to Ronda on the other side. Ronda ran the department with an iron fist for the doctors and a smile for the patients.

"Here you go," I said.

"All done, Dr. Floras?" asked Ronda, smiling at me.

I grinned excitedly. "Yes!"

"How long are you going to be gone for?" Ronda teased. She knew very well how long my trip was.

"Three weeks. Ronda, don't let Dr. Pierce go too crazy while I'm gone," I replied.

"I'll do my best. But you better go before he finds some reason to keep you!" Ronda said with a laugh.

Knowing that she was right—there had been several times I'd been on my way out the door for my day off and Dr. Pierce, the head of the pediatric surgery department and my boss, had given me a task or even another surgery—I waved at Ronda, then headed for the staff locker room to collect my things.

There were times when I regretted the trade I'd made when I accepted the two-year pediatric surgery fellowship. Instead of a traditional paid time off schedule with the big holidays off, I had offered to work those in exchange for a continuous three full weeks of vacation over the summer to break up the two years of the fellowship. Since I was single and never had holiday plans, it was a good trade. I'd get enough time to have a real vacation at Abuela's in Santa Barbara with plenty of time to surf and relax.

When I had decided to accept the fellowship at the Los Angeles Children's Hospital, I had been apprehensive about having to live in Los Angeles itself and dealing with the amount of people and traffic. Over the past year, though, I'd found that I spent so many hours in the hospital that I hadn't had time to form an opinion about the city. My apartment was two miles from the hospital, and I ran it every single day, rain or shine. The traffic *was* horrendous, but I rarely had to drive in it. The grocery store was a block from the apartment—one of the other reasons I had chosen it.

Pushing the locker room door open, I caught a glimpse of myself in the full-length mirror just inside the door: neon-purple scrubs, stethoscope around my neck, hair hidden under a scrub cap decorated with surfing cats. I stopped short when I saw Dr. Nina West, her inky-black hair in a severe bun and her doctor's coat and purple scrubs as immaculate as ever, leaning against my locker as though waiting for me. Her almond-shaped black eyes, which to me always felt cold and distant, were watching me in a far friendlier manner than I'd previously experienced. In two weeks, Nina would be done with her pediatric surgery fellowship. I wasn't sorry to see Nina go. We did not get along very well. She was abrasive and always wanted to be right, even when there were numerous ways to approach a case. I was surprised that a person who didn't like children wanted a career that revolved around them.

"Hi, Nina," I said, taking a step toward my locker, hoping she would move out of the way and not make our encounter awkward.

"Kelsey. I just wanted to say good luck. I hope you have a lovely vacation and enjoy the rest of your fellowship. I'm heading back to New York and am not sure if our paths will cross in the future." Nina held out her hand.

I took it, giving Nina's hand a solid shake. When our hands released, Nina stepped away from my locker and headed deeper into the room. *How odd*, I thought. Our relationship had been strange from the beginning. I had taken my California general surgical board exam before I began the fellowship, which meant legally I was a fully licensed and practicing general surgeon. Nina had not taken the board exam. So, although Nina was my senior in the fellowship, I was assigned surgeries that Nina had been denied based on hospital liability policies.

My choice to take the board exams before starting the fellowship was based on my intention to stay in California once I completed my fellowship. Abuela was not as young as she used to be, and I wanted to be close enough to visit more than once a year.

I opened my locker, recalling that conversation.

"Abuela, I want to move back to California permanently. To be closer to you," I had said passionately.

Abuela tsked at me over the phone. "Closer to surfing, you mean."

I gasped in shock. "No!"

Abuela began cackling. "Fine, closer to Joel and surfing."

I rolled my eyes at the mention of Joel. Abuela had always hoped we would get married one day, no matter how many times I tried to explain we were just good friends and nothing more.

"She was right," I muttered to myself. "I did want to be closer to home so I could go surfing."

After grabbing my purse and keys out of the locker, I shut it, then did one last glance around the locker room. *Three weeks.*

I went over the contents of my suitcases one last time, zipped them up, and then carried them down the three flights of stairs and into the parking garage for my apartment complex. I slid into the worn gray driver's seat in the Prius and realized as I set my water bottle in the cup holder that my hands were shaking slightly. I rolled my eyes at myself. There was no reason to be nervous about going home. The worst thing that could happen would be running into my childhood friends—Joel, Penny, and Lane. We had all grown up within two blocks of each other in Abuela's neighborhood, though Penny was the only one I spoke to on a regular basis after moving away for medical school.

Sipping the cool water, I gave myself a moment to settle before driving out of the parking lot and into the chaotic Los Angeles traffic. Forty-five minutes later, I finally made it onto the 101 freeway, and traffic lightened up. As I passed palm trees, shopping centers, and subdivisions, my thoughts drifted to Joel.

We were best friends and had lived next door to each other until middle school, when Joel's parents sold their house on Paloma Street and had bought one in a newer neighborhood ten minutes away. Until I left for medical school on the East Coast, I couldn't remember a time when we didn't see each other at least a few times a week, if not every day. Abuela and Joel's Nanna Vivian were best friends. Their families lived next to each other in their small village in Colombia and had immigrated to the United States at the same time. They saw to it from the day we were born—two hours apart—that we spent as much time together as possible.

Our senior year of high school, our lifelong friendship became romantic. We were named prom king and queen and dated through undergrad at Cal Poly San Luis Obispo. When I accepted a full scholarship to Johns Hopkins for medical school, we had decided that a long-distance relationship with my nonexistent free time wouldn't make sense. We ended it on friendly terms and did our best to stay in contact over the past nine years. Which, now that I thought about it, had resulted in virtually no contact. Even on my visits to Santa Barbara, we had failed to cross paths due to his hectic work schedule.

While Joel had supported my passion for medicine, he had chosen a completely different path for himself. He got his bachelor's in architectural engineering and stayed at Cal Poly for a master's in city and regional planning. While I was off on the East Coast working my way through medical school and surgical residency, Joel was hired by the City of Santa Barbara in their city planning and development department and was now a project manager.

It would be nice to see Joel, I thought as the freeway began to curve to the left, indicating I was approaching Santa Barbara. What I didn't want was to give Joel any wrong ideas. This trip was a chance to relax and lose myself in the joy of surfing. Once my fellowship was over, then I'd have more time and mental capacity to figure out when I could have a relationship with Joel—or any other man. Until then, I would focus on completing my education.

Thanks to the ridiculous amount of traffic I encountered, the two-hour drive to Santa Barbara took me four, but I finally made it. Turning onto Paloma Street, I couldn't help but smile as I drove by a neat row of houses—blue, gray, yellow, light pink—and then finally Abuela's house, pale green with white trim and a white picket fence around the front yard. I went around the back into the alleyway and parked next to Abuela's ancient and giant maroon Packard that was in pristine condition.

I walked up to the hunter-green back door and unlocked it. As soon as I stepped into the house, Abuela came over and gave me a big hug. She was petite, barely five feet tall, with white hair cascading loosely around her shoulders, and wearing a bright orange blouse and tan Bermuda shorts. She looked just as she had on my last visit.

"Nieta," she whispered. "Let me guess." Abuela smiled. "You are going to unload everything, put that hideous rack on your roof, and go out surfing."

I smiled. "You know me too well, Abuela."

"Let me feed you before you go out at least?" Abuela offered.

I nodded and watched for a moment as Abuela walked toward the kitchen. For all of my life that I could remember, it had been the two of us. I was the sole survivor of the car accident in Los Angeles that took my parents' lives when I was barely three years old, and Abuela had raised me herself. I returned to the car and carried my two suitcases inside while she prepared lunch.

After depositing the suitcases in my bedroom, I meandered toward the kitchen, fondly tracing the stenciled peacock feathers we'd added to the wall when I was ten. Halfway down the hallway, the feathers gave way to a freehand painting I had done when I was seventeen of Abuela and me on the beach.

Abuela was waiting for me with sandwiches on a plate when I reached the kitchen. I took the plate, sitting at the table across from her.

"Thank you," I said with a smile.

She beamed. "You're welcome, Nieta. Now eat and tell me your plans."

I ate a few bites of the sandwich before the words came spilling out. "Surfing is my only plan for the next three weeks."

Abuela chuckled. "What about your friends? I'm sure they'd like to see you."

I shrugged. I had deliberately not told anyone I was coming for this trip, though Abuela's words had me wondering who she had told. Either way, if my friends wanted to see me, it would have to be on the ocean. "They know where to find me if they want to see me."

"You have to eat and sleep too, you know," Abuela chided.

"Yes, and I promise I will eat and sleep," I said sincerely.

Abuela nodded, seemingly satisfied with my answer. "Good. You look tired. Maybe I should come down there and tell Dr. Pierce he's not letting you sleep enough."

My eyes widened and I gasped. "You wouldn't!" I said, not sure if she was joking.

Abuela grinned, her white teeth bright against her dark skin. "I've thought about it. But you're right. I won't—for now."

I patted her hand. "I know to you it might seem like I'm tired, but I promise it's worth it. The things I'm learning, Abuela. Los Angeles Children's Hospital is exactly where I need to be to fulfill my dream, and I'm so close. Three weeks and twelve more months!"

"I am so proud of you, Nieta. Your parents would be too." Abuela's voice dropped low, and I knew she missed them terribly. My mother—her daughter, Carolina—and my father, Mateo, who was her best friend's son, had been an integral part of her life for forty years until their untimely accident.

Pressing my lips together, I nodded solemnly. The food was solidifying in my stomach. I stood up and took my plate to the sink to wash it, needing the distraction. When I was done, I turned to Abuela. She was still sitting at the table, finishing her sandwich. "I'm going to go surfing."

"I didn't mean to upset you ..." Abuela started.

I shook my head. "You didn't. I'm fine. But I have been looking forward to getting in the ocean for weeks, and I can catch the afternoon high tide if I go soon."

Abuela nodded. "Okay. I will see you later."

I put the dried plate back into the cabinet and headed to my bedroom to change into my swimsuit and collect what I needed to surf.

The crashing waves, salty air, and cry of the gulls were all things that I knew I would miss terribly when I went back to finish the fellowship. But becoming a pediatric surgeon had been a dream of mine from a very young age, a dream I had fought tooth and nail for.

Snatching my surfboard out of the sand, I waded into the frothy dark blue ocean. It was easy to pick out the locals from the vacationers who were trying surfing but really had no clue. For starters, most of the locals preferred surfing without a wetsuit. Although the water in Santa Barbara wasn't as warm as some beaches on the Gulf Coast, it was a significant improvement from the frigid Oregon Coast.

I smiled as the salt water hit my legs. Long ago, I had learned the hard lesson of the risks of surfing in a two-piece swimsuit—a lesson I remembered all too well. Penny had talked me into buying a pretty pink bikini. I went surfing in it and misjudged a wave and tumbled. The bikini top had untied and come off completely. The only thing that had saved me from embarrassment was that it had been early enough in the morning that no one else was around to witness my topless dash back to my towel. But just because I surfed in a one-piece, that didn't mean it had to be ugly. Today I wore a black-and-white snakeskin print with high legs and a cutout back.

I focused my attention on the task at hand, paddling out to where some other surfers were waiting for a good wave. The angle the sun was hitting the water made it impossible to tell who they were.

"I was beginning to wonder if you were even going to show up today," Joel called to me. I sighed; apparently Abuela *had* informed my friends—or at least Joel—of my impending arrival. His dark brown hair looked as though he'd been running his hands through it. It stuck out every which way.

Not wanting to be rude or clue Joel in that I had been hoping to avoid him on this trip, I responded, "I left the hospital on time. It was the traffic that took forever."

"Well, you get to enjoy no traffic for the next three weeks," Joel reminded me, confirming my suspicion that Abuela *had* told my friends about the trip.

"Precisely why I came," I replied.

"You didn't come to see me?" Joel asked, sticking his lower lip out in a pout.

I was close enough to him that I reached over and poked him in the side.

Joel laughed. "You know that never works on me."

I stuck my tongue out at him.

"It was worth trying," I replied.

"Hey, you two! Are you planning on surfing?" demanded Lane. He was about ten feet away from us and gesturing at the wave. Not waiting for our response, Lane paddled toward it. I didn't want to miss out on what looked like a great wave and quickly followed him, with Joel matching me stroke for stroke.

One, two ... and up I went, balanced on my surfboard. I let out a whoop of excitement as I expertly guided my board on the wave and to my surprise found I was the last one up.

Lowering myself back onto the board before I got beached, I

turned around and paddled into the surf. I wasn't quite sure where Joel went, but there was a redheaded guy, one whom I hadn't seen before, heading back out with me. Out of the corner of my eye, I inspected him. He seemed normal height, a clear eight-pack of abs, well-shaped ass—and as my inspection drifted to his face, I realized he was watching me. Blushing, I turned my face away and adjusted my course to the left—farther away from whoever this new guy was.

Lane and Joel were waving to me, and I sped up. I could see another wave starting to form, and I didn't want to miss out because the newcomer distracted me.

Chapter 3: Conner

Thursday, September 5

The hour before dawn, I perched on the highest part of the roof of my house in Malibu. A light breeze ruffled the pearly white feathers on my outspread wings. Any passersby on the beach below who might look up toward the house would see nothing but the roof and sky. As an angel sworn to serve the Archangel Cassiel, who also happened to be my father, the only time a human or demon could see me was if I wanted them to.

There were times when I loved my job. Ensuring hospitals that were run by demons followed the rules when treating humans was exhilarating and gave me renewed purpose. Yet there were other times where Cassiel wanted things his way, and it was tiring to constantly have to explain why finesse was a better tool in many situations than a sledgehammer.

For the past week, we had been butting heads over a contract with the Los Angeles Children's Hospital board, and I had finally had to put my foot down, wanting space to clear my mind. I had learned over the years that if Cassiel and I were at odds, the demons could almost always sense it, and the deal either wouldn't go through, or the terms would not be favorable.

I had decided to take a few days for myself and head to Santa Barbara. Because my human cover was that I was a high-profile billionaire, it was difficult to go out in public without the media catching wind. My house in England was the ideal location to hide in, but I wanted to challenge myself with a feat that was difficult to achieve at this point in my life. A few years back, I discovered surfing, and the beaches in Santa Barbara were a short two hours away and would allow me to maintain my anonymity.

The other challenge with being an immortal angel was that only select individuals on my staff knew, and I had to keep up the billionaire façade. For the most part, that meant I got to spend ridiculous amounts of money on cool toys. I could fly or use my magic to get to Santa Barbara, but I also owned a helicopter.

To be convincing as Conner Hudson, I would fly the helicopter to the small private airport in Santa Barbara and then transfer to the old truck that came with the house rental. No one would ask questions that they didn't know the answer to.

I sat in the passenger seat of the helicopter, hoping that my plan would work and Cassiel *and* the press would stay out of my hair for four days. Fabio, my executive assistant extraordinaire, had seen to every detail, including those that, according to Fabio, would be noticed by humans if they were omitted but were inconsequential to me.

My phone rang. I grimaced as I realized I had not shut it off before I got on the helicopter. It was tempting to just ignore it. The screen flashed, and I saw it was my sister Charlotte calling. My lips twitched. When Charlie called, it could be about almost anything, especially when she chose to use a phone. Even over extreme distances, we could communicate telepathically. I still couldn't understand why she enjoyed using the limited human cell phone technology.

"Hello," I answered dryly.

"Conner," Charlie said in excitement. "Fabio said you're going off grid. I'm glad I caught you before you did."

"You know you can always reach me," I reminded her.

She huffed out her breath. "I was trying to respect your desire to ... you know ... not be reachable. But since you've given me permission, I'll make sure to chat when it's most convenient for me."

I rolled my eyes, knowing that she would pick a time when I was asleep just to be annoying. "Do you need anything?" I asked.

"Just to check in on you. It's the sisterly thing to do," Charlie replied, though I could almost hear the smirk I knew was on her face.

"I'm fine. Eager to disconnect for four days," I replied.

"You have other options to disconnect," Charlie replied sagely.

I sighed. She was the darling of the family and seemed to be able to do no wrong. Of course she'd think it would be simple to get the distance I needed.

"I have a race this weekend." I could hear the excitement in her voice.

While I understood her need to race, it wasn't the safest sport, especially since she was competing on a human race circuit and she was hiding it from our parents.

"Be safe," I said. One benefit of being immortal was that though racing cars was dangerous, it couldn't actually kill her. *But* it could expose our existence to the world, and that would be a very serious problem.

"Always. I love you," Charlie replied.

"Love you too. How about you call me in four days and tell me how it went?" I offered.

"Will do. Have fun," Charlie said, then hung up.

I drummed my fingers on my thigh. For our human friends, Charlie was ten years younger than me. In reality, she was a whole century younger, but either way she was the princess of the family. I made the mistake twenty years ago of taking her out for a drive in my Aston Martin Vantage, hooking her on fast cars. Our parents just saw it as us going for a weekend drive and sibling bonding time. Now, she moonlighted as a professional racecar driver under the name Charlie Fiore. To the public, she was an internationally known model, Charlotte Hudson.

I ran my hand over my face. *I am not going to spend my vacation worrying about my little sister. She is old enough to take care of herself.*

On our descent to Santa Barbara, I couldn't help but smile at the beautiful, empty white sand beach below us, excitement building at the prospect of no work, no women, nothing but me, the ocean, and my surfboard.

The helicopter landed at the tiny private airport. It had a handful of small gray metal hangars. Two prop planes were preparing to take off on the landing strip. Beside the hangar closest to us, a few strides away, was a worn-out blue Tacoma. The pilot put my suitcase in the truck for me.

"Anything else, Dr. H?" he asked.

I shook my head. "Nope. This is everything I need. I'll see you in four days."

"Yes, sir," came the curt reply. I waited as the pilot turned the helicopter on and then flew away.

I took a deep breath, delighting in the salty ocean air, then settled into the driver's seat of the truck. There was a sticky note with an address and brief directions on the dashboard. I turned on the truck, and it rumbled to life. Grinning, I eased out onto the road. *Four days in paradise.*

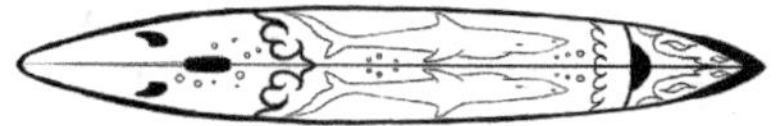

An hour after my arrival in Santa Barbara, I made it to the beach. The parking lot was only about a quarter full. A faded blue Prius with a roof rack was the only sedan in the lot, with the rest a collection of trucks and SUVs, and I found myself with some very human-like thoughts wondering who it belonged to. Shaking my head, I made my way out to the beach, setting my surfboard upright in the sand while I removed my dark green button-up shirt and set it on top of my towel.

I picked my lime-green-and-navy-blue surfboard up out of the sand, tucked it under my arm, and waded into the ocean, sighing as the salt water quieted my thoughts. The gentle push and pull of the waves calmed me into an almost meditative state. This was one of the reasons I was drawn to the ocean.

I was about knee-deep in the water when a female surfer caught my eye. She was too far out for a human to discern the details, but superior eyesight was another benefit of being an angel. Her hair was slicked back in a braid, dark from the ocean water; her arms and legs were pale olive, as though she didn't get out in the sun much. She was wearing a black-and-white one-piece swimsuit, and she had lasted the longest of the group who had ridden the last wave in.

I tried not to stare, but I was impressed by her skill—something that rarely happened, especially where humans were concerned. Clearly, she was comfortable on the waves. I was wading farther out when her eyes met mine, and it felt like a lightning bolt went through me. The sensation disappeared when she turned away, breaking eye contact. For a moment, I had wondered if she was going to come over to me, but it passed when she paddled out toward the group I presumed were her friends instead.

I let out my breath and continued farther into the ocean, mulling over what had happened when the woman had met my gaze. I interacted with human women on almost a daily basis, but none of them had ever had any effect on me. At least not one that could be considered otherworldly. *Cassiel might know*, I mused, and immediately rejected the idea. The last thing I wanted to do was let Cassiel know I needed his wisdom for anything. I had my own resources; I was certain I could figure it out without his help. A small wave formed, and my surfboard bobbed over the top—a reminder that I was out here to surf, an activity that required my full attention to be enjoyable.

I paddled until I was closer to the other single surfers but deliberately too far away to invite anyone to strike up a conversation with me. I wanted four days of solitude to relax and recharge. No father or board of directors breathing down my throat.

I knew four days was not nearly enough of a break, but it was better than nothing. A few years ago, my best friend and fellow angel, Nathanael, had dared me to take surfing lessons. Until the mid-twentieth century, I had largely stayed away from human pastimes, preferring to socialize in my free time with other angels in Ianialar, the Ash Realm. Once supercars were invented, I became fascinated with the idea of a manmade object capable of reaching high speeds. Instead of going to Ianialar, I acquired a supercar and built a racetrack at my estate in England so I could drive in private.

It was simple for me to understand my attraction to driving, but it caught Nate and me both by surprise when I thoroughly enjoyed surfing. Catching the perfect swell was just as exhilarating as going two hundred miles per hour, the primary difference being that in the ocean, I was going against Mother Nature.

However, both sports were blissfully free of people demanding my attention. I inhaled deeply and let my eyes flutter shut. When I opened them, I smiled; a wave was forming. I glanced to my right and left, making sure I had plenty of room to maneuver, and then I set myself up and rode the wave.

Chapter 4: Kelsey

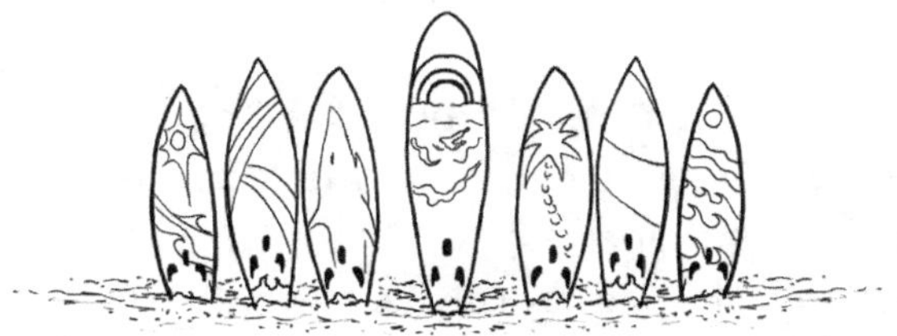

Thursday, September 5

I tugged the last strap holding my surfboard in place on the roof rack of the Prius, then scanned the area around my car, making sure I hadn't forgotten anything. Lane and Joel had carpooled and were wrapping up loading their gear into Lane's truck.

Joel caught my eye and walked over, grinning. "See what you've been missing all these years? Precisely why you should come home after your fellowship is over."

I frowned as his words caught me off guard. *Joel wants me to come home?*

Lane jogged over. "We want our own personal doctor to call upon," he said.

"Uh-huh. Does that mean when you have a hangover at three a.m. and can't sleep, I'll get the call?" I demanded.

Lane nodded. "Yep!"

I rolled my eyes. "I'm a pediatric surgeon, so unless you turn into a child with a surgical matter, I won't be able to help you."

"Well, the way things have been the past few years, it might be the only way we can see you," Lane teased.

He was right. Other than talking to Penny, I had abandoned the rest of my friends in pursuit of my career. Until now, I hadn't realized how much I missed them. *Maybe this trip shouldn't be only surfing like I planned, but also reconnecting with my friends.*

"How about meeting up at Toucan's later?" I suggested.

Joel walked over and slung his arm around Lane's shoulder. "Sounds great."

"Perfect. I'll see you then," I replied, looking at Lane.

Lane grinned and gave me a hug, then retreated to his truck, leaving me alone with Joel.

"Hey, stranger," he said casually.

"Hey, yourself," I replied, our old greeting easy on my tongue.

"You looked good out there today," Joel said.

I blinked, trying to decipher if he was complimenting how I looked physically or my rusty surfing skills. "Uh, thanks?" I said uncertainly.

"Oh!" Joel gasped, blushing. "I meant surfing ... well, and ... um ... you're fit."

I couldn't help myself. I burst out laughing, relieved that he wasn't intentionally flirting.

Joel ran his hand over his face and through his hair. "I'll see you later," he said and then made a beeline for the truck.

Still giggling, I checked my surfboard one more time and climbed into the Prius.

In the shower at Abuela's, hot water sluiced over my head and down my back. I was looking forward to seeing everyone at Toucan's, but the week was starting to catch up with me. I'd pulled a twenty-four-hour shift before leaving Los Angeles midmorning today. On a regular day, I'd have eaten lunch at the apartment and then slept till the next morning.

Stifling a yawn, I ran my hands through my long brown hair

one more time. Satisfied that all the soap was out, I turned off the water and grabbed a towel, wrinkling my nose at how rough it was. I dearly loved my Abuela, but the towel I was using had to be over fifty years old. It was threadbare and thin enough to almost see through it. My muscles were relaxed and noodly and bed was calling my name. I shook my head. *I can manage two rounds of drinks at Toucan's.* I didn't want to let my friends down by bailing on them. Not my first night back.

"Nieta!" Abuela's voice came through the door. "Tú teléfono ... Joel."

"Gracias, Abuela. I will call him in a bit," I responded, wondering what Joel wanted. Shrugging, I finished towel-drying my hair and hung my swimsuit on the towel bar to dry.

Back in my room, I rummaged through the closet. *I really need to buy some new clothes.* Rolling my eyes at the choices, I flipped through three dresses—the same three that I had taken with me nine years ago when I left for medical school. Fortunately, my figure had not changed. I was a little taller than average at five feet and ten inches. I had learned early on in medical school that going to the gym—since surfing wasn't an option—gave me the energy I needed to focus on school. Thanks to my daily workout, I had slowly developed and maintained a well-muscled body.

I picked my favorite of the three, a deep green knee-length wrap dress with white flowers. After laying it on the bed, I opened the top drawer of the dresser and pulled out a nude lace bra and panty set.

Discarding the towel, I slipped the bra and panties on, then slid into the dress. My phone rang. I realized Abuela had put it on my bed where I would see it. Sure enough, it was Joel.

"Hello?" Phone to my ear, I sat on the edge of my bed, preparing to pull on my dressy sandals.

"Hey. I got called in to work," Joel said. I could hear the frustration in his voice.

"Work on a Friday night?" I replied, trying to hide my amusement that in some ways his job was a lot like mine: unpredictable hours and being on call.

"Yes, I know. There is a big gas leak in one of the subdivisions, and the city wants all hands on deck. My supervisor has made arrangements for me and my crew to stay on-site in temporary trailers," he explained apologetically.

"Where exactly is it?" I wondered out loud.

"Do you remember the house we snuck into when we were seventeen and the owners found us making out in one of their cars?" Joel asked, bringing back a memory I often fought to forget. Not because of us making out, but because it was one of the times I had made Abuela truly angry at me.

"Yeah, I remember," I said hesitantly.

"It's in that area," Joel confirmed. "I need to go. I'm getting another call on my work phone. Probably asking where I am even though they only told me like thirty minutes ago."

"Good luck, and stay safe," I replied. During medical school, I had volunteered in the emergency room and had seen some horrific traumas caused by gas leaks and events triggered by them. The line went dead. In the past, he would've at least said goodbye. *I guess they are calling him till he answers.*

Yawning, I looked at the shoes in my hand. If Joel was not going to Toucan's, then I wondered if it even made sense to go out. My friends tended to get quite drunk and rowdy; perhaps someplace quieter or even staying in and going to bed early was a better option.

I'm dressed. I might as well go somewhere, I decided, knowing that Abuela would fuss and worry about why I was tired if I told her I was not going somewhere tonight. This way, she wouldn't fuss, but I could keep things low-key and then retire early.

Glancing at my makeup bag, I shook my head, rejecting it. If I wasn't going out with friends, there was no need to take the time. I did opt to blow-dry my hair so I wouldn't soak the back of my dress, and it fell past my shoulders in silky waves. It was rare that I could leave my hair down since I worked in a hospital and performed surgeries almost every day.

A soft knock came on the door. My hands were braced against the sink, and I realized I'd been staring blankly at my reflection.

"Nieta ... are you done?" came Abuela's strained voice.

One of the sacrifices of being so close to the beach was the house was tiny. Two bedrooms, one bathroom. One day, it would belong to me if I desired. I still wasn't sure where I wanted to end up. The end of the road was approaching, and soon I would have more control. For medical school, I had been offered a full scholarship to Johns Hopkins, a luxury I was grateful for every day because I didn't have student loans for those four years. It had also meant I was forced to leave my childhood home in pursuit of my dream career.

The year I'd spent in Los Angeles had only confirmed how little I liked the city, but I hadn't given much thought to whether I wanted to settle down in Santa Barbara or somewhere else. I laughed at that. *Who am I kidding? What use does Santa Barbara have for a pediatric surgeon? I need to live in a place that has a well-known and sought-out children's hospital.*

"Nieta, por favor!" Abuela called urgently.

"Sorry!" Gathering my things, I yanked the door open and almost walked right into Abuela with her thighs pressed tightly together. I realized she had been waiting for me to finish so she could go the bathroom. I gave her an apologetic smile and went into my bedroom. I deposited my toiletries on the bed and snagged my black leather purse off the top of the dresser.

"See you later!" I yelled through the still-shut bathroom door. I heard a mumbled phrase. Shrugging, I headed for the back door where my car was parked. If Abuela needed something, she would call me. Although many technological advances confused my grandmother, she did understand how to use a cell phone and could even text.

I tugged the Prius's door shut and then pulled out my phone

and dialed Lane's number. It rang once, and then he answered.

"Hey, Lane."

"What's up, Kel?" he answered cheerily, and I almost changed my mind about not meeting them at Toucan's.

I opened my mouth to reply, and instead of words, a yawn escaped. "Joel called and canceled, and I had a twenty-four-hour shift before I drove here, so I'm going to have an early night. Maybe we can do something tomorrow?"

"You sure? You could just come to Toucan's for an hour," Lane pressed.

I smiled and shook my head, then remembered he couldn't see me. "I appreciate the offer, but I'm sure. We have three weeks, there will be another night."

"Okay, but I'm going to hold you to that," Lane said seriously.

"Have fun," I responded and hung up before he could try to talk me into coming anyway.

Not wanting Abuela to fuss over me, I chose to go to Blue Fin, a quiet boutique restaurant with a wine room and unparalleled views of the ocean. It was on the roof of one of the older build-ings in historic downtown Santa Barbara. Climbing the worn, dark wood stairs, I savored the tantalizing smells of garlic and herbs wafting from the kitchen. Although the chef was born and raised in Santa Barbara, he had trained with many world-renowned five-star chefs in cities like Chicago, New York, and Seattle before returning home. Often, I thought Blue Fin wasn't as well-known as it should be, because the food was excellent.

I recognized the hostess with her black hair in a cute bob that was tucked behind her ears, revealing her left ear still full of earrings, just like in high school. Brittney had been in a couple of my classes, but we had never been friends. Still, she gave me a bright smile.

"Good evening. Is it just one or are you waiting for someone?"

"Just me," I replied with a tired smile. I was looking forward to a quiet meal with a book and my own thoughts for company. *A suitable start to a vacation.*

"This way." Brittney led me to a table set for two by the big glass windows. It was the last table available with the best view, so I was surprised it was being offered to me.

"I heard a rumor," Brittney said with a slight smile. "That you're back for good, and not just visiting."

Eyebrows arched, I replied, "Who told you that?"

"People," Brittney responded mysteriously.

"I don't know who 'people' are, but I'm only here for three weeks, then I will be in Los Angeles for another twelve months to finish my fellowship."

"That's closer than wherever you were out east," Brittney said. She departed, leaving me wondering who had started the rumor and why. When Brittney returned, disrupting my thoughts, she had a water pitcher.

"Would you like some wine?" Brittney inquired.

"Yes, but I would like to determine what I'm ordering first," I replied.

"Here is tonight's menu. Your waiter will be by shortly if you have any questions." Brittney presented the menu with a flourish before returning to the host stand.

I looked over the menu; every item on it sounded amazing. I knew from experience it all was too. The waiter, a blond man with a medium build in a black polo shirt and khaki slacks, walked over just as I made up my mind.

"I'm Tom and will be your server tonight. Do you have any questions?" Tom asked.

I shook my head. "No, or not about the food. I would like to get the butternut squash ravioli with sage brown butter sauce and grilled shrimp."

"House salad or soup of the day?" he asked.

"I'll take the house salad with balsamic vinaigrette. If you have any wine suggestions, I'd love to hear them."

"Sure," Tom said agreeably. "With your pasta selection I would highly recommend the Firestone Chardonnay. It's a favorite pairing among our regular guests."

"Sounds wonderful," I said with a smile.

When Tom departed with my order, I opened my book and dove into the story, barely glancing up when my wine arrived. I caught myself rereading each page, a sure indication of how tired I was. Luckily, the food came quickly, and I hoped that it would give me enough energy to not fall asleep in the middle of my meal.

The pasta was divine with the balance of the sweet butternut squash and savory sage and herb shrimp exactly as I had imagined it would taste. I was sad when I took the last bite that I had finished it, though my stomach was comfortably full. The plate was cleared away, and I slid the book into the plate's vacated spot.

Reaching for my wine glass, absorbed in my book and the beginning of the final conflict, I heard a throat clear. Startled, I jumped, and my hand hit the wine glass, causing it to spill and barely missing my book. Luckily, there was not much left in the glass.

Face flushed in embarrassment, I looked up and was shocked to see the red-haired man who had caught my eye at the beach this afternoon.

"Sorry I startled you," he said in a light tenor with a hint of a British accent, offering me a napkin to help with the mess.

I took the napkin, turning even deeper red, and mumbled, "Thanks." I finished mopping the table and realized he was still standing there.

I took a deep breath before peering up at him. "Can I help you with something?" My assessment in our first meeting while surfing hadn't even come close. This man, whoever he was, was hot. No, he was hotter than hot. He was like a walking sex machine. Tonight, he was wearing a white linen shirt that was unbuttoned about halfway down, providing a glimpse of his well-defined pecs, and beige pants. Natural red hair with the barest hint of gray, a nice tan, warm brown eyes, and cheeks covered in stubble. When he smiled, I was swooning.

"I'm Conner," he said, extending his hand.

I dropped the napkin and clumsily shook his hand, blushing again. *Get a hold of yourself!* I thought. I was not some simpering idiot who had never been around an attractive man before.

"And your name?" he asked, giving my hand a gentle squeeze that sent butterflies fluttering in my stomach.

"Kelsey," I replied, forcing myself to release his hand and return mine to my lap. I was tired and not sure I trusted my judgment around a guy who looked like Conner did. Not wanting to be rude, I prayed he would leave of his own accord.

"Can I buy you a drink?" he offered.

My stomach sank. *I should say no.* Instead, I replied, "Sure, that would be lovely. Please sit." Digging my nails into the palm of my hand, I berated myself for agreeing. *Go home. You're tired.*

Conner made a motion with his hand to the waiter. "Two glasses of the Cabernet Sauvignon." Tom nodded and dashed away.

"Kelsey, you seemed quite at home out there today in the ocean. Do you surf often?" Conner asked, clear interest on his face.

His interest caught me off guard. The fact that he had been watching me this afternoon was a little creepy. Though I had to admit, people would often sit on the beach and just watch surfers. Likely his interest had not intentionally been to make me uncomfortable. I was also surprised. Most of the men I had dated in medical school—hell, if I was being honest, any man other than Joel—were not in the least bit interested in surfing.

"When I am home, I do, but I haven't spent much time here recently. I've been in the city working and before that back east for school."

"That's too bad. You are quite skilled," Conner said.

Not sure how to respond, I hastily asked, "Do you surf often?"

Conner smiled. "No ... or I guess I should say not really. I've had lessons here and there over the years, and I do enjoy it immensely, but it's rare that I have both free time and proximity to a place to surf."

I found myself getting lost in his warm brown gaze. I tore my eyes away and stared out the window for a moment, trying to come up with something else to say. It was comforting to meet a stranger who seemed genuinely interested in my hobby. *Stick to basics.* "What brings you to Santa Barbara?" I inquired.

Tom set the glasses of wine down and disappeared before either one of us could comment or thank him. I carefully picked up my glass and took a small sip, not wanting to repeat the earlier debacle. Typically, I found I didn't like red wine, but to my delight this one was delicious.

I watched through my eyelashes as Conner took his time considering the question, swirling his wine in the glass.

"I am on vacation," Conner finally said.

Why was that such a difficult question to answer? I wondered, but I didn't even know Conner, so I chose a different, safer question that wouldn't come across as an interrogation. "Where do you call home?"

Conner arched an eyebrow in surprise. "Home? The place I call home is London."

"London, England?" I asked, eyes wide. With the British accent, it made sense.

Conner laughed. "Is there another London somewhere?"

"Yes, there is a London not too far out of Fresno," I said matter-of-factly. I knew there were lots of cities with the same names as the big famous ones. How was I to know he meant *the* London?

Conner chuckled. "Perhaps one day I will check out London, California."

I ran the edge of the napkin through my fingertips. Every time he spoke, his voice wound its way around me. Focusing on the conversation was difficult thanks to a mix of exhaustion, the alcohol, and something else I couldn't put my finger on.

I grabbed my wine glass and took a big sip, hoping Conner

wouldn't think I was acting weird. When I set it down, I asked, "What kind of work do you do?"

Conner considered the question for a while before answering it, just like he had done when I asked about why he was here. *Almost like he has a secret.*

"I'm a businessman. Would it be wrong to ask if we could refrain from talking about work? I have four days to relax and forget about the chaos."

I shrugged. "That's fine with me. It sounds like we came to Santa Barbara for the same reason, to escape our jobs for a little while."

Conner flashed the most brilliant smile. My lips parted as I imagined what his lips would feel like against mine. "Sounds like a deal. I know we are here on vacation. Tell me, if you could go anywhere in the world on an all-expenses-paid vacation, where would you go?" Conner asked.

I moistened my lips, trying to focus, though I was intrigued by his question. "Anywhere in the world?" He nodded confirmation. "Tahiti," I said immediately.

"To surf?" he guessed.

I smiled. "Absolutely! What about you? Where would you go?"

Conner tapped his lip with his finger. "Greece. I have always been fascinated by Greco-Roman history."

I wasn't sure what I had hoped he would say, but it wasn't Greece. I gave myself a mental shrug. *It's his dream vacation, not mine.*

The conversation with Conner was doing a better job of keeping me awake than my book was. It had been a long time since I'd had a real conversation with a man who was genuinely interested in me as person. Most interactions I had were either with patients and their families or the various supervisors I'd had at the hospitals I'd worked in. Over the years, I had developed a mental armor, giving me emotional distance from people until I was ready to let them all the way in. Yet after less than thirty minutes at Blue Fin with Conner, I found I wanted to tell him everything.

"Would you like to go for a walk on the beach?" Conner asked, startling me out of my thoughts.

Glancing at my watch, I took note of the time: nine p.m. I was going on no sleep for almost thirty-six hours. The walk was tempting, but I did not know him, and it was almost completely dark. Going on a walk in the dark with a stranger was not on my to-do list, ever, even one as nice and sexy as Conner.

"No, I'd better get back. I'm planning on surfing early tomorrow morning—dawn patrol—and need a good night's rest," I replied.

"I understand," he responded.

At Conner's signal, Tom came by with the check. I reached for it, but Conner snagged it from me, tsking. "I'll get it."

"Are you sure? It has my dinner on there too, not just the wine. This isn't exactly a date or anything," I protested.

Conner smiled. "You're right, it's not a date. But I do recall it was me who barged in on your clear excitement over your book. I feel it is only fair that I compensate you for that interruption."

His reasoning was not convincing, but I let it slide. The next time we went out, I would insist on paying. I paused, realizing that although Conner hadn't said anything about going out again, at least not yet, I wanted to see him again.

These weeks are for you to relax and surf. There is no room for a man. I bit my lip, knowing I was right. No matter how handsome Conner was, my trip to Santa Barbara was for me and maybe my best friends, but I didn't want to sacrifice my plans for a stranger. I did enough of that when I was working.

Mind made up, I gave him a polite smile. "Thank you for dinner, and good night," I said. Then, I departed quickly.

I rushed to the Prius and drove away before he had even made it down the stairs.

Chapter 5: Conner

Thursday, September 5

I took my time leaving the restaurant. From the large windows, I could see the quiet street below and observe Kelsey once she reached the sidewalk and was walking toward her car.

The way she rushed away made me wonder what I'd said or done that had rubbed her the wrong way. There had been a to-go menu for Blue Fin in a kitchen drawer at the house I was renting. When I arrived at Blue Fin, my intention had been to eat a quiet dinner alone and then return to the beach house. Everything had changed when Kelsey appeared at the top of the stairs. Just like this afternoon, there had been an odd, charged pulse between us that faded as quickly as it appeared.

Intrigued and annoyed that there was something magical between us that I had no idea how to explain, I made the decision to introduce myself. I was confident that she was a human, not a demon or half-demon. There had been no aura around her that I could sense. In fact, everyone in the restaurant was human. Occasionally, I would catch thoughts of demons walking by on the street below, but they were not causing any problems, which meant I had no reason to interfere with their evenings.

Startling her had been a mistake. I almost caught the glass before it hit the table, remembering at the last moment that doing so would lead to questions I wasn't permitted to answer. It was better if she thought I was an asshole than suspected there was something otherworldly about me.

She's just a human. Forget about her, I told myself as I walked down the steps. I had originally walked to Blue Fin wanting to blend in with the tourists; now, though, I felt like I owed myself a stern reminder. Instead of walking, I drew my magic around myself, becoming invisible to any passerby, human or demon, and leapt into the air, my wings unfurling a hair before my feet would've touched the ground. Flapping my wings, I headed straight out to the ocean and then turned down the shoreline the two miles to the little house.

Instead of tuning out everything and focusing purely on my joy of flight, I ran the conversation with Kelsey over and over in my mind, unable to erase the image of her long brown hair floating around her shoulders and the hunter-green dress with large white flowers. Her confidence and willingness to challenge my motives had me craving more time with her.

"I am here to surf and disconnect," I reminded myself under my breath. Except the treacherous part of my mind wanted desperately to know more about this human who had a magical connection to me. *Kelsey surfs ... We might run into each other again.*

I sighed and glided to a landing on the sandy path up to the tiny white beach house with faded yellow shutters and trim. As I approached the front door, I vanished my wings and dropped the invisibility. Then, I let myself into the house. My whole life had revolved around conforming to rules, and though this trip was bending them a little, I was not willing or prepared to go to war with Cassiel for a forbidden long-term relationship with a human woman.

The punching bag in the corner of the main room caught my eye. Fabio had had it installed for me prior to my arrival, likely anticipating that I would want to get more exercise than surfing would provide. I changed into a pair of green athletic shorts and strapped on my boxing gloves, then began my routine. My focus narrowed until my only thought was the punch combination I was executing next.

Sweat dribbled down my back and arms. I rubbed my arm across my face and it came back soaking wet, and sweat still trickled into my eyes. Growling in annoyance, I glanced at the clock on the wall and was surprised to see it was almost midnight. *Even I need to sleep*, I reminded myself. Except now I was drenched in sweat and in dire need of a shower. Wrinkling my nose at the memory of the shower earlier after I had gone surfing, I was not looking forward to squeezing into it again. If Fabio were here, he could magically alter it, but that was not a power I possessed.

Dumping the sweat-soaked clothes into a pile in the bathroom, I got into the shower and turned on the water. Cold water hit my head and cascaded over my back, quickly lowering my core temperature. I adjusted the knobs so the water was lukewarm and stood with hands braced against the wall and my eyes closed.

Today had been successful. I surfed and went to a restaurant and kept my anonymity. I was looking forward to another day of surfing and prayed that Fabio was wrong and that it wouldn't get out to the media where I had snuck off to this weekend. People always acted differently if they knew you had money—or also, in my case, if the local demons thought I was here to ensure they were in line. On this trip, I just wanted a chance to be me. The me my sister knew, not the side I presented to my father or business associates.

After toweling dry, I got into bed, and as soon as I shut my eyes, an image of Kelsey came to me. Her smile and full lips. I fell asleep dreaming of the wicked things I wanted her to do with those lips.

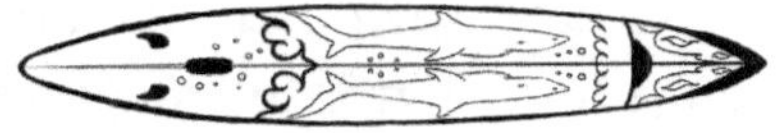

I woke with a start. The sheet was wrapped around my throat, and I struggled against it. A telltale ripping sound, and I freed myself at the expense of the sheet, which was now in three pieces.

Peering around the pitch-black room, I wondered what time it was. Then, I caught sight of the alarm clock on the nightstand. Six thirty a.m. *So much for sleeping in*, I thought, then remembered that Kelsey had mentioned going out for dawn patrol in the morning.

Grinding my teeth together, I debated whether I should attempt to go back to sleep or head out to the beach. I lay on my back for fifteen minutes in the dark before giving up on sleep. I sat up and scooted off the bed. One of the perks of being an angel was I did not need human nourishment, though I could eat if I wanted to, which was convenient for blending in.

I pulled out the top dresser drawer and selected a pair of black swim shorts with large blue palm trees over the pockets and a tan linen button-up shirt. After donning the clothes, I recovered my sandals from the corner I'd tossed them into and headed out to where the beat-up truck was parked.

My gaze lingered on the faded black electric scooter, mottled with rust, propped against the back wall of the house. Wondering if it was even drivable, I darted into the house and snagged the key marked "scooter" off the peg by the front door.

Cautiously, I put the orange key into the slot and turned. To my shock, the engine started with an electric hum. Feeling a little reckless, I threw my leg over the seat and sat down.

"Here goes nothing," I muttered under my breath, and with the twist of my wrist, the scooter shot forward, sending gravel spraying at the truck. "Oops." I was lucky the truck was old and any damage I had caused was nothing compared to what was already there. Steering the scooter out onto the path at the front of the house, I eased it onto the beach.

The longer I drove down the beach, the noisier the scooter became. The whirring sound started soft and then grew so loud it drowned out the engine's hum. Not sure what it meant, since I was not well versed in electric vehicle mechanics, I decided to ignore it. I enjoyed the breeze hitting my face and the chatter of the seagulls as I sent them scattering from whatever treasures they'd found in the beige sand.

Ahead, I could see a parking lot, empty except for one faded blue Prius. As I returned my attention to the sand in front of me, my heartbeat raced a little faster when I recognized Kelsey walking toward the ocean with a clear plastic water bottle in her hand. I lifted my hand to wave at her when the scooter started wobbling, and I quickly put my hand back on the handlebars. Instead, I lightly tapped the horn and was rewarded with a childish *beep, beep*.

Wanting to slow down so I wouldn't rocket past Kelsey, I applied the brakes, but nothing happened. I tried again, and the scooter started swaying side to side. One last try and to my shock, the scooter tipped all the way over on top of me, shoving me into the sand.

"Are you okay?" Kelsey shouted, her voice high.

I opened my mouth to shout back and was met with a fistful of sand flooding my mouth. Coughing, I fought the urge to remove the sand from my mouth with magic. Since the sand was affecting my ability to breathe, it fell within the classification of healing.

"Are you okay?" Kelsey called again, her voice moving around me. I felt the sand shift when she knelt beside me and delicately settled her hand on my shoulder and probed with her fingers—I presumed to determine if anything was broken. Her fingers digging into my shoulder felt like I was being zapped with lightning. When she let go, the sensation ceased.

"I'm fine," I said, roughly lifting my head just enough to spit the sand out.

"Conner?" she gasped. I felt her shifting beside me.

"Yes, it's me, Conner," I replied.

"Did you get sand in your mouth?" she asked, amused.

I refrained from replying. Instead, I rolled over onto my back and gave a thrust with my legs, shifting the scooter enough to free them.

"Much better ... and yes, I did get sand in my mouth," I said.

Kelsey laughed. "Here," she said, passing me her water bottle. I took a drink, rinsing the grit from my mouth and turning away from Kelsey to spit it onto the sand.

"Thanks," I said, giving the bottle back.

"What were you doing out here on the scooter?" Kelsey asked.

"I couldn't sleep," I explained.

"You're lucky I'm not a cop. It's illegal to drive on the beach," Kelsey pointed out.

"Oops," I said. Unable to help it, I flashed her a smile. My stomach was flipflopping, and I could feel my pulse quickening the longer we gazed at each other. I was sitting in the sand and she was kneeling next to me, our faces almost level. To make matters worse, I could feel Kelsey's blood thrumming in her veins, the way her breath hitched as her gaze flicked down to my lips and then back to my eyes.

Knowing I shouldn't, but with an excuse at the forefront of my mind—*it's just a weekend fling*—I leaned forward and brushed my lips against hers tentatively. Kelsey's lips were soft, full, and fit mine perfectly, and she returned the kiss without hesitation. I ran my hand through her damp hair and deepened the kiss, until she had to pull back to take a breath. Our eyes met, and my throat constricted as I wondered what she was going to do next. I could tell she wanted me to kiss her again. I wanted to kiss her again, but we were also sitting on the sand—not an ideal spot for anything romantic, and it was close enough to the parking lot that we could draw attention to ourselves. Deciding to be responsible, I rocked back on my heels and stood up, careful not to knock Kelsey over in the process. Then, I awkwardly picked up the scooter and gave it a shake, trying to dislodge as much sand as I could. I held it upright by the handlebars, removed the key from the slot, and blew it out before returning the key and turning it. To my surprise, the scooter started right up.

Kelsey giggled behind me, and I glanced over my shoulder. "What?"

"Honestly, I thought you broke it," she replied.

"Me too," I said, relieved that I wouldn't have to explain to Fabio why we had to replace the ancient scooter.

"You said you couldn't sleep. Bad dreams?" Kelsey asked.

I pressed my lips together. I doubted she was looking for honesty when it involved admitting I'd dreamt of having sex with her. "I was having a nightmare about work."

Kelsey made a face, and I wondered if she also had nightmares about work. Instead, she asked, "Did you have a plan beyond experimenting with the scary scooter and surfing?"

I shook my head. "No. Surfing and being unplugged are all that's on the agenda this weekend."

Kelsey nodded as though she knew exactly what I was talking about. "Same here." Then she checked her watch, and I wondered if she had somewhere to be.

"I promised Abuela I would be home for brunch," Kelsey explained.

"Abuela?" I asked. I was fluent in all languages that had ever existed, including those humans had forgotten, but I didn't want to assume the woman she spoke of was a blood relative.

"My grandmother," Kelsey replied.

It dawned on me that when she had mentioned "home" in our conversation yesterday, she meant her home was *here*. How ironic that she wanted to vacation at home, while I wanted to be as far away as possible from my own.

"Then I won't keep you any longer." I slid my leg over the scooter and settled myself on the seat. I put my hand on the throttle, then Kelsey stepped close enough that her leg was brushing mine. It sent chills up my spine. *Get ahold of yourself.*

Kelsey leaned over, giving me a brief glimpse of her breasts before her lips were on mine, demanding. I returned the kiss, letting the tip of my tongue tease her lips open. She was willing, straddling my leg, her thigh brushing tantalizingly against my balls. A low moan escaped from my lips, and I pulled back.

"Unless you want me to take you right here, we should stop," I said softly, trying to slow my breathing.

She reluctantly took half a step back, but my leg was still between hers. I met her gaze with mine and could see her eyes were dark with desire.

"I need to go," she mumbled.

I nodded, waiting for her to move from my leg. Moments ticked by where she seemed frozen with indecisiveness. "Do you want to have dinner?" What I had really wanted to ask was *can I have you for lunch*, but she had already made it clear she had to return to see her grandmother. I did not want to intrude.

"I'll think about it," Kelsey replied and then scooted the rest of the way off my leg. Without a backward glance, she retreated to her car.

I drove the scooter down the beach, mulling over Kelsey. It was obvious our attraction was mutual, but I was struggling to figure out why this human woman whom I'd now had two conversations with was affecting me this much. I had had plenty of one-night stands with humans and longer relationships with other angels, but my interactions with Kelsey didn't really fit into any experiences I'd had previously.

It wasn't until I was back at the tiny house that it dawned on me that we hadn't set a time or a place for dinner, and I had no idea how to contact her.

Chapter 6: Kelsey

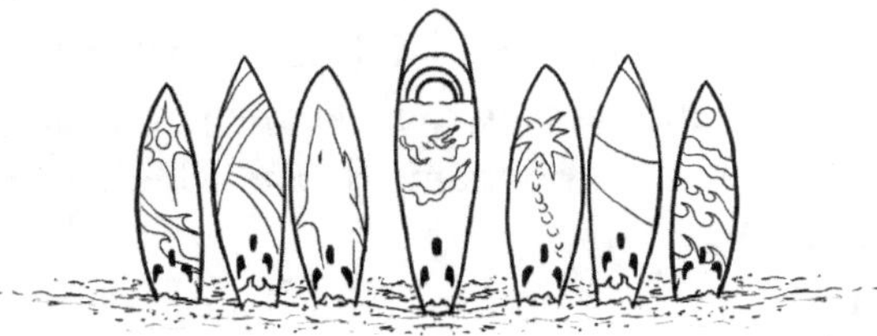

Friday, September 6

"Hola!" I called to Abuela as I entered the house from the back door, the screen door slapping shut behind me.

"Hola!" came her clear response from the kitchen at the front of the house.

I was famished, as Abuela anticipated I would be after morning surfing. I also knew she wanted to spend some time with me before I got too busy with my friends. *Am I going to be too busy? We all have jobs and responsibilities now. Look at Joel. He had to cancel last night because he was called in to work for an emergency.*

I decided to eat first and then shower. I snagged a clean towel from the linen closet and wrapped it around my hips to protect the floral chair cushion from any remaining sand I might shed.

"How was your morning?" Abuela asked over her shoulder as she pulled silverware out of the drawer. She was wearing her favorite red shirt and black pants with her long white hair in a braid down her back.

I hesitated by the table. "Good." I thought about how Conner's lips had felt when we kissed and that he had left me wanting far more than a kiss. My cheeks warmed. "Can I help?"

Abuela shook her head. "No, please sit."

I sat down at the round table. The tablecloth was maroon with a mix of pink and white roses and matched the chair cushion covers.

"I heated up some tamales," Abuela said and put a plate with two of them in front me, followed by a glass of orange juice.

"Gracias," I replied, then took a bite. Abuela's tamales were divine. She had taught me how to make them, but I still thought hers were better. It was an ongoing debate whether or not mine were as good as hers.

I was aware she was watching me while I ate and only picking at the tamale on her own plate. I finally set down my fork. "What?" I demanded.

"You are different," Abuela said.

"Different how?" I asked. I hadn't seen her in almost a year, so it was not a surprise she thought I was different.

"Happier," she replied.

I smiled. "I'm twelve months away from being able to get my dream job. It has been a long, intense journey, but totally worth it. That must be what you're seeing."

Abuela shook her head. "No. No. Feliz desde esta mañana."

I raised my eyebrows. "I was happy last night too."

She just smiled and waved me off. I found it interesting that Abuela noticed a change in me from my arrival yesterday afternoon till now, twenty-four hours later. *Surfing.* That was the biggest thing that had been missing from my life. My plan was working if Abuela noticed already.

"I promised myself I would do everything possible while I am here to relax. Simply enjoy three weeks of surfing and friends. No plans, no expectations," I said.

Abuela dug into her tamale and a companionable silence filled the room. I missed this; how easy it was to live here with her. The comfortable routine we had had when I was growing up settled around me as though I'd never left. *Maybe I should find a way to move back in with her when I'm done with my fellowship.*

After lunch, I took a nap, a luxury I rarely had time for working at the hospital. I knew in a few days my internal clock would adjust to vacation hours, and until then, I would rest as needed. I had nowhere to be.

I woke up to fading light through the window, and I remembered that I had agreed to go out to dinner with Conner. I reached for my phone and scrolled through my contacts, then slapped my forehead. "We never exchanged numbers." I had no idea where he was staying or what restaurant he might prefer. Which left me with nothing to go on. I didn't even know his last name. I couldn't exactly call every hotel around and ask if they had a Conner staying there.

I nibbled on my lip, trying to decide what to do. It was a Friday night. Everywhere was likely to be extremely busy. *Maybe I should go to Toucan's and keep my promise to Lane.*

I sent Lane and Penny a quick text saying I was going to head over to Toucan's for a few drinks. I showered and put on clothes, passing over the dresses in favor of a pair of dark-wash skinny jeans and a black tank top.

Abuela was going over to a friend's too. I was pleased she had plans of her own and wouldn't be hanging around the house while I was busy the whole visit.

"I don't know what time I will be back. Don't wait for me if you're returning tonight," I told her and gave her a quick kiss on the cheek.

Abuela smiled. "Have fun. Don't worry about me."

The drive to Toucan's was slow going with Friday night traffic, and the parking lot was already jam-packed. Thankfully, the Prius was small and could fit into almost any size parking space. I carefully squeezed between a red lifted Dodge dually and a lime-green Mustang convertible. The band was already playing, though from out here the sound was muffled.

I pulled out my ID and flashed it at the door. The bouncer, Tiny, pulled me into a bear hug. "You're back!"

"Sorry, but it's only for three weeks," I responded.

Tiny shook his head. "I always knew you'd go out and do big things. Have fun tonight. Penny is at your usual table."

"Thanks," I said and walked past Tiny into Toucan's.

Chapter 7: Kelsey

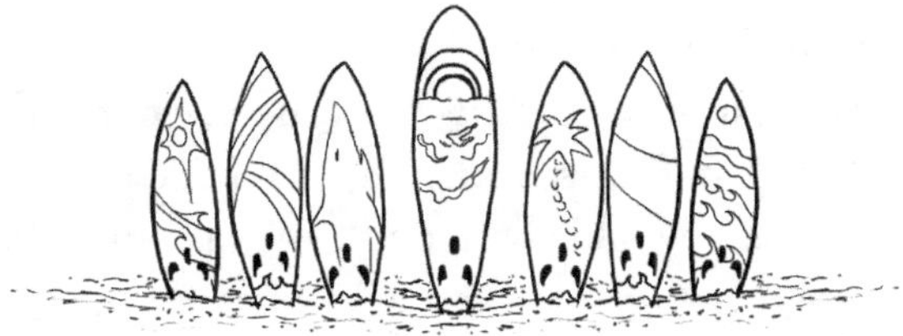

Saturday, September 7

I smacked my alarm as it screamed at me that it was five thirty a.m. Saturday morning. I groaned, wondering why I hadn't changed my plan to surf dawn patrol this morning, especially after an energetic night of drinking and dancing with Penny and Lane. *I still have the better part of three weeks. Plenty of time to wake up crazy early.* Reaching for my phone to turn off the alarm was enough to wake me up the rest of the way. Sighing and vowing to sleep in tomorrow, I sleepily went through the motions of getting ready and eating breakfast without waking Abuela.

Thirty minutes later, I was pulling into the parking lot at a remote beach that was known for dolphin sightings—though at the moment, the marine layer fog was thick enough that I couldn't even see the waves lapping at the sand. I unstrapped my surfboard, then plucked it off the roof rack and tucked it under my right arm. Grabbing my towel and water bottle with my left hand, I set off across the bike path and down to the slightly damp compacted sand. Then, after discarding my towel and water, I strapped the tether to my foot and waded out into the ocean.

The water was chilly and goose bumps rippled across my skin, but by the time I was out far enough to wait and catch waves, I had acclimated to the temperature. Gripping the edge of the board, I pulled myself onto it and settled in to wait. I let my focus narrow till the only thing I was aware of was myself, my board, and the swells. Wave after wave; some were perfect, some I made mistakes, but it was thrilling nonetheless.

One of the largest waves yet this morning began to crest. I went for it. As soon as I stood up, I knew I had made a mistake. I was angled wrong, and it was likely to end badly. I took a deep breath and tried to correct the board anyway. Sure enough, the wave crashed over, sending me spinning through the air, and I landed on my back in the water with the wind knocked out of me.

I rolled over, breathing heavily, trying to recover as the surf tugged me to and fro. Getting my feet under me, I stood facing the shore and was surprised to see Conner wading out toward me, his surfboard abandoned on the beach.

"Are you okay?" he asked roughly.

I found myself blushing at his concern. "Yeah, I'm fine," I said, trying to force my breathing to return to normal. Seeing him jogging toward me through the water had not helped my heart rate. I closed my eyes, and when I reopened them, I found myself gazing into his warm brown eyes. His hand was reaching for my face as though to reassure himself I was okay.

I could feel my heart pounding even louder in my chest and prayed he wouldn't be able to hear it too. I wasn't sure how long we stayed like that, staring deeply into each other's eyes. Our bodies close but not touching. My fingers were cramping from how hard I was clutching the surfboard to keep it from drifting away or slamming into us.

"Kelsey ..." he murmured, his voice wrapping seductively around me. Unable to resist, I found myself peering up at him through my lashes. As though that was all the invitation he needed, Conner kissed me, and I melted against him, eagerly returning the kiss and finding myself desperate for more.

An unexpected surge of the surf tugged on the surfboard and forced me to take a step back so I wouldn't unbalance us both. It also gave me a chance to sort through my feelings. Though I'd had a few very short relationships with men since Joel, I'd never done anything as bold as having sex before the third date. Conner and I hadn't even had *one* date. But his charm, combined with how amazing it felt to be desired, was pushing me into stepping outside my normal comfort zone. I picked up my surfboard and slogged through the water back to the beach. Splashing behind me indicated Conner was following. When I got up to my bag, I unstrapped the board's tether from my foot and set the board upright in the sand.

Turning around, I saw Conner watching me a few feet away next to his lime-green-and-blue surf board. Not sure how to do this, I decided on the first thing that came to mind. I marched right up to him, gave him a quick but intense kiss on the lips, then jogged out into the ocean. When there was enough distance between us, I turned to see if he was following. He wasn't. He just stood there oozing sex appeal.

"Have you ever body surfed before?" I called. He shook his head no. "It's easy, I promise," I assured him, turning away from the beach and wading farther into the ocean, not checking to see if he was coming or not. When the water was about chest height, I glanced around. Conner wasn't on the beach, and I couldn't see him in the water. *Did he leave?* I wondered, admitting it was quite possible I was misreading Conner.

Then, I felt featherlight hands on my hips from behind. As the hands slowly worked their way up, I could feel the rest of Conner pressing against my backside as he surfaced. When his hands reached my breasts, his lips were on my neck, nibbling. My body was melting under his touch, and all I could think of was wanting his hands on more of my bare skin.

Licking my lips, I tried to convince myself to focus. "Body surfing?" I squeaked.

Conner laughed a deep throaty laugh and shifted so he was standing in front of me. He wrapped his hands around my waist and pulled me close. He tilted his head down and nibbled his way up the column of my neck and to my earlobe. "Is that what you really want to do?" he whispered before capturing my lips with his.

No, I don't want to body surf, at least not in the ocean, I thought, but I was enjoying his attention too much to want to speak out loud. With our bodies pressed so tightly together, it was impossible not to notice how hard he already was. The wild side of me wanted nothing more than to have him take me here and now in the ocean. The logical side warned me about what people would think if someone came across us.

Conner ran his hand down my back, cupping my buttocks, and then he slid a finger under my swimsuit. Caught completely off guard, I tensed. To my relief, Conner immediately removed his hand and placed it lightly on my hip, then met my uncertain gaze. "What's wrong?"

I shook my head, blushing. My voice was thick with pent-up desire. "Nothing's wrong per se. I wasn't expecting you to touch me like that."

"I'll keep my hands to myself," Conner replied and let both his arms drop to his sides.

Worried he might think he'd pushed me further than I was comfortable going, I wrapped my arms around his shoulders and pulled his face back down to mine. His tongue brushed lightly on the edge of my lips, and I parted them, inviting him in.

Blood thrumming in my veins and desire coiling in my stomach made the choice to tip my head back and breathe a difficult one. "Maybe we should go to a hotel?" I whispered, my heart skipping a beat as I suggested something so out of character for me.

"The beach house I'm staying in is much closer than the hotels," Conner replied gently. He cupped my face in his hands and kissed me lightly on the lips.

Impulsively, I dipped my hand between us, brushing against his hard cock. "How fast can we get to your beach house?"

Conner grinned. "Fast."

As we waded back toward the beach and our stuff, Conner was slightly ahead of me, and I stared openly at him. Waves of desire rippled through me, and I belatedly wondered if maybe trying sex in the ocean would have been okay after all.

We collected our gear and headed to the parking lot. He loaded his gear in a beat-up Tacoma, and I put mine in the Prius. I followed him to a white beach house with yellow trim. He was right. It was not very far away, and it was on the street with the park that my friends and I would hang out at after surfing when we were in high school.

We parked at the back of the house. From the outside, it looked smaller than Abuela's and likely only had one bedroom. I followed Conner inside. The pale blue walls were hung with seashells at regular intervals. My towel was wrapped around my hips and I had my purse hanging on my shoulder. I hadn't brought any spare clothing because my original plan was to surf and then return to Abuela's, not go anywhere else. The short time in the car had stifled my desire, and I was tempted to go home. The whole idea of sex with a deliciously hot stranger was what you'd find in a romance novel, not here in real life. Conner paused at a door on the left and then cast a glance over his shoulder at me, a hungry look on his face, as though he had read my mind. He quickly closed the gap between us and crushed me against his bare chest, then kissed me passionately. As our bodies pressed together, I wrapped my hands around him, my desire rising as his hard cock bumped the apex of my thighs. A moan escaped my lips.

"Are you sure about this?" Conner asked between kisses.

"Absolutely, as long as you're willing to wear a condom," I said with confidence, praying he wouldn't reject the idea of protection. While I might know who had been in my bed recently—no one—I knew very little about Conner and didn't want to take a chance.

Conner nodded. "Of course. I have some in the bedroom."

I kissed him again, relieved; the last thing I needed was to gamble my health with a stranger.

Conner took a step back and pushed open the door to the bedroom with his foot. I followed him.

Once inside the bedroom, I unzipped the front of my swimsuit and peeled it off, discarding it in a heap. Conner did the same. I slid a condom out of my purse and placed it on the bed. I took a step toward the bed, then another when he didn't stop me. I lay down on my back, and Conner gazed at me from the end of the bed, eyes dark with desire. My eyes drifted from his face down to his erection, the tip already glistening with fluids.

"Are you coming?" I teased and crooked my finger, motioning for him to join me.

Conner nodded and climbed onto the bed next to me. He ran his hand through my damp brown hair. "You are so beautiful," he murmured, then began trailing kisses from my neck to my navel.

A gasp escaped my lips, and he quickly put the condom on, then rolled over on top of me, his arms braced so I wasn't bearing any of his weight. I spread my legs wider, and his cock brushed my entrance, sending a shiver down my spine. He dipped his head down and kissed me, and then used his finger to flick my clitoris. I arched my back as my need intensified, demanding, and he flicked again.

"Please," I whispered against his lips.

"Please what?" he said.

"I need you inside of me." I gasped as he plunged his finger into me and began a steady rhythm.

"Like this?" he asked. I whimpered when he pulled his finger out. "Needy, aren't you?"

I wasn't sure how to answer as he spread my legs farther apart and guided his cock into me. My body tightened as he moved in and out; a small spasm rippled through me, and he stopped moving.

I kissed Conner, wanting him to keep going. Desperate for the release that was tantalizingly close. He pulled partway out. Not sure what he was doing, I opened my mouth to vocalize my thoughts. Then, he slammed back into my channel, driving his shaft as far as it could go into my core. The intensity of his thrusts was driving me wild, making me realize that it had been far too long since the last time I'd had sex. My body clenched almost unbearably, and a cramp started to form in my foot. Then, he placed his right hand over my breast and began massaging. I hit my climax, but still Conner continued to thrust. His fingers circled my nipple, and then he pinched it. Pleasure exploded around me, and I almost blacked out it from the intensity. Conner's arms were vibrating as the spasms of his own release surged through him.

Conner slid off and lay beside me on the bed. I couldn't remember having an orgasm that intense, ever.

"Now what?" I asked. I was out of my wheelhouse. *What are you supposed to do with a guy like this? Especially after sex like that?*

"A nap?" Conner suggested, waggling his eyebrows.

I swatted at him playfully, but he twisted out of the way just in time. "Are you hungry?"

"Maybe," he replied as his stomach let out a crazy-loud gurgle.

Giggling, I replied, "If your stomach is making noises like that, you must be hungry." We had been two consenting adults who had sex, but we weren't dating. Hell, I didn't even know his last name. Not wanting to let food distract me from the answer I was looking for, I moved onto my side, using my elbow to brace my head. "Before we do anything else, can you at least answer a question?"

Conner smiled and replied agreeably, "Of course."

"What is this between us?" I asked, then held my breath, half afraid of what he might say.

Something I couldn't recognize flickered in Conner's eyes before it disappeared. "A nice weekend with a beautiful, sexy woman."

"And after this weekend?" I pressed.

Conner sighed. "We probably should have discussed this before I brought you here. I wasn't trying to give you the wrong idea. I'm only here this weekend and would like to keep what's between us as our weekend of fun. Then, when I depart, we can go our separate ways. No harm, no foul."

His proposal was a solid one and would be made easier by the fact that we had already omitted identifying details such as our last names and places of work. "Okay." My stomach gurgled, and I giggled. "Back to the topic of food. I would say that would be a good idea. I know a place we could eat."

"I would kill for a shower. I don't know about you, but I have sand in all sorts of places it doesn't belong," he said with a grimace.

Unable to help it, an image of Conner naked in the shower lathering himself with soap popped into my mind.

Attempting to keep my voice normal, I replied, "I could give you the address, and we could meet at the restaurant, in say, an hour?" I wouldn't mind a chance to shower and change either.

"Or, what about this? We stay here, shower, and I will cook for you?" Conner proposed.

"Yes, that sounds wonderful," I replied. Staying at his house would also resolve the issue of me not having any clothes.

Chapter 8: Conner

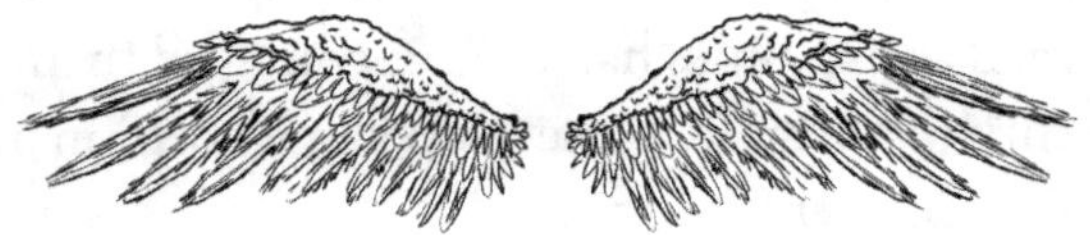

Saturday, September 7

I leaned over and gave Kelsey a kiss, then slid out of bed and headed to turn on the shower for us. However, when I walked into the bathroom, it dawned on me that there was no way two people could fit in the shower when one person barely managed. For the first time since my arrival in Santa Barbara, I found myself wishing I could go to my house in Malibu. *Technically, we could*, I reminded myself. *Yeah, and then the whole point of this trip would be wasted. I am here not to flash my money around, but to be me without all the bells and whistles for once.*

I returned to the bedroom with a towel wrapped around my hips. Kelsey hadn't moved from the bed. I could feel my desire stirring already and was glad that I wouldn't have to explain my inhuman libido to her. "The shower is only big enough for one. I will go first, and then I can cook while you shower."

"Sounds good," Kelsey replied amicably.

With an iron will, I made myself retreat to the bathroom. I climbed into the shower and let the hot water roll down my back. The sex with Kelsey had been far more intimate than any I'd experienced with a human before. There had been a moment as I reached my climax that I thought I was going to lose my grip, and she would've seen my wings. I'd never lost control like that before, and I wasn't entirely sure what it meant.

My response to her question about what the two of us are doing was the plan I had to stick to. *It's only a weekend fling.* No matter how different she was from the other women, I could not afford to see her beyond this weekend—or act upon the strange connection developing between us. Cassiel ignored the trysts with human women and at times had even encouraged them, especially the past twenty-five years as we developed my position in society as billionaire Dr. Conner Hudson.

Except Cassiel expected me to marry an angel, and time was running out for him to maintain that amount of control over my life. For humans, my upcoming thirty-eighth birthday would mark when I would be the sole executor of my inheritance, thereby giving me financial independence. The same day was also my fifteen hundredth birthday, which was the day I would ascend the Ianialar stairs and become an archangel, equal to Cassiel and no longer required to follow his orders.

I rinsed the last of the soap out of my hair. *If my purpose is to be me, why did I seduce Kelsey this morning? How is my behavior any different from the way the media perceive Conner Hudson?* Growling to myself, I yanked on the faucet forcefully to shut it off. To my surprise, the handle popped off. Taking a deep breath, I studied the handle and quickly reattached it, crossing my fingers that I hadn't just broken the shower.

Wrapping a towel around my waist, I made a beeline for the bedroom. Kelsey was lying on the bed with the sheet tucked around her.

"Your turn," I said with a smile and then snagged a pair of boxers out of the top dresser drawer before meandering into the kitchen. *Hopefully, she doesn't have any grand expectations of my cooking.* The list of things I knew how to cook was short, but not because of a lack of skill. I just had never had a reason to try, especially since angels didn't require food. My family had always employed at least one cook in each of our houses to ensure any human staff had the nourishment they required and to have food available for entertaining purposes. It had seemed natural when I set out on my own to follow suit.

Collecting the ingredients from the fridge and cupboards, I got to work preparing farm fresh scrambled eggs and turkey bacon. When the bacon finished cooking, I set it to the side and started the eggs, using what little grease was in the pan to add more flavor. As an angel, I had exceptional hearing, and I was aware of Kelsey's movements as soon as she exited the bathroom. I tracked her throughout the house by sound, aware of her rummaging through the closet as well as the dresser drawers. I wiped off the edges of the plates and placed a garnish of fresh strawberry slices.

Finished, I looked up from the plates to where Kelsey was hovering by the hallway. Trying not to be rude, I met her eyes with mine and smiled before subtly scanning the rest of her. She had selected one of my white long-sleeve button-up shirts, and the water dripping from her hair made the fabric nearly see-through as it clung to her perky breasts.

I let my eyes linger as Kelsey walked over to one of the silvery metal chairs by the glass dining room table. She sat down, and to my amusement almost jumped right back up when her bottom touched the chair.

"Shit," she gasped.

Worried that perhaps there had been something sharp that had stabbed her, I rushed over to her side to inspect the chair while she was hovering behind it.

"What's wrong?" I asked, running my hands over the chair, but there was nothing wrong with it that I could tell.

"It's embarrassing," she muttered and cautiously sat back down on it.

Arching my eyebrows, intrigued, I replied solemnly, "I promise I won't laugh." As if to prove my point, I grabbed the plates off the black granite counter and set one in front of Kelsey and the other at the open chair. "Well?" I asked, desperate to know as her blush deepened.

"Your boxers … don't fit," she finally managed to say.

Confusion filled me. *What do boxers have to do with her jumping out of a chair?* Humans had strange behaviors all the time, but this one was new to me. "I don't follow."

Kelsey twisted her hands together and placed them in her lap, hesitantly. She replied, "I had to raid your closet for clean clothes."

My mouth formed an O as her meaning hit me, that she was *only* wearing the see-through shirt. Kelsey started to eat. I took the hint and sat down in my chair, following suit. I went through the motions of eating, refusing to let myself do what I desperately wanted, which was to have Kelsey sit in my lap and ride my cock. Thankfully, her eyes were shut as she ate, and she had a satisfied expression on her face, so I assumed that she was enjoying the meal.

"What are you thinking about?" I asked, unable to bear the silence.

Kelsey shrugged and poked at the eggs on her plate. "Only how amazing your eggs are, and how my cooking wouldn't hold a candle to this."

"My eggs might be amazing, but I assure you that my cooking talent ends there," I said with a smile.

"We could always have a cook-off and see who is better," she suggested.

Curiosity piqued, I replied, "That sounds intriguing. What do you suggest we cook for our cook-off?"

"It would have to be something fair. I doubt engaging you in a cook-off for tamales would result in anything other than you losing," she retorted.

"Tamales, eh?" I asked, eyebrows arched in mild surprise.

"Yes … my abuela made sure I could make them just as well as she can. She's from Colombia," Kelsey explained.

"Ah. Well … cook-off aside, what if I just want to try your … tamales?" I questioned, at the last moment substituting *tamale* for the word on the tip of my tongue—*pussy.*

She took a sip of orange juice. "You would need a lot of patience."

I smirked, wondering if she had caught my meaning after all. "I can be patient."

"It usually takes about two whole days. But we make a huge batch. They freeze well. It's well worth the time if you enjoy tamales. If you are serious about the tamales, I can plan on making dinner next weekend ... if you'd like to come over," she offered.

"I appreciate the offer and would love to try them, but I am working next weekend," I replied smoothly. Likely it had been a mistake when she mentioned next weekend, temporarily forgetting about our discussion earlier about not seeing each other again after tomorrow.

Taking my words in stride, Kelsey replied, "I could always mail you some. They ship well."

"Okay," I replied, then took a sip of orange juice and the last bite of eggs.

We slipped into companionable silence. Kelsey drained her cup and stood up, picking her plate up and moving toward my side of the table. Her thigh brushed my arm as she reached for my plate. Unable to resist, I gently squeezed her hand and took the plates, setting them back on the table.

"What are you doing? You cooked. I clean," Kelsey said uncertainly.

Throat constricting with pent-up desire, I tugged her onto my lap, then shifted my hips so she was straddling me. Using the barest touch of magic, I slid the fly of my boxers open enough to free my throbbing shaft. Keeping my gazed fixed on Kelsey's, I settled my hands around her waist to keep her balanced and tilted my hips, causing my cock to brush her inner thigh. A gasp escaped her lips, but she didn't protest. Intent on my objective, I unbuttoned her shirt quickly, then gently massaged her breasts, lightly pinching her nipples between my fingers. She squirmed in my lap, bumping my cock and almost driving me into her folds. A moan escaped her lips and sent blazing hot desire to my core. Kelsey draped her hands around my neck and captured my lips. Releasing her breasts, I set my hands on her waist again and thrust upward with my hips, sliding effortlessly into her drenched pussy.

Kelsey's channel tightened, and my whole body quivered. Lightly lifting Kelsey's hips, I encouraged her to find her rhythm, this position allowing me to drive even deeper than before. Sharp sparks flowed down my spine. They were painful, yet seemed to be heightening my desire at the same time. Kelsey plunged downward, and I held her close as our orgasms shuddered through us.

Kelsey fell asleep in my arms. Not wanting to disturb her, I picked her up and carried her over to the couch, then laid her down. I removed my now-useless boxers and curled up alongside her. I had less than forty-eight hours left with no one demanding my attention or arranging my schedule for me. I fully intended to make the most of what I had left. As Kelsey slept, each rise and fall of her chest caused her nipples to rub against my rib cage.

Minutes trickled by, and it became increasingly difficult to ignore the desire once again rising within me. Throwing caution to the wind about any questions Kelsey might have regarding my sexual stamina, I dipped my head down and took her breast into my mouth. Kelsey whimpered softly, sending a jolt of need straight to my cock.

Her eyes opened the barest of slits. "You want more?" she asked in a teasing tone.

Opting to answer with action, I let my left hand trail a path from her breast down to between her thighs while I lightly grazed her nipple with my teeth. Though my own need was borderline painful, I enjoyed watching Kelsey's body respond to my ministrations. With a calculated flick to her clit, Kelsey's body spasmed with release, and my hand was slick with her fluids. Releasing her breast, I met her gaze and lowered mine, hoping she would watch as I took my left hand and wrapped it around my shaft, stroking. My gamble almost failed as each touch of my hand sent me dangerously close to my own release.

Kelsey covered my hand with hers and scooted closer. I allowed her to guide my cock into her entrance. Then, I loosened my hold on my cock and drove myself deep within her folds. Kelsey shifted so she was entirely on her back, her fingers loosely encircling my shaft, adding another layer to the multitude of sensations I was feeling. Beneath me, I could tell Kelsey was worn out from our morning together but clearly didn't mind. Her eyes were glazed with pleasure.

I leaned down to kiss her, sensing we were both close. I froze mid-thrust when there was a sharp knock on the door. Growling in frustration, I stood up and snagged the throw blanket off the back of the couch, wrapping it around my hips as though it were a towel.

I offered Kelsey a hand to stand. "Who is that?" she asked.

Frustration filled me that I had not been able to finish for both of our sakes. Usually, I was attuned to when people were approaching. The fact that I wasn't meant one of two things: either Kelsey was a massive distraction or the visitor was an immortal. Selecting my words carefully, I replied, "I'm not sure. Why don't you go to the bedroom and find something more suitable to wear, and I will figure out who it is and how to get rid of them."

Kelsey snatched the discarded shirt off the floor and quickly headed to the bedroom. When I heard the bedroom door shut, I yanked open the front door and stepped onto the stoop, closing the door firmly behind me. I faced the visitor, cursing under my breath when I recognized Octavio, fellow angel and my father's right-hand man and official third-in-command. Octavio's human form was a tall, reed-thin man with deep brown skin and tightly curled midnight-black hair. His attire of choice was always a black-on-black tailored suit with a dark, solid-colored tie. Today the tie was navy.

"Conner, I am pleased to have found you," Octavio began. I ground my teeth together. *I'm sure he's so pleased.* "Cassiel needs you to return immediately."

"No," I replied harshly. I still had almost two full days left; I refused to let him renege on our agreement.

Octavio inspected me from head to toe, his eyes lingering on the blanket wrapped around my hips. "You can find another woman to fuck back in Los Angeles. This is not a polite request. He is ordering you to return now."

Curling my hands into fists, I stepped forward menacingly. "My answer is no. I will not return until Monday morning as previously agreed. What I do while I'm here is neither his business nor yours."

Octavio's eyes flashed bright gold for a moment before returning to normal. As long as I stayed here in the human realm, Octavio could not force me to do anything. Nor could we allow humans to see our true selves. Going to Ianialar, the Ash Realm, would level the field between us, but it was a fight I had been avoiding for centuries because I wasn't certain I could win.

"Perhaps I should solve the issue," Octavio said and sniffed the air pointedly. "I shall go in there and kill the human woman, and then you can return."

I lunged forward and threw a punch at Octavio's stomach, except he vanished and reappeared behind me. His arm wrapped around my throat, cutting off my airway. Flailing my arms, I did every maneuver I knew to get out of his hold to no avail. Unlike me, because Octavio largely served as an enforcer to prevent humans from discovering the existence of immortals, he could take a human life as long as he could prove it was to protect the secret.

Octavio's breath was hot on my ear as he whispered, "You never cared about a human before. I'm going to find out who she is, and then I'll be back. You have two choices: return to Los Angeles and I'll leave her be, or stay here and watch her suffer."

The pressure around my throat disappeared when Octavio used his magic to travel back to wherever he came from. Breathing heavily, I braced my hands on my thighs, trying to sort out my next move. I would not get another warning from Octavio or Cassiel.

Of that, I was certain. However, Octavio and I had a complicated history, and there had been more than a few times where, to get under my skin, he had escalated the urgency of Cassiel's orders.

I reviewed what I knew. It was early afternoon on a Saturday morning. The hospitals we had been in recent negotiations with made a point of not setting meetings up on the weekends. Which meant whatever had come up was either a more personal matter to Cassiel *or* a sharp reminder that he was still in charge at least for another two months. Remembering Kelsey was waiting for me, I spun on my heel and ran back into the house, trying to leash my temper so Kelsey wouldn't see this side of me.

Taking a deep breath, I let my anger at my father dissipate. If I was only going to have the rest of the day to spend with Kelsey, I didn't want to waste it. *Now I must decide. Do I try to get to know her better and make leaving her that much more complicated?* I paused. Why *do I care if it's complicated? As soon as I leave, I will forget her.*

"Kelsey?" I called into the silent house. After checking the bedroom, I peeked into the bathroom and noticed her swimsuit was missing. Running a hand over my face, I searched each room again, looking for a note or something. *I could call her ... except we agreed to not share that information.*

There was a short note sitting on the counter.

Conner,

I can't thank you enough for the amazing morning.

See you around,

Kelsey

Octavio's appearance and Kelsey's departure were stark reminders of why I had originally wanted to not interact with anyone this weekend and what had led to the previous decision not to exchange any useful contact information with Kelsey. The current turn of events also provided me with nothing that would truly keep me here. I had no idea how to find Kelsey using human technology and was not willing to breach our agreement and use magic to find her. *Perhaps I should return to Los Angeles. Do I have any reason to stay?*

Chapter 9: Kelsey

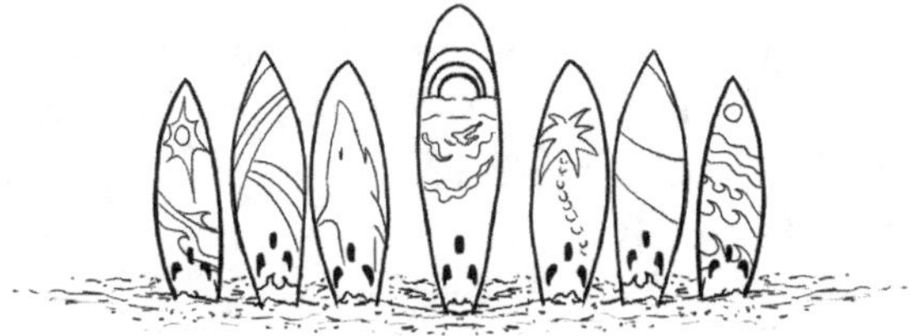

Saturday, September 7

Returning to Abuela's house, I was relieved when I recalled she was gone for the entire day helping a friend at one of the local Saturday markets. Which meant she wouldn't ask me why I was wearing a man's sweats and shirt after returning from surfing. Though I had hoped when Conner went to answer the door that he would handle the visitor swiftly and return so we could finish what we'd started, I knew that it was better this way. He had been clear about his intention to keep whatever was between us exclusively tied to this weekend, which I was coming to terms with. I didn't have a way of contacting him, but it no longer mattered. Our time together was over. My phone buzzed as I parked behind the house, flashing that Penny had texted me.

I turned off the engine and reached for the phone to send her a quick response that I would love to meet her at Toucan's that night. Checking that my alarm was shut off and wouldn't wake me up for dawn patrol tomorrow, I climbed out of the car and set about hosing off my surfboard.

When the sand was washed away, I propped it up at the back of

Abuela's house to dry.

A yawn escaped my lips as I unlocked the house. *Maybe I should take a quick nap.* Decision made, I locked the back door and made my way straight to the bedroom. Yawning again, I climbed into bed and slid under the covers. As soon as my head touched the pillow, I was asleep.

The phone rang, and my eyes popped open. I was shocked to see the room was pitch black. *What time is it?* I grabbed my cell phone and stared at it in disbelief when I saw it was seven p.m.!

"Hello?" I said groggily.

"Did you forget?" Penny nearly shrieked in my ear.

"Forget what?" I asked, rubbing the sleep from my eyes.

"That would be a yes, you did forget. We texted a few hours ago … to meet at Toucan's tonight?"

Fumbling around, I turned on the lamp at the side of the bed. "Sorry, I took a nap … a really *long* nap."

"Well, you better hurry. I'm already here saving our table," Penny said excitedly.

"I will hurry. Promise. See you shortly," I said. I looked down at my clothing—*Conner's clothing*—then caught sight of my hair in the mirror. My hair was like a rat's nest. Groaning, I debated what I should do. A shower would be the best option, but it would also make me even later. *I don't want to scare Penny away because I smell like sweaty sex.*

An hour later, cleaned up in a cocktail-length little black lace dress with my hair pulled back in a messy bun, I hurried inside as Tiny waved me through the doors to Toucan's. Every Friday and Saturday night throughout the year, they had live music and dancing. The band usually played a mix of current country and rock songs as well as some older favorites from the seventies and eighties.

Penny was at what used to be our favorite booth on the right side. Tonight, it was covered in a dark red shimmery tablecloth with a small LED candle flickering in the center. Weaving my way through the throng of people, I finally reached her. Penny gave me a thorough inspection, smiling in approval. I did the same to her, falling into our old habit. She was wearing a calf-length empire waist dress with a black top and gold bottom.

"I can't believe you still have that dress!" Penny giggled. "And it fits you!"

I laughed. "Your dress doesn't look too shabby either."

Penny rolled her eyes. "Thanks. I really do appreciate it. You'd be amazed at how often your body does the strangest things after popping out two kids."

"While you're right, I don't have any firsthand experience with that ... but I do work with a lot of young children, and therefore interact with their mothers. So I'm not as naïve as you might think," I remarked.

"Has it changed your mind about wanting children at all?" Penny asked.

"No, I still want children," I said with a sad smile. It was one of the things I worried about. I was thirty-two, and other than the relationship with Joel years ago, I had never had a steady boyfriend. Nor had I ever met anyone that I could see myself sharing a life with. Reproductive assistance techniques had evolved by leaps and bounds, but at times I couldn't help feeling as though my clock was ticking for my ability to become a mother. At least if I wanted to be pregnant.

"How old are they now?" I asked.

Penny smiled. "Eight and five."

"Are you going to have any more?" I asked hesitantly, knowing for many it was a sensitive topic.

Penny chuckled. "Hell no. That second pregnancy almost killed me twice. I don't mean figuratively either. After that, Ken agreed to have a vasectomy so we wouldn't risk going through it again. Two is enough. A third is not worth gambling my life."

"I'm sorry. I didn't realize you had complications," I said, feeling like a terrible friend.

"You were just starting your surgical residency. I didn't want you to screw up your future by having you rush home when there was nothing you could do for me," Penny said, patting my hand. "Now enough of this soppy shit. Let's go dance!" Penny snagged my hand and dragged me onto the dance floor just as the Eagles' "Hotel California" wrapped up.

Light on my feet, I swayed to the music, easing into dancing when "Hotel California" ended. I was surprised and pleased that the band transitioned into Black Sabbath's "Paranoid," enthusiastically swinging my hips, the beaded hem of my dress swishing against my legs. Losing ourselves in the music, Penny and I danced to song after song. When the band took a water break, I inhaled deeply the smell of beer, a few nearby fruity cocktails, and cooking oil from the limited menu of fried finger foods such as fries, chicken bites, and mozzarella sticks.

We retreated to the table to avoid the throng of people cramming around the bar. A waitress brought two glasses of ice water over and asked if we wanted anything. I declined, fully intending to go back on the dance floor when the band's break ended.

Penny set her mostly empty cup down and smiled at me. "Are you going to tell me why you were so tired this afternoon you took a nap for over three hours?"

Amused at her question, I gamely replied, "I went surfing on dawn patrol. This was the second morning in a row."

Penny shook her head. "I know what your crazy surgical schedule is like. I am not convinced it was simply a matter of you getting up early to surf."

I raised my hands. "You got me. I met a guy. Conner."

"Met him where? Tell me more," Penny said, eagerly leaning toward me.

Her questions had me blushing and wondering how stupid I was going to sound when I explained it. Taking a deep breath, I decided, why not? "At Blue Fin, but he is here for the weekend to surf. We hooked up this morning with a promise that it's just for this weekend, so we didn't exchange any contact information."

"Go, girl!" Penny cheered. "You deserve to have some fun every once in a while."

"Even with a stranger?" I asked, a little surprised that Penny was this happy about my weekend antics.

"That makes it easier. No baggage to unpack or deal with," Penny replied.

Listening to her, I let her words sink in, realizing how right she was.

The band settled themselves on the stage as a big throng of people moved toward the dance floor. I opened my mouth to ask Penny if she wanted to dance more when she popped out of her seat.

"Bathroom!" she gasped and took off.

Wrapping my hand around the damp cup of ice water, I was content to observe. The band opened with a particularly loud number, and I tapped my foot in time to the drum beats, watching a purple-haired couple vigorously jumping near the middle of the dance floor.

I heard a throat clearing, drawing my attention away from the dance floor. My eyes widened as I took in Conner—the last person I expected to see tonight. He was dressed as though he was going to a business meeting, wearing a gray tailored suit and red tie.

"What are you doing here?" I asked, fiddling with my cup.

He gave me a charming smile, and my stomach started doing flip-flops as he spoke. "The guy at the gas station suggested it would be a great place to grab a drink and enjoy live music before I leave town."

Not sure how to reply, I looked toward the bathroom, hoping Penny would return soon.

Then, the music shifted to a slow song, and he asked, "May I have this dance?"

Pressing my lips together, I considered the question. He was on his way out of town, and after I'd left his beach house this morning,

I had come to terms with the likelihood we wouldn't see each other again. *Then one dance won't matter.*

I set my glass down and rose from my seat. "One dance," I agreed, then placed my hand in his and let him lead me to the dance floor.

We pushed our way through the people till we found a small open pocket. I stepped close to Conner, put my hand lightly on his shoulder, and placed the other in in his hand. I was careful not to eliminate the gap between us, ensuring we weren't touching anywhere except our hands.

Conner spoke. "How was the rest of your afternoon?"

"I took a nap," I replied softly.

"I was being serious," he responded.

"Yes, I know, and I did in fact take a nap," I said defensively. "Do you have something against naps?"

Conner shrugged. "No. I was just surprised. I don't know very many people who take naps during the middle of the afternoon." A smile formed on his lips when he said, "I do know people who are in bed at that time."

"That's the same thing," I replied matter-of-factly.

"No ... trust me. It's not." Conner's gaze dropped from my eyes to my lips, and I held my breath, guessing what he was going to do. He tipped his head down and captured my lips with his.

As we kissed, I realized what he meant. "Oh!" I gasped, and my cheeks heated.

Behind Conner's shoulder, over at the bar, I could see Penny waving to me. "Excuse me," I murmured before slipping away through the crowd. Thankfully, he let me go. I enjoyed the dance with Conner, but tonight was my chance to hang out with Penny. I didn't want to ditch my best friend, no matter how hot the guy was.

"Who was that?" Penny asked, eyebrow arched.

"No one important," I mumbled.

"If you say so ..." Penny replied with a smirk. "I just ordered a snack. They're going to bring it to our table. C'mon." Penny linked arms with me, and we wandered back over to the table, saying hi to Lane, Genevieve, and few other familiar faces along the way.

"See, everyone missed having you around," Penny retorted as we slid into the booth together.

"I think you're imagining things. They were just saying hello to me to be polite because they're *your* friends," I replied.

"Maybe, maybe not," Penny said. Just then, our snack arrived. A fresh veggie platter and pita bread with hummus.

"Great choice!" I said appreciatively.

"See, I do remember what you like," Penny said.

"I never implied otherwise. I mean, I did practically live at your house every summer for what? Ten years?" I remarked.

"Something like that, yeah," Penny agreed. She opened her mouth to say something else when a cough interrupted her.

"Excuse me," Conner said from the edge of the table.

"Why hello," Penny replied in a much deeper, more sultry voice than she usually used.

I stared at my friend in surprise before glancing at Conner. The dance had been nice, but he was leaving tonight, and I was not sure I wanted to give him any more of my time. "Penny, this is Conner. He is leaving," I said firmly.

"Nice to meet you, Penny," Conner said, offering Penny his hand.

"Likewise," she murmured, taking his hand and studying it. I rolled my eyes.

"He's not a specimen in the lab, Penny," I muttered, embarrassed.

Conner laughed. "What do you do, Penny?"

Penny dropped his hand before replying. "I'm the lab manager of a chemical engineering firm. What do you do?"

Conner smoothly replied, "I'm in business."

"Very nice," Penny said. Then, her phone started vibrating, and she glanced at the screen. "Ken is calling me. I need to take it."

I watched as Penny picked up her purse and headed toward the door to the parking lot. I ran my fingers over the edge of my dress, not sure what to say to Conner.

"What do you do?" he asked, breaking the silence.

I jumped slightly, not expecting him to say anything, especially not a question that went against our agreement from the morning. Deciding to keep any useful details out, I replied, "I'm a surgeon." I glanced toward the door, worried about Penny, when my phone vibrated. Peering at it, I read Penny's text. "Penny had to go home. Both kids are puking," I informed Conner.

"Sounds unpleasant," he murmured.

I sighed. I agreed it did sound disgusting, but someday I wanted children of my own—badly enough that even dealing with sick ones sounded better than none.

"Would you like to dance again?" Conner asked.

I bit my lip, indecision coursing through me. On one hand, I was annoyed with Conner for barging in on my friend-date with Penny, but was it really his fault? Penny had to go home to take care of her kids. I knew Penny would think I was crazy if I left without at least one more dance with Conner. *If I like him as much as I think I do, why would I not want to dance with him?* Taking a deep breath, I looked him straight in the eyes.

"Yes, I will dance with you. But ... I need a moment. I'll be right back." I stood up, gathering my purse and phone, then quickly headed for the bathroom.

Chapter 10: Conner

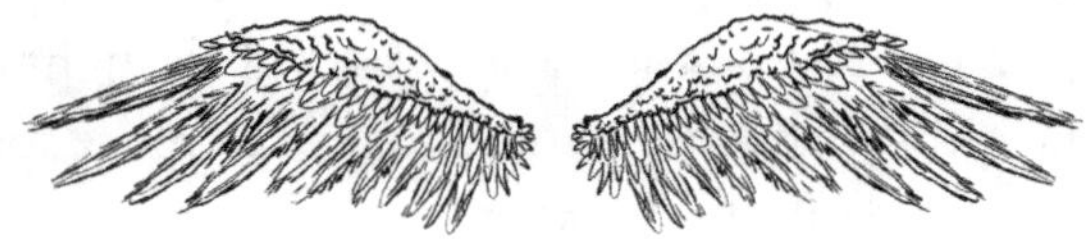

Saturday, September 7

While Kelsey went to the bathroom, I waited at the table she had shared with Penny, absently running my fingers over the shimmery tablecloth. I was curious about the live music, and the gas station clerk had suggested that I come here to check it out. The last thing I had anticipated was running across Kelsey again, especially after she had departed in haste during Octavio's visit.

I wasn't entirely sure what I was doing. The helicopter was waiting for me at the small airport, but I was reluctant to leave. Seeing Kelsey here had me seriously considering ignoring Octavio's threat. At the very least, I wanted to say a proper goodbye. I was gazing blankly at the table when Kelsey walked right up to me and gave me a light kiss on the lips, then slid her hand into mine and tugged.

"You said you wanted to dance, right?" she asked. Nodding, I allowed myself to be guided back onto the dance floor. The music was fast-paced, but by the time we found space among the dancers, it had changed to another slow song. Kelsey wrapped her arms around my neck, and our bodies brushed lightly. With slow and deliberate movements, I set my hands loosely on her waist.

"I'm sorry," she murmured.

My eyes narrowed in uncertainty. "Sorry for what?" I asked.

"Earlier at the beach house ... you had someone show up, and I left," Kelsey said softly. "I wasn't sure what was going on, and I thought it would be better if I left. I had some matters to attend to."

"Matters like your nap?" I teased.

Kelsey blushed. I tipped my head down and kissed her. Then the song changed, and Kelsey took a step back. I thought she might leave, but she didn't. She just wanted to give us more space.

We danced and danced. Her arm would bump my arm. Then, her hip brushed my thigh, sending an electric shock through me from head to toe. I stumbled slightly and cast her a worried glance, but thankfully Kelsey was too absorbed in the music to notice, and clearly she wasn't feeling whatever magical phenomenon was affecting me. A blessing so I wouldn't have to explain the existence of magic to her tonight.

The band eased into "Stairway to Heaven," and I pulled Kelsey tight against me. I could feel her heartbeat in sync with mine, and I ran my hand down her back. My cock was hard enough to be painful. To my surprise, Kelsey crushed her lips against mine, demanding. I eagerly responded, needing the contact, when she began grinding against me. A moan escaped my lips. If I wasn't careful, I was going to lose control here on the dance floor.

Breathlessly, Kelsey murmured, "Do you want to go somewhere?"

Instead of answering her with words, I kissed her again.

Giggling, Kelsey let go of me and led us toward the table where her purse was. "We could go to my place." She snagged her purse off the bench and rifled through, pulling out a few bills and setting a glass on top to ensure the waitress would notice.

I was surprised at the offer, but it solved the problem of me not having anywhere to go. All my stuff was in the truck; I had already turned in the beach house keys.

"What about ... what about your grandmother?" I asked, following her to the Prius.

She didn't respond until we were both in the car. "On the weekends, she helps her friend at the farmers' market and usually spends the night since they have to start cooking at four a.m.," Kelsey said, keeping her eyes on the mirror as she backed out of the parking lot. Usually, I wanted to be the one behind the wheel, but I decided for one night I could relinquish that small bit of control. Kelsey driving gave me a chance to enjoy the view she provided without coming across as rude. I studied the lines of her jaw, the shape of her lips, and the stray piece of brown hair curling around her face.

Toucan's was a few blocks away from the beach, making it easy to understand why it was popular for surfers. My eyes flicked away from Kelsey's face as we approached a signal turning yellow. Instead of driving through the light as I would have done, Kelsey took the cautious choice and stopped. I immediately recognized the intersection since it had the gas station at the corner where I'd gotten the advice to check out Toucan's hours ago. Now, with the late hour, the lights flickered over the empty parking lot.

A tingling sensation at the back of my neck warned me another immortal was approaching. Subtly looking around, I saw no other vehicles or pedestrians in our vicinity. I shrugged it off. There were enough others living in the human realm that one being nearby was not overly concerning.

Our light turned green, and the Prius made a loud whirring noise before shooting forward abruptly and then slowing down. I peered at Kelsey and teased her, "Maybe you need a new car. I think this one is on its last legs."

Kelsey stuck her tongue out at me as we crept forward out of the intersection. "It serves its purpose."

I leaned over to kiss her lightly on the cheek when a large red dually truck that hadn't been there seconds ago barreled through the intersection, heading straight for us.

Horror in her eyes, Kelsey stomped on the gas pedal, but the Prius wouldn't go any faster.

Through the window, I could see Octavio's dark face, glowing gold eyes, and his vicious expression. The need to protect Kelsey overwhelmed me, and without thinking through my actions, I unfurled my wings and wrapped myself protectively around her as a shield.

I must have blacked out. When I opened my eyes, my wings were still wrapped around Kelsey, but the Prius was on the sidewalk blocking the driveway to the gas station about twenty feet from where the initial impact had happened. Kelsey moaned, and I withdrew my arms, once again hiding my wings. She was bleeding profusely from a wound on her head, and her eyes were closed.

"Kelsey," I said.

"Mmmm," she replied.

"Open your eyes," I ordered, concern for her overriding my fury at Octavio and Cassiel for orchestrating the accident.

She opened her green eyes and gave me a confused look. "Who are you?"

My throat constricted as I realized Kelsey had a concussion.

"Here to help," I replied calmly. "You were in a bad accident."

Kelsey gave me a bewildered look, then gasped sharply. "It hurts."

"Can you tell me where?" I asked, my hand hovering over her arm.

"Everywhere," she whispered.

I laid my hand lightly on her arm, careful not to apply any pressure, and summoned my magic. I could feel it under my skin, but it wasn't working to heal her. *Fuck, they're blocking me.* I blew out my breath, trying to keep my emotions out of my voice and not alarm Kelsey. "I'm going to call for help. I will be right back, I promise," I told her. Kelsey gave me the barest of nods, and I got out of the car.

I yanked my phone out of my pocket and powered it on. "Call nine-one-one," I told it, then held it to my ear.

"Nine-one-one, what's your emergency?" the dispatcher's voice said.

"I'm at …" I looked around for street signs. "The BP gas station on Main and Eleventh Street. There was an accident. A red dually truck ran the red light and T-boned a Prius."

"Help is on the way. Is there anything else you can tell me?" the dispatcher asked.

"The red dually that caused the accident fled the scene," I growled.

"Did you get a plate?" she asked.

I shook my head, then realized I would need to give a verbal answer. "No. But I do see police and an ambulance approaching." Flashing lights were coming from two directions.

I hung up. I knew I probably should have stayed on the line, but I was worried about Kelsey and wanted to make sure she stayed conscious. Walking up to the decimated driver's side, I couldn't see much of anything. The glass on the windows was cracked to the point that it obscured her from view. I went around to the passenger side, where the window was undamaged. To my dismay, Kelsey's head was lolling forward and her eyes were shut. She'd passed out.

"Help is coming," I told her through the door, hoping my voice would wake her up, but she didn't move. Only the rise and fall of her chest confirmed she was still breathing. I felt helpless waiting for the emergency services to come, a feeling I didn't like, not when I was used to having my healing abilities at my fingertips.

As a fire truck, ambulance, and police car drove up from different directions, I realized I needed to decide what I was going to tell them. Kelsey had no idea who I was, and it would be difficult to explain how I had walked away unscathed when she was severely injured. I stood watching with my arms crossed over my chest as the firefighters conducted a full inspection of the exterior of the car, then selected the tools they would need for her extraction.

The police officer waved to get my attention. "A word," he called. I nodded and walked toward the broad-shouldered, average-height man with a blond mustache and hazel eyes.

"Yes, Officer," I said calmly.

"I'm Sergeant Pete Hunter. Can you tell me what happened?" he asked, a pad of paper and a pencil in his hand.

"I was waiting at the crosswalk next to the gas station when the light turned green and the blue Prius started across the intersection. It was having some obvious mechanical issues and not moving very fast. The light cycle was long and still green when the dually came out of nowhere going extremely fast and ran its red light. It slammed into the Prius, and then when both vehicles stopped moving, the truck backed up and left. You can see the skid marks there," I said, indicating black lines on the pavement from where the dually had peeled out. "I did not get the license plate number."

"We have cameras for that," Sergeant Hunter reassured me.

I stayed silent. Since Octavio had caused the crash, I assumed that likely the traffic cameras had been off or obscured. My phone buzzed in my hand. I glanced down at it. It was my father. I sent the call to voicemail, but I knew I needed to go soon. "I must go to an emergency meeting. I hope the woman is okay," I said.

Sergeant Hunter nodded in understanding. "Thank you for being so prompt in calling about the accident. If you think of anything else that could be useful, don't hesitate to call my number." He pulled out a business card and handed it to me.

I stuffed it in my pocket. "Will do."

I glanced over at Kelsey's car. The jaws of life had been used to pry open the driver-side door, and she was being wheeled away on a gurney toward the ambulance. My hands were shaking. I shoved them in my pockets, hoping Sergeant Hunter was too distracted by the accident scene to pay attention to me. I wanted to go to the hospital with Kelsey but was afraid that if I did, Octavio would return to finish the job.

Instead, I turned my back and walked away. Each step was almost painful, but I had no other option. I refused to put her in more danger than I already had. *This was my plan, to leave after the weekend*, I reminded myself, throat constricting. *Then why does it feel like I'm doing the worst thing I've ever done in my life?*

Leaving Kelsey in the hands of the EMT was one of the most difficult things I'd ever done in the fifteen hundred years I'd lived. It was good that once I got in the helicopter, the pilot had been in charge of flying us to my house in Malibu; otherwise, I'm certain I'd have landed on the helipad at the hospital. Deep down, I knew never seeing her again was the only way to keep her safe. It didn't make it any easier.

Wisely, I'd chosen to stay away from Cassiel Saturday night, not trusting myself to keep my temper in check. I was confident the pilot had informed either Cassiel or Octavio I had returned and that was all that truly mattered.

Taking a deep breath, I tugged the cuffs of my pale gray suit jacket down and strode into the office, where Cassiel was waiting for me. He'd chosen to meet Sunday morning in one of our high-rise mixed-use buildings in Newport Beach, California. The large window Cassiel gazed out of provided a spectacular view of the beach, and the ocean appeared to stretch endlessly.

Cassiel was wearing an impeccably tailored dark gray suit with subtle pinstripes, his shoulder-length dark gray hair immaculately styled. His back was to me, a deliberate jibe. "You're late," he growled.

Choosing my words carefully, I replied, "Traffic was terrible per usual. You frequently press upon me how important it is that the humans we interact with see us behaving normally, which is what I did."

Cassiel turned around to face me. His piercing blue eyes missed nothing. His jaw tightened, and I was surprised when he dropped the matter. Instead, he said, "Fabio has updated your schedule with any necessary adjustments. I need you at meetings for the next two weeks here in Los Angeles, and then you'll be heading back to

London."

He offered me a piece of paper. I took it and skimmed the contents, a rough list of meetings and topics. "Azinak and Tolmon have been getting antsy the closer we get to your birthday. There have been some whispers among their clans about whether you are going to pull out of your contracts after your birthday. I want you to reassure them that you will not."

I kept my mouth clamped shut to hide my amusement. Azinak and Tolmon were the board chairs for two different hospital groups that had holdings within Southern California. Both had been vehemently opposed to dealing with Hadriel again after an emergency had caused her to take my place. Hadriel preferred to force demons to bend to her will, whereas I found negotiating worked better, especially with the demon clans who ran the hospitals.

If I did part ways with Cassiel and my current responsibilities, then Hadriel would take over. While I enjoyed working with Azinak and Tolmon, their needs were not going to supersede my own, and I had yet to decide if anything would change after my birthday. Or at least change as far as the demons were concerned.

The meeting with Azinak was at the Los Angeles Children's Hospital, where my father was chief financial officer for the corporation that owned the hospital. Previously, the LACH board of directors had not been interested in allowing me a permanent position on their board despite the gaping vacancy. *But Azinak hadn't been involved.*

"Other than these meetings, is there anything else you need me for?" I asked, careful to keep my voice neutral.

"The Los Angeles Children's Hospital is planning a gala fundraiser. The theme is a Halloween masquerade since it is on October thirty-first. I also felt it would be appropriate to celebrate your birthday at the same time, since it is the same day," Cassiel announced.

I sighed. *Yay, another Halloween birthday party.* This would be the fifth Halloween birthday party Cassiel had required me to attend in the past decade, and I was over it. Though if Azinak was involved, the demon would be thrilled to have a chance to celebrate with me. *Except for the small matter of the humans who would also be in attendance.*

"Do you have a problem with that?" my father asked, giving me a sharp look.

I shook my head. "No, I will be there. Now, if that is all," I said, glancing at the piece of paper again, "it seems as though I have a meeting this afternoon, and I would like a chance to prepare for it."

Cassiel nodded a dismissal. Paper in hand, I exited the conference room. The receptionist waved hello. I ignored her. Typically, I spoke to all the office staff, but today, I just didn't have spare time. Mashing the elevator button, I waited impatiently for it to take me to the ground floor, where Fabio waited with the car.

Fabio, in a black suit with a lime-green button-up shirt and white tie, opened the door to the black limo. I slid onto the white leather seat, and I let my eyes close before Fabio got in. I startled awake as the car glided to a stop in front of my Malibu house.

"Are you okay, sir?" Fabio asked.

"Fine. There were just things that occurred in Santa Barbara that I am still trying to make sense of," I replied and led the way into the house. Our footsteps echoed on the white marble in the entryway. The house was eerily quiet, reminding me that the staff wouldn't be returning until tomorrow afternoon, when I was originally supposed to return.

"Meet me in the gym in ten minutes. I'd like to run a few things by you," I said, making a swift decision to loop Fabio in on the strange events of the weekend. I had about three hours before I had to be ready to go. Not time for me to do much, but I could work out and review my meeting notes on the way there.

"Will do," Fabio responded.

I headed up the sweeping marble staircase to the second level, where the master suite was. The staircase on the opposite wall went down into the subterranean third level comprising the garage and gym.

The master bedroom alone was about the size of the entire beach house I had rented. Though at times the Malibu house felt borderline excessive, many people I rubbed elbows with would kill for an invitation. Rummaging through the closet, I found some workout shorts and discarded my suit in a heap. *Good thing I have enough clothes to wear for over a month without doing any laundry.* After sliding into the black athletic shorts, I headed down the three flights of stairs and into the gym.

When I was in town, Kory, or Korelas, fellow angel and longtime friend, would come four days a week to supervise my workouts. We would vary our training, ranging from hand-to-hand combat, strength training, and occasionally working with my favorite weapon, the glaive.

I walked over to the hidden panel and laid my palm flat on it. There was a shimmer of gold magic and then it disappeared, revealing an assortment of weapons that humans would consider medieval. I selected the glaive. It had a thick, well-oiled oak shaft that was topped by a two-foot-long steel blade. Carrying the blade over to the large square mat on the left side of the gym, I set it on the rack, then began my warmup stretches.

Fabio came in when I was about halfway through. I focused my gaze on him and continued stretching.

"I heard a rumor about what happened in Santa Barbara," Fabio started.

I changed position and started on my crunches. "Oh yeah?" I replied.

"Octavio is usually full of shit, so I was hoping you'd set the record straight," Fabio responded.

Keeping my breathing even, I worked my way through a set of crunches, then paused. "The short version is that Saturday morning Octavio delivered orders for me to return to Los Angeles immediately. Around midnight, he crashed into the car I was in with a human woman."

Fabio sucked in a sharp breath, and I could almost hear his questions in my mind. "That's risky ... but I must ask, why were you in a car with a human woman at midnight?"

I closed my eyes and sat upright, abandoning my second set of crunches. I opened my eyes again and Fabio was giving me a strange look. "There is a connection between her and me. The best I can explain it is that numerous times over the weekend it felt like I was hit by a lightning bolt when I was near her. I knew it was Octavio driving toward us, and I shielded Kelsey. Otherwise, she would have died. He was driving too fast in a massive truck, and she had an old Prius."

Fabio ran a hand over his face. "Does she know who you are?"

I shook my head. "We only exchanged first names. Our agreement was to have a fun weekend and then never see each other again."

"That's good. Then what is the problem?" Fabio asked.

"There are a couple. The first is that an angel attacked a human for no reason, and given she was driving an almost fifteen-year-old car, I'm not sure she can afford to replace it. The second is that I've never heard of angels being directly connected to humans in any way," I replied.

"I see. Well, I should be able to hack into the police records and see what information they were able to discern from the intersection cameras. That will give us an idea of what we have to work with. Most likely Octavio orchestrated it so he was untraceable. If that's the case, I can fabricate a man who has auto insurance to take the fall, and that will get Kelsey an insurance payout as well as remove any odd questions from coming up. In my experience, human police accept things that may not be quite natural if they have a very real person to blame," Fabio responded. "As to the lightning bolt thing between you and the woman, I'll see what I can dig up. I'd suggest you ask Cassiel, since he might know, but I know the two of you too well to expect that to be a solution."

Relieved that Fabio would help out with these two pressing matters, freeing me to handle the meetings Cassiel had set up for me, I resumed my warmup. Fabio waited until I stood up and retrieved the glaive from the stand before departing.

Taking a deep breath, I moved into the middle of the mat and started a basic drill with the glaive. High, low, and middle strikes and blocks. On each set, I increased the speed until it was too fast for humans to discern. I was confident Fabio would sort out the matters tied to Santa Barbara, which meant it was up to me to move past whatever was between me and Kelsey and focus on my work the next two weeks in Los Angeles.

Chapter 11: Kelsey

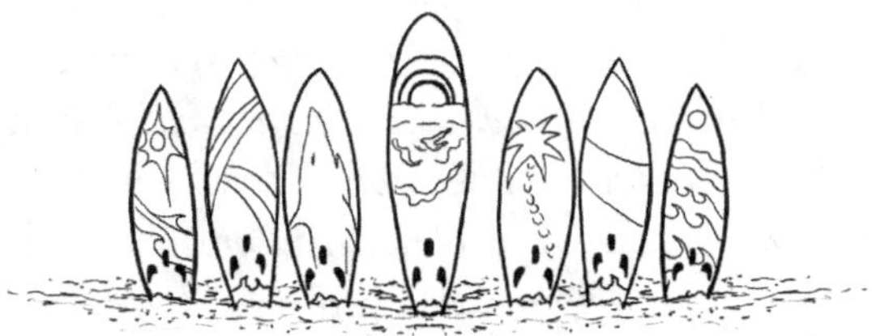

Sunday, September 8

Beep. Beep.

I gradually became aware of the sound of a machine near my head. I thought I could feel a seatbelt-like strap across my shoulders and legs, but I wasn't entirely sure since my whole body was screaming at me, particularly my head. I cracked my eyes open a slit. A woman in a uniform was leaning over me. Slowly, I opened my eyes the rest of the way. The black uniform with the blue medical patch meant the woman was probably an EMT. Peering straight up and to the sides, I saw lights and cabinets. Then we hit a bump, and I realized I was in an ambulance.

"Dr. Kelsey Floras?" the EMT said.

I tried to turn my head toward her but realized I was in a C collar and couldn't.

"Yes," I said, though my words sounded strange to my own ears, and I wasn't entirely sure I had spoken audibly.

"I'm Tonya, your EMT. We're taking you to the hospital," Tonya explained. Her face was becoming fuzzy and then darkness closed around me.

I was sitting on my hot pink surfboard, my hair draped over my shoulders in double French braids. Joel was next to me on his surfboard. We were alone on dawn patrol, surfing before our first day of senior classes. The waves were quite flat, and we spent more time chatting than we did surfing.

Joel's leg brushed mine. Butterflies fluttered in my stomach. His eyes met mine, and he leaned over. I was angled toward him, hoping he was going to finally kiss me, when his board started to tip. He straightened to correct the board's momentum. Instead, it sent him flipping over into the ocean. A giggle escaped my lips. I waited for him to get back on his board, hoping he would try to kiss me again, but he didn't. He continued our conversation like nothing had happened.

I opened my eyes a crack and was blinded by insanely bright lights. I waited for my vision to adjust and cautiously opened my eyes a little more. A blurry pink face hovered over mine for a few moments. My vision wasn't clearing, but I was starting to be able to hear the words being spoken. I thought I recognized the voice, though I couldn't put my finger on his name, when there was a sharp pain in my side, and everything faded out again.

Joel and I were sitting on a green-and-white striped picnic blanket on a secluded part of the beach, hidden from view by a large pile of gray boulders. It was a spot we had discovered by accident but sought out when we wanted privacy and the chance to be intimate without any interruptions. I was fiddling with my graduation cap.

Joel took my hand in his. "I love you, Kelsey," he said. This wasn't the first time he had said it, though the words felt different this time. Maybe because we'd graduated from high school.

I licked my lips. "I love you too, Joel." I had loved him for years, but now it finally felt like it was real. If we wanted to get married, we could. I turned eighteen two weeks ago. Legally we were adults, and no one could object.

He leaned over and kissed me. I returned the kiss, hoping he'd want to do more. The next few days were going to be crazy with all the celebrations. I wasn't sure when we'd be able to have more alone time.

There was a plastic thing digging into my side and someone was holding my hand. Opening my eyes, I was surprised when my vision was blurry. I could see a person sitting next to me and the pink blanket that was pulled up to my shoulders. I blinked a few times, and my vision cleared enough that I could see who was sitting next to me. Joel.

He had dark circles under his eyes, and his relief was palpable as his face appeared hovering over mine. Looking over his shoulder, he called, "She's awake!" I wasn't sure who that was directed to.

I licked my parched lips. "Joel," I rasped. He hastily grabbed a cup of water with a straw from a small table by his elbow. I took a sip, grateful for the cool water that ran down my parched throat.

"Joel," I said again, my voice sounding mostly normal to me. "What happened?"

Joel frowned. "You were in a car accident. A bystander witnessed it. He said your car was having mechanical issues and wasn't accelerating very fast, and then a dually truck ran the light, hit you, and fled the scene."

I conducted a self-evaluation. My whole body was sore. There was a bandage taped to my forehead and an IV line in my arm, but otherwise the sharp pain I had felt was gone. *Or I'm on that much medication.* "What day is it?" I asked.

"Thursday, September twelfth," Joel replied.

"I've been unconscious since Thursday, September fifth?" I gasped, hoping that the reason all I felt was soreness otherwise, the accident would've been quite severe.

He frowned. "Your accident was Saturday around midnight."

"Did anyone else come by?" I asked, mind still reeling over how many days I'd been here and the Friday and Saturday before the accident I had somehow also misplaced.

"Just the friends and family you have here. Oh, the doctor said that you will heal just fine. It was a minor concussion and lots of bruising, including your ribs from the seatbelt. He highly recommends that you *rest* for your remaining two weeks of vacation though. So, no surfing or other strenuous activities."

My eyes widened in surprise. "That's it? Just take it easy, and I'm fine?"

Joel nodded. "Yeah. You're lucky, Kel, that it wasn't worse. Given the state of your car, everyone is surprised that you're walking away with only a minor concussion. I even overheard the doc saying that usually in crashes like this, anyone in the vehicle on the collision side suffers from multiple fractures. They did every test they could come up with but ultimately decided that there wasn't anything that rest wouldn't fix. The bruises might not be entirely gone by the time you go back to Los Angeles, but the overall soreness should be."

I sighed in relief. My biggest fear was that this accident ruined my shot at becoming a pediatric surgeon.

Joel squeezed my hand. "There are others waiting who want to see you, especially Abuela. I'll be back tomorrow to pick you up."

"Wait," I said as he withdrew his hand.

"Yes?" Joel asked curiously.

Frowning, it felt strange to make this admission, but I plowed on. "The last thing I remember is when you called to tell me you couldn't meet us at Toucan's Thursday, and then waking up here and having this discussion. I have no recollection of the accident at all."

"The doctor talked about amnesia and memory loss. Only time will tell if you will remember the accident. Given you have been unconscious since your arrival at the hospital, I'm not sure there are many memories you'd recover from your stay here," Joel explained.

I yawned. Joel leaned forward and kissed me on the cheek. "I'm going to go so you can see Abuela before you fall asleep again. I'll see you later."

"Okay," I replied tiredly.

Abuela walked in the door. She gave Joel a hug as he left. I gave her a wan smile. My eyelids felt heavy.

"You scared me," Abuela said softly.

"I'm fine," I reassured her, debating if I should ask to look at my medical chart so I could assess myself.

"The doctor said they have to run more tests now that you're out of the coma, and then they will decide how soon you can go home. Joel offered to pick you up," Abuela said and patted my hand. "He missed you."

I gave her a tired smile. "I know I realized on Thursday how much I missed all my friends, and I remember deciding I would make a bigger effort on my vacation to spend time with them *and* surf."

"Nieta, no surfing." Abuela shook her finger at me in warning, then leaned down and gave me a kiss on the forehead. "Get some rest. I'll be back in the morning to keep you company."

"You don't need to do that. I'm fine," I replied.

"Carolina and Mateo died in a tragic accident. Coming here to see you is for me too, Nieta. To be certain you are doing well. I cannot bear the thought of losing you too," Abuela said, her lip quivering.

I sat up and wrapped my arms around her in a tight hug. "You won't. I promise."

Abuela untangled us and got me settled in the bed, then left. When the door shut, I closed my eyes and fell asleep.

I woke up to the sound of a bag rustling. Blinking, I took in the off-white paint on the ceiling that was peeling in the corner and the faded turquoise-and-white chevron wallpaper.

"Hi!" the nurse said cheerily as she changed out my IV bag and looked at the monitors I was hooked up to.

"Hi," I replied. My stomach rumbled, prompting me to ask, "Can I get some food?"

The nurse turned toward me. She was petite with tan skin and brown hair with blond highlights. She was wearing navy-blue scrubs and had a name badge that said Susan. "Yes, the doctor told me that if you woke up hungry, you're allowed to eat. Your vitals have been stable for twenty-four hours," Susan said.

There was a small tray on wheels that had a pitcher and a couple of cups. Susan poured clear liquid out of the pitcher. "Here's some water, and I'll be back with a snack in a little bit. If it stays down, you can order off the full menu," Susan said, offering me the cup and setting the menu on my lap.

"Any dietary restrictions?" I asked, gratefully taking the water.

"No, you can order whatever sounds appealing. Just dial zero-zero-two on the phone, and it'll connect you to the kitchen. I'll let Dr. Winters know you're awake, and he'll come in and talk to you." Susan gave the monitors one more inspection, then bustled out.

I heard a light tap on the door, and then it opened to reveal who I assumed was Dr. Winters. He was tall and lanky with light gray hair and a white goatee. His white doctor's coat covered fire-engine-red scrubs.

"Good morning, Kelsey," he said in a welcoming voice.

"Good morning, Dr. Winters," I responded.

He sat on the edge of my bed. "I don't know how much your friends and family told you, but now that you are awake, I will go over everything with you. Your abuela told me that you're a surgical fellow at Los Angeles Children's Hospital. Congratulations. That is a very competitive program to get into."

"Thanks," I said, worry creasing my forehead as I wondered if he was about to tell me I wouldn't be able to operate again.

He patted my leg. "You arrived at the hospital unconscious and with a laceration to your forehead as well as significant bruising across your shoulder, ribs, abdomen, and left arm. A few of your ribs have hairline cracks, but otherwise you have no broken bones, though you do have a concussion, and that is likely why you were in a coma for four days."

I swallowed, realizing how lucky I had been. "Am I cleared to return to work?"

Dr. Winters chuckled. "Given you have two weeks left of your vacation, yes, I will clear you before you leave Santa Barbara, but you must rest and stay away from strenuous activities. No surfing, no dancing. I have been made aware you are a runner. Over your time here, I give you permission to ease back into running, though I would highly recommend taking it slow. You are going to be sore for a while."

"I understand. Since Joel said I could leave tomorrow, I'm assuming your plan now that I'm awake is to make sure over the next twenty-four hours that I'm eating and functioning properly?" It was the protocol at the hospitals I'd worked at over the years, though sometimes they would require forty-eight hours depending on the severity of the surgery or trauma.

"Yes, that is correct. After you eat, as long as the food stays down, we will disconnect the fluids, though I'll leave the port just in case. Susan will also remove your catheter at the same time."

"Sounds like a plan," I replied.

The door opened, and Susan entered carrying a tray of snacks. She set it down next to the water pitcher.

Dr. Winters smiled. "This is my cue to leave. Don't be afraid to ask if you come up with any more questions or concerns."

I nodded, mouth watering, as Susan removed the lid from the tray, revealing a biscuit, a bowl of fruit, and a small plate of cheese with crackers. Dr. Winters departed, and I used the buttons on the bed controller to sit more upright. "It looks amazing."

Susan chuckled. "I'm glad you're hungry. I'll be back in about fifteen minutes to remove the IV and catheter."

"Thank you," I said and tugged the tray closer. Susan smiled and walked out, pulling the door shut behind her.

I stood and stretched, wincing as the motion pulled on my ribs. Unzipping a black duffle bag, I removed the clothing Abuela had left for me. A black T-shirt, jeans, white bra and underwear, socks, and a pair of navy-blue running shoes. After tossing the hospital gown in the bin marked Dirty, I slowly got dressed, then tucked my discharge papers into the duffle bag where they would be safe.

There was a knock on the door as I finished tying my last shoelace. "Come in!" I yelled, lowering my foot to the floor and pivoting to face the door.

Joel poked his head in with an uncertain expression on his face. "Are you presentable?"

I giggled. "I wouldn't have told you to come in otherwise."

Joel gave me a bashful grin and stepped all the way into the room. "How are you feeling?" he asked, then snagged my bag off the bed before I could grab it.

"Better," I replied. "Ready to go home, though."

"Then let's go," he said. I nodded and followed him out. Then Susan buzzed open the door for us and waved.

There had been times over the past two days that I had had a nagging feeling I was forgetting something important about the accident and the weekend. It was more frustrating than anything because practically the whole weekend was a gaping hole.

I stumbled slightly when we got to the stairs but caught myself on the railing before I could fall. Joel threw me a worried glance. "Are you sure you're okay enough to go home?"

I chuckled. "Yes, I just have to watch where I am putting my feet."

"Which is totally you," he replied.

When we got to the car, I climbed into the passenger seat, my thoughts churning, and a feeling of shyness crept over me. I swallowed, then asked, "What happened to my Prius?"

"It was totaled. Your insurance sent you a letter. It's at Abuela's house," Joel replied.

I nodded, then closed my eyes. We had been inseparable for over half of our lives and then the reality of adulthood and our career dreams had forced us to be realistic. The past nine years, I had had almost no time to myself for anything. An occasional text confirming Joel was alive was about all I had been able to muster. To be honest, I hadn't thought much about him. Until I'd come back on Thursday.

As we turned onto Paloma Street, I broke the companionable silence. "Maybe tomorrow we can look at cars."

"I would love to take you," Joel said and stopped at the back of Abuela's house. He gave me a light hug but did not ask to come in. I was grateful. I went straight to my room and climbed into bed, succumbing to the overwhelming need to sleep.

Sunday morning, Abuela agreed to take me to Penny's before she went to the late church service. I found myself sitting in Penny's modern kitchen, a mix of white painted cabinets and dark wood with sharp edges and angles, sipping a cup of coffee. It was too hot, and each time I tried taking a sip, I ended up scalding my tongue again. Penny's husband, Ken, had their kids out in the backyard to give us privacy for our "girl talk."

Penny smiled at me. "Abuela mentioned in one of her updates that you don't remember much from the weekend either before or after the accident. Is any of it coming back?"

I shook my head. "No. But the accident was only a week ago. Memory loss after a concussion can take months to come back, or never come back."

Penny gave me an odd look before taking a sip of her coffee and then speaking. "How is Joel?"

"Fine, or at least he seemed fine when he drove me home from the hospital," I replied, dreading the direction I thought the conversation might be going.

"Don't hate me for saying this, but it has been on my mind since you told me about coming here for your three-week break in the middle of your fellowship. Have you considered giving Joel another chance? Everyone thought you were going to get married. Even after you left for medical school, there was a running bet on how long before he proposed," Penny said.

I arched my eyebrows. This was news to me. "How come you never said anything before?"

"Because, silly. If I had told you then, you might have done something that wasn't right for you. But ... that was years ago. Now that you're back in Cali ..." Penny let her words trail away.

My lips twitched in amusement. "Originally, when I planned this trip, I didn't want it to be about reconnecting with old friends. One of the few things I do remember from Thursday was that the friends I made while growing up have left a gaping hole in my life, and it's time for me to put in an effort to fill it. Though I'm two hours away, it's not an impossible distance if we are all making an effort." I took a breath. "As far as Joel goes. We parted ways for many reasons. I'm not looking for more than friendship right now."

"Well, the next two weeks are the perfect time to get to know each other again and see where it goes," Penny said.

I shook my head. "Why do you want us back together?"

"Is there anything wrong with wanting my best friend to be happy?" Penny replied softly.

"No. But I have been happy without Joel for the past nine years. Why does that need to change now?" I replied.

Penny tapped her fingers on the counter. "Except moments ago you admitted there was a hole in your life where our friendships had been. You're telling me conflicting things."

I stuck my tongue out at her. "Maybe I'm feeling conflicting emotions. Joel is going to take me car shopping."

"See, you're off to a good start. You already have a date!" Penny said with a smirk.

I rolled my eyes. "It's car shopping. Far from a date."

Penny patted my hand. "Make sure you give me all the details afterward."

"I will text you about every single car I see," I replied dryly.

Penny winked at me. "I'm sure you will."

Chapter 12: Kelsey

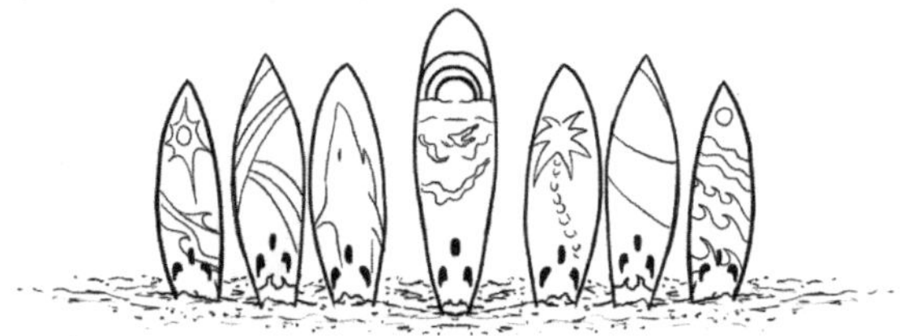

Wednesday, September 18

I didn't know whether Abuela had told my visitors to wait until next weekend so I had more time to rest or if everyone was just busy. But I spent the next two days napping and reading without being disturbed. On the third day, I was finally feeling more like my usual self, and I wanted to get out.

Abuela offered to take me anywhere I wanted to go, but as much as I loved her, I did not want to hang out with her outside of the house. If I wasn't allowed to surf—not that I felt up to surfing anyhow—I wanted to spend time with my friends.

I picked up my phone, debating who to text to see if they wanted to go out for lunch. Just as I was scrolling through names, a text flashed at the top of my screen.

Joel: Do you want to go car shopping? I have today off.

I smiled. It was almost as though he had read my mind. We used to do things like that. We had once been so in tune with each other that we were able to finish each other's sentences and anticipate what the other wanted to do before it was ever spoken aloud. It annoyed all our friends.

Me: Sounds great. What time?

I could see that Joel was typing something, but it was taking him forever to hit send. *He's writing a textbook.* While I was waiting, I decided I could at least change into proper clothes to leave the house. I'd been wearing baggy sweats and an oversized T-shirt the past few days.

I thumbed through the clothes in the dresser, not entirely sure what seemed comfortable for car shopping. *Jeans and a blouse.* I selected a pair of cropped jeans and a pink V-neck shirt.

I started brushing my hair, gazing out the bedroom window. When a hand touched my shoulder, I jumped straight into the air and gasped.

Joel started laughing. I whirled toward him and smacked him on the arm with the flat side of the brush. "That wasn't funny. Why'd you sneak up on me like that?"

Eyes twinkling in amusement, Joel grinned. "For old times' sake."

I rolled my eyes. "I hate it when you do that."

"I know," Joel replied.

"Why didn't you just text me back?" I demanded.

"I wanted to surprise you," he said with a huge smile.

A big red dually barreled toward me, and try as I might, the Prius wouldn't accelerate. Gasping, I dropped the brush and backed up a few steps.

Joel stepped toward me, and my gaze flicked up to his, then away. "Is something wrong? We can go car shopping a different day."

I bit my lip and wrung my hands together.

"C'mon, Kelsey. You can always talk to me," Joel pleaded. He took another step closer and pulled me into a hug.

The warmth of his arms around me was too much. I started sobbing. I clutched his shirt and let the tears fall.

"Hush, you're safe," Joel said softly, gently rubbing my back.

I had no idea how long we stood there, Joel holding me, the lifeline I didn't know I so desperately needed. I loosened my grip on him and leaned back so I could meet his eyes. "Something was wrong with my car. It was only creeping across the intersection," I whispered.

"You're alive. That's all that matters," Joel said and kissed my forehead.

I bit my lip, trying to work through my emotions. "I am grateful I'm alive. But this vacation was supposed to be a chance to relax and reconnect with myself and my friends as well as surf. Now ..."

Joel rubbed my arms in an attempt to comfort me. "Just because you can't surf doesn't mean the time is wasted. Besides, most of your friends, including myself, work. We're lucky if we can get out to the beach more than once a week. I know Penny sometimes goes for an entire month depending on the kids' schedules."

I frowned, feeling hopeless. "What else am I supposed to do? I am confident the doctor would not be happy if I decided to work out at the gym."

"What do you do for fun when you're in Los Angeles?" Joel asked.

I laughed, but it came out more like a bark. "You say that like I have free time to do fun things."

Joel nibbled on his lip for a moment in thought. "Fine. What would you *like* to do if you had free time for fun things? Don't say surfing."

"Watch a movie, walk on the beach, read a book," I replied automatically.

"Well," Joel said. "I don't know what your doctor would say about going for a walk on the beach just yet. Reading a book is more of a you-time thing, but if you don't want to go car shopping today, we could watch a movie."

"Here?" I asked uncertainly. Abuela did have a TV, but I almost thought a movie theater might be better than trying to see things on the tiny screen.

"We can go to my place or the movie theater, your choice," Joel offered.

"How big is your TV?" I questioned.

Joel chuckled. "I promise it's larger than Abuela's."

I took a deep breath, evaluating how my body felt and being honest with myself. "Your place sounds better. That way, I can change how I'm sitting without disturbing anyone in the theater."

"Great. You're dressed, so is there anything else you need to do before we go?" Joel asked.

I reluctantly let go of Joel and took a few steps back to survey the room. He was right. I was dressed. Other than my purse and phone, I couldn't think of anything else I might need. It wasn't like I was going to spend the night or anything. I picked up my purse and shoved my phone into it. "I'm ready."

Joel nodded and led me out the back door. I locked up and turned to his car. It was a new—or I thought it was a new—black Chevy Tahoe. I opened the passenger door and climbed into my seat. I was surprised when I realized it was leather.

"This is fancy," I muttered.

Joel chuckled. "It's the company car. One of the perks. They allow me to use it for my personal stuff too, and I get a new one every two years."

I stayed silent, not sure how to reply. As a surgeon, unless I worked at some fancy high-end private hospital, company cars were not a thing. Not that I cared.

"Where do you live?" I asked, trying not to dwell on how different our lives were and would continue to be.

Joel gave me a sly smile. "You'll see."

"Hmmph," I muttered and folded my arms over my chest. I immediately regretted my choice as my arms dug into my ribs where some of the worst bruising was.

When I agreed to go to Joel's place, I wasn't sure what to expect. I recalled at some point he had told me he bought a house and gave me his address in case I wanted to mail him anything, but I'm not sure if I even saved that information. We drove through town toward the mountains. *He must not surf much anymore if his house is this far from the beach*, I pondered.

After a few more turns, Joel pulled onto the street that led into the Riviera neighborhood. My eyes widened in surprise. "You live in Riviera?" The houses in the lower part of the subdivision were small, but I knew the lots got larger higher up the hill. Most of them were Spanish in style, though occasionally a few rebellious builders did something entirely different.

Joel turned onto Las Alturas Road and slowed down as we approached a house that had a wavy stone wall. "Here we are. Home sweet home."

We pulled up into the driveway, and I saw the house was Mediterranean style with off-white stucco and rich orange terracotta roof tiles. He even had a tower, a house feature that had always been one of my dreams that Joel had thought was silly. *Yet who has the house with the tower now?*

"C'mon, let's go inside," Joel said and got out to open my door for me. I stepped out and we headed inside, up the stairs to the main level. It had an open-concept living, dining, and kitchen area, and large windows with mountain and ocean views.

My gaze settled on the TV against the wall. It was huge. *Taller than me*, I thought. Before Joel could say anything else, I sat down on the couch and sank into it.

"This is much better than a movie theater," I said, smiling at Joel.

"Thanks," Joel said. "I'll get us some drinks and popcorn. The remote is on the coffee table. You can pick any movie you want."

I flipped through the offerings of the various streaming services he had on his TV. Our usual would be an action flick with lots of big explosions, but I wasn't sure I was in the mood for that. In the end, I decided on *The Proposal* with Ryan Reynolds and Sandra Bullock.

Joel sat down just as the opening credits finished, a steaming bowl of popcorn in his hands.

I sniffed. "Smells amazing."

We polished off the entire bowl of popcorn. When we removed the bowl between us, I snuggled against Joel.

I must have fallen asleep during the movie. When I woke up, I was on the couch with a fuzzy gray blanket tucked around me. I could hear Joel's voice coming from the other room, as though he was on the phone.

The shadows in the room were lengthening, but the room wasn't dark yet. I stood up and stretched. Then, I went on a hunt for a bathroom. I knew there had to be one somewhere, though Joel hadn't told me where when we arrived. I opted to try the stairs in the tower. I was surprised when at the top of the stairs I found myself in what I presumed was Joel's bedroom. A flash of sunlight caught my eye, and I turned and saw the bathroom mirror.

I hurried into the bathroom and took care of my business. As I washed my hands, I looked around the bathroom. The Spanish theme of the exterior continued to the interior. White and warm neutrals.

As I exited the bathroom, I noticed the balcony. I pushed the door open and smiled at the breathtaking view of the mountains and the ocean. The sun had sunk about halfway into the ocean and was casting brilliant red-and-pink hues across the water. Growing up with Joel, the closest we ever got to discussing our ideal house to settle down in was that we both hoped for an ocean view, a box Joel's house checked.

I heard Joel's footsteps in the bedroom before he stepped through the door and onto the balcony. I glanced over my shoulder at him and then back at the sunset. "I'm not sure anyone would be able to convince me to leave if this was my house, not with a view like this."

Joel chuckled and joined me at the rail. "It's the primary reason I bought the house."

My stomach rumbled. "Did you have any ideas for dinner?"

"If you want to stay, I can cook, or we could order something," Joel offered.

I shrugged. "Whatever is easiest."

"I'll cook. Then you can just relax," Joel replied.

"Okay," I said. I was not sure how long we stood there in companionable silence watching the sun set.

It must have been a while because Joel gasped when he looked at his watch. "I guess if we want dinner, I actually need to cook it."

I grabbed his wrist and peered at his watch. It was almost eight p.m. "We can just order in."

Joel chuckled. "It's fine. It won't take me any longer to cook than it would for us to order food. C'mon, let's go back downstairs." He slipped his hand into mine and led me back to the living room and kitchen area.

While Joel bustled around the kitchen with honey-colored wood cabinets and black granite countertops, I sat on one of the stools, watching him. "What time do you go in to work tomorrow?"

Joel glanced up from dicing chicken on a cutting board. "I took the next two weeks off."

I sputtered. "You did what?"

Joel shrugged, not meeting my eyes. "I did what any friend would do. You were injured and need to get rest. I wanted to keep you company. Besides, we haven't spent this much time together since you left for medical school. We have a lot to catch up on."

I bit back the sharp response to his statement that I had left. Like it was my fault we broke up. *We discussed it, and he chose not to follow me east. It was a joint decision.* I folded my hands in my lap. "Do you have a girlfriend?" I asked, startling even myself.

Joel's lips twitched in amusement, and he met my gaze for a moment before focusing on dumping the chicken into the skillet. "No. Since I got this job with the city, the mayor has been supportive of my desire to be in a supervisor position, and my journey to where I am now has been filled with many long days. I have some casual dates here and there. What about you?"

I blushed, realizing I should've known he would turn the question on me. "Too busy for much. As I said earlier, I don't have free time. I haven't had free time since I started medical school. Depending on where I get a job when I finish the fellowship, I might finally have some downtime, or it could be just as chaotic."

"Where would you like to end up?" Joel asked. He chopped bell peppers and onions and added them to the skillet with the chicken.

"I'd love to work in a children's hospital and have regular hours. I knew when I chose this path that it would mean a lot of sacrifices for many years but that it wouldn't have to be that way all the time. Otherwise, I'm not sure I would have pursued it," I admitted.

Joel snorted. "I can't remember a time when you didn't want to be a surgeon." He bustled around the kitchen, stirring the contents of the pan and adding more things to it. Whatever he was making, it smelled amazing. I had to keep reminding myself my mouth needed to stay shut; otherwise, I might start drooling.

"Believe it or not, I have missed you terribly while you've been gone all these years," Joel admitted as he gave the pan one final stir and then removed it from the stove.

My lips twitched. "You knew exactly where I was. You could have come for a visit."

Joel sighed. "Every time I bought a plane ticket, work scheduled something or an emergency came up. I tried four times. I even made it to the East Coast last time, but when I landed, they called and demanded I come back immediately to solve whatever problem had arisen overnight."

"It sounds like you need a new job," I said, not sure what else to say. The last thing I had expected Joel to tell me was that he had made plans to come see me four times. His revelation caught me off guard.

"I would be inclined to agree with you, except it's a really good position, and they pay exceptionally well," Joel replied.

I couldn't see why he would keep a job that wouldn't let him use his hard-earned vacation time when he wanted. Frustration curled through me, though I couldn't decide if it was directed at myself or Joel. As he set the table and motioned for me to take my seat, I rubbed the bridge of my nose. He had never told me he tried to visit. There wasn't anything I could do about it now.

Silence spread though the room as we ate with only the occasional clink of silverware on the plates to indicate anyone was even in the house. Exhaustion washed over me. Not that I was surprised; the accident had been very traumatic. It was likely going to take the full two weeks before I could operate at my normal energy levels, maybe even longer.

When my plate was empty, I stood up and carried it to the sink. "Thank you for dinner. If you don't mind giving me a ride, I'd like to go home now," I informed Joel when he walked into the kitchen.

"Okay," he replied.

I must have dozed off in his Tahoe because when Joel lightly touched my shoulder, it startled me. "We're home. I'll call you tomorrow, and we can decide if we're going car shopping or waiting."

I nodded groggily, trying to make my eyes focus on Abuela's house, but it was dark, and the back porch light wasn't on. I opened the Tahoe door, then slowly made my way into the house. Belly full of the delicious dinner, I was confident I would sleep well.

Chapter 13: Conner

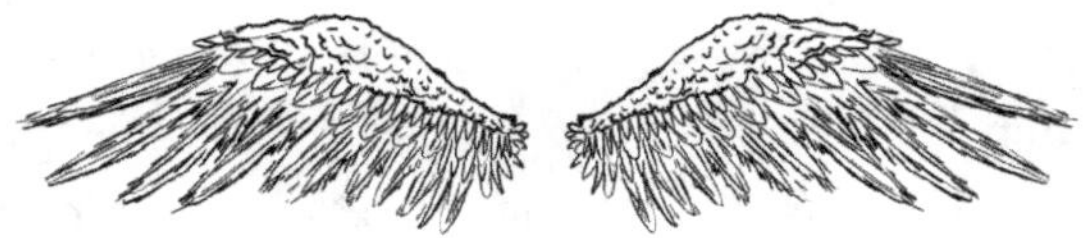

Monday, September 16

Leaning against the railing of my bedroom balcony at my house in Malibu, I stared out at the ocean, wishing I could surf. Technically, it was possible, but I didn't have the time. Sighing, I forced myself to turn my back on the gray waves as I walked into my bedroom. I paused in the doorway as the air shimmered with my magic and an image of Kelsey walking toward me in my white button-up shirt appeared. The fabric, damp from her hair, clung to her curves, leaving very little to the imagination. Shaking my head, I willed the magic away, wondering what had caused it to escape my control.

Clenching my jaw, I snagged my suit jacket off the chair and headed toward the garage. *Octavio's warning was very clear*, I reminded myself. My footsteps were heavy on the staircase, the sound echoing around me. My temper flared that it had been just over a week since I left Santa Barbara, and I still had trouble keeping myself focused on work. Kelsey kept invading every part of my day. As I strolled down a bustling downtown street, I'd swear I caught a glimpse of her. The idea was ridiculous. She hadn't told me what city she worked in. Los Angeles was not the only large city that you could reach within a day's drive from Santa Barbara. It was easy to assume she could have come from San Francisco or any of the cities dotting California's Bay Area.

I entered my garage and peered at the cars, trying to decide which one suited today's mood the best. Just as I was about to snag the keys for the Audi R8, the door to the driveway opened and Fabio walked through, wearing a light pink dinner jacket and magenta slacks with a black button-up shirt.

My eyes narrowed. "Why are you here? We were supposed to meet for lunch."

"Sorry, Conner. Cassiel gave me express instructions to collect you," Fabio replied with an apologetic frown.

Swallowing my frustration and inclination to refuse Cassiel's orders, I shut off the lights and then followed Fabio out onto the driveway. A satin-black Bentley Flying Spur was waiting for us. The chauffeur stood at the passenger side door, beckoning me to get in. I wrinkled my nose at my father's car choice, for I was one hundred percent certain this was his personal vehicle. Cassiel refused to buy anything other than a Bentley. It was one of the few human luxuries I had seen my father indulge in.

They were remarkably comfortable—I had to give him credit for that—but their exterior styling was not to my taste. I settled into the luxuriously soft charcoal leather with white piping and waited for Fabio to tell me why he was here.

My patience was wearing thin as we merged onto Highway 1 and were still cocooned in silence. I turned so I was facing Fabio. "Spill. What is so important that Cassiel had to send you and this damned car to retrieve me?"

Fabio's fingers twitched in his lap. My nostrils flared. *He's nervous.*

Fabio ran his hands over his pants before meeting my gaze. "You're supposed to meet with Agatha Frierson this morning."

My interest was piqued at the mention of my long-time friend and fellow angel, whose work in the human world had her rubbing shoulders with models and movie industry celebrities whom I tried my best to avoid. "Agatha is here in Los Angeles? I haven't seen her since we crossed paths in Dubai a few years ago."

"Yes, she's here. However, your father has been in discussions with her parents about ... marriage," Fabio said, the last word barely a whisper.

"Fuck," I snarled, slamming my fist into the console. "Why does he *have* to interfere in my life?" Anger washed through me that my father was always looking for a way to control me. He would never be content to allow me to live how I saw fit.

Fabio spread his hands wide. "He's likely just worried about you. Almost fifteen hundred years old, you don't have a wife or children, and you're the last of the male Hudson line."

"We are immortal. Fifteen hundred years means nothing to us," I muttered.

"I know, but we're both aware that being immortal doesn't mean we can't die. I'm just the messenger," Fabio said softly.

Forcing my fingers to unclench, I slowly let out my breath. "Does Agatha know?"

"I think so, but I am not privy to those details. Given she is your friend, I didn't think you wanted me to pry into her life unless you expressly requested it. How about this? Approach your meeting with Agatha this morning exactly as it is. A chance for old friends to meet. Nothing more, nothing less," Fabio recommended.

He was right. It wasn't Agatha's fault our family members were colluding behind our backs. "Where is the meeting happening?" An early morning appointment with an old friend seemed strange. *Unless her schedule is too busy.* I could relate to that problem.

"The Manhattan Beach Pier," Fabio replied.

My eyes widened in surprise. The restaurant on the pier wasn't open on Mondays, especially not this early in the morning. They only offered breakfast on the weekends. The helicopter would have been much faster than driving from Malibu down to Manhattan Beach, especially at eight a.m. on Monday morning. *This is a calculated move on Cassiel's part.* It seemed a little odd that he would choose today of all days to bring up a potential marriage. And through a proxy, no less.

As the car slowly made its way through traffic and Fabio didn't seem to have anything else to say, I let my eyes shut—not because I was tired, but simply to shut out the physical proof of the power my father still had over me. A car with my assistant in it showed up, and I allowed myself to follow my father's directions. I could have easily refused and attended the meeting I had originally scheduled this morning, but I didn't. *One more week and I can return to London and be away from his direct influence.*

I opened my eyes just as we pulled up to the pier.

"Is there a set time you're returning, or do I just call?"

"Call. I'll be nearby," the chauffeur replied as I stepped out of the car.

I took a deep breath and squared my shoulders. *I can do this. A casual breakfast and coffee with an old friend.*

The Bentley drove away. I wasn't sure if Agatha was even here yet. The street and parking lot were empty—no surprise since it was Monday morning. Giving the edge of my jacket one last tug, I made myself walk toward the restaurant.

Just as I reached for the door, it swung open. Inside the doorway was Agatha. Her black hair was surprisingly tamed into an elegant chignon, and her cream pantsuit showed off her olive skin perfectly.

Agatha smiled and gestured at our attire. "I guess our families surprised both of us with this meeting this morning."

I stepped close, lightly gripping her elbows, and kissed each cheek. "It's good to see you."

"What were you told about our meeting?" she asked as we turned toward the waiting host.

"Cassiel believes we still live in an age where I'll agree to an arranged marriage," I replied.

Agatha snorted. "Clearly they don't understand our friendship."

I flashed her a smile and focused on not tripping as we went up the dark wood staircase and into a large dining room, where a floor-to-ceiling glass wall offered an expansive view of the ocean. The hostess led us to a table set for two overlooking the water. As we sat down, I had a strong sense of déjà vu. The last time I had sat at a table for two with an ocean view was when I had intruded on Kelsey at Blue Fin.

A warm hand gripped mine, drawing me out of my thoughts. "Are you okay, Conner?"

I gave her a half smile. "I'm fine, promise. What have you been up to since Dubai?"

Agatha chuckled. "The better question would be, what haven't I been up to?"

"I've seen some of the new spreads you've done for *Vogue*. You're quite the world traveler now," I said appreciatively.

"Well, for my job, I go where I'm told. The fashion business has gotten more creative with their photo shoots. A mix of staged photos using green screens and wanting me to be on location for the authentic feel. For the most part, it has been refreshing to have the opportunity to travel the world on someone else's dime. Part of my deal requires them to give me four personal days so I can explore," Agatha explained.

I whistled, impressed. I remembered when Agatha had been originally tasked with making a place for herself in the human world as a model, wanting to experience the process like a human would and not rely on her magic abilities to influence her rise in the world. She resorted to begging for jobs and often was overlooked in favor of a white woman. Now the human society's views had shifted and embraced women of color.

"Wonderful," I replied.

Agatha pursed her lips in thought. "I was going to wait until later to ask, but since we're on the topic ..." She still hesitated.

"You know you can ask me anything," I reminded her.

"Yes, I know. The studio has this idea, and they want you to do a photo shoot with me," Agatha said.

I couldn't help it. I burst out laughing. "Me? Model!" I took a sip of water to let my laughter subside. "I'm sure there are plenty of other male models who would be far better partners than me."

Agatha shrugged. "I told them you'd respond like this, but they are determined to have you." She paused. "Think about it. To the humans, you're more than just a billionaire. You're the epitome of an English gentleman, rich and sexy as hell."

I sniffed and made a face. "Oh really? 'Sexy as hell' ... Did you say that or did your boss?"

Agatha slapped my hand playfully. "It's true. Just because you're not my type doesn't mean I can't appreciate you all the same."

At that moment, the waiter approached. I expected to order, but small plates of various pastries and fresh fruit were set out before us as well as a large carafe of coffee. I was grateful for the distraction. Agatha's request had caught me completely off guard. *A photo shoot?* A long time ago, Charlie had tried to talk me into a photo shoot for one of the magazines, but I had vehemently declined. I strongly disliked being in the spotlight and it would do nothing to assist my ability to accomplish the work I did with the hospitals. *What will my sister think if I accept Agatha's request?* I wasn't sure Charlie would even care, especially since I kept her career as a racecar driver a secret. *But what do I think about the request?* I took a sip of my pitch-black coffee, inhaling its bitter aroma.

"What do they want me to do for the photo shoot?" I finally asked.

Agatha flashed me a brilliant smile. She knew me well enough to guess that if that was my first question, I was on board. "They want us to be a couple for the shoot. The idea was floated that we could possibly use your estate, but I warned him that you would likely say no."

"That would depend on which estate they're referring to. The Malibu house?" I asked, nibbling on a piece of croissant.

"Unfortunately, no. They want it to be at your estate in England," she said, eyeing me.

I frowned. A photo shoot was the last thing I wanted to happen at my home in England, though I understood why it would be appealing as a backdrop. "I will have to think about it."

Agatha nodded. "Sounds good. Now, what have you been up to lately? Rumors are flying about where you were last weekend."

I debated what to tell her. As Charlie's best friend, she wouldn't keep anything I said just between the two of us. "Just needed some breathing room, so I went surfing." I paused, then added, "Anonymously."

"Were you able to pull it off without being recognized?" Agatha asked, leaning forward.

"As far as I know, yes," I replied. Then I took a long sip of my coffee.

Agatha met my gaze. "You're telling me that Cassiel and Octavio are all fussing about you spending four days doing nothing but surfing on a remote beach? I am not entirely sure I'm inclined to believe you."

I wrinkled my nose to stave off a sneeze. When I was certain it was gone, I replied, "You know Cassiel likes to control everything I do. Especially when we're in the same city together. But if you really must know, my *plan* was to only surf, and then ... I met a woman."

Agatha's lips parted and formed a delicate O. Her eyes sparkled in delight. "A human woman who caught your fancy without trying. How intriguing."

I rolled my eyes. "It's not like it's never happened before."

"Hmph," Agatha muttered, then looked away, peering out the window at the waves crashing against the pier.

Taking time to let us both think over what I had just revealed, I ate several slices of melon and finished my croissant. When it was clear that Agatha was waiting for me to divulge more information, I decided to give her what she wanted, knowing that Agatha of all people might at least understand the situation I was in and the choices I had made. *Maybe.* I took a sip of coffee to wash the last of the croissant down my suddenly dry throat, then said, "Her name is Kelsey. We first officially met at a restaurant, where I intruded on her nice dinner and date with a book."

Agatha gave me an incredulous look but stayed silent. I continued, "We had a few glasses of wine and just spoke of easy things. We crossed paths a few times over the days I was there." A sense of deep longing filled me as I pictured Kelsey straddling me on the metal chair as thrust into her, and then the final image I had of her when she was wheeled into the ambulance.

"You're falling for her," Agatha said in a low voice.

I blew out my breath noisily. "Am I?" I should have known Agatha would be able to sense my feelings. It was one of her magic abilities.

Agatha nodded and reached over to squeeze my hand. "If you could hear the way you talk about her, then you would agree. Why haven't you called her if you feel this way?"

My cheeks heated up. "A few reasons. The first is that it's forbidden to have a deep relationship with a human. She ... *we* were in a severe car accident. I shielded her." Agatha sucked in a sharp breath. I continued, "Octavio was driving the truck that hit us. He had come to tell me to return, and I didn't leave Santa Barbara quick enough. The accident was a warning. While I regret not getting Kelsey's last name or phone number, at this point, I am worried that Octavio will kill her if I attempt to reestablish contact, and I am not willing to forfeit her life. Besides, we agreed it would just be a weekend and that was it. No strings."

"Conner, life is fleeting. If you feel this deeply for her after four days, then go after her. Surely there is some way you could find her again, especially with the resources you have—Fabio," Agatha cajoled.

"You would disobey Cassiel's orders for a human?" I replied incredulously.

Agatha shrugged. "It's time you put yourself first."

"I am sure one day I'll find an angel female who is meant for me." I tugged my hand out of her grip and refilled my coffee cup, ending the discussion about Kelsey.

My phone buzzed in my pocket. I pulled it out, glancing at the screen. It was Cassiel. "Now what?" I muttered, then answered. "Good morning, Cassiel."

"How is it going with Agatha?" Cassiel asked.

I frowned at the question, uncharacteristic for my father. "Fine. Why?"

"Just checking in to see if you're going to make our lunch meeting or if I should push it back," Cassiel replied.

Glancing at my watch—it was only ten a.m.—I wondered why my father was concerned that I wouldn't make a noon meeting. *Does he think we're going to get married right now at breakfast?* "Don't worry. I will be there on time. Goodbye." I hung up and shoved the phone back in my pocket.

"Problems?" Agatha asked.

I shook my head. "Nothing to worry about." Using my father's interruption as an opportunity to shift the conversation away from Santa Barbara, I asked, "What brings you to Los Angeles?"

Agatha shrugged. "We have a photo shoot scheduled at sunrise tomorrow up in Santa Ynez."

"Picturesque location choice," I murmured, recalling the green rolling hills with the long, neat rows of wine grapes growing for miles in the Santa Ynez Valley.

"We have a couple of different shoots. The first one is at the beach. Then, we're doing sunset in the hills at a vineyard. There was a brief mention of horses being involved as well," she replied.

"How long has it been since you've ridden a horse?" I asked. A few summers in a row, Agatha and Charlie had hung out at my estate riding for hours on end. Then, duties had made them go their separate ways. I knew there were also horses in Ianialar, but I had no idea with Agatha's busy schedule how often she was able to go to the Ash Realm.

"A few weeks," Agatha said.

"On your own horse? I thought you traveled too much to keep one," I replied, surprised.

Fiddling with her napkin, Agatha took a few moments to formulate her response. "I wish I had my own horse. Over the years, I have made many friends around the world, and some happen to have horses that they allow me to borrow when I am nearby. Not quite as good as owning my own, but better than nothing. And less temperamental than convincing an Ianialar horse to allow me to ride it."

I opened my mouth to reply when the waiter appeared again. "Ms. Agatha, you requested we notify you when it has passed ten thirty if you were not preparing to leave."

"Thank you," she said with a smile before turning to me. Based on the waiter's comment, I knew she had appearances to keep up, as did I, and relying on magic transportation did not work if we were trying to maintain the charade that we're human and not immortal.

"It was so good to see you. If you have time before I return to London, we should have dinner at my place," I offered, standing.

"I will have to check my schedule and get back to you," Agatha said, stepping close and pulling me into a hug. "Don't be a stranger," she whispered into my ear, then slid out of my grip.

I stood there frozen as the waiter returned. "Is there anything else I can do for you?" he asked.

Blinking, I focused my gaze on him. "No. Thank you for your discretion," I replied, then saw myself out.

The chauffeur was waiting for me in the parking lot. He opened the car door, and I climbed in. I relaxed in the seat of the Bentley as the chauffeur drove me to my meeting with Cassiel. *Maybe if Agatha and I play my father's game, he'll get off my back about marriage for a while.* I knew Agatha and I would never get married; we were not the right fit for each other, but she was brilliant at acting and one of my closest friends.

The photo shoot at my estate, I mused. It would be an excellent way of selling our relationship, especially when the magazine Agatha worked for already wanted me to participate. If Agatha could get things scheduled so that the photo shoot could occur while I was in London, it would prevent me from needing to make an exclusive trip home.

The Bentley stopped in front of a large skyscraper. I frowned as I got out, wondering why Cassiel wanted to meet here. The chauffeur opened the door for me. I grabbed my briefcase and stepped out of the car. Peering up at the building, I wondered how I was going to figure out where my meeting was. To my surprise, my father walked out of the large glass doors. In the bright noon sunlight, I almost would've sworn I could see his white wings spread out behind him and his skin shimmering gold. Shaking my head, I knew I had to be mistaken. There was no way Cassiel would allow himself to be seen in his true form in the middle of a human city. When my gaze drifted back to him again, the wings and gold skin were gone, replaced with lightly tanned skin and a black tailored suit. His salt-and-pepper hair was neatly styled.

"Thanks," I murmured to the chauffer, then strode toward my father.

"Conner," Cassiel said, holding his hand out for me to shake.

I took it as expected, trying not to roll my eyes. "Cassiel," I replied. My father had never been one for hugging or any show of affection. Even in the privacy of our home in Ianialar, Cassiel had left that as my mother's duty. *Thank goodness she showed me that not everyone has to be that cold.* I would admit I mimicked Cassiel's demeanor, but only in business dealings. With those who belonged in my inner circle, I was far warmer and more informal.

"How was breakfast?" Cassiel pressed.

"Fine," I replied, not wanting to get into details if I could avoid it.

"Glad to hear it. Let's go inside," Cassiel said and led the way into the building.

Once inside, I realized the lobby was still under construction. The tint on the glass from outside had made it impossible to see the scaffolding. I scanned the room. The significant number of windows provided substantial natural light. But with painting underway, there was no clear indicator of what the building's purpose was.

When it was clear my father was not going to offer an explanation, I finally asked, "Why are we here?"

"I have been looking at a location for a new office," Cassiel replied.

I sighed. "We have an office downtown already."

"This one will give us more space. I wanted you to take a tour with me and see for yourself," Cassiel said.

I took a deep breath. One of the downsides of our human identities being billionaires was that Cassiel found it entertaining to continuously expand the assets of Hudson Corporation. Nothing I said would change the fact that he was going to give me a tour. We started on the first floor. There were two office suites that could be built out. Each boasted close to twenty thousand square feet by my estimate. The building was large and high-end. *So is our current office.* Instead of using the elevator, we went up a large, sweeping metal-and-glass staircase to the second floor, then toured the three suites on that level. Two were around ten thousand square feet with the third once again twenty thousand. From the exterior, I knew the building had at least thirty floors.

"Are all the floors like this? Forty thousand square feet in various customizable arrangements?" I asked, trying to wrap my mind around why he chose this building.

Cassiel shook his head. "Not quite. The top three floors have condos. But yes, otherwise there are twenty-seven floors of office space."

"We don't need a new office *or* a new building," I replied firmly. *We can afford it.* But there was no logical reason Cassiel had to buy this building. For Hudson Corporation, the most we would use would be one of the first-floor office spaces.

"I bought a new business," Cassiel said, his eyes on my face to gauge my reaction.

I tensed, then forced myself to relax. I operated as a consultant to public and private hospitals, serving on boards of directors. The public purpose was to help them modernize their organizations from top to bottom and then bottom to top. The private purpose was to ensure the demons who owned the hospitals were not taking unfair advantage of the humans the hospital served. Ultimately, I ended up performing a mix of duties. Though the demons as a whole were enthusiastic and well-versed businessmen, there were times when their choices made sense for demons but did not meet the needs of their customers—humans—as well as they should.

I actively supervised over one hundred private hospitals around the world.

"What is the new business?" I asked carefully.

"A tech services company that is using magic to develop artificial intelligence solutions for the medical industry. They are quite a bit more advanced than what the humans have come up with, and I am certain your clients will be eager to implement these solutions into their hospitals. This building would serve as its new home and allow for significant growth, as well as opportunities for us to lease out some of the floors to other businesses, and the condos, of course," Cassiel replied. His answer sounded rehearsed. *I suppose after fifteen hundred years he would know what my questions would be—and the answers that would appease me.*

"Did you already buy the building, too, or did you *want* my opinion on it?" I asked, unable to keep the tightness from my voice.

"The commercial broker agreed to hold it for twenty-four hours so I could get your thoughts," Cassiel explained.

I frowned. Twenty-four hours was not very long, and a building of this size in downtown Los Angeles came with a hefty price tag. "Does the purchase price include finishing the construction or will that cost us extra?"

My father held his hand out and a large file folder appeared, which he handed to me. "They are going to finish it according to the specifications in this file. The ground-floor offices will be completed to my specifications with the remaining floors' offices following a generic layout. The lessees will have the opportunity to customize their own spaces and foot the cost. The condos will be completed as well."

I opened the file and saw there was a front page with a QR code that went to a digital version of the documents in my hands. I sighed with relief. I didn't want to go through several hundred pages of paper. "How long do I have to review this before you have to give the broker an answer?"

Cassiel smiled. He knew just based on those words that I was likely going to agree with his decision to purchase the building. "Five p.m. tonight."

Glancing at my watch, I noted it was almost two, giving me three hours. "Is there anything else you need from me, or can I go?" I said, shaking the file slightly.

"You can go," Cassiel said.

I wished he'd wipe the satisfied smile from his face. I needed to review the file before giving my approval.

Chapter 14: Kelsey

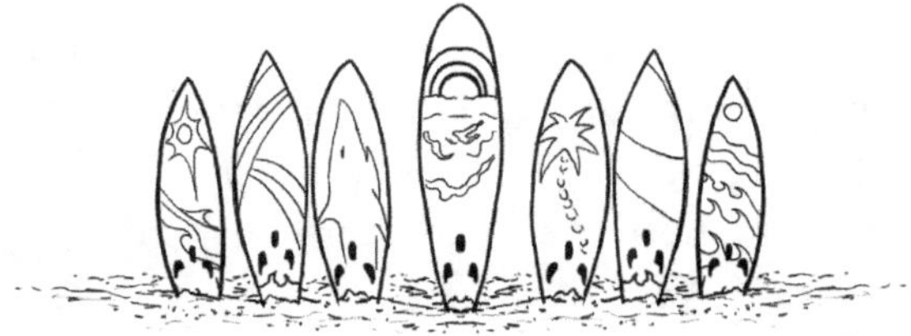

Friday, September 20

My phone vibrated and fell off the nightstand. I rubbed my eyes and blinked at the sunlight creeping through the curtains. *What day is it?* I wondered, praying I hadn't spent more than just Thursday asleep. There were a few times that I thought I heard Abuela's soft footsteps at the bedside while she checked on me, but I opted to keep my eyes shut instead of encouraging a conversation.

Relief washed through me as my phone flashed that it was Friday, eight a.m. The phone buzzed again, telling me Joel had just left a message. I took my time getting out of bed and retrieving the phone from the floor. I felt much better, though my medical intuition was concerned about something as simple as dinner and a movie with Joel sapping my strength enough to require a full thirty-six hours of rest afterward.

As I tugged a soft brown sweater over my head, my phone began buzzing again. *Persistent today.* I grumbled, then answered it. "Kelsey." My voice lacked its normal cheer, but honestly I didn't care at the moment.

"Everything okay?" Joel asked. I could hear his concern.

"Fine. I just woke up," I explained.

"Abuela said you slept most of yesterday. Are you up to car shopping, or did you want to just hang out and tackle that another day?" Joel asked.

Running my hand over my face, I considered the reality that not having a car wasn't an option. At the very least, I needed it as transportation to return to Los Angeles for my job. It wasn't like I had other pressing matters to attend to today. "Might as well get car shopping over with sooner than later."

"Have you eaten?" Joel inquired.

I opened my mouth to reply when Abuela poked her head in my room. "Breakfast is on the table."

I giggled. "Well, by the time you get here I will have eaten. Abuela made breakfast for me."

"I'll see you in thirty minutes," Joel informed me. We hung up, and I wandered down the hallway to the dining room. Sure enough there was a heap of eggs, bacon, and strawberries on two plates.

Abuela sat across from me and picked at her food. "Nieta, are you sure you're okay?"

Mouth full of eggs, I nodded and swallowed. "Yes. Recovery from an accident like the one I was in can take weeks. I promise if anything changes, I'll make an appointment with the doctor."

Abuela nodded, and we ate in silence for a while. I realized Abuela had given herself about half as much as she'd given me when she finished far before me. "A letter came for you while you were in the hospital. It's from the insurance company. You should read it."

Abuela slid the large manila envelope across the table to me. I took it, wondering why she wouldn't just tell me what it said.

September 12

Vincent Forge, Adjuster

Ianialar Insurance

P.O. Box 4319

Los Angeles, CA 90210-4319

Re: Kelsey Floras - 03/29/1990 Oscar Kiev Claim number: AO111110Date of accident or injury: September 7

Dear Kelsey Floras,

Pursuant to the documents provided, please allow this letter to confirm Ianialar Insurance, representing Oscar Kiev, have agreed to settle your claim that is referenced above. The claim is settled in full for the amount of $100,000.

Please see the attached check in the amount of $100,000. The release form releases Oscar Kiev and Ianialar from any further damages related to the accident. Sign and return the release form to me at the following address:

Vincent Forge P.O. Box 4319

Los Angeles, CA 90210-4319

If you have any questions, please do not hesitate to contact me.

Sincerely,

Vincent Forge

213-383-7625

vforge@Ianialar.comVictor Fox, JD In counsel for Oscar Kiev

I riffled through the rest of the documents. Sure enough there was the release form as well as a few other documents explaining how they came up with the sum of money. My eyes were wide in disbelief when I looked up at Abuela. "Is this real?"

Abuela nodded. "Yes. I called my friend José, who is an attorney, and he verified that this is a legitimate offer. After the police said that the video footage was messed up, I did not think they would find who hit you."

"One hundred thousand dollars." I said each word slowly, letting it sink in. The sum of money was absurd. The Prius had been worth less than five thousand dollars. *But I should be dead*, I reminded myself. Still, it was a lot of money, more than I'd ever had at one time before.

"You could buy a car and have a down payment for a house, Nieta," Abuela said with a smile.

I had no reason to not accept the offer. I had no doubts in my mind that regardless of what this paperwork said, this was a one-time offer, and if I refused it, there would be no second chances. "Do you have a pen?"

Abuela slid one over to me. "Of course."

Flipping to the release form, I read through the letter and the whole form, then signed it. To my surprise, at the end of the packet was an addressed and stamped envelope for me to return it in. Pulling out my phone, I took a photo of the signed release form next to the settlement offer, then stuck it in the envelope.

Abuela snatched it. "I'll take it to the post office."

"Thank you," I replied, then stood up and gave Abuela a hug, still reeling over this check.

Joel arrived as I was washing the plates in the sink.

Abuela pried my fingers off the plate I was holding. "Go. I can finish here."

"But ..." I protested. She smiled and waved her free hand at me.

Joel tugged lightly on my arm. "Come on, before she changes her mind and ropes me into dishes too!"

I chuckled. He was right. There had been many times we had lingered too long and ended up doing a mountain of dishes that had mysteriously appeared in need of washing.

"See you later," I said with a smile before turning to Joel and following him out.

Before climbing into the Tahoe, I walked around it, conducting a more in-depth inspection. *Way too big for me.*

"Thinking of getting a Tahoe?" Joel said curiously.

I laughed. "No. It's huge! How would I ever find a parking spot without hitting anything?"

"You adapt," Joel replied.

"Then let's go to the Hummer dealership," I replied with a straight face.

Joel chuckled. "Those things are horrible—not reliable and even worse fuel mileage than the Tahoe." He paused. "Now in all seriousness, what kind of car are you looking for? Are you leaning toward getting another Prius?" Joel asked, turning on the Tahoe and backing out of the driveway.

I blew out my breath. There was no reason to not tell Joel about the turn of events this morning. "That was my plan, a used Prius."

"I sense a *but* coming," Joel teased.

"The person who caused the accident, I guess they were able to figure out who it was. His insurance sent me a settlement, and you're not going to believe it ... one hundred thousand dollars!"

"You're kidding, right?" Joel asked, staring at me.

I shook my head. "No. Abuela even verified it with her attorney friend. I signed the letter that says I accept the settlement and release them of any other responsibilities, so the money is mine."

"You know, you could really get any car you want," Joel replied.

"I know. But the Prius is so practical. I'd rather keep the settlement as savings and use it on something other than a car. Especially since I don't drive that much," I explained.

Joel shrugged. "How about this? We can go to the Toyota dealership and then see what we find. Maybe try out a few other cars, not just a Prius?"

"Sure," I agreed.

We drove to the Toyota dealership in companionable silence. One thing that kept running through my mind was how lucky I had been to recover from the accident without surgery. *What if the outcome had been different? Have I lived my life the way I want?* I nibbled on my lip, staring blankly at the dashboard. *Maybe I should take my own advice from this past weekend and live more. I only have one life to live.*

I peeked at Joel out of the corner of my eye, then went back to gazing at the dashboard. *Penny was right. I should give him another chance. Or at least be open to rekindling things. Especially since that seems to be something Joel is interested in.*

A speed bump jolted me out of my thoughts, and I blinked, noticing we were at the dealership. Row after row of brand-new vehicles, mostly white and silver, flashed in the sunshine.

"Just go over to the used side. No reason to park over here," I said, fluttering my hand dismissively at the new cars.

Thankfully, Joel followed my instructions and found an open spot on the used side.

On first glance around the used car section of the dealership, I didn't see any Priuses, but I was still optimistic they would have at least one.

I strolled down the row of cars, ahead of Joel, and sure enough just ahead of me was a Prius. I eagerly sped up, so I was almost jogging until I was at it. *Am I going to be lucky enough to go to one dealership and find exactly what I want?*

It was a Prius, faded red, with a large crack in the back window. I walked around the car, my hopes plummeting as I caught sight of the sticker. They wanted eight thousand for it because of the low mileage, but it was a 2008, two years older than mine had been. I frowned.

"What's wrong?" asked Joel, inspecting the car.

I grimaced. "It's overpriced and older than the one I had."

He shrugged. "You're the one who said you wanted something used."

"I was hoping to at least be able to upgrade slightly from my old one," I replied.

"I have an idea," Joel said with goofy grin.

"Uh-oh," I said. We had gotten into *so* much trouble as teenagers when he uttered those very same words.

He pulled out a bandana from his back pocket. I raised my eyebrows and shook my head. "No way."

"Trust me," he said, taking a step forward.

I sighed. *We are adults now. He's not going to let me get into trouble.* When I didn't say anything else, Joel stepped behind me and slipped the blindfold over my eyes.

"No peeking," he warned.

I pinched my lips together as Joel guided me down the aisle between the cars. The minutes kept ticking and weariness began to weigh upon me, a sharp reminder that I was still not recovered from the accident. I raised my hand to remove the blindfold because I was tired of walking and not being sure of where I was, when we halted. Joel set his hands on my shoulders and turned me ninety degrees. "You can take it off."

I removed the blindfold and blinked, trying to adjust to the too-bright sunlight. We were standing in front of a silver Prius that had been pulled out of its spot and had its doors open, waiting.

"Why are you showing me this? Clearly someone is already looking at it. Besides, it's new." I was afraid to look at the sticker to see how much it was.

Joel gave my arm a light squeeze. "It is waiting for you to look at it."

My eyes widened. "For me?" I repeated, confusion swirling through me. *What did Joel do?*

He nodded. "Yes. Now, humor me and check it out, please."

I was obliged since he added the please. After conducting a thorough inspection of the exterior, I decided to try sitting in it. I was surprised by how comfortable it was and how shiny and new all the buttons and knobs were.

"Do you want to go for a test drive?" he asked and tossed the key in my lap.

I picked it up and inspected it. The little tag listed the age. I was wrong; the car wasn't brand new. It was a 2023, so one year old. Suddenly, I felt nervous, like I shouldn't be there and didn't deserve to try a new car.

I growled under my breath at myself, *Fuck that.* I yanked on an invisible cloak of confidence. "Yes, I'd like to drive it."

"Let's go!" Joel said, grinning and climbed into the passenger seat.

I was pulling out of the dealership when I glanced over at him, remembering how buying a car normally plays out. "Aren't we supposed to have a salesman with us?"

Joel shrugged. "Not all the time. Don't worry about it. Just drive."

I eased us out onto the street. The first thing I noticed was how quiet this car was. My old Prius had been quiet, but this one was *silent.* It was unnerving. Visibility was about the same. We slowed down at a light, and the brakes were responsive.

"Seems nice," I mumbled.

"What did you say?" Joel asked, cupping his hand to his ear as though to hear me better.

"Nothing," I replied, though I swear I caught Joel giving me a satisfied smile.

I focused on the road. Since it was my first time behind the wheel since the accident, I had to admit that staying on task while driving was a challenge. I constantly had to fight the feeling that any second the dually truck was going to come barreling down the road.

We drove about a mile, and then I chose the shorter route back to the dealership. I drove back to the precise location where we had gotten into it. There was still no salesman to be seen.

"Be honest. What are your thoughts?" Joel prompted.

I sat quietly, tracing the buttons on the steering wheel, trying to formulate my thoughts about the car. "It's nice, but too expensive," I finally managed.

"Okay," replied Joel. He got out and came around to open my door.

"That's all you're going to say?" I queried, meeting his eyes. It wasn't like him to just back down when he clearly had an opinion about how used the next car I bought should be. As I stood up, I became aware of how close we were to each other. I tried taking a step back but bumped into the car door. Joel didn't say anything. We stared at each other. Butterflies fluttered around my stomach and goose bumps that had nothing to do with being cold broke out along my arms. As the urge to kiss him hit me, I had to look away, blushing.

"Kelsey, it's your car. You must drive it. I want you to pick what's right for you. If it's not the right car, then it's not the right one," Joel said, then backed up enough steps to give me room to move away from the car.

Suddenly, a wave of exhaustion crashed over me. Unable to find the energy to tell Joel what I was feeling, I started walking toward the Tahoe, worried that if I didn't sit down soon, I was going to just collapse into a heap and fall asleep. My feet felt like they were filled with concrete. I was about halfway there when Joel slipped his hand in mine and gave me a light squeeze.

"Driving was too much, wasn't it?" he guessed correctly. "I'm sorry. I didn't think this through. It's only been a week since you left the hospital."

I bit my lip and nodded. He pulled me close and I leaned into him, then we made our way back to the Tahoe.

As soon as I laid my head on the soft black leather headrest of the front passenger seat, I fell asleep. I woke up when the Tahoe's engine cut off and was startled to see we were across the street from Blue Fin.

"Hey, sleepy," Joel said and leaned over and kissed my cheek.

"Hi," I said softly. "What are we doing?"

He gently flicked my nose. "Eating dinner."

"Oh, isn't it only two or three?" I asked, then I caught sight of the clock in the middle of the dashboard. *Six p.m.* I did feel more awake now than I had been.

"See, it's dinnertime. C'mon," Joel encouraged me.

We made our way up the stairs, and they seated us right away at one of the small tables for two at the window. This one was in the corner away from the bustle of the bar and other guests. We sat down, and I browsed the menu, memories returning of the first night I had been in Santa Barbara at Blue Fin, alone and with a book for my date. I closed my eyes and opened them, trying to focus. I was with Joel, not a book. Joel, who had been kind to me the past two weeks and was, at one time, my best friend.

Joel was perusing the wine menu, and I found myself openly ogling him. His light brown hair was messy. He had a short beard and blue-gray eyes. His short-sleeve shirt did nothing to hide the muscles rippling on his arm. He looked up and caught me staring, I blushed and looked down at my menu.

I ran my finger down the list of appetizers and entrees, trying to decide what I wanted to eat. I found I was rereading each item multiple times. I could not make my brain focus. Instead, I kept thinking about Joel, how his hand had felt in mine earlier. Then, my thoughts drifted to things those very hands had done to me. I blushed.

"Kelsey," Joel said. I met his gaze.

I took a sip of my water, trying to get myself to focus on what I wanted to eat, not on the many wild nights we'd shared together as teenagers. *Besides, if I can barely handle a few hours of car shopping, I doubt anything that requires more physical exertion would be a good option given my current state.*

Just then, the waiter came over. "Would you like any appetizers?"

I shook my head, declining. Joel winked at me and then faced the waiter. "We would like to get the crab and artichoke dip." *He remembers.* Blue Fin used to be our preferred restaurant if we wanted a quiet date without our friends getting into our business.

The waiter took our appetizer order to the kitchen and then returned. "I'm ready to take your dinner order."

"Hmmm," I mumbled, running my finger down the menu. "Parmesan-crusted halibut with seared asparagus."

"You stole my order," Joel teased, then addressed the waiter. "I will take the basil pesto salmon with potatoes au gratin."

The waiter nodded. "I will get these in. Your appetizer should be out shortly."

I sipped my water, watching Joel over the rim. I couldn't decide how to start a conversation with him. *He's still the same person*, I reminded myself.

Joel began talking about how busy Santa Barbara was becoming with people wanting to leave Los Angeles and find places to live that were slower paced. How much real estate prices had soared and that some of the families we had known when we were growing up were selling their beautiful homes and moving, away from the beach that we loved, to somewhere more remote without a beach like Boise or Reno, where they could buy a mansion at a fraction of the cost and retire in luxury. *Yet here I am wanting to stay in California.*

Dinner was delicious. My halibut was flaky and flavorful, and the asparagus had just the right amount of crunch. As I ate, I couldn't help peering at Joel over my fork. Biting my lip, I tried to steer my thoughts away from kissing Joel. The last thing I wanted was to muddy the waters between us, especially when I was returning to Los Angeles and my fellowship in a few days. I didn't have time *or* energy, I admitted, to have a romantic relationship with anyone. *After the fellowship ends, I can decide if I want to explore things with Joel again.*

I excused myself to the ladies' room. I washed my hands in the sink and peered at myself in the mirror. The bruising on my face was thankfully gone.

Inhaling deeply, I returned to our table.

"I'm just waiting for the receipt," he said casually. We had both polished off our entire plates. In high school, we had always ordered dessert, but he hadn't said anything, and honestly, I was too full to care. Before I could sit, the waiter brought the receipt and Joel's card back. I belatedly realized I wasn't originally planning on letting him pay for dinner if we ended up eating out.

"I was going to pay ..." I said softly.

He stood up and captured my hand, bringing it up to his lips. It was something he used to do when we were dating. As his lips brushed the back of my knuckles, goose bumps rippled across my skin. I must have made a noise of some sort, for when he looked up at me, a slight smile was at the corner of his lips.

"You were too slow," he replied and brushed his lips across my hand again before letting it fall between us. My lips parted. It was tempting to kiss him. *Does he still kiss the same?* But I held back. I had to keep my priorities straight. Finish the fellowship. I turned away and headed down the stairs, having an odd feeling of déjà vu that I couldn't place. Who else would have been watching me walk down these stairs other than Joel? Last time I was here, I was by myself.

I considered walking home. It would be manageable from Blue Fin and would be a welcome chance to clear my head. I hesitated at the bottom of the steps, uncertain, feet pointed in the direction of Abuela's house.

"You can't walk home," Joel said from behind me.

I turned, frustration bubbling to the surface. "You aren't allowed to tell me what to do," I replied stubbornly.

"I have a perfectly functional Tahoe. There is no reason for you to push yourself and walk back," he said, keeping his tone neutral.

He remembers all the times he challenged my decision and I went ahead anyway. No matter how reckless it might have been.

"No thanks. I'll walk," I responded and took a few steps toward the corner, intending to cross, when Joel stepped in front of me, blocking my way. I frowned, not wanting this to blow up into a real argument. I wanted space to breathe and think without Joel hovering. Running always helped me clear my head, and I hoped walking would too. Besides, it was less than two miles. I could manage. *If I can't, then should I really be returning to my fellowship this soon?*

"Kelsey ..." he started.

"Is there something wrong with wanting space? The accident, being here in Santa Barbara, it's overwhelming," I replied, my voice hitching.

I tried to step around him. He wrapped his arms around me and pulled me close. Then, to my shock, he kissed me. I tensed but soon found myself leaning into his embrace, parting my lips, and returning the kiss.

I tipped my head back, trying to catch my breath. Joel gave me a few moments at best before our lips met again. He ran his fingers through my hair, sending tingles down my spine. I pressed my hips tighter to his as my need intensified.

This time, he pulled back to breathe. "Do you still want me to leave you alone?" he said, his lips tickling my ear.

I swallowed and made myself step backward, meeting his gaze. "Yes ... No. But the timing is not good. I'm returning to Los Angeles to finish my fellowship. I don't have the energy right now to do a relationship with you justice and stay committed to the fellowship. I've worked too hard to get the fellowship to let it fall apart now. I hope you can understand."

Joel nodded. "If that is what you want to do, then I respect your decision."

I licked my suddenly dry lips. "It's not a forever no," I said softly.

Joel gave me a kiss on the cheek. "I understand. You don't need to explain yourself to me, Kelsey. I will be here when you're ready." Then, he turned and walked back to the Tahoe.

Squaring my shoulders, I headed across the street and walked back to Abuela's.

Chapter 15: Conner

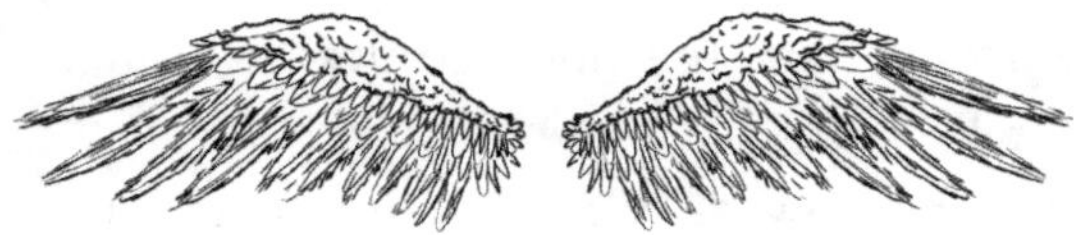

Monday, September 23

Cassiel had said I was to depart in two weeks, after I concluded the endless stream of meetings he had put on my schedule. I was tired and ready to be back in London—though deep down, I knew it was because I wanted to be away from my father, not because I disliked being in Los Angeles.

I checked the clock as I pulled up to the curb in front of the Los Angeles Children's Hospital. The day was gloomy with cloud cover and the promise of rain. I tossed the keys to the valet, then strode inside. I had three minutes to get upstairs before I was late. I took the stairs two at a time, ignoring the looks some of the doctors gave me as they went about their tasks.

The meeting was in room 2000. I could see 2000 etched in the glass doors just ahead. I pushed them open just as the clock struck ten a.m. I felt a fleeting tightness as I crossed the threshold, which I knew was a shield to prevent any humans from seeing the demons' true forms.

"Conniel," a demon in a black suit and tie said, stepping forward with his hand outstretched. He had dark blue skin, bloodshot yellow eyes, and bright yellow hair slicked back on his head.

I shook his hand. "Azinak," I said confidently. Like me, he was immortal, but had chosen to go through human schooling. Humans knew him as Dr. Malcom, a licensed pediatric surgeon.

He smiled, flashing his sharp bright white teeth. "I'd like you to meet some of the other board members." Azinak gestured at the three demons in the room and began introductions. Sonnamed was the same kind of demon as Azinak. He merely gave me a curt nod. Vol'gar's skin was a vibrant orange with bright blue spots, much like a poison dart frog, and harmless to humans but deadly to an immortal.

Vol'gar rose and bowed. "Conniel, son of Archangel Cassiel, it is an honor to finally meet you," he said formally.

I inclined my head. "The honor is mine, Vol'gar, son of Kor'oron." Though I'd never met Vol'gar, I had plenty of dealings with Kor'oron, who had mentioned his son on several occasions. Their clan was one that always erred on the side of formality when dealing with me or my father. Though their skin was deadly, they did not enjoy being the center of conflict.

The last demon was Jazonar. She was the most humanlike, and I thought of her kind more akin to what humans considered "vampires" than the other demon types. She had bright red eyes and her skin was pale white, and straight black hair hung down to her waist. The tailored white pantsuit made her look even paler.

To my surprise, she walked around the table and offered me her hand. "Good morning, Conner," Jazonar said in a deep, rumbling voice.

I took her hand and shook it. "Good morning, Jazonar." Her gaze roved over me from head to toe before she released my hand and returned to her spot at the table.

"Archangel Cassiel was quite persistent in encouraging me to set up this meeting. As I am sure you are aware, previously when his firm has made proposals for you to obtain a seat on our board, we have graciously declined. We are not entirely sure what skills you offer that we do not already have," Azinak stated.

I smiled. "Well then, let me show you what I can offer."

I walked to the head of the table and then stopped in my tracks.

Originally, I had expected humans to be in the group. Given there were none, there was no need to show them the computer presentation.

"After reviewing your financials, employee handbook, and the results of a survey I had sent out, it is obvious that you have let your personal needs cloud your decisions with the operations of the hospital. The majority of your staff are humans, and you only treat humans; therefore, it is critical that *humans* are your priority.

"Let's start with the employee handbook. It reads like it was written thirty years ago. Though thirty years may not feel long to immortals, there have been immense changes in human businesses. Employee retention rates for LACH have dropped year over year in the past five years. Low retention rates mean the hospital is spending more money than it should on recruitment and new hires."

I went on to discuss the details of the survey and particular areas of concern, then launched into an analysis of their financials. None of them looked surprised at anything I was saying. *Perhaps that was why they agreed to meet. They know the hospital is suffering.*

"There is one more matter, though it is not a high priority. I will be addressing it if I join your team. That is security. As crime rates are continuing to increase across Southern California, I believe we should also upgrade our security measures. To protect our staff and our patients." I glanced at my watch. "I am certain you have much to discuss. You know how to reach me if you have any questions. Thank you for your time."

Azinak rose and escorted me to the door. He shook my hand. "I will be in touch soon. Thank you."

The valet driver must have gotten a heads-up from someone inside that I was heading out because my car, a bright blue Lamborghini Revuelto, was sitting out in front, visible through the large glass doors.

The drive to the private airport was uneventful. One of the downsides of having this car here in Los Angeles was the lack of nearby opportunities to take it out for a drive and put it through its paces. Now, I was returning to London, which meant that task would have to wait until I returned.

I recalled the resigned looks on the faces of the four demons from the LACH board. They had not overhauled their hospital's business structure for many years, and it was overdue. There was a reason why my father couldn't afford for me to leave his team. The unique combination of degrees I had obtained—undergraduate in biology, master's in law, and PhD in international business, along with my immortal language ability that made me fluent in all human languages—gave me a different perspective on how businesses operated. When traditional approaches were outdated or no longer as successful, I had an uncanny ability to turn things around without needing to use force to acquire a position within the hospital allowing me to spearhead the changes.

Their reaction was precisely why I enjoyed my duties to keep peace between immortals and humans, all while ensuring humans remained oblivious to our existence. The demons running hospitals often became complacent in their responsibilities, focused more on the profits they were using to indulge in human luxuries and not on ensuring the humans in their care were properly managed.

I slowed down and drove straight into the hangar where the Hudsie II, the smaller of the two family jets, was waiting. The Gulfstream G650ER could accommodate up to twelve people and easily perform a nonstop flight from Los Angeles to London.

The pilots and crew greeted me. I left the keys in the Revuelto and grabbed my suitcase and briefcase out of the passenger seat. The suitcase was whisked into the plane by one of the crew members, but I held on to the briefcase.

"Good evening, sir," the pilot said.

"John, remember our conversation last time? Just call me Conner, please," I replied.

"Yes, si— Yes ... Conner," John responded.

I smiled and headed up the short set of stairs inside, then plopped down in one of the two pairs of chairs and set the briefcase in the chair next to me.

Diane, the crew member primarily responsible for providing food and drinks, walked over. "I have a turkey club sandwich ready for your dinner, and then the suite is set up for you whenever you choose to retire."

"Perfect. I'll take the sandwich now," I said, settling back into my chair.

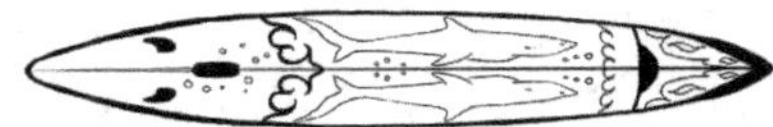

I was sitting on the dark brown leather couch in my condo in London, gazing at the landscape painting of the sun rising in the English Channel. Taking a deep breath, I ran my hand over my face. Two days ago, I closed the deal with the Los Angeles Children's Hospital. My position would become official on October first, and they would formally announce during the Halloween gala. I frowned. I had tried to dissuade them from adding something else to the agenda for the gala, but it was obvious Cassiel had used his influence.

I had a couple of appointments to attend to tomorrow in London, and then I would be free to head to my estate. About half of the work I did with the hospitals could be accomplished remotely with the other half requiring me to have a physical presence. The good part about retreating to my estate was that I had the freedom to come and go as I pleased without using human transportation.

My temples tingled a fleeting warning before Nate's amused voice was in my head. *"Are you coming?"*

"Shit," I grumbled, realizing I had forgotten I'd agreed to meet Nate and our other friends.

"Ya work too much, mate. Come down to the pub. We'll wait for ya," Nate cajoled.

I blew out my breath. He was right; I did work too much, and right now a chance to drop the pretense of being human and hang out with other immortals was appealing.

"See you shortly," I replied. I took a quick shower and changed into a clean blue button-up shirt and khaki trousers. Confident I looked less formal, I made my way to the pub. It was only two blocks away. One of the rules was that customers were required to walk through the front door, and it was neutral territory, so no fights were permitted, or the offenders would be banned for two decades.

I think my friends favored it because they were more likely to get me to agree to it than meeting in Ianialar.

Strolling down Ely Court, I took in the small shops with their colorful awnings. Ahead was Ye Old Mitre with its dark gray stone and black-trimmed windows, a popular destination for local humans. One door down was The Dapper Lamb. Its black-painted door was unadorned, though I could see a shimmering gold lamb with a cheeky grin and hat. I pushed open the door, and there was a light tug as I passed through the barrier that blocked humans.

Directly in front of me was Mavin, a demon with a reptilian appearance. Though he had a human shape, his skin was made of dark blue iridescent scales, and his golden eyes had slit-like pupils. He gave me an appraising but silent inspection and then waved me through the next door. I hesitated at the entrance, opening my wings to their full span for a brief moment before folding them closed.

The walls were paneled in dark wood with a white ceiling broken up with thick walnut beams. The bar spanned the entire far wall and had an assortment of stools with burgundy leather seats set along it. Mavin's brother, Verve, ran the pub and also served as its primary bartender. I was surprised that the crowd was pretty light, though mused perhaps it was because it was a Thursday.

Nate was waving and shouting "Hello!" from a high-top table to the right. His pale gray wings were a stark contrast to his dark gray bomber jacket and jeans. His pale blond hair and blue eyes always attracted women, human and immortal. Jordan was sitting across from Nate. His wings were white like mine, but his skin was blue-black, as was his hair. Coupled with his gold eyes, of the three of us Jordan had to alter his appearance the most to fit in with the humans. But here at The Dapper Lamb, we were free to be ourselves.

I flashed them a grin and made my way to their table. Nate offered me a glass that looked like it was not as full as it had originally been, though as soon as I wrapped my hands around it, the amber liquid was at the brim. I lifted it, saluting Nate, and drained the whole glass in one swallow. The bourbon burned a welcome fiery trail down my throat. Luckily, the server came back over with a fresh round before I could lift a finger.

Jordan scooted his stool over and made space for me next to him.

"What have you been up to?" Nate asked.

"Same old stuff ... demons and hospitals," I said with a shrug.

Nate didn't look convinced by my response but didn't press me. He knew enough about what I did to know it was not of interest to him. Unlike me, Nate wasn't charged with managing demons. Similar to Agatha, Nate, who had a fascination with human technology, had pursued a "career" in the computer engineering field, becoming invaluable to the firm he worked for.

Jordan eyed me. "Meet anyone new in Los Angeles?"

I considered saying yes, but I knew that would prompt more questions. Given we were in a pub with other immortals, this was not the right place to share my weekend fling at the beach with them. "Not in the way you mean," I replied. I figured they didn't want the who's who of any of the various boards I belonged to.

"Well, we need to change that. I should hook you up with—" said Jordan.

I smacked his arm. "I don't need to be hooked up with anyone."

I slowly sipped my bourbon, taking time to enjoy it. I was too lost in my thoughts to catch what they were talking about, but I realized Nate's last sentence was directed at me. "What did you say?" I asked Nate.

"Are you and Agatha dating again?" Nate pressed.

I sighed, knowing that if they were saying these things about Agatha and me, then they didn't know she preferred females. Though I knew her preference was not a secret, I was not going to be the one to tell Nate and Jordan. But Agatha and I had also agreed to pretend to be dating and getting engaged, so I had to keep up the ruse. "Yes, we are."

Jordan smirked, and Nate handed him a five-pound note.

I frowned. "You made a bet?"

Nate nodded. "Yep, and I lost. I didn't think you'd say yes since you and Agatha obviously broke up previously."

"Cassiel seems to think that Agatha and I need to get married," I added.

Jordan rolled his eyes. "He hasn't figured out yet that the two of you are better as friends than lovers?"

I shook my head. "No. Her family is even in on it. While I understand it would be a prestigious marriage for both of us, I'm not inclined to jump because I'm told."

Nate chimed in, "After October, you'll be free."

I let out a gusty breath. "I know. Except I must make it through the next month."

Nate laughed. I was the oldest of the three of us, just shy of turning fifteen hundred. Nate and Jordan were a century younger.

My father had married my mother when he was three centuries old, and I was conceived shortly after his fifteen hundredth birthday. Over the centuries, he had tried to pressure me into settling down, citing that as the son of an archangel it was my duty. There were only two archangel bloodlines still in existence, and mine happened to be one of them. Unfortunately for Cassiel, I disagreed, and though I had had several lengthy relationships with other angels over my lifetime, for the most part my relationships had been arm candy and bedroom partners. One of the disadvantages of being the archangel's son was everyone knew who I was. That was all they saw, a link to the famous Archangel Cassiel, not that the son was his own angel.

Then, there were the humans who in the past two decades had been chasing after Dr. Conner Hudson, the illusive billionaire.

No matter how much I disliked the firm hand my father took with me and the company, he had never once hurt me. Angered me, absolutely. Once I had left for college, I found I was no longer willing to accept his decisions that I disagreed with without discussing them. Occasionally, he would agree that I had a valid point and would alter his plan accordingly.

"Enough of this ... What have the two of you been up to?" I asked and drained my glass. I came here to have fun, not let my two best friends analyze my life.

Chapter 16: Kelsey

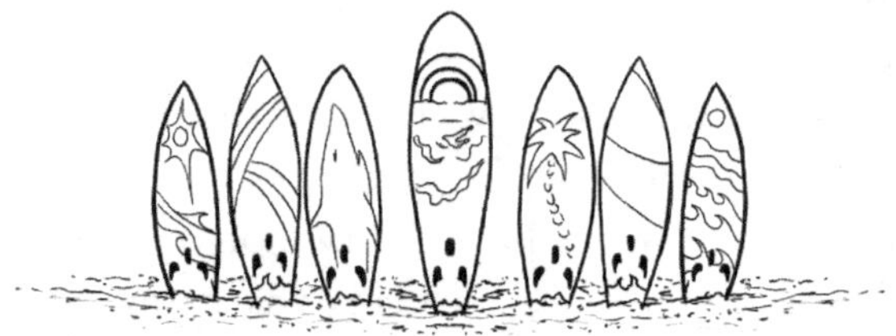

Saturday, September 28

I was performing a hernia repair on a five-year-old girl whose dog was named Rover. Two third-year surgical residents were assisting me. I made the cut and then stopped. I could feel everyone staring at me, waiting, but try as I might, I could not remember what the next step was. My panic rose.

My eyes snapped open. I was in bed, a discarded book beside me. Breathing heavily, I sat up. *It's just a dream*, I reminded myself. My thoughts drifted to my accident. I remember stopping at the traffic light next to the gas station. Then, my next clear memory was waking up in the hospital bed. I knew I had been on my way home after an evening at Toucan's, but I couldn't remember who I was at Toucan's with or anything before that. I was sure that I had gone surfing twice, but the details of those first four days of my vacation were blurry. Joel and Penny had filled in a few gaps, but I still felt as though I was missing something important—I just had no idea what. Without my ability to ask the right question to help remember, none of my friends or family were offering the details to confirm that I *was* forgetting something.

As a doctor and surgeon, I knew that sustaining memory loss was common in accidents such as mine. Often, it would return days or weeks later. *I will just have to be patient and wait for it to return.*

I swung my legs off the bed, deciding I felt good enough to run five laps around the block. I knew it was still going to be awhile yet before I could run the two miles from my apartment to the hospital, but I could build up to it. I was still tiring quicker than normal. *At least what would be normal for me after a typical twenty-four-hour shift.*

Dr. Pierce had called earlier this morning to check in on my progress and assure me that if returning full time was too much at the end of my vacation, I could ease back into my normal schedule. I appreciated the gesture, but I did not want them to baby me.

Mind made up, I pulled on my shoes and headed out the back door for my run. It was my last day in Santa Barbara. Abuela had wanted me to relax today, but I insisted on going for a run. The doctor had made me promise not to surf, even though he had given me the all-clear to return to work full-time if I felt ready on Monday. It was tempting to disobey his orders and head to the beach anyhow, but deep down I knew if I did and something went wrong, I could sacrifice my dream of becoming a pediatric surgeon.

Only half paying attention to the direction I was running, I came to a halt at the signal and peered around. Realization slammed into me, and I found it was hard to breathe as I stared at the scene of the accident. All debris had been long since cleared away, and it was impossible to determine if the black skid marks were from the dually that had hit me or someone else braking hard.

Trying to control my breathing, I closed my eyes.

My whole body hurt, but my head was the worst. I could feel blood trickling down my forehead. A red-haired man was sitting next to me in the car.

"Kelsey!" he kept saying in a British accent.

How does he know my name? *I found myself wondering. The*

red-haired man disappeared and was replaced by firefighters armed with the jaws of life.

I opened my eyes, blinking in the sunlight. *Who was that man?* Confusion filled me. I couldn't recall ever meeting a red-haired Brit while in Santa Barbara, but clearly he had known me. *Or*, I mused, *I am just daydreaming. Wouldn't it be romantic if instead of the firefighters, I had been rescued by a guy with a British accent?* Shaking my head, I noticed the light had turned green, and the crosswalk signal indicated I could cross. I took off at a run and headed into the neighborhood on the other side of the street.

Not paying attention to where my feet took me, I halted in front of Penny's house. It was two p.m. on a Saturday. With an active family, I wasn't sure if she would even be home. Steeling myself, I strode up to the bright turquoise door and knocked on it. From inside, I could hear the distinct sound of running feet and a child shouting, "Mom!"

I guess they are home.

Eventually, the door opened, revealing Penny. Smudges of flour were on her face and black sweatshirt.

I giggled. "Baking today?"

"If you want to call it baking," Penny grumbled, then waved me in. "Is everything okay?"

I smiled. "Yes, I'm fine. I was just out for a run, and my feet carried me here."

We sat down on the couch. "Do you need to finish baking?"

Penny shook her head. "No, we just put the muffins into the oven. Ken has it handled from here."

I ran my hand over my hair, but it was still secure in its ponytail. I felt nervous, but I wasn't sure why. This was Penny I was talking to. I'd been friends with her since we were both in diapers, even longer than Joel.

"Are you worried about going back to the hospital on Monday?" Penny asked.

I let my hand drop into my lap. "No. Well, I'm a little apprehensive about driving back into Los Angeles. I haven't been behind the wheel for more than ten minutes since the accident, but I'm going to have to get over it. I can't let the accident prevent me from living my life, and driving has always been a part of that. Mostly just for the independence it affords me."

"An understandable concern. At least now you have the new car. I'm glad Joel encouraged you to go with an almost-new one. I feel better knowing you have more safety features," Penny commented.

Twisting my hands in my lap, I debated if I should tell her about the daydream. It was no secret I was still having nightmares about the accident. "Have you seen a red-haired British guy before?"

Penny's eyebrows shot up, and her mouth parted. I swallowed, my throat feeling tight with apprehension. *What does she know?*

"When we were at Toucan's, you danced with a red-haired Brit," Penny said.

"I what?" I rose partway in my seat before sitting back down.

"You said it was just a weekend fling. You're an adult and perfectly capable of taking care of yourself. I know you've gone on dates. Hell, even slept with other men besides Joel. I don't like prying into your business unless you want me to. I assumed that since you hadn't mentioned him, you didn't have any interest in staying in touch," Penny replied. Her voice was low, and I could tell from her expression she felt defensive.

"I'm not blaming you for anything, Penny," I said and patted her hand in what I hoped was reassurance. Frustration welled up within me. *What else am I forgetting?*

A sliver of fear worked its way into me. *What if I get in the operating room and I don't remember what to do partway through a surgery?* I gasped. My hands were shaking as that possibility had just become far more real.

"Concussions often result in short-term memory loss," Penny said, reciting the exact words my doctor had several times over the past few weeks. I just hadn't realized the missing memories weren't just hanging out with people I know. It was also meeting a new person.

Penny must have noticed I was falling apart. She scooted onto my part of the couch and pulled me into a warm hug. I melted against her, sobbing. "Hush, Kelsey, you're fine." She rubbed my back and rocked me gently while I cried. I felt better after a few minutes and sniffled, realizing she'd probably calmed her children the exact same way hundreds of times over the past eight years.

"Muffins are done!" an excited girl's voice screamed from the kitchen.

I laughed and loosened my arms from around Penny. "Thanks. Should we go eat a muffin?"

Penny scrunched her nose up. "If you dare. They most likely don't taste very good."

I shrugged. "I'll at least try a bite. A great cook doesn't start off great."

Chapter 17: Kelsey

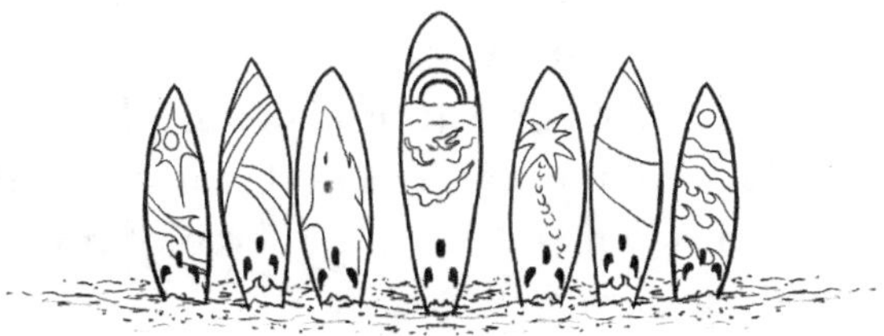

Monday, September 30

Opting to be cautious on my first day back at the fellowship post-accident, I made the decision to drive to the hospital rather than walk or run. Descending the stairs to the parking garage, I couldn't help but smile as I laid eyes on my new-to-me car, the 2023 silver Prius. I opened the door and slid onto the slick black faux-leather seat. I placed my coffee cup in the cup holder and my purple backpack in the passenger seat.

I was pleased with my decision to listen to Joel's encouragement and get an upgraded-model Prius, splurging a little but still able to put the majority of the insurance payout into a high-interest savings account.

Yawning, I sipped on my coffee and waited impatiently for the light to change so the cars in front of me that were blocking the parking garage entrance would move. The traffic was a sharp reminder of why I rarely drove to work.

An hour later, I was able to turn into the parking lot. It was five a.m. The parking lot was about halfway full, and I quickly found a spot.

Taking a deep breath, I grabbed my coffee out of the cup holder, swung my backpack over my shoulder, and locked the car, heading toward the hospital and the next twelve months. Though I spent much of yesterday worrying about how today would go, now that I was here, I felt energized. *Twelve months.* I could recall feeling this way throughout the years. My senior year of high school as I walked through on the first day, thinking, *One more year.* Senior year might have been the last year of high school—and of being considered a child—but it was not the end of my education track. Today, though, truly marked the last stretch of my journey to becoming a pediatric surgeon.

Using my keycard, I entered through the staff entrance, bypassing any possible run-ins with patient families. I wanted to get oriented before interacting with a patient. Over the years, I had learned how quickly the status of a patient could change, either for better or worse. Three weeks was a long time to be out of the loop. The last thing I needed was to say the wrong thing to a patient.

Taking the stairs to the third floor in the west tower, I noticed the fresh coat of paint on the walls.

Scanning my card again, I pushed through the double doors and was greeted by a throng of smiling nurses in light blue scrubs. At the back of the bunch, I spied Dr. Pierce in navy-blue scrubs and his white doctor's coat. He offered me a slight smile.

"How are you feeling?" asked Ronda. "We heard about your accident."

I smiled and moved back a step, so I could have room to breathe. "I got lucky. It could have been far worse." Everyone kept peppering me with questions. A bouquet of flowers was thrust into my arms, and I nearly dropped my coffee.

"Enough!" Dr. Pierce shouted over the din of voices.

Ronda gave me a bashful smile. "Sorry. We just missed you."

"I appreciate it. Really, I do. I promise I'm fine and ready to work," I said, hoping they would get the hint and go back to whatever they were doing before I arrived.

They reluctantly trickled back to their stations, leaving me alone with Dr. Pierce. His brown hair was hidden under a plain black surgical cap. He looked me up and down, assessing. I raised my eyebrows, wondering if he was going to find a visible issue and require me to go home.

Finally done with his inspection, Dr. Pierce met my gaze. "You look tired."

I wrinkled my nose. "I promise I have had lots of sleep, and I followed all of the doctor's orders, easing back into my normal routine and not surfing. Injury-wise, I was given the all-clear on Friday."

"How was driving?" he pressed.

"Manageable. Though I could do without the Los Angeles traffic," I responded.

"Come, let's look at the surgery board together." He motioned, and I walked over to the board. Shoulder to shoulder, we gazed at it. I waited for him to explain what specifically he wanted me to look at.

"Colin Masey is having a Ross procedure on Wednesday. I would like you to scrub in and assist Dr. Hoover," Dr. Pierce said.

Dr. Hoover was a pediatric cardiovascular surgeon. The last time he had a Ross procedure, I had had a liver transplant arrive two hours beforehand and had to bow out of the opportunity to assist. As one of the larger children's hospitals in the country, LACH had the resources to be able to do a lengthy Ross procedure, which was an option for children with congenital aortic stenosis. It was typically offered when, like in Colin's case, a balloon valvotomy had been done and the aortic valves became leaky over time.

"Given that I want to ease you back into work slowly and the Ross procedures are very uncommon, I would like to keep your workload today and tomorrow very light so that you will be well-rested and able to participate in the Ross procedure. If any surgeries that are simple come in, like an appendectomy or something similar, you are welcome to take those, but don't feel like you need to push yourself into a larger surgery. You have twelve months. There is plenty of time," Dr. Pierce said firmly.

Deep down, I knew he was right. There were a couple other surgeries on the board for today and tomorrow that were tempting to take, but they were long and would be very draining. "I will do as you suggest. I would love to be able to do a Ross procedure."

"Very well. Why don't you spend the next hour getting up to speed on your cases and then we can do rounds?" Dr. Pierce suggested.

"Sounds good," I said and took my leave.

Chapter 18: Kelsey

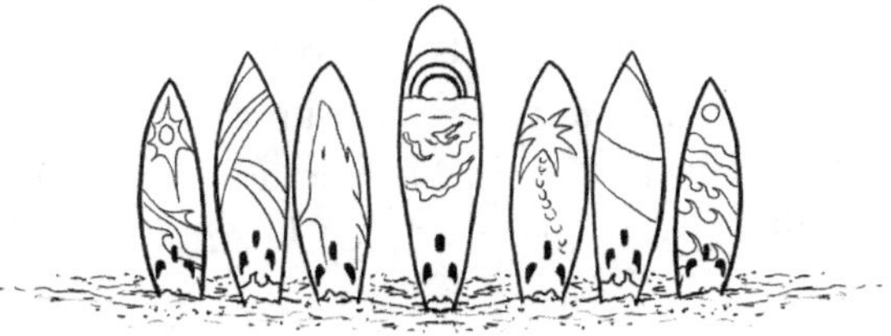

Friday, October 4

On Friday, the end of my first week back at LACH, I walked home slowly. I was exhausted but thrilled by how well the week had gone. Despite my apprehensions of returning after my accident, I had slipped back into my fellowship responsibilities as though the accident had never happened. The Ross procedure had been as amazing as I had hoped, but the twenty-hour-long surgery had sapped what was left of my energy. Thankfully, Dr. Pierce let me have an easy day afterward, handling consults for surgeries that had yet to be scheduled or were slated for next week. It did feel great to be back in the hospital. *Where I belong.*

I was heading home for the weekend to recharge. I was looking forward to sleeping in my own bed and not taking power naps in the doctors' lounge. The walk felt great. An opportunity to move freely was a welcome change. Though by the end of the walk, I made the wise decision to take the elevator up to my apartment. My feet squeaked on the freshly mopped tile in the entryway. To my surprise, the elevator was waiting on the ground level. I stepped inside and pushed the button for the fourth level. The interior of the elevator was simple stainless steel panels. The elevator dinged and the door opened on my floor. I stepped onto the thickly carpeted hallway and walked to my apartment, 4B, and let myself in.

The first thing I noticed was the lights were on. I hung my keys on the hook and set my backpack by the door. Sniffing the air, I could smell something amazing wafting out of the kitchen. Wondering which of my friends had borrowed Abuela's key, I called, "Hello?" I wandered toward the kitchen.

Smiling, Joel strode out of the kitchen. His hair was messy, and there was a red towel in his hands. "Hey, beautiful." He came over and gave me a hug.

I relaxed into his embrace, then let go when curiosity got the better of me. "What are you doing here?"

"I wanted to surprise you, and you have tomorrow off. I thought you could use the company." He walked back into the kitchen. "Besides," he called over his shoulder, "Abuela was certain you have been eating terribly this week. She sent me with a batch of tamales too."

I followed him into the kitchen, but I had to peer around him because he was broad enough to block my tiny stove from view. He was sautéing chicken and had a pot of penne boiling. "It smells wonderful."

"It's almost ready. Why don't you just sit down and relax?"

I nodded and ran a hand over my face, hoping I would be able to stay awake through dinner. My plan had been to eat a protein bar, take an ibuprofen, and go to sleep. *I can still take an ibuprofen and go to sleep.* But with Joel here, my plans would have to change. It would be rude if I went to sleep without at least trying to hang out for a bit.

I sat down and yawned. I started to lay my head down on the table when Joel came in with plates full of food. "Here you go."

I sat up straighter, covered my yawn with my hand, and gave him a tired smile. "Thanks. You really didn't have to do this."

"Sure I did," he said and gave me a kiss on the forehead before taking his seat across from me.

I focused on the food on my plate. The chicken had some sort of pink sauce on it and the penne had alfredo sauce and spinach. I cut up the chicken into manageable pieces and took a bite. I closed my eyes, savoring the flavors. It was alfredo, but there was also the slight tang of gorgonzola, parmesan, and other cheeses I couldn't identify. When I opened my eyes, Joel was watching me.

"What?" I demanded.

"You're beautiful," he said softly.

I rolled my eyes. "I'm sure I look like shit. I just ended my first week back and probably should have taken today off after the long procedure on Wednesday."

He gave me a crooked smile. "I'm not joking. It doesn't matter how exhausted you are. You are still beautiful to me," Joel insisted.

I blushed at the compliment and began eating again, not entirely sure how to respond. Exhaustion was making it difficult to think. When I finished eating, I stood up and took my plate into the kitchen, intent on my task of putting away the plate and going to sleep. I could worry about cleaning the kitchen in the morning.

Joel came up beside me and dried the plates that I had washed, then put them away in the cabinet. "Thanks," I said, meeting his gaze.

Joel shrugged. "I know you're tired. I will head to my hotel and see you in the morning."

I pressed my lips together. I felt bad that he had to pay for a hotel when I had a perfectly good sofa bed. "You're welcome to stay here."

Joel raised his eyebrows. "Are you sure?"

I nodded. "Of course. Let me set up the bed for you." I turned and walked out of the kitchen. Joel snagged my hand.

"If you tell me where it is, I can set up the bed," Joel replied.

I sighed and agreed. "Okay." Leading the way, I gestured to the closet. "Sheets, pillows, and blankets are in there. As are spare towels."

"I know you're tired, and we will have plenty of time to hang out tomorrow. Go to bed, Kelsey, before you fall asleep on your feet and I have to carry you."

I gave him a tired smile and headed into my bedroom.

I sat up in bed, confused, the green sheets wrapped around me. I heard a cough in the living room. My eyes flicked to the door, and then I remembered. *Joel surprised me with dinner.* Happiness spread through me. My best friend came to visit for my weekend off.

I chose to take a shower, since I had forgotten that part of my plan last night.

A knock on the door broke me out of my thoughts. "Want some company?" Joel asked.

I choked on a few droplets of water that ran into my mouth. *I must have heard him wrong.* "What did you say?" I called.

The door opened a hair. "Want some breakfast?" Joel asked.

I started giggling at my mistake. How I had heard *company* instead of *breakfast* I wasn't sure, but it was far better than Joel trying to test my boundaries.

"Breakfast would be wonderful. But you don't need to cook again. I have cereal," I replied.

Joel chuckled. "A sad excuse for breakfast. It'll be ready when you're out of the shower."

Chilling in the apartment with Joel over the weekend was just the lowkey two days that I needed. We watched movies and played a couple of different card games. Sunday, we made a triple batch of lasagna, enough for us to eat for dinner, and both of us could keep some to freeze for future meals.

Purple backpack over my shoulders, I walked briskly to the hospital, smiling as I watched the cars creep by.

I almost started running the last block but held myself back. *Tomorrow*, I promised myself. It was easy to forget how exhausted I had been on Friday after an easy weekend. I needed to pace myself and not get overzealous and cause more problems.

When I reached the pediatric surgery wing, I could hear voices buzzing on the other side of the door. Curiosity warred with concern as I pushed my way through the doors into the scene awaiting me.

"Morning!" I called to Ronda. She gave me a slight wave before returning her attention to the conversation Dr. Hoover and Dr. Pierce were having. Reluctant to barge in unless asked, I headed for the staff locker room to deposit my gear.

Dr. Pierce walked in just as I was pulling my white doctor's coat on. "Good, you're here. Dr. Hoover wanted to page you an hour ago, but I urged him to wait. We didn't have all the bloodwork yet, so there was no need to call you early."

I waited for him to tell me who the bloodwork was on, not wanting to cut in on the middle of his explanation. I had done that a few times at the beginning of my fellowship and learned quickly that he did not appreciate being interrupted.

"Hannah George, eight, presented this morning with an arrhythmia. Her mother says she's been seen at Sinai Hospital by a cardiologist, but her concerns were not taken seriously. The past twenty-four hours Hannah has become sluggish with a very slow heart rate, so she brought her into the ER, and they referred her to us immediately. With the patient's history, we're assuming she is going to need a pacemaker. The test results should be in shortly. I know you've placed pacemakers in adults. I thought you would like the opportunity to do one in a child," he explained.

I understood why Dr. Hoover disagreed. He didn't want to wait to start the procedure. He was confident it was the solution. I was just grateful they wanted me to do the surgery. To complete my board certification, I would have to take an exam, and one of the most critical aspects was to be comfortable with all types of pediatric surgeries. Though I had some cardio experience from my general surgery residency, there had been few opportunities so far during my fellowship.

"What room is she in?" I asked. If I was going to do surgery, I wanted to meet the patient and her family. They weren't just a number; they were individuals with feelings. I also liked getting to know them because sometimes I found I would learn tidbits that had not been thought relevant to the health history but had a significant impact on the outcome of the surgery. Knowing Johnny's dream was to play basketball, for example, I made choices that would maximize the potential for him to do that.

"Three sixteen," Dr. Pierce replied. "Oh, and you're flying solo on this one."

My eyes widened. "I am?"

"Yes, you're ready. Don't worry. You will have a fourth-year surgical resident to assist, but Dr. Hoover and I agree that you did an exceptional job assisting on the Ross procedure and are ready to tackle a surgery such as Hannah's on your own," Dr. Pierce replied and gave me a smile. "If you have questions, we're available, but you've got this, Dr. Floras."

"Thank you," I replied, voice soft. As soon as he left, I couldn't help grinning. Snagging my water bottle off the chair, I tucked my surgical cap in my pocket and departed for room 316.

Chapter 19: Conner

Saturday, October 5

The long, winding road out to my estate was peaceful and quiet—two things that were nearly impossible to be either in London or Los Angeles. The leaves on the trees were a vibrant mix of reds, oranges, and browns, a nice contrast with the still-green grass and the grayish rocks. With modern amenities, I could just as easily work at my estate as I could from the flat in London. I had no meetings for the next three days that required me to be in the city, and I intended to use the time to relax and get back into a routine of sorts.

The large wrought iron gates swung open, and I pulled around the cobbled circular driveway with a large fountain in the middle. Taking a deep breath, I exhaled slowly.

Ring. Ring. Ring.

I sighed. *Now what?* I tugged my phone from my pocket and hit accept without figuring out who it was. "Dr. Hudson," I answered, opting for professional. I never really knew who was going to call me, human or immortal, friend or business associate. The last thing I needed was to piss off an executive at a hospital I worked for.

"Conner." Agatha's silky voice was a relief.

"Agatha." It dawned on me that I had not gotten back to her

with dates for the shoot. "I forgot to check my calendar."

"Yes, I am aware. But I am also a step ahead of you. Cassiel said you're working at your estate for a few days. Would tomorrow be a good time to do the photo shoot?" Agatha asked.

I slid out of the car and peered around. The large eighteenth-century Edwardian manor house was a welcome sight. The door to the house opened, and Fabio stepped out. I pointed to my phone, and without asking, Fabio removed my suitcase from the trunk and led me into the house.

"I will have to make sure everything is presentable. But I don't currently have a meeting scheduled around sunset if they want to time the shoot around that," I replied. The last thing I wanted to do right now was a photo shoot, but I had promised Agatha, and I didn't know when I would be back. My schedule was more erratic than I liked to admit. Even when I attempted to set a schedule, it always shifted. *Or perhaps the issue is everyone is used to me being flexible, and I need to retrain them if I no longer wish to alter my plans at the drop of a hat.*

"Wonderful. I'll see you tomorrow," Agatha replied, then hung up.

Belatedly, I realized I should have asked for more details. They wanted to use my estate, but I had no idea which part. *Inside the house? The exterior of the house? The forty-some acres?* I supposed it didn't entirely matter. The pixies serving as my house staff kept the manor and grounds in pristine condition. The housekeeper came by once a week when I wasn't home, and the groundskeeper came twice a week to ensure that everything was in top shape.

If I was going to be residing here for any amount of time with humans for company, then a cook would stay in one of the guest houses and ensure the humans were fed properly.

With one more glance around the front, I strode into the house. High-arching dark wood beams and wood paneling greeted me. I sighed, relieved to be home. This manor was the only house I owned where I felt like I could truly be myself.

"Do you need anything?" asked Fabio when I didn't make a move to exit the foyer.

I glanced at him. "Agatha is bringing a photo crew here tomorrow afternoon."

"They're already here," replied Fabio.

My eyes widened in surprise. "I just spoke to Agatha ..."

Fabio chuckled. "Yes, I know. She set things in motion as soon as you gave her the okay in Los Angeles. I've been working with her supervisor to plan everything and coordinate when you'd be available."

"Of course," I replied. *I should've known Fabio had it handled.*

"What's your agenda for the rest of the day?" Fabio asked, though I suspected he probably knew the answer already. After five hundred years together, it was hard to imagine my life without Fabio. He knew me better than I knew myself and thankfully was working for me and not Cassiel.

"I was going to drive on the track. Then, who knows," I replied, hoping that at least for the next few hours I could be left to my own devices.

Fabio gave me a knowing look. "The McLaren is waiting for you."

I chewed on my lip, debating if I wanted to drive the McLaren or take something else out. In the end, I opted to keep it simple. My track was a mile long with a half mile straight and the other half mile a set of well-planned curves inspired by the Monaco F1 track. The McLaren, though not my fastest car, was adept at maneuvering through my track. Of my options, it was probably the "safest," at least as far as humans were concerned—if one considered driving 150 miles per hour safe.

"I'm going to unpack, and then I'll head over to the track," I responded. The garage that housed my car collection was next to the track. Most people would never know there was a track on my property. I had deliberately positioned it and landscaped around it so the track blended in. The last thing I wanted was an eyesore, and I knew I would never hear the end of it from my neighbors. Because I had human guests and most of my neighbors were human as well, I had to make sure that the track—part of my human persona—was a real part of my estate.

I climbed the emerald-green carpeted stairs two at a time and crossed the short distance down the hallway to my bedroom. The doors opened automatically upon my approach, a bit of magic that Fabio had put into them when I purchased the estate years ago. Inside was a massive four-poster bed, large enough for me to sleep with my wings out. Today, it was covered in a green-and-tan plaid coverlet that matched the drapes surrounding the windows.

My suitcase was sitting on the stand, waiting for me to unpack it. I crossed the room, and then a flicker of movement caught my eye out the window. On the edge of the walled garden was a large red kite, mesmerized by a rabbit nibbling on the grass below. The wildlife was one of the things I enjoyed about being out here. My father had never understood my preference for solitude in the human world, how I could sit for hours watching a hawk hunt or a herd of caribou crossing the field.

Blinking, I returned to the suitcase and lifted out the clothing, placing it in designated drawers in the small white dresser across from the bed. Having a suitcase and taking time to unpack was another activity that I had picked up from my time among the humans. I could dress myself with a mere thought if I wanted. But I kept company with humans and immortals, requiring me to be comfortable and versed in these human activities.

When the suitcase was empty, I zipped it up and set it on the floor. Fabio would put it away while I was out on the track.

Taking a deep breath and letting my hands settle at my sides, I visualized the inside of my garage by the track and a moment later I was there.

The building was split into two sections divided by a thick glass wall that prevented anyone from seeing or hearing what was going on in the workspace if they were in the showroom.

The showroom had black marble floors with the occasional veins of white. The back wall was covered in an assortment of historic Ferrari racing memorabilia and a series of immaculate white leather couches. I gazed wistfully at the bright blue Aston Martin Valkyrie AMR Pro on its pedestal. *Another time*, I told myself. Next to the Valkyrie was a red 1962 Ferrari GTO and on the far side a green 1962 Aston Martin DB4 Zagato.

Trailing my fingers lightly over the hood of the Valkyrie, I focused on the door between the showroom and the workspace. It swung open, and I stepped through onto the grippy black epoxy floor with its swirls of silver. Sure enough the McLaren was waiting at the door, a fresh set of tires on it. A 2003 Honda NSX was on the car lift waiting for the new clutch to arrive so it could be installed.

I opened the door to the McLaren. A fresh driving suit was sitting on the driver's seat under my helmet. I snagged the driving suit, and with a quick glance to ensure the very human mechanic was not nearby, I used my magic to don it.

I slid into the lime-green-and-black racing seat, buckled the harness into place, and tugged my helmet on. The garage door opened, and I started the car, unable to help smiling at the engine's purr. Shifting into first gear, I eased out of the garage and onto the road that would lead me the short distance to the track.

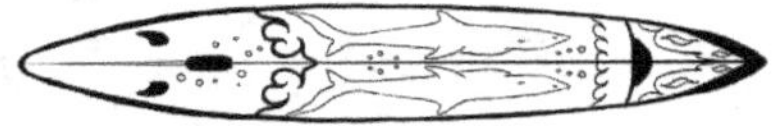

To my surprise, Agatha was waiting for me when I pulled off the track and headed back toward the garage. I rolled down the window and peered up at her.

"What are you doing here?"

Agatha shrugged. "Is there something wrong with watching you drive?"

I shook my head. "No. Did you want me to drive you around the track for a lap?"

Agatha laughed. "Absolutely not. The last time Charlie offered and I stupidly accepted, I got extremely carsick, a shock to both of us. I'll stick to riding horses, but thanks for asking."

I turned off the car and climbed out, ditching the helmet on the seat. A second later, I was clean and dressed in a pair of comfortable khaki slacks and a hunter-green polo shirt. I offered her my arm. "Let's walk back to the house, and you can tell me all about this photo shoot I've agreed to."

Agatha flashed me a brilliant smile. "Sounds good."

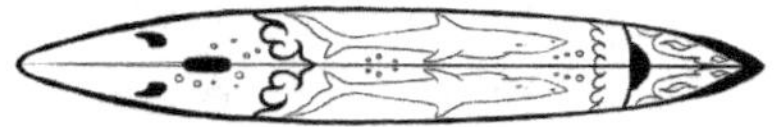

The photo shoot ended up being what I thought of as a lifestyle shoot. I was wearing a black suit from my own closet; Agatha wore a white sweater and a tweed knee-length pencil skirt. Her hair was straightened and fell in sheets just past her shoulders.

The makeup artist had finished the few touchups needed on me and was double-checking her assistant's work on Agatha. Since we were outside instead of in a studio, there was slightly less equipment. *Only slightly.* It still felt as though everywhere I walked outside of the house I was tripping over a tripod, bag, or cord belonging to the photo crew. If it had been in one of the family offices, I would have demanded they move things. But the only person it was annoying was me, and it was only temporary.

Sunset was only an hour away. *The photographer better be ready.* I had gotten a request this morning for a Zoom meeting with LACH today. Due to the photo shoot, I had to ask to push the meeting to tomorrow. Which meant the shoot *must* happen today, or we would need to scrap the idea.

Agatha walked over and smiled. "Marco is always on time," she said reassuringly.

"On time to begin preparations or to ensure he captures the right lighting for a sunset shoot?" I asked tartly.

"The latter. This is not the only location he's worked where we had one set window of time and then we would no longer be welcome," Agatha replied.

I sighed. "I trust you."

"Yes, you do. This plan helps both of us, remember?" Agatha said, patting my arm.

I brought her hand up to my lips and kissed it lightly.

"That is just what I need! Bueno!" Marco chirped excitedly. He was a short-statured Italian man with darkly tanned skin, coal-black hair, and dark brown eyes. A large camera hung around his neck, and another was in a holster at his hip.

I dropped Agatha's hand as though it burned me. I hadn't realized I had an audience.

Marco frowned. "You need to relax. You're best friends, no?"

I nodded. "Yes. We're best friends."

"Then why are you so stiff? You look like you're going to a funeral," Marco replied.

My jaw tightened. I inhaled deeply, nostrils flaring. Marco had been the one who asked if I had a black suit. I hadn't chosen what I was wearing any more than Agatha had.

Agatha must have sensed I was getting annoyed; she stepped between Marco and me. "Marco, are you ready?"

Marco nodded. "Yes."

"Then where do you want us?" Agatha stuck her arm through Marco's, and the two of them headed toward the front of the house. Occasionally, Marco would wave his arm in the air to emphasize his words.

I followed them, knowing if I didn't, Marco would blame me for missing the sunset.

Chapter 20: Kelsey

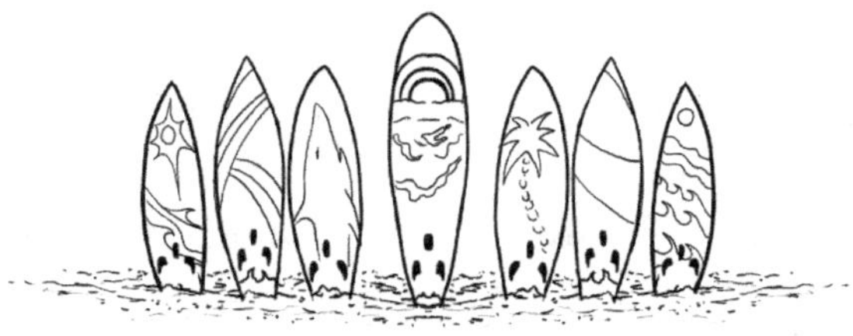

Friday, October 11

The comforting beep, beep, beep *of the monitors indicated the patient in front of me on the operating table was stable. I did one last suture and set my instruments on the tray, then stepped back. The entire appendectomy had been textbook and I glanced at the clock.* Even faster than my last one!

"We've got this, Dr. Floras. Why don't you go eat your lunch?"

I nodded and was almost to the door when the monitors went wild. I spun around and blood was shooting straight up out of a gaping wound in the patient's chest.

I woke up with a start, jumping to my feet, when I realized I had fallen asleep on the blue vinyl couch in the staff break room at the hospital. My seven a.m. orthopedic surgery had gone better than anticipated. Everyone was pleased—the parents and Dr. Pierce. This past week, it seemed like every comment Dr. Pierce made to me was negative, a stark contrast to my first two weeks back. But his congratulations were genuine about my creative approach to placing the pins in a complex fracture at the ankle. *Maybe he has something going on in his personal life that is spilling over to his professional relationships.*

I glanced at the large digital clock with giant red numbers hanging on the wall. I had two more minutes before I was due at my next appointment, a consultation, and if the mother approved, Dr. Pierce and Dr. Hoover, with me assisting, would be doing the grueling surgery to split conjoined twins tomorrow. I hadn't been given another solo surgery since the pacemaker. Dr. Pierce had scrubbed in on my procedures, and a few times even taken the lead—not that I would have been comfortable leading this surgery. It was too complex. The boys needed it, but it was a hard sell to the mother. Not that I blamed her. There were many risks involved with surgery, especially when you added a rare heart condition into the mix. I was confident she would make the best choice for her sons. I just had to ensure my presentation covered every angle.

My pager buzzed, flashing 911. I frowned and stashed my brown snack bag in my locker, then ran to the nurses' station. Ronda was there waiting for me with a chart. "Robby coded. The nurses are in there now, but Dr. Pierce wants you to take point."

I choked back a sob of frustration, my stomach sinking at what this meant. The ankle repair had gone extremely well. I should have known it wouldn't be that simple. Taking a deep breath, I threw my shoulders back and took the folder.

"You've got this," Ronda called encouragingly as I dashed down the hallway. I could hear the beeping and found myself praying that he would make it.

As I skidded into the room, everyone paused their efforts and their sad eyes met mine. "One more time," I said, and the nurse nodded and readied the paddles.

"Clear," she called and then pressed them onto Robby's motionless body. We all held our breath, until we heard it. *Blip, blip.* The sound we had been waiting for. His heart was going again. We exhaled a collective breath.

"What happened?" I asked. But no one knew. One moment he was fine, and then he wasn't.

"Let's rerun the blood panels and do a full body scan. Maybe we missed something."

They nodded, and I walked out, knots in my stomach. I knew it was going to be a long day.

Ring. Ring. Ring.

My eyes snapped open, and I looked around blearily. I had been dreaming about surfing, having the perfect ride on an insanely huge wave, and when I made it into the shallows, a red-haired man was standing there and offered me a gold medal.

Ring. Ring. Ring.

I reached for my phone. I had to rummage around the nightstand before my fingers grabbed it. "Hello," I said groggily. I turned on the light with my free hand.

Dr. Pierce's gravelly voice came over the line. "Kelsey, we got the results back on Robby. I need you to come in now. He's getting prepped for surgery as we speak."

I swung my legs over the bed, instantly awake, red-haired mystery man momentarily forgotten.

Dr. Pierce continued speaking. "The results are surprising given he came in for an ankle injury. He has a tumor on his spleen. It should be a straightforward splenectomy."

"Give me thirty minutes, and I'll be there ready to go," I said when he finally paused.

"Don't be late," he replied, then hung up.

I set down my phone and stretched. I considered myself lucky that I had gotten five hours of sleep before the hospital had called me. I wondered how many tests they had done before getting Robby's mother to agree to a splenectomy. I was also shocked Dr. Pierce wanted me to do it. *Maybe he doesn't want to stay longer than he must.* While our shifts overlapped, they were not always the same. Since I was in the second half of my fellowship, I was being given some autonomy.

I got dressed and did my hair in two braids that I could easily tuck under my surgical cap. I ate a bowl of cereal while my coffee was brewing and then filled up a thermal cup. It was early enough that I opted to drive my car.

I hummed to myself as I drove to the hospital and found a parking spot. *I guess there is an advantage to arriving at three a.m.*

I briskly made my way through the hospital to our floor. Dr. Pierce saw me and followed me as I went into the staff room to put on scrubs.

"Good, you're here. Prep is almost done. I'm going to head out. If you need me, don't hesitate to call. However, I don't think you'll need me. Pathology is ready to analyze the spleen and tumor as soon as we have them. You might get preliminary results by the time you've settled him in his room again. You're in surgery four."

I nodded. "Sounds good. I'll keep you posted."

As I tied my surgical cap on, I ran the steps of a splenectomy through my head, including all of the warning signs of things going wrong. I had done about ten of them in the past five years, though most of those had been adults, not nine-year-old boys. I wasn't worried, though.

As I started scrubbing for the surgery, my fear rose. *I still have memory loss. What if my nightmares come true and I forget how to do a splenectomy when Robby's on the table?* I closed my eyes and took a deep breath, counting backward from ten as I released it. *I can do this.* I repeated the words in my mind as I finished scrubbing, knowing if I started the surgery thinking positively, it would affect how the whole surgery went—or at least the parts in my control.

My fears had been unfounded and the surgery was a success. The tumor was tiny, and I was hopeful that we had caught it early enough to prevent it from spreading. We were taught to give patients hope that it was not a malignant tumor, but I was not optimistic after examining it. The pathology report would be able to give an in-depth analysis.

I sat on the couch in the staff break room, sipping my lukewarm coffee. A flyer on the announcement board caught my eye. *Halloween Fundraiser Gala.* If I could judge the event from the flyer, it was going to be way out of my league. I thought Halloween was a long way off, but when I peeked at my phone, it informed me that Halloween was in just under three weeks. *When did that happen?*

I closed my eyes and imagined soft grains of sand between my toes. *They got firmer as I walked closer to the water. Inhaling deeply, I smelled the salty ocean air and the cry of seagulls as they swooped and dove overhead. Out on the water, waiting for a wave, was a redheaded man. Conner.*

A cough startled me out of my reverie. I raised my coffee cup to my lips and disappointment filled me when I realized it was empty. *Mystery man's name is Conner?* I peered up at whoever had interrupted my daydream.

"Ronda," I squeaked.

"I've been trying to find you. The pathology report is back," Ronda said and handed me the file, then hurried back out toward her station.

I skimmed the report. The pathologist agreed that the tumor was malignant but was refraining from identifying the stage until he had the full slate of tests back, which would take a few days. I stood up. I was going to have to see if one of the pediatric oncologists would be able to go with me to discuss the news with Robby's parents. Once he healed from the splenectomy, the pediatric oncologist would take over his care.

I closed the file and set it down on the couch. Technically, it was still my day off, but I couldn't just leave Robby's parents high and dry. I stood up and tucked the file under my arm, deciding I would see if I could find the oncologist, talk to Robby's parents, and then go relax for a bit at home. I looked at my watch. It was eleven a.m.

Chapter 21: Conner

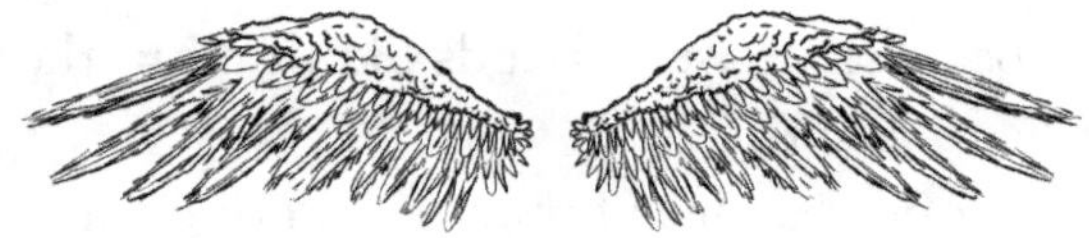

Saturday, October 12

A week after the photo shoot with Agatha, needing to keep up appearances for our families, we coordinated a date. Our schedules did not align very well; since the new arrangement with LACH, I had a lot of meetings at the end of the day to accommodate the time difference.

I took a deep breath and closed my eyes, visualizing Ianialar, the Ash Realm. When I opened them, I was no longer in front of my estate in England with its vibrant grass and fall-colored trees. Ianialar was shades of gray; the only spots of color came from the immortals who lived here. Large sentinel trees lined the stone path to the dance hall I'd agreed to meet Agatha at. Up ahead, I could hear the sounds of laughter and music as other angels gathered. We had chosen a neutral meeting location and out of the prying eyes of humans. I climbed a short flight of three wide stairs, and then the dance hall was beyond the first set of columns.

I was just past the columns when I spotted Agatha. Her black hair was straightened tonight and brushed the top of her shoulders. She was wearing a tight-fitting black cocktail dress that accentuated all the right places.

"Agatha," I said and kissed her lightly on the cheek. "Did you want to sit and talk?" I asked, glancing at the tables along the edge of the dance hall.

"Sure," she replied, giving me a curious look.

I sighed. It had been a long time since I'd gone on such a visible date with another angel or even been in the Ash Realm. I could feel the pulsing of magic in the dance hall thrumming in my veins, and I almost suggested we dance, except I was worried what it would lead to. Just because we were friends didn't mean the chemistry between us had vanished.

We walked along the edge of the dance floor until we found an empty table in the corner. A light breeze ruffled Agatha's hair, and a flicker of desire wound through me. Digging my nails into my palm, I pulled a chair out for Agatha and then sat facing her.

"How was your day?" I asked, trying to be conversational.

Agatha smiled. "Busy, but it went well. I finalized a multi-shoot contract with *Vogue*."

"Congratulations," I said, genuinely happy for her.

Just then a silvery wisp floated over to our table, a musical voice emitting from it. "Drinks?"

I glanced at Agatha, then back at the wisp. "I'll take a bourbon on the rocks."

Agatha ordered a glass of the fairy wine. When the wisp departed, she focused on me. "Thanks. I'm excited my hard work is paying off."

Just then, our drinks arrived. I picked up my bourbon and took a small sip.

"How are things with the new hospital?" Agatha asked.

"Still tense," I replied.

I drained my glass. It glowed gold briefly and then refilled.

"Conner, you really need to answer your phone," came the annoyed voice of Cassiel.

I blew out my breath. *"I'm in Ianialar. My phone doesn't work here. You know that."*

"I need you to go to Dublin tonight," demanded my father.

"Can't this wait?" I ran my hand over my face and glanced back

at Agatha. She caught my gaze and smiled. I was certain she had figured out I was talking to someone telepathically.

"No. The CEO of CM Hospital was just murdered. I need you onsite to manage things," he said.

"We have a disaster manager for this. Not me," I growled.

"You have more finesse than Octavio has," my father pointed out. I could not counter that. He was right. Octavio tended to come in like a jackhammer, which in certain situations was perfect; in others, it backfired and caused an even larger problem than there was before.

"Fine. I will go, but once I have it handled, since you ruined my trip to Santa Barbara, I want twenty-four hours at my estate without being bothered," I snapped. I felt bad that I was going to have to bail on Agatha, though to be fair she likely half expected a call like this. It was fairly common when we were dating years ago.

"Give me an update when you get there," my father ordered. Then, his presence in my mind disappeared.

I gave Agatha an apologetic smile. "Agatha, I hate to do this to you, but duty calls. I need to leave for Dublin immediately to handle a client emergency."

Agatha stood and kissed me lightly on the cheek. "I understand. Just reach out when things quiet down."

I smiled. "Will do."

I nodded and used my magic to return to my estate. I wanted a few minutes to collect what I needed to take with me. As I moved around my bedroom, putting together my briefcase with my laptop and a few other odds and ends, I thought about how this was not how I had envisioned my evening ending. Bailing on a date that had taken weeks to set up. I closed my eyes and was surprised when an image of Kelsey entered my thoughts. An ache surged through me as I conjured memories of how my cock had felt when I thrust deep inside her when she was straddling me in the chair, and I fought the urge to palm myself. Now was not the time or the place.

The throbbing continued. I bit my lip hard enough to draw blood and tried to force my thoughts to anything else. *Murder. The CEO was murdered.* A wall spattered in blood and brains. *If the press caught wind of a violent murder, the hospital will be in trouble.* Given the urgency of the trip, I was going to use my magic to get to Dublin and have Fabio take the jet to keep up appearances.

I grabbed a suitcase and threw a few days' worth of clothes into it, then changed into a black tailored suit with a white shirt and green tie. Regardless of the circumstances for my visit, I had appearances to keep up. To the humans, I was a member of the board of directors of CM Hospital—a "suit," so to speak.

Running my hands over my face, I tried to figure out if there was anything I was forgetting that I would need to take with me, but nothing came to mind.

Ready to go, I snagged my suitcase off the bed and closed my eyes, imagining the storage closet in the basement of CM Hospital. My whole body tingled, and then I opened my eyes, and a metal shelf filled with old records boxes was about an inch from my face. Taking a deep breath, I rolled my shoulders back, then cautiously opened the closet door and peered into the hallway. Confident no one was around, I stepped out and softly shut the door behind me. Then, I ran up the stairs two at a time till I reached the main level.

Keeping my stride casual, I headed into the main lobby. The first person to notice me was the guard talking to the greeter behind the large, green-countered front desk.

"Dr. Hudson!" he called. I could see palpable relief on his face.

"Mr. Shores," I replied. "Where was the incident?" I knew the guard would know the details and likely had been told to watch for my arrival. I had no idea if the greeter knew anything was going on. From the looks of it, the lobby was carrying on business as usual.

"Sixth floor," Mr. Shores responded. "They're waiting for you."

I nodded. "Thanks." I proceeded briskly to the elevator. Thankfully, it was empty. The elevator dinged and then opened onto the sixth floor. A guard I didn't recognize was standing just outside of it, hand on the holster of her gun.

"Dr. Hudson, you're here much quicker than we expected," the guard said, lowering her hand to hang by her side. "I'll let them know you're here, and someone will come get you." The guard spoke into her walkie-talkie.

A few minutes later, Newton appeared through the door at the far end of the hallway. His face was drawn, and I could feel his tentative hold slipping on the glamour that kept the human guard from seeing his true self. When Newton was close enough to me, I took a deep breath and laid my hand on his shoulder. He bristled initially at the contact, then realized that I was using my magic to keep his glamour in place.

"Thanks," he said under his breath. I shrugged. It wouldn't do either of us any good if the guard saw what Newton *really* looked like—pure white pebbly skin with glowing blue eyes and a long, thin tail that ended in a cluster of bright blue feathers.

"Can you take me to the scene?" I inquired.

"Of course," Newton replied.

I removed my hand from his shoulder, and he led the way through the door and into the large conference room on the other side.

The first thing I saw was the cracks spiderwebbing around the small hole in the window. A difficult but not impossible shot to take from one of the buildings across the street—especially if an immortal had magically enhanced a human sniper rifle, as I suspected. Then, I peered around the room, taking note of the large pool of drying purple blood and rainbow-colored brain matter. The body had been moved and covered and was in the far corner of the room. I didn't need to look at it to know what I would see. Boark was the only demon at CM Hospital whose bodily fluids would not pass as human, and it explained Cassiel's urgency.

Human police could not come in this room until I had gotten rid of the evidence that an immortal had been murdered—though in this case, I didn't want to do a full purge of the space. At least not yet. Instead, I was going to glamour the entire room. My magic was powerful enough that the only immortal other than me who could see through it would be Cassiel.

Newton was watching me, wringing his hands together nervously. "Well, can you help us?"

I gave him a reassuring smile. "Of course." I cleared my throat and indicated everyone needed to come closer. When they had arranged themselves in a semicircle around me, I spoke. "Because of the type of demon Boark was, I have only one option available to me. I have to glamour this entire room. Once the police have done their own investigation, I will purge it. What that means is the blood and brain matter will become human in appearance. Your story is still the same: A sniper assassin shot him."

"What about Boark's family?" asked Vizalia, the chief operations officer. She was half-human and half-demon and physically favored her human half with dark brown skin, green eyes, and curly black hair. Her telekinetic magic had been inherited from her demon parent.

"I will ensure that his body is returned to his family once I've confirmed that it was a human bullet and there was no poison," I responded. "Now, you need to head upstairs and start working on the statement for the press. I will call the police and handle whatever they need. It's going to be a long couple of days, but I trust we're all up to the task."

Newton, Vizalia, and the others murmured in agreement and filed out.

When they were gone, I took a deep breath and shut my eyes, letting my magic flow out of me as I got to work setting the glamour in place.

Chapter 22: Conner

Tuesday, October 22

The murder of Boark, the CEO of CM Hospital, was a PR nightmare. I had been in Dublin for ten days and was still wading through red tape. The entire board and hospital management were terrified that another assassination would happen if they stepped into the CEO position, so no one wanted to take on the role. *Well, that's not true. I am taking over his duties.* The odds of the assassin being bold enough to make an attempt on my life were pretty low. The few times over the centuries demons had tried it, the outcome had not been in their favor. I killed one, and Cassiel took care of the other two, then gave Octavio orders to ensure there were no clan members remaining who would decide to take revenge.

I was tempted to call my father and tell him I was done. But then he'd accuse me of giving up. I wasn't giving up; I just needed a break. The terrified staff kept calling me at all hours of the night and any time I was trying to take care of my duties with other hospitals. Azinak in particular was unhappy, given they had just hired me and I was unavailable.

Fabio was in the kitchen of the rented condo, preparing something on the large gas stove. I sniffed the air, intrigued. He rarely cooked. I wandered over to see what it was. A gigantic batch of scrambled eggs.

"Why are you making enough eggs to feed an army?" I asked.

Fabio chuckled. "I *am* feeding an army—or at least a group of humans. I figured maybe the hospital staff would chill out if we babied them. Starting with a hearty meal of breakfast burritos."

I tapped my fingers on the counter. "It's worth a try."

I poured myself a cup of coffee and sat down on the stool, taking a small sip.

"I have a scheduled meeting with all of them today. I will find out if feeding them breakfast helps them calm down," I told him.

"Good. Elsewise, you're going to get sick. Then you'll be no good to anyone," Fabio said.

I wrinkled my nose. I hardly ever got sick, but when I did, it was the worst, making my magic do odd things and forcing me to stay in Ianialar until I recovered, so I wouldn't blow my cover to the humans. I hoped he was wrong. I finished my coffee and then collected my things I would need for the day.

My phone was back in the bedroom. I went to retrieve it, and a missed call flashed on the screen. *Kelsey*, it said. I blinked and looked at it again. Not Kelsey; Agatha. I swiped the screen open and listened to her voicemail. She was asking if I was still interested in having her come to the country estate and said she'd be free tomorrow. I sighed, then sent her a text.

Conner: I'm still in Dublin doing damage control.

Agatha: Sorry. I'll check back in a few weeks when my schedule is open again.

Conner: No worries. I'll keep you posted.

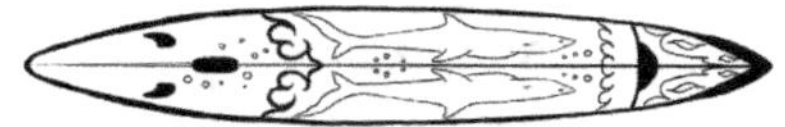

While I waited for the elevator to take me to the fifteenth floor—the executive suites of CM Hospital—I could not stop thinking about Kelsey and how I still did not have an answer about the weird spark between us. Fabio had not had any luck, and I was afraid of doing anything that would alert Cassiel or Octavio that there was anything *more* between the two of us.

The elevator beeped as the doors slid open, revealing the reception area, which was designed to deter anyone who wasn't on the executive staff or board of directors from going through the glass doors.

The receptionist smiled but stayed silent. I strode through the doors and went straight ahead into the largest conference room. The massive sweeping windows offered a spectacular view of Dublin, especially on a clear day. About half of the people I was expecting were in the room already, along with four security guards. I had hired about twenty additional guards, two of which were angels, to help prevent another assassin from getting close and to give the perception of safety to both staff and patients within the hospital. Over the years, I had discovered that perception was more important than anything else, especially when it came to an incident involving a safety concern.

The long glass table showed the remnants of the breakfast burritos Fabio had brought by. I was pleased to see that the board was less agitated today. *Maybe Fabio's idea is working.*

"Good morning, Dr. Hudson," Vizalia said and walked over to me, smiling.

"Good morning, Dr. V," I replied, using the name she went by when in the company of humans.

"We have voted that I will fill in as temporary CEO while the board is reviewing all of the candidates," Vizalia announced.

My eyes widened in surprise. I had been prepared to require them to make that vote in this meeting. Relief coursed through me. *With that decided, I should be able to wrap up here tonight and depart for Los Angeles.*

"Excellent choice," I said. "Now why don't you get everyone to sit down, and you can explain to me what your plan is going forward, and we can smooth out any issues before I leave."

"Sure," Vizalia replied and motioned for me to take a seat at the table.

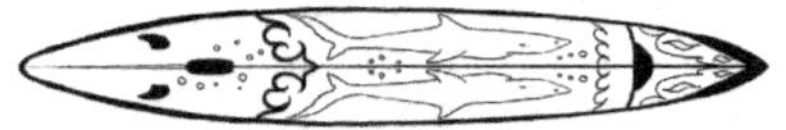

I spent the flight to Los Angeles reviewing the steps I had already set in motion at LACH. My intention was to have Sunday to recover and then jump headfirst into being a presence at LACH to ensure the changes were implemented. I had already updated the employee handbook and had been assured it was distributed to all the employees. But I knew that wasn't enough. I needed to make sure it was taken seriously. My schedule the week after the gala was rapidly filling; I planned to meet with each of the departments within the hospital to go over the changes to the handbook in person. From past experience, I knew that if we just handed over the new handbook, it would likely get ignored. If I had open discussions with the staff about the changes, then I could address any concerns or questions and impress upon them how critical it was that they follow the changes.

I must have dozed off. Someone was trying to wake me up. I blinked and found the pilot lightly shaking me. "Sir, we're here."

"Thanks," I replied and stuffed my laptop into my briefcase, then exited the plane.

Fabio was waiting for me with a car. Though his magic was different than mine and he couldn't travel directly here, he was able to do so quite a bit faster than the plane flew.

"How was the flight?" he asked.

I shrugged. "I was working and dozed off. Not terribly eventful."

"Agatha is at the house," Fabio informed me, then opened the driver's door before hopping into the front passenger side of the Revuelto.

I climbed in, smiling as the engine purred to life. "Great choice," I commented.

"I figured since you didn't have time to return to your England estate that you'd want to drive *something* that can go fast," Fabio replied.

I chuckled. He knew me well. "What is Agatha doing at the

house?" I inquired.

"She has the proofs from that photo shoot you did a few weeks ago and wanted to discuss it in person," Fabio replied.

I was surprised Agatha hadn't met up with me in Dublin. She could use a combination of her magic and the Ash Realm to go anywhere in the human world she wanted to in an hour or less. I kept my thoughts to myself and eased us into Los Angeles traffic.

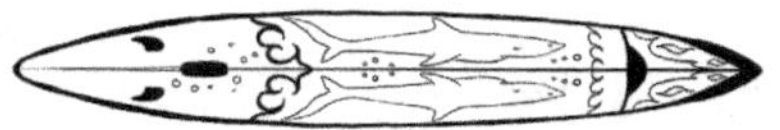

An hour later, in the enormous great room that had large windows looking out to the ocean, Agatha sat in the white leather chair opposite me. Between us was a table strewn with the proofs for the magazine spread.

"These turned out better than I had hoped," Agatha gushed, running her fingers over the glossy pages.

"Hopefully, it'll get both of our fathers off our backs about a wedding," I replied.

My favorite photo was the one of the two of us holding hands, smiling, as we strolled through the garden. The sun had just dropped below the house. I felt like it captured us perfectly. *Best friends.* Other photos were more romantic, including the one of us kissing. My back was leaning against one of the columns to the entry of the garden.

I was glad the shoot was over. Kissing my best friend had felt strange, and more difficult to be convincing than I had anticipated. Marco had even started shouting at me. I had to imagine Agatha was Kelsey to make Marco happy.

"Are you sure you don't want to accompany me to the gala?" I teased.

"Very sure," replied Agatha. "For one, I'm busy. I have a meeting with a *Vogue* editor at six p.m. that day, and that would cut it too close. And anyway, hospital functions are not my thing."

I chuckled. "Yes, only the most glamorous of events for Ms. Agatha."

She smacked me on the arm. "It's not that they aren't glamorous. I just don't enjoy talking about doctors or medicine, and Charlie told me all about the one you conned her into attending."

"Charlie has her own reasons to not like them. You shouldn't let her cloud your judgment," I responded. I knew it was futile. If Agatha had a meeting with a *Vogue* editor, then there was nothing I could entice her with to skip out on it. For an immortal or human, that was a huge opportunity.

"Instead of being sad that you're not going to have me as your date, why not celebrate instead that you'll be fifteen hundred, in control of your human inheritance, and an equal to Cassiel?" Agatha suggested. "Besides, I *will* be at your ascension. I wouldn't miss that for anything."

I had to concede she had a point. I was dwelling on the annoyance of having to attend yet another Halloween masquerade for my birthday, instead of focusing on what would happen that morning: my ascension and becoming an equal to Cassiel. Which meant he would lose his ability to force me to do things, like marry.

Technically, it also meant that the photo shoot being published in the magazine wouldn't matter. Agatha had negotiated us into a last-minute opening in the December edition of *Vanity Fair*. It would come out in mid-November.

I frowned. I blew out my breath and studied the photos a while longer before lifting my gaze to Agatha's face "I suppose you're right. The ascension is more important, and if Cassiel sees you there, he probably won't suspect anything if you don't come with me to the gala. He won't be happy when he finds out that we lied to him about the engagement, but after my ascension, it won't matter."

Agatha nodded. "Tell him as soon as you can after the gala. I think it will go better if he hears it from you. Now, how did things wrap up at CM Hospital?"

I made a face. "The CEO was a demon, and he was assassinated by an immortal using a magically enhanced sniper rifle. Octavio is supposed to be hunting for whoever it is, but currently the individual is still at large. Motive is unknown. Vizalia was voted into the interim CEO position."

"Good for her!" Agatha replied with a smile. Five years ago, Agatha and Vizalia had collaborated when I had decided CM hospital needed to up their marketing and advertising plan, which included a "lifestyle" photo shoot at the hospital. "Should we set up another date?"

"After my birthday it won't be necessary, and between now and October thirty-first, I need to focus on my work at LACH. The board has been unhappy about my limited availability, and I have to smooth things over," I said.

Agatha slid the photos into a stack and then stood up. "I will let you get to it then. I'm heading to New York."

I stepped over to her and pulled her into a hug. "Thank you for stopping by."

Agatha gave me a squeeze and stepped back. "I'll see you at your ascension." Photos in her hand, the air shimmered briefly, and then she disappeared.

Chapter 23: Conner

Thursday, October 31

Ancient columns of white stone circled the bowl-like space where ascensions took place. At the very bottom was a staircase that connected to the tallest column. Demons were banned from being inside the columns for the ceremony. Long ago, Cassiel had told me it was because a demon had interfered with an ascension ceremony and the angel had unexpectedly died. A policy had been put in place to prevent it from happening again. *If the demons even had anything to do with the death*, I mused.

The space felt crowded with the number of angels in attendance, and I was itching to get back to the seclusion of my house in Malibu. My mother set her hand on my arm, and I looked at her—tall, with long red hair, bright green eyes, lightly tanned skin, and black wings. For the ascension ceremony, she was wearing a simple white robe tied at the waist with a gold rope. "It's almost time. Don't embarrass your family by leaving."

I frowned and took her hand in mine. "I wouldn't dream of leaving. I have been waiting for this moment my whole life."

I caught Agatha's eye. She was stuck at the back of the group and didn't have any room to maneuver closer.

"We can chat afterward," she said into my mind. I nodded, and then my father came alongside my mother.

"Are you ready?" Cassiel demanded gruffly.

"Yes," I replied.

"Then come with me," he said and turned toward the stairs. We stopped in front of them and turned to face everyone. A hush fell over the crowd.

"On the day of an angel's fifteen hundredth birthday, he or she may ascend these stairs and receive their full powers and title that is their birthright. Today my son, Conniel Eylon, will make his ascension," Cassiel said, his voice carrying throughout the bowl and beyond the columns to the spectators beyond.

I stayed silent. Once Cassiel began speaking, I was not permitted to utter a word until the ascension was complete. The air felt heavy as a shimmery gray mass of magic, much like fog, slid between the columns and into the bowl. I shivered in anticipation.

"Me ti dýnami ton theón, o gios mou tha anévei aftí ti skála kai tha apodechteí ta prototókiá tou," Cassiel spoke.

By the gods' holy power, my son will ascend and accept his birthright, I translated in my thoughts.

When Cassiel stopped speaking, I bowed to him and then turned to face the staircase of pristine white marble. I took a deep breath, spread my wings out wide behind me, and took the first step. My foot tingled as tendrils of magic wrapped around me. I did my best to ignore the sensation and let my feet carry me up the one hundred fifty stairs to the top.

I reached stair one hundred forty nine, and the air around me was humming. My whole body was encased in magic, and my feet were incredibly heavy. I lifted my right foot to take the last step and found it was nearly impossible to move. Gritting my teeth, I slowly raised my foot and set it on the step. Then, I repeated the process with the left. It felt like it took an absurd amount of time to accomplish this small feat.

Straight ahead was the grayness of Ianialar. To the right and left, the columns marched away from me to complete the circle. Taking a deep breath, I rotated. The platform at the top of the staircase was the same size as the stairs—narrow. I had no idea what would happen if I fell off and if I'd be permitted to break my fall by flying.

Shakily, I raised my head and realized I had completed the turn. The edge of my wing brushed my arm, and it felt different than it had a before the climb. Glancing down, I noticed that it had taken on more of a metallic sheen. I reached out a finger before lowering it, realizing that everyone was waiting for me down below. Squaring my shoulders, I swallowed, and with my chin held high, I made my way down to the base of the staircase.

When my feet were firmly on solid ground, my mother dropped to her knees and was quickly mimicked by the others within the bowl. The only exception was my father, who bowed deeply to me. I followed his example and bowed to him at the precise angle he had.

"I present to you Archangel Conniel Eylon," Cassiel announced.

Were this a human ceremony there likely would have been applause, but angels did not feel such outward emotion was necessary. My thoughts buzzed with their emotions, excitement, pride, and even one or two overcome by bitterness. I wrote it off as unhappiness that I was now my father's equal and nothing more. The crowd split in half, and I walked through them alone, out of the bowl.

Chapter 24: Kelsey

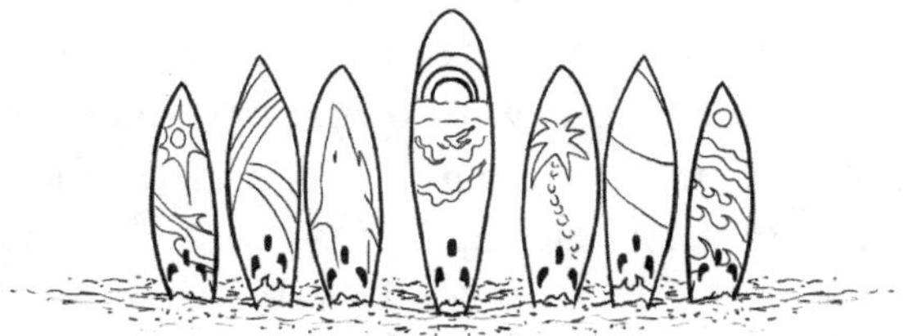

Thursday, October 31

As I was preparing to cut into Brandon, a red-haired six-year-old boy, to remove his appendix, one of the nurses started gossiping.

Chloe, the anesthesiology nurse, said, "Have you seen the new employee handbook?"

"Yes! They've actually updated it to include clear policies on how the rules will be enforced and what the repercussions are for breaking them," Mark, the surgical nurse, replied.

I kept myself from rolling my eyes, certain they were going to bring up the policy on personal cell phone usage. Though I frequently saw nurses and doctors in other departments spending time on their cell phones, I never had the issue. For two reasons: No one texted or called me during a work day, and I was too busy with my patients to spare more than a glance at my phone on my breaks.

I worked my way through the straightforward procedure, focused on my task, while the nurses continued their chatter. I paused, though, when they mentioned why the changes were taking place.

Chloe said, "The hospital has a new board member, Dr. Hudson, and he's responsible for the changes to the handbook and others that are rumored to be coming over the next year."

Double-checking my work, I swallowed hard when I looked down at the opening in Brandon's body and had no idea what I was doing. My hands shook slightly. I closed my eyes and took a deep breath, counting backward from ten. When I opened my eyes, the next steps came back to me, and I declared the appendectomy a success and started closing.

"I've heard he's not a *real* doctor," Mark said.

I looked up, the comment pulling me out of my worry that I had just frozen in the middle of a surgery. I caught his gaze with mine. "What do you mean, not a 'real' doctor?"

I could tell from the way Mark's eyes changed that he was likely smirking under his face mask. "He doesn't have a medical degree."

"There are many individuals who use the title 'doctor' who don't have medical degrees. Not all doctorates are focused on medicine. It doesn't mean they don't deserve the title," I replied. Then, I resumed my task of closing the surgical site. Two more stitches and I was done. Surgery complete, I retreated into the surgery prep area, took off my surgical gown and my gloves and mask, and stuffed them in the biohazard bin.

I was annoyed that the nurses were so offended by the idea of a person without a medical degree being called a doctor. Over the years of extensive education, I had met many people who had PhDs who deserved the title of doctor just as much or even more than I did when I earned mine.

As I headed toward the waiting room to update Brandon's parents, Ronda stopped me as I passed her desk. "Did you hear about Dr. Hudson?"

I sighed. "Yes. That's all Mark and Chloe could talk about during the surgery. I really don't want to hear more about him."

Ronda chuckled. "Well, I just thought you might be interested to hear that he will be formally introduced to everyone at the gala tonight. It probably doesn't matter to you, since in ten months you'll complete your fellowship and be long gone, but the rest of us will be affected by any changes he implements. It might be nice to find out who *Dr. Hudson* is."

"How about this? You do the research and let me know what you discover," I replied. I had already decided to attend the gala at least for the dinner, a decision that had nothing to do with whether or not I met Dr. Hudson. I didn't want to use a fancy dinner as a reconnaissance mission on the newest suit at the hospital.

Midafternoon, I was just closing my patient, Cora, a six-year-old girl with a complex spiral fracture in her left humerus. I could feel Dr. Pierce's eyes on me as he followed each stitch, making sure I did everything correctly.

"Excellent work, Dr. Floras," he praised.

I finished the last stitch before looking up at him. "Thanks." I gave a nod to the nurse on standby and stepped away from the patient, relieved that I hadn't frozen in front of Dr. Pierce like I had this morning in the appendectomy surgery.

Together, we walked out of the surgical suite and to the sink to scrub. "Are you planning on going to the Halloween gala tonight?" he asked over the sound of the running water.

"Don't we all have to go?" I asked. The chief of surgery had strongly encouraged me to attend, implying that I could lose my fellowship if I didn't. While fancy parties were not my usual style, I didn't hate them enough that I'd risk losing my fellowship over one.

Dr. Pierce shook his head. "No ... it has been highly recommended to the surgical staff and department heads. Mostly because it is the best way to secure funding for future projects. We have the opportunity to rub elbows with the superrich, who, if they decide they like your conversation, might very well buy that million-dollar piece of equipment you've been waiting for."

"Really?" I asked, intrigued.

Dr. Pierce nodded vigorously. "Yes! Dr. Frederickson had been badgering the board for three years to get a new MRI. She had one dance with some bigwig during which she mentioned the upgrade, and a week later, there was a new MRI delivered."

I gasped, impressed. I wondered if there was more to the story that Dr. Pierce didn't know, like if Dr. Frederickson had slept with someone as part of the deal, but I wasn't going to ask my boss to gossip about another doctor. Besides, *I* was most definitely not going to stoop that low. "I will be there. Since I have a few hours, I was going to go home to refresh and get ready."

"Wonderful," Dr. Pierce said.

I tossed my paper towel into the trash, then pulled open the door before looking over my shoulder. "I'll see you later." Heading to my locker to retrieve my stuff before someone could wrangle me for another task, I was relieved when no one found me. I slung my purple backpack over my shoulder and headed out of the hospital. When I reached the sidewalk, I took off at a brisk run, smiling as I felt my body loosening up after standing so long during the surgery. The run felt great.

Thankfully, the chief of surgery had given me enough of a heads-up about the requirement to attend the gala that I had been able to go shopping. As much as I hated to buy a fancy dress that would be worn once and that was it, I did not want to look like a fool in front of the hospital's investors.

The theme was a Halloween masquerade. My initial thought was to dress up as a witch, as I had for years. But then I realized that this was a very formal event. If I wanted to be taken seriously, I needed to dress that way. My choice was something I considered a safe costume: a princess. I had found a stunning pale pink satin dress with a plunging V neckline and halter straps. It was a mermaid cut with the skirt flaring out into a short train. I was able to find a mask in matching fabric and an inexpensive princess crown to go with it.

After eating a light snack and taking a long, hot shower, I was ready to begin getting ready. The gala would start with a formal dinner, followed by cocktails and dancing, then at the very end an auction. I had heard over the years that fundraisers like this always made the most money if they plied the guests with alcohol before the auction began. Then, everyone was a little looser with their money. I had perused the tentative auction list and had quickly discovered there was nothing that was even remotely in my meager budget.

As a staff member of the hospital and an unimportant guest, I was able to enter through the side doors to the banquet hall and skip the hubbub of the red carpet. Relief washed over me as I stepped inside the ballroom and into the crowd of people. Ropes of orange lights were strung from end to end of the room, with tiny glittering skulls seemingly suspended in thin air. I was shocked at the number of guests mingling. The tables swathed in layers of black and gossamer "spider webs" had little name cards on them, and I knew mine was somewhere among them.

My hands were shaking slightly. I bit the tip of my tongue, hoping to still them before someone noticed. I wasn't expecting to be nervous. *I'm just out of my element*, I reminded myself. I took a breath and held it before exhaling, trying to settle my nerves. I knew that most of these guests had no idea—and likely didn't care about—who I was. Which meant as long as I didn't behave too crazy, I could just be myself.

I giggled, resulting in a few glances in my direction. *How am I supposed to be myself when I've never been to anything this fancy before?* I didn't know any fancy proper dances or what types of conversation were considered appropriate for an event like this.

Maybe I should go.

My fingers absently stroked the smooth satin of my dress, and I gazed around the room indecisively. Near the front of the room, I caught sight of a red-haired man in a tailored gray suit with a black Batman mask on.

A bell tinkled, and the maître d' announced into the microphone that we should all take our seats so dinner could be served. I scanned the room, trying to figure out how, aside from looking at every single name card, I was supposed to find my assigned seat.

Near the entrance, I saw a table and an easel set up next to it which had a diagram. I realized that must be a seating chart, and I wove my way through the tables and guests who were still mingling until I was able to get a look at the seating chart. I had to wait my turn. I tried peering over the two ladies, but they were a tad too tall for me to do so.

When I stepped up to the diagram, I scanned for my name. Thankfully, they were organized mostly alphabetically, and I found my name without much trouble. I turned to walk away, my eyes on the tables ahead of me trying to trace my path, and I bumped into whoever had been standing behind me.

"Sorry," I mumbled, lifting my eyes up. I gasped as our eyes met, his warm brown ones catching my green ones. The red hair, brown eyes, and set of his jaw were shockingly familiar. I took a step backward and bumped into someone else. Blushing, I muttered apologies and hurried away toward my table, mind spinning. By the time I reached the table, I knew exactly who I'd bumped into—Conner.

I just saw Conner. The man from my daydream is real. Confusion filled me. I sat down at the table, which was empty for the moment, and tried to get control over my emotions. I was poised on the edge of my seat, about to leave, when the chair next to me scooted out and someone sat down. I jumped in surprise, jolted out of my thoughts, and nearly fell out of my seat, blushing deeply. I recognized one of the other fellows, though I couldn't remember her name or department.

"Hi, I don't think we've formally met. I'm Marina," the blond-haired, blue-eyed woman said, sticking her hand out to shake. I took it. Her grip was firmer than I expected.

"I'm Kelsey. Nice to meet you, Marina. What is your specialty?" I asked politely.

"Neonatal surgery," Marina replied. That explained why we didn't cross paths. She was on a different level of the hospital altogether.

"Are you okay?" Marina asked.

I hastily grabbed a glass of water and took a large drink. "I'm fine. I think I saw someone I met a few months ago that I wasn't expecting to see again. It was quite a shock."

"I can relate. The first year of my surgical residency, there was this fourth-year resident who kept trying to ask me out. I saw him over the Fourth of July weekend this year in Chicago. It was definitely awkward to bump into each other after so much time," Marina said.

I nodded. It wasn't quite the same, but I appreciated Marina's attempt to help out. Unsure of what else to say, I peered around the table. So far it was just the two of us.

"Excuse me," I said with a smile and stood up. I needed a chance to breathe and figure out what was going on alone.

Deciding to aim for the ladies' room, I had to find someone to ask where it was. Since I hadn't come in through the front, I wasn't sure which one we were supposed to use. One of the servers gave me very precise directions, and I was able to find it easily. For reasons unknown to me, there was a lounge chair in the ladies' room. Since it was empty, I sat on it and closed my eyes.

I was carrying my surfboard and a water bottle, intent on returning to my car, when a red-haired man with a green unbuttoned shirt flapping in the breeze came zipping down the beach on an electric scooter, sand flying in its wake. I watched in apprehension as the scooter toppled over on its side, pinning the man.

Dropping my surfboard, I sprinted toward him, doctor instincts taking over. "Are you okay?" I called.

When he didn't respond, I knelt beside him, praying he just had the wind knocked out of him from the fall. I touched his shoulder, unable to see his face due to the position of the scooter.

"I'm fine," came a somewhat muffled tenor voice with a British accent.

"Conner?" I gasped, rocking back on my heels.

"Yes, it's me, Conner," he replied.

I opened my eyes slowly, emotions swirling as bits and pieces of memories that had eluded me for almost two months started trickling back. I blushed as a very vivid memory of sitting on Conner's lap in a damp white button-up shirt—and nothing else—wiggled into the forefront of my mind. *There has to be more I'm forgetting.* Frustration at myself flared up, but I knew it was futile. Memory loss and concussions were different for every patient. Time often helped, but there were some people who never got their memories back, even decades later.

My stomach felt heavy, as though I'd swallowed rocks. My feelings for Joel were still unclear, and now to muddy the waters I had stumbled across Conner, my brief weekend fling. I had lots of questions and no answers. *Conner might have the answers,* I told myself. But this was an odd place to ask a virtual stranger questions like *How much sex did we have over that weekend we hooked up?*

I shook my head, trying to rid myself of these confusing thoughts. I was supposed to be here to enjoy the dinner and dancing, not hiding in the bathroom. Standing up, I straightened my shoulders and returned to my table in the ballroom.

Marina looked up from her phone. "Oh, there you are. I was wondering if I was going to have to send a search party," she joked.

"During your residency or medical school, did you have any patients with memory loss from concussions?" I asked.

Marina shook her head. "No, I haven't."

"I have a patient who was in a car accident and had a severe concussion. She's still missing memories from the four days prior to the accident," I explained, substituting a made-up patient with myself just in case Marina decided to share the information with anyone else at the hospital.

"Sounds like a difficult case. I'm sorry," Marina said kindly.

I took a sip of water and settled into my seat, deciding I'd see if I could get through the dinner and then politely excuse myself. The servers came with our first course, a Caesar salad. Two other fellows sat at our table: Daniel, who was in plastics, and Frank, who was in cardio-thoracic. Guests continued to trickle into the ballroom. I had no idea if it was normal for people to skip the meal and arrive late for the party or the other way around.

Our table filled up with more fellows I hadn't met, and the servers brought each course out. The food, as expected, was delicious. I had a few polite conversations about weekend plans with other people at the table.

When the table had been cleared, the live band started playing and Marina invited me onto the dance floor.

"Sure, why not," I agreed.

I followed Marina onto the dance floor, and I was able to forget about the memories and Conner. Instead, I enjoyed dancing with Marina, realizing that some of our dance moves were the same, trending toward more Spanish origin. The music spanned the decades, ranging from tunes from the forties all the way to the newest Taylor Swift songs and everything in between. Sweat trickled down my back, and my feet were getting sore in my heels. The wine from dinner was going straight to my bladder. Quickly, I excused myself and went toward the bathroom. We were on the other side of the ballroom, and I exited the closest door, which put me in an unfamiliar hallway. With the doors as a barrier, it was surprisingly quiet in the burgundy-carpeted hallway.

I slowly wandered down the hallway, pausing in front of a door that was slightly ajar. I went inside, hoping maybe there was an un-marked bathroom. Instead, it was an office, with a small bookcase.

One last glance and I decided there was no bathroom, and I needed to keep looking.

I heard a scraping sound behind me and turned. My jaw dropped when I saw Conner there in his tailored gray suit. His dress shirt was unbuttoned slightly at the top, allowing the Batman symbol on his undershirt to peek through.

"Conner?" I said hesitantly, not sure I believed that the memories were real and not figments of my imagination.

"Hi, Kelsey," Conner said with a smile. He stayed by the door, keeping a large gap between us. I wasn't sure if that was because we had had a falling-out over that weekend in Santa Barbara I didn't remember or what.

"Why are you here?" I asked awkwardly.

Conner's smile faded. "I can leave if you want me to. I saw you earlier and was hoping for a chance to talk."

My bladder clenched, and my face got hot in embarrassment. "Yes, I would like to talk, but ... is there a bathroom?"

A low chuckle escaped Conner's lips. "Of course. This office has a private bathroom. It's just through that door." He gestured to a door I had missed because it was covered in the same floral wallpaper as the rest of the walls.

"Thanks!" I dashed to the bathroom.

When I emerged, Conner was leaning against the desk, arms crossed over his chest. Butterflies fluttered in my stomach as I remembered what it felt like to kiss his full lips. "You said you wanted to talk, but I must warn you that I don't remember most of the weekend. I had a concussion."

"What do you remember?" Conner asked.

I licked my lips uncertainly. "You falling off the scooter on the beach ... sex in your rental house ... surfing."

Conner's eyes widened slightly. "Hmm ... What about the accident?"

I shook my head. "Nope. Though I'm hopeful if I can remember the other things that it'll come soon."

"Are you healed, from the accident?" Conner asked, genuine concern in his voice.

"Yes. I've been back at work for over a month now. I even aided with a Ross procedure," I replied.

"A Ross procedure ... That's right, you said you're a surgeon," Conner said.

I nodded. "Yes. I guess we had agreed to not share who we are. But I suppose that doesn't matter anymore." I stuck my hand out for him to shake. "I'm Dr. Kelsey Floras, pediatric surgical fellow here at LACH."

I watched as Conner swallowed, his Adam's apple bobbing up and down. I waited for him to take my hand and started to lower it when he grabbed it firmly in his grip. "Good to meet you, Dr. Floras. I'm Dr. Conner Hudson."

I gasped and dropped his hand as though it had burned me, rapidly backing up till I hit the wall. "You're Dr. Conner *Hudson*?" Shock and anger filled me. *How could I be so stupid?* No wonder he wanted to stay anonymous. He had been embarrassed to be seen with someone like me, especially when he was a billionaire and I was nothing.

"I need to go," I said abruptly and practically ran out of the room, not giving him a chance to say anything.

I walked briskly down the burgundy-carpeted hallway and back into the ballroom, mind churning. I wasn't sure what to think. Conner's name had been mentioned several times tonight, but other than knowing he was insanely wealthy, I still didn't know much about him. Ronda hadn't finished doing her research on our newest board member because we had been swamped with urgent cases.

I heard an odd noise as I sat down at the table. It took me a moment to realize it was my phone vibrating in my clutch. There was a text with 911 from the hospital line. *So much for a night off.*

Concern at why the hospital was calling overwhelmed me. I was not on call because of the gala, which meant it had to be a severe issue for them to reach out. Thankfully, a taxi was waiting outside the main doors, and it was a quick three-minute ride down to the hospital.

I thanked the taxi driver and climbed out, then walked briskly inside. As soon as I reached the nurses' station for the surgical department, Ronda shoved a tablet into my hands. "Cora's oxygen levels dropped. I put in an order for updated bloodwork, but I figured you'd want to come check on her yourself."

"Thanks. I appreciate it," I replied.

Reading the bloodwork on the tablet, I quickly changed out of the dress and into scrubs and running shoes and then headed to Cora's room.

Chapter 25: Kelsey

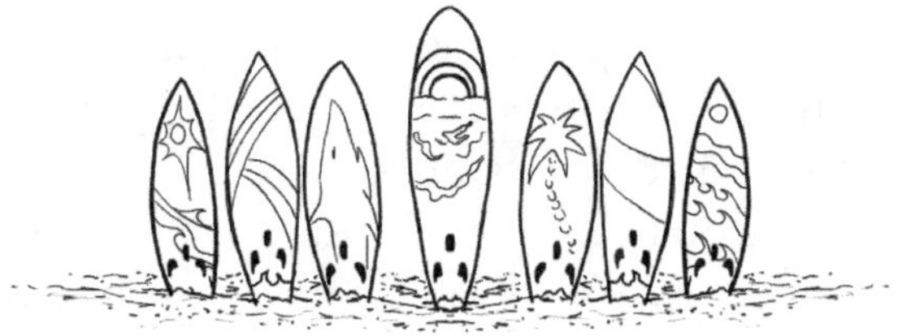

Monday, November 4

I was sitting in the staff break room sipping my water, tired but pleased with the outcomes of the four surgeries I had performed in the past three days. My patients had kept me on my toes, leaving little time to consider that I had over half of the memories from my accident weekend back—including the identity of the man I'd had a weekend fling with.

Taking a deep breath, I examined what I knew. *Conner and I had spent almost four days together and had really hit it off.* But he was so out of my league, it wasn't even funny. *There is no way we can make it work. We're too different. Unlike Joel and me …* Except I couldn't wrap my thoughts around that either.

Dr. Pierce coughed behind me. I turned toward him, and he spoke. "The parents of two of the kids you performed surgeries on this weekend sent letters to the hospital commending you on your excellent skills and service. You are well prepared for each of your procedures, even the ones you are not leading or doing solo, such as the successful separation of the conjoined twins. Your dedication to your patients and the hospital is noted," Dr. Pierce said.

I blushed at the praise. "Thank you."

Dr. Pierce disappeared around the corner, leaving me to my own thoughts. My stomach rumbled. Glancing at my watch, I realized it was lunchtime. *To the cafeteria.*

The cafeteria was six floors below us, and I opted to take the elevator. I stepped inside, and it was empty. I hit the button for basement floor three and leaned against the back wall, closing my eyes. On floor one, the doors opened. I cracked my eyes to see who it was and was surprised to see Conner.

"Hi," he said, stepping into the elevator.

My throat was dry. I swallowed, making it worse. "Hi," I squeaked.

The elevator started to move. Then, he reached over and hit the big red button, and it ground to a halt.

"You can't do that," I protested.

Conner chuckled. "Sure I can. Besides, I've been wanting to talk, and you're a very busy woman, Dr. Floras."

His voice sent shivers down my spine. I glanced at his brown eyes and then looked away, blushing.

"Kelsey, you're all that I can think about, and it's driving me crazy," Conner said softly. He kept his hands loose at his side, keeping his distance.

"I..." I made the mistake of meeting his eyes. My lips parted, and my heartbeat sped up. I took the few steps between us and kissed him.

Conner wrapped his arms around me, pressing our bodies close together, and deepened the kiss. I leaned into him, wishing that instead of being stuck in an elevator, we were in a room with a bed.

A voice came over the speaker. "Is everything okay in elevator three?"

Conner groaned and pulled away from me. "Yes, this is Dr. Hudson. Everything is fine. Thank you for checking." Giving me an apologetic glance, he hit the red button. The gears of the elevator ground together, and we resumed our descent.

"What does your schedule look like for the rest of the day?" Conner asked.

My lips twitched, wondering what exactly he was thinking. "I have a two-hour break right now. I am heading to get lunch at the cafeteria. It's not enough time for me to go home, but I might take a power nap on the cot in the staff room."

"Perfect," Conner said.

"Does that mean you're joining me for lunch in the cafeteria?" I asked.

Conner smiled. "No. Your apartment might be too far, but my office isn't."

Butterflies fluttered in my stomach, followed swiftly by nerves. The last thing I wanted was coworkers to start rumors about me and the newest member of the board of directors.

"It'll be more discreet than us eating lunch in the cafeteria," he replied, almost as though he'd read my mind.

He does have a point about the cafeteria. "Fine," I acquiesced. "What floor is your office on?"

Conner smiled and pulled a hospital badge out of his pocket, swiping it on the black panel below the floor numbers. The elevator stopped moving and then, instead of continuing our trek to the basement, it took us back up.

People are going to wonder what the hell is going on with elevator three! Conner didn't seem concerned though. *Must be nice to be above reproach.*

The elevator identified each floor till level ten, and then the numbers stopped increasing. The elevator did not halt though. Finally, it glided to a stop, and the doors opened with a ding. I stepped out and peered around the room. It was a reception area with a desk for a secretary, but no one was there. Silence filled the hall.

"You have the whole floor as your office?" I blurted.

Conner shook his head. "No. That would be silly and a waste of space. This floor is for the board of directors. Each of us has our own office, and then there's a large conference room. The board was here the day before and the day after the gala, but they had other matters to attend to *or* are practicing medicine downstairs. Other than the last week of each month, there isn't anyone up here."

His explanation made sense but was still strange. *Why would the hospital dedicate a whole floor to people who aren't here seventy-five percent of the time?*

Conner led the way. We wound through the corridor and stopped in front of a door labeled 1501. The plaque underneath said Dr. Conner Hudson, confirming we were indeed at his office. Using the badge, he unlocked the room and ushered me inside.

The office was on the corner of the building with huge floor-to-ceiling windows spanning two of the four walls. There was a large mahogany desk at an angle, a single bookcase that had a Merck Index and a dictionary, and an oversized black leather couch with a glass coffee table in front of it. Three chairs were arranged around the front of the desk. Otherwise, the room was just excessive open space. *It might even be larger than my apartment*, I mused.

"Is this private enough?" Conner asked.

I glanced at him in surprise. I had gotten lost in my examination of the room. "As long as no one comes looking for you," I replied.

"They won't. Other than Fabio bringing us lunch, which should arrive any moment, we won't be disturbed for the remainder of your break." He glanced at his watch. "Which, if you were accurate in how much time you had when we initially met, means we have about ninety minutes."

Now that we were alone in Conner's office, I was nervous. I hoped agreeing to come up here wasn't sending Conner the wrong signals. I opened my mouth to speak when the door opened, and Fabio walked in bearing a full bag of food. I sniffed and caught a whiff of a burger.

Fabio laid out the food in front of us on the coffee table and then took his leave. Conner smiled at me and popped open the lid of both boxes. "One has blue cheese and bacon, the other has cheddar cheese. As you can see, you can add lettuce, tomato, and onion to your liking as well as the sauce. I wasn't sure what kind of burger you liked, so Fabio thought these would be sufficient."

"I'll take the one with blue cheese, thanks," I replied, pulling the box with the blue cheeseburger to my end of the table. I added lettuce but left the tomato and onion off.

"I did not bring you up here with the assumption that we would have sex during your break," Conner said.

I swallowed the suddenly tasteless piece of burger in my mouth, and then I carefully set my burger down before I dropped it. He certainly was direct.

"LACH is not a small hospital, and people talk. Whatever this is between us, if it's important to you to keep it private, then I will do everything in my power to assure we do so," Conner explained.

"What exactly do you do? I know in Santa Barbara you said you're a businessman, but clearly that was intentionally vague," I asked, then cautiously took a dainty bite. The burger was delicious.

Conner hadn't touched his burger yet; instead he was studying me. "I help hospitals examine every aspect of their management and fix areas that have problems or areas that could be better than they are. Most recently, I had to help handle things after a murder of a board member."

I forced myself to keep chewing the bite of burger in my mouth. It wouldn't look good if I just let it fall out of my mouth. When I finished chewing, I responded, "Are you referring to the murder in Dublin?"

Conner nodded. His mouth was now full. I took a sip of water and waited.

"Yes, I had to spend almost two weeks getting everything sorted out in Dublin," Conner said.

"How does it work if you are helping so many hospitals? You can't be in five places at once," I asked.

Conner shrugged. "Technology is phenomenal. I have weekly video meetings with at least one member of each of the boards I serve on. Quarterly in-person visits, unless more are necessary, or if I am just initiating the plan, then I will typically be on-site for two to three months and then reduce my direct involvement."

I wiped my hands on my napkin. "You're telling me that you won't be able to go home to London for two to three months while you help LACH?"

Conner wrinkled his nose. "You said that like it's a bad thing. Besides, I have a house in Malibu."

"Oh," I said, swallowing hard. *He has two houses.*

"Luckily, there are several hospitals I am contracted with in Southern California, and it was the first city I started in, so I felt at the time it made sense to buy a house if I was going to spend lots of time here. London isn't that far. It's just an eleven-hour flight. Not much longer than if you drove the whole length of California," Conner said.

"It takes far longer than that when you're dealing with LAX. Nowadays, it's impossible to have less than two hours to make it through security," I muttered.

Conner patted my hand in reassurance. "We have two private jets."

I gasped. *Not one, but two?* "Who is we?"

"My family. My father and I are joint owners of Hudson International," Conner replied patiently. I noticed that he had finished his burger while I had barely made it through half of mine, but I was no longer hungry.

Why does a man with this much money want anything to do with me? I wondered. Conner was being candid, but I was afraid to hear his answer to my question. To discover that it wasn't because he liked me for me, but because it was just a sex thing.

Chapter 26: Conner

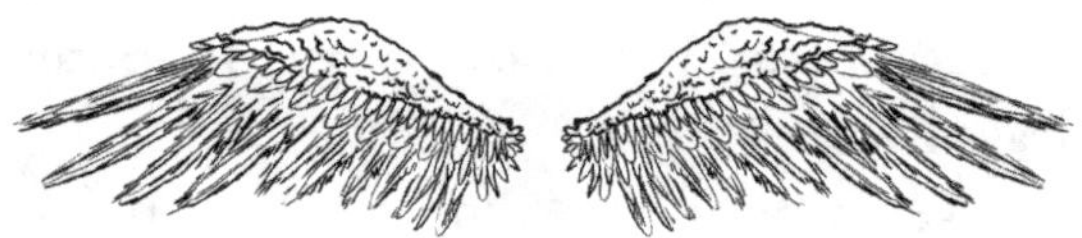

Monday, November 4

I had been hoping I would run into Kelsey at the hospital to make it less stalker-like and more casual to get a chance to talk to her. I couldn't have planned our meeting in the elevator any better. Now that we were in my office, I could tell Kelsey was nervous. Which was the last thing I wanted. I was used to women getting nervous around me, of course. Those who struggled to think of me as anything other than an aloof billionaire.

I racked my mind for ways I could get her to relax. I had hoped the food would help, but I didn't think it worked as well as I had intended.

"How have you been?" I asked, settling on something simple.

Kelsey met my gaze briefly, then looked out the window. "Mostly good. I was in a coma for four days because of the accident. A concussion and lots of bruising, but otherwise nothing major. Everyone has told me how lucky I was. I'm grateful the accident did not cause me to lose my fellowship."

"Do you remember the whole weekend now, or are your memories still in bits and pieces?" I inquired

Kelsey's eyes wandered back to mine. "I think I remember most of it. Including that you were in the car with me during the accident and yet you walked away completely unscathed ... and disappeared."

"I'm sorry. My father is quite overbearing, and I had to get home as soon as possible for an urgent problem at work. Given we had agreed it was a simple weekend fling, I did not think you would want to see me again anyhow," I replied. Even now that I was face to face with Kelsey, I was afraid to admit the truth: that there was a connection between us. It would be better for both of us if she told me to leave her alone.

I could hear Kelsey's pulse speeding up as she spoke. "Honestly, I don't know what I feel or think anymore. I *should* be angry that you left, and part of me is."

I appreciated her honesty, but it was a struggle to figure out how to salvage things. Her anger was justified. I shouldn't have left her behind after the accident regardless of what Octavio's threats were. Smoothing my hand over my pants leg, an idea came to me. "Would you consider starting over?"

"Starting over?" she repeated in disbelief. I held my breath, afraid she was going to reject me and knowing that if she did I would have no choice but to honor her decision.

"Yes, if you're willing. We can get to know each other properly, without leaving out any important details," I said. Realization sank in that if I was going to be completely honest with her as I was promising to do, that meant I would have to tell her about my immortality. *Not today*, I consoled myself, but I could not hold off forever.

Kelsey gave me a hesitant smile. "I am willing to give it a try."

I barely stopped myself from pulling her into a hug. *She wants to start over!* "Brilliant! I'm Dr. Conner Hudson, board member of LACH." I stuck my hand out for her to shake. Thankfully, she took it.

"Nice to meet you, Conner. I'm Dr. Kelsey Floras, pediatric surgery fellow at LACH," Kelsey replied and let go of my hand, setting hers lightly in her lap.

"Would you like to have dinner with me tonight?" I asked. A

subtle glance at the clock on the wall told me we were rapidly running out of time for her break. If I wanted Kelsey, then I knew I was going to have to play by the rules and not interfere with her job. Which meant she needed to get back on time, not have a board member give her a late pass.

Kelsey nodded. "Yes. But I'm going to warn you now, I've been working back-to-back twenty-four-hour shifts the past three days. I am not sure how much fun I'll be."

I shrugged. It didn't matter to me. I just wanted a chance to start fresh with her. "I'm not worried. What time are you done today?"

"You want to pick me up from the hospital?" she said with a slight shudder.

I realized my mistake. If she'd been taking back-to-back shifts, likely she hadn't been home in a few days and had just been resting in the staff room.

I backtracked. "I can pick you up from your apartment. How about two hours after your shift ends?"

"Yes," Kelsey agreed. Then, she pulled her phone out of her pocket and unlocked it. She handed her phone to me. I took it and saw she had started adding me as a contact. I obliged the unspoken request and added my phone number, then had her phone send me a text so I'd have hers.

"I guess now you won't be able to get rid of me. I know your last name, and I have your phone number," I teased.

Kelsey surprised me with her response. "I'm okay with that." She glanced at her phone as I handed it back to her. "I do need to go. I have rounds with Dr. Pierce as soon as my break is over."

I stood up and offered her my hand. She took it and pulled herself up to standing. I led her to the elevator and pushed the button. "Once you get inside, you can just hit the button for the third floor, and it'll take you straight there. You don't need to swipe your badge or anything. That's only to get up to this floor."

"I see," Kelsey replied.

We waited in awkward silence as the elevator made its way up.

When the doors opened, I bit my tongue. None of the words that were waiting to come out would have done me any good. Not if I wanted to truly have a fresh start. Kelsey entered the elevator, and I gave her a slight wave.

"I'll see you tonight," she said as the doors slid shut.

I retreated into my office, thoughts churning. My fifteen-hundredth birthday and the ascension had passed, which meant I truly could do what I wanted without Cassiel having the ability to punish me for it. Except for one small matter ... marrying a human was not permitted. I knew I was getting ahead of myself. I would never force Kelsey to marry me, and I had no idea if she felt the same way I did. I spent enough time around hospitals and LACH to know how competitive the pediatric surgery fellowship had been, and I doubted Kelsey would do anything that would compromise her ability to finish it. There was also the small matter that, as far as I could tell, Kelsey was oblivious that immortals existed.

As a species, humans did better assuming anything that could be considered "magical" was science performing at its very best or a miracle. The last human I knew of who had discovered that angels and demons existed had been executed for trying to blackmail Cassiel. That was over three hundred years ago.

There was a light tap on the door, then it opened. Fabio, wearing a plum suit with a white button-up shirt and a silver tie, walked over to me. "How'd it go?"

I gave him a slight smile. "We're going to try starting over."

"And Cassiel?" Fabio inquired.

I shrugged. "It's none of his business."

Fabio coughed. "What about everything going on with Agatha?"

"I'm meeting with Cassiel in an hour. I'll tell him then. Though given she was not at the gala, I'm sure he already knows that Agatha and I are not going through with the engagement. I will make sure I am very clear on the matter," I responded.

"Do you need me for anything else?" Fabio asked.

I shook my head. "No. I'll let you know if that changes. Promise."

Fabio collected the containers from our lunch and carried them out. I moved over to my desk and settled into the chair, sorting through my emails while I waited for the meeting with Cassiel.

The hour went by quickly. I had a couple of urgent matters to deal with, and it sounded like I would need to return to Dublin for another issue at CM Hospital that could only be handled in person.

Unlike Fabio, Cassiel did not knock. He simply pushed the door open and came in. Not that I would have stopped him. LACH was not the right place for a battle of wills. As soon as the glass shut, I felt a pulse of Cassiel's magic. My eyes widened as his appearance changed from a smartly dressed businessman in a black suit and tie with gray hair to a seven-foot-tall angel with gold wings, bronzed skin, and a head of golden curls. He held a large, gold-plated staff with a diamond globe at the top.

I stood and moved away from my desk, my iridescent white-and-silver wings unfurling as I approached Cassiel. We were the same height and our gazes were even, a change since my birthday. Previously, I was about a head shorter, which had forced me to look up at Cassiel when we were in our true forms. Now, though, even he could not deny that we were equals.

"I heard that you and Agatha were messing around with the photo shoot at your estate as a way to appease me, but even then, you weren't intending to go through with the engagement," growled Cassiel. I stayed silent, knowing I had to hear him out. "Instead of being upfront that she prefers women and is even considering marrying one, you made me look like a fool."

Lip curling in annoyance, I replied, my voice sharp, "I would have told you if you had given me a chance. But like everything else, you only wanted to tell me what would happen instead of listening to my thoughts on it. Just like instead of letting me return from Santa Barbara on my own, you sent Octavio to demonstrate how intolerant you are ... nearly killing a human in the process."

Cassiel blinked and his jaw tightened. "Octavio interprets my orders to achieve the desired results."

"Perhaps you should consider using someone whose interpretation doesn't always resort to violence. If I hadn't been in the car, she would've died, and that would have been an even bigger mess," I said in a clipped voice.

Cassiel's eyes darkened. "If she would have died without you there, that means you risked her seeing you use your magic. Equally dangerous for us. Did you tell her what you are?"

I bit my cheek, coppery blood flowing into my mouth. I hadn't intended to tell him about Kelsey yet, but now I couldn't decide if it would be better to lay all my cards on the table or keep that to myself. *We're equals now*, I reminded myself. Deciding to take a chance that Cassiel would give me answers for once instead of reacting in anger, I said, "Have you ever heard of an angel experiencing the sensation of lightning or electricity when touching a human?"

Cassiel's eyes narrowed. "You mean like a Fien bond?"

My mouth went dry. "I never paid much heed to the details of a Fien bond. Mother always said they were legends and weren't real."

Cassiel shook his head. "That sounds like Samara, telling you they're not real. But a Fien bond is very real, though they are rare. I only know of three, and the last Fien bonded pair died a century before you were born."

Curiosity piqued, I dared ask, "Can you tell me what you know about them?"

"Yes. A Fien bond occurs between two individuals, though the nature of their relationship can vary significantly, from sharing a deep friendship to a couple that seeks marriage. There are three things that always happen. First, the sensation of a Fien bond developing is like being hit by lightning, or, for some species, similar to the sensation of being zapped by human electricity. Second, the bond can be felt by one or both of the individuals, sometimes taking a long time to develop to its full strength. Three, they can occur across species. As I mentioned, I know of three pairs of Fien-bonded individuals. The first was a female angel and a male demon, the second two male demons, and the third was between two dragons. As you can see, Fien bonds are in a class of their own," Cassiel explained.

My throat went dry when he said an angel and a demon had a Fien bond. In many ways, an angel becoming romantically involved with a demon was worse than a human. *Perhaps there is hope for Kelsey and me if what I'm experiencing is a Fien bond.* "How do you know for sure if it is a Fien bond?"

Instead of answering the question, Cassiel dropped his staff and stepped forward, gripping my forearms. When he touched me, I could feel the connection between us. Cassiel used his magic to look through my memories. I stifled the desire to block him, knowing that would only make things worse. Aside from his anger when he arrived, Cassiel was being fairly amenable.

"A human?" Cassiel hissed, letting go of my arms and stepping back.

I shrugged. "You said yourself that Fien bonds can defy logic, if that's what it is."

"It certainly is a Fien bond. But ... a *human*? Did you tell her?" Cassiel demanded.

I shook my head. "No, she doesn't know anything. But we are going on a date tonight."

"Telling humans about us is tricky. If the Fien bond finishes forming, she will find out soon enough. I would recommend telling her before then."

"You're not going to punish me?" I asked.

Cassiel laughed. "Punish you? Son, we can't control when a Fien bond forms. Besides, if I punished you for such a coveted and rare circumstance, it would not go well with the gods."

I sighed in relief. My biggest fear had been Cassiel taking out his anger on Kelsey. Knowing that the Fien bond would protect her from Cassiel and the wrath of other immortals made me feel significantly better about the whole matter. Except I was likely getting ahead of myself. Kelsey had agreed to start over, which meant we were going on our "first date" tonight. I doubted that she would be open-minded if I told her about the Fien bond and that I'm an angel on our first date. But I could take things slow and feel her out first.

We stood in companionable silence for a while, then I remembered that we'd set up the meeting to talk business. "Toruk, the chairman of the board at CM Hospital, quit. I'm going to need to go back out there and figure out who can take his spot. Vizalia is the temporary CEO, but without a chairman, she's struggling to keep everything together, and it sounds like rumors are flying. I need to personally oversee things until it settles more."

"That's unfortunate. The LACH board was expecting you to be here this month," Cassiel reminded me.

"I know. That's why I'm bringing it up to you. It's possible your presence at CM Hospital would be sufficient," I suggested. Personally, I'd never liked the angel Toruk. He preferred threatening humans and demons to achieve results whereas I would negotiate. Typically, the outcome was the same, except Toruk ended up with coworkers and subordinates who despised him.

"I can go. Your position at LACH is too new to risk you being gone for a month in Dublin. At the gala, many of the doctors expressed interest in your hands-on approach and were looking forward to having a chance to meet with you informally," Cassiel said.

"Very well, I will stay here. I'll send you the details you'll need while in Dublin," I replied.

"Excellent. I'll depart in two days. We can meet again before I leave if there's anything else you want to talk about," Cassiel said. He turned toward the door, resuming his human form, then looked at me over his shoulder. "Good luck with the human."

My jaw dropped open in surprise, but he was gone before I could figure out how to respond. Cassiel and I were usually at odds. With this turn of events, and knowing that I was experiencing a Fien bond, I wondered if Cassiel and I would finally be able to set our differences aside. For the time being, it seemed that way. Taking a deep breath, I returned to my desk to get more work in before my next meeting.

Chapter 27: Kelsey

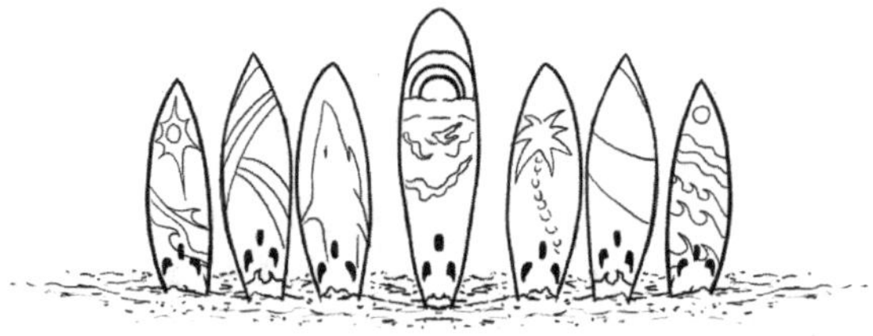

Monday, November 4

The unexpected lunch with Conner had been on my mind all day. I liked the idea of starting over with him properly, but I was not willing to get my hopes up that it would turn into anything. *There's no way a man like him would ever be serious about dating me.*

Slinging my backpack over my shoulder, I left the hospital and started my two-mile trek home. Wearing my earbuds, I dialed Penny's number and then shoved my phone in my pocket. I had no idea if she would answer at six p.m. on a weeknight or if they were busy with after-school activities.

"Is everything okay?" Penny asked in concern.

"Yes!" I replied quickly. "I didn't mean to alarm you. I'm just running home and thought I'd call you and talk, unless it's a bad time."

"Now is fine. What's up?" Penny asked.

"Do you remember the red-haired guy that I met before my accident?" I inquired.

"Mmmhmmm," Penny replied.

"Well, I had lunch with him today, and he asked if we wanted to start over," I explained.

Penny chuckled. "I'm assuming you said yes and are now having second thoughts?"

I sighed. She knew me too well. "Yes and yes ... I'm tired. I have had back-to-back twenty-four-hour shifts for three days. Hardly enough time to sort through the memories of my weekend with Conner."

"Did you tell him that you're tired?" Penny asked.

I nodded, then realized she couldn't see me. "Yes. I did, and he still wanted to go out for dinner."

"Kel, it's just dinner. If you're truly starting over, then there should be no expectations," Penny told me.

"But last time ..." I started.

"Nope. Forget whatever happened between you. This is a clean slate. Think of it like you're going on a blind date with someone you've never met before. Try to get to know each other. Besides, I know you too well. If you had hated the few times you went out together previously, there's no way you'd have agreed. Tonight will be a chance to see if you can enjoy each other's company outside of the bedroom," Penny said sagely.

"What about the fact that he's a billionaire?" I squeaked.

"Since you gave me his full name after the gala, I did research on him for you, Kel, and I honestly think that if he wants to get to know you better, then good for you. He could be a keeper," she said.

I blew out my breath. I was only a block from my apartment. "Thanks for the advice, Penny. I need to go if I'm going to have time for a shower."

"Any time, love ... and text me later to let me know how it went!" Penny said excitedly.

"I will. Love you too," I said and then hung up.

I took a long, hot shower when I got home. Part of me wanted to text Conner and ask for a rain check. I was exhausted, and the draw of sleeping in my own bed, which was merely through the bathroom door, was tantalizing. But I also knew that if I canceled, I wasn't sure I'd have the guts to ask him out. While I liked the idea of starting over, it was hard to get past knowing that he was a billionaire and the worry that I'd never be good enough for someone like him.

Towel wrapped around me, I perused my walk-in closet. Flipping through the dresses and skirts, my gaze settled on a pair of jeans. *Not exactly screaming "date."* I yawned. *If I can even keep awake long enough to have a conversation.*

Mind made up, I grabbed the jeans. They were a very dark, almost black wash. I paired them with a shimmering green blouse and black flats. I carried the clothes into the bedroom, then moved over to my dresser and chose my favorite black lace bra with matching underwear. All my selections were chosen primarily for comfort, then for looks.

I towel-dried my hair and braided it, not wanting to deal with a blow dryer or having it hang damply on my shoulders, then donned the clothes. I hung up the towel and looked around the room, trying to figure out if I was forgetting anything. My cell phone started ringing. I snagged it off the nightstand and saw it was Conner. *Is he here already?* "Hello?"

"I'm in the visitor parking space. Just come down when you're ready. No rush," Conner said.

"Give me five minutes, then I'll be down," I replied quickly.

"See you shortly!" Conner said, then hung up.

I dashed into the bathroom and brushed my teeth. Confirming my keys were in my purse, I locked up and headed down the stairs to the parking garage.

Sitting in the visitor parking spot was a black Audi SUV. If Conner hadn't told me he was in the visitor parking space, I likely would have walked right past it. I saw enough black Audis downtown that I would never have pegged it as Conner's car.

The driver side door opened, and Conner came around to greet me. "You look lovely, Kelsey."

I gave him a smile. "Thanks." He was wearing the same dark blue suit he'd had on earlier, though he was no longer sporting the tie. "Did you stay at the hospital?"

Conner shrugged. "My house is in Malibu. Since I drove today instead of flying the helicopter, I didn't want to drive home and then turn around and drive right back."

I swallowed, digesting the information he had just let drop as if it were no big deal. He had a house in Malibu *and a helicopter*! "Smart choice. Traffic can be a beast even just the two miles from the hospital to the apartment. I can't imagine the drive all the way to Malibu."

"Which is why I usually fly," Conner explained.

His reasoning made sense. I struggled to wrap my mind around the fact that not only did he have a helicopter, but he also knew how to fly it. Swallowing hard, I focused on Conner's face. "Where are we going to eat?"

"There's a small Italian restaurant in Malibu I wanted to take you to. It's off the radar, and we can just enjoy a quiet meal," Conner replied.

"Sounds good," I said.

He opened the door for me, and I noticed the honeycomb stitching on the black leather seats and the RS logo before I slid into the passenger seat. It felt like sitting in a luxury office chair, not a vehicle seat. Conner shut my door and got into the driver's seat.

He must have noticed I was running my finger along the leather. "Are you comfortable?" He sounded worried.

"I was just admiring the feel of the leather. I've never been in a car this fancy," I replied.

Conner chuckled as he pulled out of the parking space, and we started what I was certain would be a long trek to Malibu. It was seven thirty, and traffic was still going strong. "Do you like cars?"

I shrugged. "I'm not a huge fan of driving, and prior to the accident, I had an ancient Prius, so I would say not really. Why?"

"Cars are one of my hobbies," Conner replied, then paused. "Well, I guess I should be more specific. I like to drive on a track when I have time. At my country estate, I have my own track."

I licked my lips. He must really like cars to have a track at his house. "The only hobby I've ever had is surfing. From the time I was five years old, that's all I ever wanted to do when I had free time. Of course, it helped that Abuela's house was near the beach."

"I like surfing too," Conner responded. "It has some similarities to racing but also distinct differences."

"What was your childhood like?" I wasn't sure it was really a good first date question, but this wasn't *really* our first date. It was more like the third or fourth.

Conner glanced at me, then back to the road. We were almost to the Pacific Coast Highway. Traffic was heavy, but it was moving faster than I had expected.

"I was sent to boarding school when I was ten. I'd come home over the breaks. I hated it at first, until I realized it was a chance for me to figure out who I was without my father dictating. I would have stopped returning home over the breaks if it hadn't been for my sister. She's ten years younger than me. Once she turned three, we got really close. Still are."

"I didn't realize you have a sister," I replied.

Conner nodded. "Yes. Charlotte Hudson."

The name didn't ring a bell, but he said it like it should. We had already determined I had no idea what it was like to live in his circle, rubbing shoulders with the richest of the rich on a regular basis.

"I went to public school in Santa Barbara all the way through high school and then attended UC Santa Barbara for premed," I said, not sure how else to respond to his tale of boarding school. I had nothing to really relate to that.

"Valedictorian in both high school and undergraduate," Conner said.

"You pulled my records?" I asked, then realized Penny had essentially done the same thing—or as much as she could get off of an internet search.

"I did. You were also top of your class at Johns Hopkins, and when applying for your LACH fellowship, you were the top candidate by quite a significant margin," Conner replied.

I realized he must have looked up my application to the LACH fellowship if he knew I was the top candidate, information even I hadn't been privy to.

"My coworkers have been put off by the fact that you're a doctor but have a PhD, not a medical degree. What is the story behind your college education?" I asked as the freeway made the sweeping curve and transitioned from Interstate 10 to the Pacific Coast Highway. Surprisingly, the Pacific Coast Highway was empty. The sun had already set, and the ocean was dotted with small lights from the various cargo ships and oil rigs.

"The short version, because we are almost to the restaurant, is I did undergraduate in biology with premed. I originally thought I would pursue becoming a doctor, but I had the opportunity to spend a summer working in a law office in London. They focused primarily on business law, and I was fascinated. I decided to pursue law school, and then after practicing law for two years in that same firm, I opted to return to school and get my PhD in international business. Drawing on my interest in medicine, plus education and experience in business law, it was a good fit. The doctorate allowed me to become a business consultant for the medical profession," Conner explained.

Up ahead on the right, tucked against the steep Malibu bluffs, was a tiny restaurant on the side of the highway. We pulled into the parking lot. There was only one open spot. I wasn't sure we would fit, but Conner maneuvered the Audi in without any problems.

"Why international business?" I asked.

Conner opened the door and got out. I scooted out my door before he had a chance to open it for me. He gave me a slight grin. "The business I co-own with my father, Hudson International, existed before I got my PhD, and given it was already an international business with offices in London and Los Angeles, it seemed to make the most sense if my degree would cover topics already important to me. I'm also fluent in Spanish, German, and Japanese, which allowed me to do a cultural comparison as part of my thesis. It's far easier to get a feel for business in a different country where English isn't the native language if you speak the language."

"Fair enough. Now, I guess we should go inside if we want to eat," I said. We were still standing beside the Audi.

Conner took my hand in his and brought it to his lips. I blushed at the gesture. "I was merely answering your questions, madame."

I tugged my hand out of his grip. "I know, I know. But I'm tired and hungry, so please, let's go eat."

Our conversation over dinner ranged from favorite classes in college to surfing techniques. As the waiter cleared away our plates, I was struggling to keep my eyelids from sliding shut.

"I will take you home," Conner said, running his thumb over my knuckles.

"I warned you earlier I am tired," I replied with a sleepy smile.

The waiter brought the check, and Conner paid. Arm in arm, we walked back to the car. The parking lot was empty. My watch told me it was ten p.m. *No wonder it's empty.* As a surgeon, I didn't always get weekends off. Sometimes, this week included, I had odd days off—like tomorrow. Legally, the hospital had to ensure its doctors and surgeons had enough sleep to be able to properly provide medical care to the patients. If a surgeon was too tired to do their job, mistakes happened, and that was when lawyers had to get involved.

I fell asleep once we pulled onto the Pacific Coast Highway.

Conner's hands ran down my hips and thighs as I fumbled with the key to my door. I almost dropped the keys when he pinched my breast.

"Stop!" I hissed. "Someone will see us." He didn't stop. I finally managed to get the key in the lock and turned it. We burst through the door. He kicked it shut behind us and then pushed me into the wall, demanding.

I tugged my shirt up and over my head, forcing him to take a step back. He ran his fingers under the edge of my bra and unhooked it, letting it drop to the floor with my shirt before he pressed against me again.

"Missing something," I teased. We were both still wearing pants and underwear.

Conner kissed me, our tongues dancing, and I focused on our mouths. He slid my underwear and pants down so I could step out of them, then slid his own off too.

"I want you," I said breathlessly against his lips.

He ran his finger through my soaked folds and then placed his hands under my tush, picking me up. I wrapped my legs around his waist and moaned in pleasure as he thrust deep into me. He pressed my back into the wall to support me, and his strokes became more intense. I tightened as the pressure built. He sped up more, and I screamed as he sent me spiraling into bliss. Conner kept driving himself deeper and deeper, until I felt him surrender to his release.

"Kelsey," Conner's voice called.

I didn't want to open my eyes. I was having the most delicious dream.

"Kelsey, we're at your apartment," Conner said again, then brushed his hand along my cheek, sending shivers down my spine.

My lips parted, and I opened my eyes. Conner was standing in the open door, half leaning over me as though he was going to unbuckle the seatbelt like I was a child.

Still not sure I was entirely awake, I wrapped my arms around

Conner and pulled him toward me, crushing my lips to his. It took him a moment before he kissed me back. The dream was still fresh in my mind, and exhaustion had been replaced by hot desire.

Conner broke off the kiss. "I thought you were tired."

I stuck my tongue out at him. "I was, I am ... I just ..." My cheeks heated up, and I looked away, embarrassed. I unbuckled the seatbelt, and Conner stepped back to give me room to get out.

When I shut the door and met him at the end of the Audi, Conner said, "Good night, Kelsey." He gave me a light kiss on the cheek and walked toward the other side of the car.

"Wait!" I called.

Conner poked his head around the end of the car. "Yes?"

I moistened my lips with the tip of my tongue and gave him what I hoped was a sexy smile. "Would you like to come up to my apartment?"

"If that is what you want," Conner replied. His expression looked hopeful, though his tone didn't betray anything.

I nodded. "Yes, that is what I want."

Fumbling with my purse, I pulled my keys out and then dropped them. Conner stooped down and swept them off the floor, offering them to me. "Are you sure you are okay?"

I blushed again. "I don't know how to do this."

"Do what?" Conner asked.

I waved my hand between us. "Us."

"You didn't seem to have any problems that weekend in September," Conner replied.

"I had a sex dream," I blurted out, then covered my mouth with my hands. *Why did I just tell him that?* Embarrassed, I turned on my heel and rapidly walked toward the elevator. Thankfully, the elevator car was in the garage, and the doors opened. I turned around and Conner was there.

Before I could say anything, he pulled me into the elevator and kissed me. Need wound through me. "There's nothing wrong with having a sex dream about me," Conner whispered against my lips.

"Let me tell you a secret ... I have them about you too."

The elevator dinged, then opened on my floor. I extracted myself from his arms and led him toward my door. Unlike my dream, he kept his hands to himself as I opened the door, and we went inside. I deposited my purse on the table next to the door and then locked it.

Conner wrapped his arms around me, and we kissed again. My whole body was thrumming with desire. I parted my lips, inviting his tongue in, desperate for more. Conner ran his hands down my back and then slid them under my blouse, unclasping my bra. He stepped back half a step and lifted the hem of my shirt up, I obliged and raised my arms, allowing him to slide the blouse and bra off.

He cupped my breasts with his hands and then lightly pinched my nipples between his thumb and forefinger. A low moan escaped my lips. Conner's hands dropped from my breasts. I gave him a quick kiss.

"Let's go in the bedroom," I suggested.

Conner followed me into the bedroom. With my back toward him, I tugged off my jeans and let my underwear fall to the floor. I turned slightly to see how far he had gotten with his clothes, when he wrapped his arms around me from behind. I could feel his cock pressing into my butt. He ran his hands down my sides, circling my breasts, before his right hand went lower. I hissed in pleasure as his fingers plunged into my folds, swirling and teasing. I arched against Conner's chest as he sent pleasure rolling through me.

Satisfied with my response, he turned me around to face him and then pushed me back lightly. I took the hint and lay down on the bed. Conner knelt between my legs and guided his cock into me. I moaned at the feel of him as he pressed deeper and deeper into my core.

He struck up a moderate rhythm, in and out. Intense pressure was building inside of me. As though he knew, Conner quickened his strokes. My bed began to shake, and I tried to tune it out. I tipped my hips, allowing him to plunge even deeper.

"Conner!" I screamed as a wave of pleasure crashed over me, strong enough I thought I might black out.

One more thrust and I felt Conner spasming inside of me as he got his release. He dipped his head down and kissed me. "You're amazing, Kelsey."

I gave him a sleepy smile. "You're not too shabby yourself."

Conner chuckled, and I wondered if we were even talking about the same thing. He rolled to the side, freeing me. I tugged the sheets up around us and fell asleep.

Chapter 28: Conner

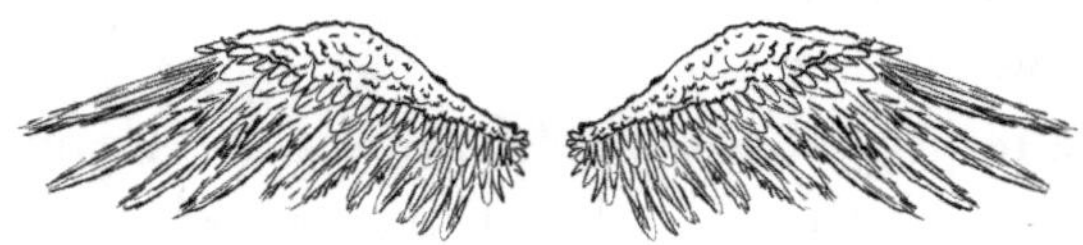

Tuesday, November 5

I woke up with a start. Then I remembered where I was—in Kelsey's apartment. Carefully, so as not to disturb her, I checked my phone. It was eight a.m., and I had several texts from Fabio asking where I was and if he should cancel my morning meetings. Glancing at Kelsey, I reluctantly got up. I found my clothes in a heap near the foot of the bed and took them with me out of the bedroom.

I had no intention of disappearing on Kelsey again, but I did need to respond to Fabio. I got dressed and walked into the kitchen, so I was as far from the bedroom as possible, then called Fabio.

"Hey, I saw your messages. I'm sorry I didn't give you a heads-up last night, but the plan was originally that I was dropping Kelsey off and returning to the house," I explained.

"You're still at her apartment?" Fabio asked. I knew he wasn't judging me. It was just an inquiry that would impact my schedule for the day.

"Yes, and yes to your next question. There is a bag that has a clean change of clothes in the back of the Audi," I replied.

"Your first meeting is in thirty minutes. Can you make that, or should I push it? How far back do you want me to reschedule everything?" Fabio asked.

I scratched my chin, debating. I had no idea what Kelsey did on her days off, or if she wanted me here. "What if I make the ten a.m. meeting, and you adjust anything before that. Then, I can see what Kelsey wants to do today."

"I can't believe she invited you into her apartment," Fabio said, voicing my own thoughts.

I decided to keep Kelsey's revelation of the dream to myself. That was more information than Fabio needed—*or likely wanted*—to know. "Last night went better than I expected. Maybe the Fien bond is starting to affect her too."

"Just don't chase her away," Fabio said in warning.

I knew he was right, though after how our date went, I wasn't too worried about chasing Kelsey away. We shared a few interests and conversation came naturally between us.

"I will do my best. Now please apologize to the doctors for the changes in our schedules. I will check in with you when I head over to the hospital," I said.

"Sounds good. Bye," said Fabio.

I sighed. This week was full of meetings, and moving the ones from this morning would potentially push others into the following week, something I'd been trying to avoid. Hopefully, Kelsey would wake up soon, and I could eat, shower, and leave on good terms.

Poking my head into the bedroom to check on her, I noted she was still in the exact same spot as when I'd gotten out of the bed. My keys and wallet were in my pants pocket. Snagging her apartment key off the hook by the door, I made a quick decision. I ran down to the parking garage, grabbed the duffle bag out of the trunk, and, taking the stairs two at a time, raced back to the apartment.

I shut her apartment door behind me just as Kelsey exited the bedroom, rubbing her eyes. She had put on an oversized T-shirt that hung to the top of her thighs.

"Good morning," she said softly.

"Morning," I replied and set the bag down. "I keep at least one change of clothes in all of my cars."

"You have that many unplanned sleepovers?" Kelsey asked, amused.

I coughed and my face flushed. "No. But you would be surprised how many people accidentally spill things on me. Since I like to get to know the hospitals and medical staff I'll be working with, I'll sometimes shadow doctors during their rounds, and I've had some very unpleasant things splashed on my clothing. I quickly learned to keep at least one spare," I explained in what I hoped was a convincing way.

"I guess if you wear suits all the time it's not as simple as just getting a new pair of scrubs from the staff room," Kelsey replied.

"Exactly. I did make the mistake once of putting scrubs on as a last resort, and because people at the hospitals know me as Dr. Hudson, I almost ended up in assisting in a surgery before I could extract myself," I said.

Kelsey gave me a slight smile. "Nurses can be very pushy sometimes."

"Yes, they can," I agreed.

"Did you want to eat or take a shower first?" Kelsey asked.

"Can I eat you in the shower?" I asked, wondering how she'd respond. In Santa Barbara, Kelsey had been just as eager as I was to have sex. I wasn't sure if she had been behaving that way because it was *only* a fling or if she always was that way with her boyfriends.

She tapped on her lip, taking her time to consider my question. "Maybe, but if you want to do that, then I'd highly recommend feeding me real food first."

"Okay, what do you have here?" I asked as I walked into her kitchen. I browsed the contents of her cupboards before turning my attention to the fridge. She had a carton of eggs, a basket of grapes, and some salad mix. *Not much to use.*

Kelsey strode past me and bent over, rummaging through a cupboard. Her shirt scooted up and revealed that she wasn't wearing underwear. I sucked in my breath and shoved my hands into my pockets to stop myself from touching her. *She said she wanted to eat first, but damn. Did she forget she wasn't wearing anything before she bent over? Or is this a test?*

Kelsey stood up, a skillet in her hands between us. She gave me a knowing smirk. *Planned*, I decided. I took the skillet, set it down on the counter next to the carton of eggs, and pulled her to me. I ran my hands along her back down to her butt and cupped it, then kissed her fully on the lips.

Breathless, she tipped her head back. "You agreed to wait until we eat."

"You changed the rules when you bent over, and you know it. If you wanted to eat, then you should have come out with underwear or pants on," I scolded her lightly.

"I couldn't decide," Kelsey admitted.

"Is your shower large enough for two people?" I asked.

"I think we'll fit. I've never had a reason to experiment," Kelsey admitted.

Happiness welled within me that she hadn't had a reason to invite anyone else into her shower.

"I can get creative if I need to," I replied.

Kelsey kissed me, then brushed her hands along my cock before waltzing out of the kitchen, sashaying her hips. I followed eagerly, hoping her shower was large enough for two.

Kelsey discarded her shirt, and I quickly undressed. Following her into the bathroom, I came up behind her and cupped her breasts while I trailed kisses from her ear down to her shoulder. She leaned against me for a moment before stepping forward to check the water.

"It's ready," she said, turning toward me while she stood under the water, getting her hair wet.

I stepped in and closed the door behind me. Our bodies were touching, the water cascading between us. I took a step backward and the cold glass met my skin. I retracted my foot and peered past Kelsey. She didn't seem to have much more room than I had.

"It will work. I promise," Kelsey said.

I was surprised when she lowered herself to her knees in front of me. Her eyes were on my cock as she moistened her lips, then took the tip into her mouth. I bit back a moan as she sucked. It had been a long time since a woman had felt like being generous enough to give me a blow job.

She took my whole length into her mouth, and my body tensed as pleasure rolled through me. I closed my eyes. She dragged her teeth lightly on my sensitive flesh as she drew me in and out. I set my hand lightly on her shoulder to brace myself, and with one last rake of her teeth, she sent me over the edge. My whole body spasmed as the orgasm rolled through me. I sagged against the wall.

Kelsey kept my gaze locked with hers as she swallowed my seed and stood up. I kissed her, feeling as though I needed to somehow make up to her the gift she had given me. An image entered my mind of her legs wrapped around me, her back against the wall, but not wanting to press Kelsey against the cold glass in the small shower, I decided to use other ways to wring every last drop out of her.

Chapter 29: Kelsey

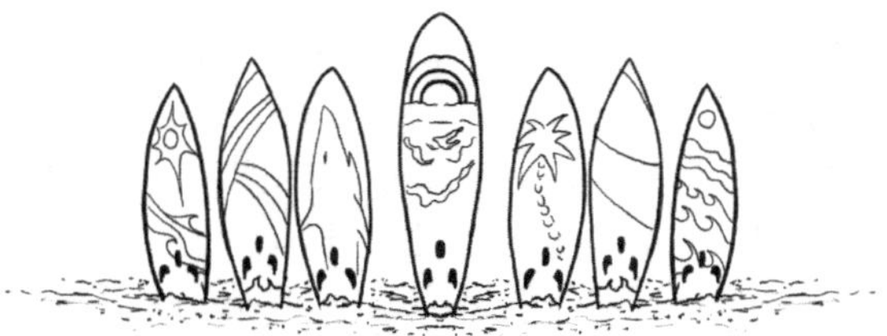

Tuesday, November 5

I felt like a noodle after Conner gave me not one, but two orgasms in the shower. Lifting my arms to wash my hair was almost more than I could manage, but I knew I needed to do it. *Getting clean is why I wanted a shower*, I reminded myself. I glanced over my shoulder at Conner, who did not seem to have the same issue. His arms were working just fine as he lathered his hair and body with soap.

"Is everything okay?" Conner asked when he caught me looking at him.

I giggled nervously. "I'm very wobbly."

"I can wash your hair for you if you'd like," Conner offered.

Before I could stop myself, I nodded. "That would be great."

Conner ran his fingers through my hair and then began massaging my scalp. I hissed in pleasure as his fingers worked their magic. Desire wound through me. I bit my cheek, trying to tamp it down. I could barely move my arms. What would more sex do to me? *Not like I have anywhere else to be*, I reminded myself.

I reached behind me and ran an experimental finger over the tip of Conner's cock. He chuckled. "I thought you were wobbly."

I sighed and dropped my hand, knowing he was right. *Maybe once we're out of the shower I will be able to be more convincing.*

"You can rinse now," Conner instructed. I inched under the water and let him work the soap out of my hair. "All done."

"Thank you," I said, turning around to face him.

Conner stuck his arm out of the shower door and retrieved two towels. I shut off the water and shivered in the cold air. He wrapped the towel around me. "It's not that cold."

"I know. It's just how I am," I muttered.

Conner stepped out of the shower to give me more room to dry off. He picked up his pants and withdrew his phone from the pocket, then cursed.

"What's wrong?" I asked.

"It's nine thirty. I need to go. I have meetings," Conner said.

"Oh," I replied as disappointment welled up inside me. He hadn't said anything last night about having to work today, so I had just assumed he had the day off too. *Or would exert his billionaire powers to clear his schedule.* I turned so he couldn't see my face and continued to vigorously dry myself off.

"Next time we go on a dinner date, I can make sure I don't have meetings the next morning," Conner said. "With our conversation in my office yesterday and how tired you were when I picked you up, I had no expectations that I would end up spending the night."

I gave myself a mental kick. *Of course. I had said I wanted to take things slow. That usually doesn't involve sex on the first date. I can hardly blame him.* "It's fine. I understand."

Conner wrapped the towel around his waist and snagged his dirty suit off the floor, then disappeared into the front room where his duffle bag was. Not wanting to cause him to be late for his meeting, I got dressed in my bedroom. Baggy sweats and another old T-shirt. This time, I was wearing a bra *and* underwear. Not that it would matter if I wasn't, since he was leaving anyhow.

I emerged from the bedroom to see him finishing up brushing

his teeth in the kitchen sink. When he finished, I asked, "What does your schedule look like the rest of the week? I have today off and then work Wednesday through Saturday with Sunday and Monday off. Followed by another set of twenty-four-hour shifts."

"Meetings," Conner replied.

"Even on the weekend?" I asked incredulously, earning me a laugh.

"No, not the weekends. Most of the department heads at LACH work Monday through Friday. They would not appreciate coming in for a weekend meeting unless it was an emergency," Conner replied.

"We could do a date on Sunday then?" I suggested. It was the only day that had come up between our two schedules that seemed like it was clear.

"Sure, Sunday is open for me. What would you like to do?" Conner asked as he stuffed his dirty clothes and toiletries into the duffle bag and zipped it up.

"See your house in Malibu. I'm assuming you have an ocean view?" I replied.

"I have more than an ocean view. I have a direct pathway down to the beach," Conner revealed.

I gasped. I hadn't expected him to own one of *those* houses. "I just need your address."

"You said you hate driving," Conner replied.

"How else am I supposed to get to Malibu? It doesn't make sense for you to come pick me up just to go back to your house," I said.

"It's your lucky day then, because the hospital has a helicopter pad," Conner responded.

"You're going to pick me up in a helicopter?" I squeaked. I had only been on an airplane a few times in my life and still wasn't sure I was entirely comfortable in them. A helicopter was an entirely different matter. *And they're very dangerous.* In medical school, we had learned about a famous helicopter crash in Boston, and then during my surgical residency I had observed an amputation on a helicopter pilot when things had gone wrong.

"I promise it is very safe. I'm not only licensed, but I'm certified to fly a search and rescue helicopter for the state of California and in the United Kingdom," Conner said.

I whistled, impressed that he was that invested in his flying skills. It also helped me feel marginally better about the idea of Conner flying me in his helicopter.

"Okay, then I will meet you at the helicopter pad at ten a.m., Sunday," I suggested.

"I will be there," Conner said. He gave me a kiss full of passion before reluctantly stepping away. He grabbed his duffle bag. "See you Sunday." Then, he departed.

I shut the door behind him and leaned against it. *Wow.* Taking a deep breath, I realized that we had never actually made breakfast, and I hurried into the kitchen, my stomach rumbling in protest.

Going through the motions of making scrambled eggs, I revisited the past twenty-four hours, marveling at how I had shifted from wanting to take things slow and getting to know Conner to practically dragging him into bed. But I had to admit, being with him felt right, which sounded ridiculous. *Penny would know.* But when I reached for my phone, it told me that it was Tuesday, the middle of the week. *I'll call her later,* I promised myself.

I sat at the dining table, eating my scrambled eggs and drinking a mug of coffee, mulling over what I wanted to do today. My first thought was surfing, but I quickly rejected that since my surfboard was at Abuela's and I didn't want to spend my entire day off driving. Conner had mentioned that his house was in Malibu, and the restaurant we went to was also in Malibu. *A run on the beach?* I mused. The idea was appealing; I could spend time near the ocean and clear my head. Decision made, I polished off my eggs and coffee, then cleaned up.

An hour later, I found myself pulling into Zuma Beach State Park in Malibu. As I had expected, the parking lot was deserted. I parked, then double-checked the contents of my backpack—water, a protein bar, small bag of nuts, and a tiny first aid kit. Smiling, I slid my AirPods into my ears, locked the car, and settled my backpack on my shoulders. Then, I took off at a jog heading north.

Humming to my music, I lost track of the time when eventually the sandy beach ended and made way for rocky cliffs. I chose a large boulder to sit on and checked my watch; I'd been running for about an hour. Munching on mixed nuts, I considered my options. I knew there was a bike path that followed alongside the Pacific Coast Highway, or I could turn around and head south. Opting to head south so I could choose whether to return to my car when I reached the parking lot or to continue on, I took off at a run. The slightly damp sand was compact enough to give me a comfortable running surface with more give than a concrete sidewalk would have.

I noted my car when I barreled past the parking lot. If anything I felt like I had more energy than when I started, which seemed strange. Shaking my head, I pressed onward. In the distance, I could see large houses perched on the edge of a small cliff. One even had a pathway that had been cut into the cliff instead of a sketchy-looking staircase that a few others had had.

It was a gorgeous fall day today with the brilliant blue sky and seventy-degree temperatures. I halted when I reached Paradise Cove and selected a spot on the small beach to sit down. My hands were shaking slightly, and I realized I likely should have eaten my protein bar sooner. Rolling my eyes at myself, I ate the protein bar and took several sips of water. My watch told me I'd gone ten miles and that my car was two miles away.

I was tired, though, and even two more miles seemed a daunting task. *I can walk*, I reminded myself. There was no one I needed to prove anything to. Today was supposed to be enjoyable. Putting the wrapper of my protein bar into my backpack and replacing the water bottle, I rose to my feet and began the two-mile walk back to my car.

I was about halfway around the peninsula and my phone rang.

Tapping the accept call button, I kept my eyes on the shoreline. "Hello?"

"Hey, Kelsey. It's Joel," Joel said.

I sighed, realizing I hadn't spoken to him since before the gala. "Hey, what's up?" I replied casually.

"Do you have any plans next weekend?" Joel asked.

"I love you as my friend Joel, but I—" I stumbled on a rock and almost landed on my knees in the sand.

"I get it. You met someone, right?" Joel inquired.

"I did meet someone, but I also am walking on the beach and I tripped on rock," I said.

Joel chuckled. "Sounds about right. As far as you meeting someone, good for you. I hope it works out, and remember we're still friends." He paused, and I could hear another phone ringing. "My supervisor is calling, I gotta go. Don't be a stranger!"

The line clicked, and my music began playing again. Peering around me, I realized the parking lot was just up ahead. As soon as the Pacific Coast Highway merged into I-10, I realized I had misjudged when traffic would start and I was now stuck in afternoon traffic a few miles too far from my apartment. Traffic crept along, and I finally made it into the parking lot for my apartment complex.

Sighing in relief, I pulled into a parking space. As I rode the elevator up to my level, I decided I would splurge tonight and order takeout for dinner. It was either that or going to the grocery store. I didn't feel like eating eggs twice in the same day.

Thirty minutes later, food had been ordered and I was drying off from a shower. Noting that it was already five o'clock, I realized it was close to dinnertime anyhow. I started a load of laundry and then settled on the couch, flipping through the streaming channels to figure out what show was most appealing tonight.

A loud knock on the door—my food was here. I opened the door, eyes widening when I saw Conner holding the bag of my Chinese food and a bag of what looked like groceries. I could see the top of a bundle of celery sticking out.

"What are you doing here?" I asked, opening the door wider and motioning for him to come in.

"I was getting ready to go home and thought I'd stop by. Is that okay?" Conner inquired politely.

I smiled. "Sure. As long as you don't stay too late. I need to sleep tonight."

"Of course," Conner said.

I shut the door behind him and followed him into the kitchen. He placed the bag of Chinese on the dining room table and started unpacking the groceries. Celery, sweet onions, spinach, two packages of chicken breasts, and a top sirloin steak. Combined with the eggs I had left and the dry goods in the pantry, it was enough to feed me for the next week.

"Thank you for the groceries," I said, removing the Chinese from the bag, belatedly realizing that Conner would want to eat and I had only ordered enough for one person.

I heard the fridge open and shut, then Conner walked over to the table with two plates and silverware. "Don't worry, I had a giant lunch. I won't eat much."

I shrugged. "How was your day?" "Filled with meetings—the director of fellowships and residents, head of surgery, and a handbook review session with the entire cardiology department," Conner replied.

I wrinkled my nose as I imagined sitting through those meetings. "Is that all your job is? Meetings?"

Conner chuckled. "It does involve a lot of meetings. But most of them are not lectures. I prefer to have interactive discussions since it allows me to get to know who I'm meeting with and get a sense of how they would behave in their work environment."

I took a plate and opened the box of chicken lo mein, scooping out about half of it onto my plate. Conner might not be hungry, but I was starving. I sat down and watched as Conner put a few forkfuls onto his plate and sat too.

"Let's eat while the food is hot," Conner suggested.

Not needing a second suggestion, I dug in. Even though Conner's plate was empty in a total of three bites, he stayed silent while I ate my fill. I polished off the entire container of chicken lo mein.

"Instead of talking about work, why don't we talk about something else?" Conner asked.

"What do you want to know?" I inquired.

"What places have you traveled to?" Conner asked.

I tapped my fingers on the table in thought. "The week before I started medical school at Johns Hopkins, I went on a trip with Abuela. We went through Washington DC, New York City, and Boston. I also did another foray into Manhattan on my first spring break. Growing up in Santa Barbara, I've traveled up and down the California coast. Honestly, I haven't been very many places. Abuela provided a good home for me, and there wasn't much money for extras. Once I was in college, time was a factor as much as money. What about you?"

Conner patted my hand. "I've been too many places to count. The hospitals I work for are located around the world."

"Fine, then what are two of your favorite places that you've traveled to?" I asked.

"Monaco and Alaska," Conner responded.

I wasn't sure what I had expected, but Alaska was not it. A question bubbled forward before I could stop it. "Why Alaska?"

"The wildlife and the quiet," Conner said.

I stood and collected the plates and silverware, then packed them into the kitchen and proceeded to wash them. Now with a full stomach I could feel how tired I was. I'd spent the past six years on constantly changing sleep cycles and longed for the near future when I would no longer be a student or fellow, but an attending and have a regular work schedule.

"Are you okay?" Conner asked from the kitchen doorway.

I turned around and smiled tiredly at him. "Yes, I'm fine, merely tired."

Conner closed the distance between us and wrapped his arms around me in a hug. I leaned into the embrace, then yawned into his shoulder. "Thank you for the groceries," I said, tipping my face up toward him.

"It was my pleasure. Now, I am going to go, so you can get sleep before your early shift in the morning," Conner said and kissed me lightly on the lips.

I returned the kiss then reluctantly stepped back. "I'll see you Sunday."

"See you Sunday," Conner replied and then departed.

Chapter 30: Kelsey

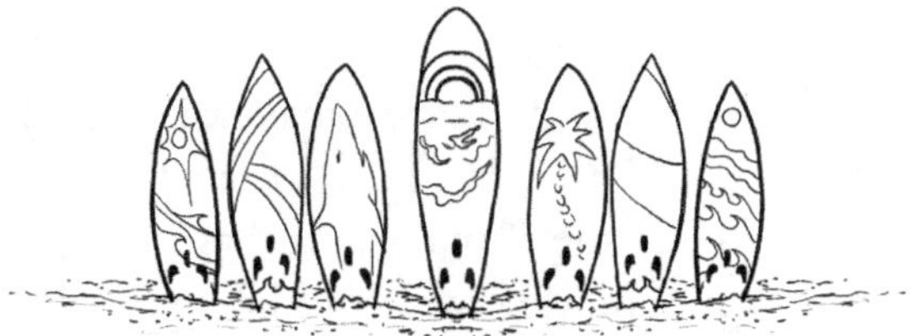

Thursday, November 7

Rumors had started circulating around the hospital about the changes that Dr. Hudson was planning to put into place. I tried to ignore it and focus on my job. From what Conner had told me about his job on our date three nights ago, his agenda was solely focused on ensuring the hospital was being managed properly and meeting the needs of the staff and the patients.

I had read the handbook in its entirety before accepting the fellowship and then read the new one when it was released two weeks ago. The changes were expansive but needed. The hospital had had policies in place that were two to three decades old. LACH was far from the only hospital that had undergone major management revamping in the past five years.

Strolling down the hallway toward the break room, I considered my options for lunch. Conner was still stuck in meetings and our relationship was too new for me to want to interrupt him with an offer of going out to lunch. A few minutes later, I was reaching into my locker for my phone when it started vibrating. Penny's name came up on the screen.

"Penny, is something wrong?" I asked, unable to keep the concern from my voice. It was unusual for her to call me in the middle of her work day.

Penny laughed. "I appreciate that you're worried about me; however, nothing is wrong. In fact … I was hoping you'd be available for lunch."

My eyes widened in surprise. "I'm available, but I don't have a spare four hours lying around today to make the round trip."

"I'm here, silly goose. In Los Angeles. A few blocks away from you, in fact. My boss sent me down here this morning to pick up a piece of lab equipment and told me I could have lunch with a plus one on the company if I desired," Penny replied. I could imagine her smiling on the other end of the phone.

"Yes! I'd love to do lunch. I have two hours today for my break," I replied.

"Perfect. How about I pick you up in ten minutes outside the hospital entrance?" Penny suggested.

I nodded before realizing she couldn't see me. "Sounds great. I'll see you in ten!"

Unable to contain my excitement, I removed my surgical cap and shoved it in the locker, then swapped my doctor's coat for a sweatshirt. I slid my purse out of my backpack, locked the locker, and made my way toward the main entrance.

When I arrived out front, Penny was just pulling up in her silver Toyota minivan. I raced out to meet her and eagerly opened the door, practically throwing myself into her arms. We both were squealing in excitement.

"I can't believe you're here!" I exclaimed.

"I can't believe you answered your phone," Penny said as we hugged tightly.

I'm not sure how long we sat there, but when other vehicles started honking, I released my best friend and put on my seatbelt.

Grinning, I said, "I think we should go before they push your van out of the way."

Penny burst into a fit of giggles but wisely put the van into drive and eased out of the hospital's loading zone.

Fifteen minutes later, we parked near a well-rated Chinese restaurant a few blocks from the hospital. Ronda and a few of the other nurses had told me about this restaurant, but I'd never had a chance to try it, because either I was too busy or the restaurant had an hour wait, and I didn't want to do that when it was only me.

When the waitress took our order, Penny grabbed my hands and smiled knowingly. "So, spill the details."

I blushed. "Conner and I went on two dates and ..." My words trailed off.

"You slept with him," Penny guessed.

I stuck my tongue out at her. "Is it that obvious?"

"Only because of how deep your blush is," Penny replied. I sighed. Penny kept talking. "How were the dates?"

"Amazing. He's easy to talk to, and even though we don't have a lot in common, he is genuinely interested in what I have to say," I explained.

Penny squeezed my hand. "Good for you. You deserve to be happy, Kel."

"Does it sound strange for me to say that I feel a deep connection with him already, almost like it's meant to be? Even saying it out loud makes it seem ridiculous. Who ends up with the guy they have gone out on only three dates with?" I asked.

Penny shrugged. "Love doesn't always have to make sense. Ken and I despised each other for a long time until we had a company team-building event that paired us off and we discovered every-thing we have in common."

"Unfortunately, though, Conner is not just an ordinary man. He's worth billions and is in the media. I have no idea what his family is like, if they'd be willing to accept me," I said uncertainly.

Penny opened her mouth to respond when our food arrived. Instead of diving into her meal, she squeezed my hand. "If you're worried about Conner's family, ask him about them. I doubt you have to worry about Abuela. As long as Conner treats you respect-fully and makes you happy, she will be pleased."

I sighed. Penny was right. I should just ask Conner these questions. "I promise I will ask him about his family the next time I see him."

"Good, now let's eat before our food gets cold!" Penny said and shoved a big forkful of chow mein in her mouth.

Chapter 31: Conner

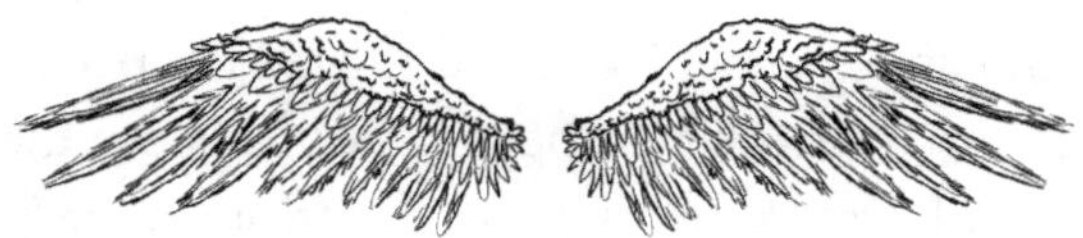

Saturday, November 9

The past three days had been borderline painful to bear without seeing Kelsey. I couldn't determine if it was the Fien bond or something else at work, but the minutes had ticked by excruciatingly slow. Twice, I had picked up the phone to call Fabio and ask him to clear my schedule and Kelsey's, but I had stopped myself. I knew that in order for things to work between Kelsey and me, I was going to have to allow her to have her fellowship and future surgeon position without interfering. She had told me this had been her lifelong dream, and I loved her too much to stand in the way.

The other reason was personal. I had given LACH my word that I would help them resolve the issues I had identified. Voiding our contract would not go over well with the demons, and word would spread throughout the Ash Realm that now that I had ascended, I was no longer the same angel.

I was in the elevator heading down to Kelsey's floor to invite her over to my place for dinner in. I'd flown the helicopter and thought since we both had the day off tomorrow it would be a good opportunity to show her my house.

The elevator door opened and to my surprise, Kelsey stepped in. Her green eyes lit up as she met my gaze.

"Hi," she said.

"Good evening, Dr. Floras," I replied formally as another doctor stepped into the elevator on Kelsey's heels.

Kelsey stood next to me, her hands loosely at her sides. I itched to grab her hand, but decided waiting till the elevator was empty would be better. At the main floor, everyone got out. Kelsey started to leave when I snagged her hand and tugged her back inside.

"My apartment is that way," she said, pointing out the side door.

"I know. But I wanted to ask you a question, *alone*," I replied.

Kelsey's face filled with confusion, then understanding. "I see. What is the question?" she asked as the elevator doors slid shut and we were finally alone.

"Would you like to come over for dinner?" I asked.

"Uh, sure? Would I be able to do laundry? I don't have another set of clean clothes with me," Kelsey said.

I shrugged. "Of course. My whole house is at your disposal."

"Did you drive?" Kelsey asked, eyes traveling to the elevator level indicator that displayed we were now going up.

I shook my head. "Sorry to disappoint you, but I flew the helicopter."

Kelsey swallowed, then gave me a hesitant smile. "I've never been in a helicopter before."

"I promise it's safe. The flight is short, ten minutes at most. Driving on a Saturday night, especially with the holiday festival at the Santa Monica Pier, would be a disaster," I explained.

The elevator reached the sixteenth floor of the hospital and opened, revealing my helicopter sitting on the roof.

"Here we are," I said and took Kelsey's hand in mine. Side by side, we walked over to the helicopter. I tugged open the passenger side door and helped her up into the seat.

"You'll need to put the headset on once you're buckled," I instructed, then shut the door and walked around to my side.

I climbed in and checked Kelsey's buckles and headset before getting myself settled. I glanced over at her, and she was nibbling on her lower lip. "It'll be over before you know it," I reassured her.

Kelsey grimaced and kept her eyes forward. I shrugged and turned on the helicopter. The engine fired up, and the propeller began whirring. I set my hand on the control, and we lifted into the air. I guided the helicopter toward Santa Monica, and we flew over the bumper-to-bumper traffic clogging most of the streets below us.

When we cleared the high-rise buildings and could see the ocean, Kelsey seemed to relax more. We flew past the Santa Monica Pier and out over the ocean. The sun was sinking beneath the water with the last few tendrils of purple and dark magenta trailing through the sky.

"Wow, this is amazing!" Kelsey murmured, sitting forward and peering out of the window.

"Told you," I replied. I could see the lights of the helipad at my house just up ahead. I slowed our speed as we descended, timing the touchdown perfectly.

"That was fast," Kelsey replied, her eyes wide as she took in the cobbled area that I had landed in. "I understand now why you would choose the helicopter over traffic."

I smiled and shut off the helicopter. I wasn't entirely sure what we were doing tomorrow and wanted to keep it here in case Kelsey decided she'd like to fly again. By the time I got to Kelsey's side, she was standing next to the helicopter, her purple backpack over her shoulder.

"Let's go inside," I said and led the way. We left the helipad and followed a gray cobblestone pathway lined with palm trees that had small white lights wrapped around their trunks. The pathway opened up onto one of the balconies overlooking the ocean. Though there was not much light to truly appreciate the view with, I paused, giving Kelsey a chance to look around, then put my hand on the wrought iron handle on a glass door and pulled it open.

Straight ahead was the elite chef-sized kitchen, with medium-stained alder cabinets and black marble counters with veins of warm brown. Everything was oversized, which made it a great space for entertaining, but not terribly practical for an angel who didn't need to eat to survive.

"What do you think?" I inquired.

Kelsey moved ahead of me, walking in a large circle. "It's massive," she replied, though I could tell she was distracted; her eyes lingered on the floors—a mix of dark stained wood and cream travertine stone throughout the house—then traveled across the room.

"What would you like to see or do first?" I asked. I knew what I wanted to do first, but no matter how I felt about Kelsey, we had agreed to take it slow and really get to know each other. Which meant ignoring the Fien bond pulsing under my skin and letting Kelsey take the lead.

She dropped her gaze down to her scrubs and wrinkled her nose. "Change and a shower. Though we'll need to wash my clothes too. Maybe eat and then later we can shower, so the clean clothes won't matter if we're getting in bed."

I couldn't help but chuckle. I pulled her into my arms and gave her a kiss, meeting her gaze and keeping my tone serious. "No one else is here. It's just the two of us. We can do whatever makes you the most comfortable. You are beautiful as you are."

Kelsey blushed, then kissed me back, lightly running her tongue over my lips. I parted them, and she deepened the kiss. Wrapping my arms around her, I held her close, desperate for her to do more than kiss me. *I can be patient*, I chided myself. Closing my eyes, I lost myself in her lips.

I returned to myself when I felt her fingers clumsily unbuttoning my pants. Trying to let her take the lead, I finally took matters into my own hands and undid the button and zipper. Kelsey ran her hands along the edge of my underwear and then tugged, sending my pants and underwear into a heap at my feet. I started to step out of the clothes when she stroked my shaft with her nails. My body responded instantly, my cock hardened more, and I was certain cum was beginning to leak. I inhaled sharply as Kelsey ran her finger over my tip, then brought it up to her lips and sucked on her finger as though it was my cock.

Gently, I tugged Kelsey's pants and underwear off. They pooled at her feet, and she stepped out of them. I followed suit, not wanting to trip. I reached for the hem of her shirt and she lifted her arms over her head. I helped remove her shirt and then unclasped her bra. Her eyes flicked between my cock and my lips as though she was debating what she was doing next. My whole body throbbed with desire. I was about to make a suggestion when Kelsey spoke.

"Where do you want me?"

My eyes lit up at the invitation. I guided Kelsey backward a few steps, and the back of her legs bumped into the sofa. She gave me an inquiring look.

"On the sofa?"

I smirked and shook my head. "Not quite. I want you to brace your arms on the back of the couch, but bend over, so your back is to me."

Kelsey let her hand trail down my chest until her fingers encircled my shaft and she stroked. Wondering if she had changed her mind and had her own idea, I opened my mouth to speak. She kissed me and then released her hand and turned around, facing the couch with her back to me. I stepped close, letting my cock lightly brush her buttocks, and then I shifted so it was between her soaked thighs. Leaning over Kelsey's back, I massaged her breasts with one hand, and with my other hand, I plunged my fingers into her deliciously wet folds.

Expertly, I swirled and flicked, driving her toward her climax and testing my control. Kelsey arched against me, and I could tell she was almost there. I withdrew. Her hands twitched and dropped as though she was considering pleasuring herself. Not wanting to lose my opportunity, I nudged open her legs and slid myself deep inside of her. That was all it took, and I sent her spiraling over. Her body went limp, and I was glad I had suggested bracing against the couch.

Needing to get my own release and careful not to hurt Kelsey, I maintained a steady in-and-out rhythm. Kelsey's channel tightened around me, and I was thrilled that this time I could satisfy both of us. She moaned as I sent us both exploding into our climaxes. I held her tight against me, wanting to savor the feel of being inside of her. I lightly brushed my lips around her shoulder.

"Was that okay?" I asked.

"Mmm," she said.

I kissed her on the cheek and withdrew. I knew she was hungry, and we would have plenty of time to cuddle after I was able to satiate that too.

Chapter 32: Kelsey

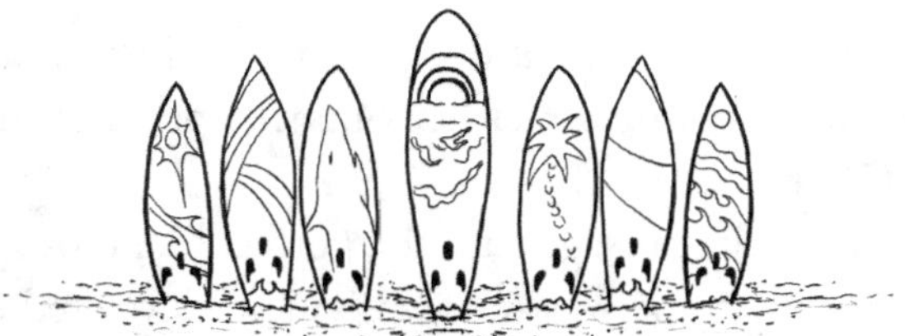

Sunday, November 10

Side by side, Conner and I made breakfast at the huge gas stovetop. I was in charge of the eggs, and Conner was cooking the sausage patties. I was wearing one of his white button-up shirts and a pair of his sister's sweatpants that he'd dug out of his closet from one of her visits. Conner wore a fire-engine-red T-shirt and khaki shorts. I felt strangely at home here in this mansion of a house, cooking with Conner.

"Sausage is done," he declared and turned his burner off, then removed the skillet, dividing the sausage patties evenly between two plates.

"So are the eggs," I replied. Conner held the plates while I split up the eggs and then carried the plates over to the high-top bar. I poured two glasses of orange juice and joined him.

Wanting to make sure I learned more about Conner—who he was, not just how creative he could be about sex—I took a large drink of my orange juice, then dove in.

"I know you've mentioned your sister Charlie. Where does she live? Do you have any other siblings?"

Conner smiled and set his fork down. "Charlie lives in London, though she travels a lot for her work as a model. No, it's just Charlie and me. No other siblings."

Not wanting it to come off as an interrogation, I provided details about myself. "I'm an only child. Though my best friend Penny and I are extremely close, like sisters."

"I believe there are pros and cons to growing up as an only child versus with siblings. Neither one is superior. They're just different." Conner said.

I took a bite of the sausage, and the perfect blend of spices with the barest hint of maple was simply divine. I devoured the whole patty before I could bring myself to ask him another question. "Do your parents live in England too?"

Conner nodded. "Yes. My family has lived there for generations. Though everyone except my mother travels extensively for work."

I wanted to ask why his father wasn't retired yet. Clearly, the family had money and didn't need to work for a living. But I felt like that was a question for when we knew each other better—or perhaps for his father himself.

"What about you? Did you grow up in Santa Barbara?" Conner asked.

I smiled. "Yes, I was born and raised there. Abuela was born in Colombia and immigrated when she was sixteen with her mother."

We fell into a comfortable silence, both eating our eggs and sausage until our plates were empty.

"Do you get along with your family?" I assumed he did with his sister the way he'd spoken of her, but I couldn't get a sense for his relationship with his parents.

Conner grimaced. "My father and I are usually at odds. My mother says we're too similar, but I'm not sure I believe her. He's what I've heard people refer to as 'old school' and has tried to mold me since I was young so I'll follow directly in his footsteps. I wouldn't describe what I've done as outright rebelling, but I'm definitely putting my own unique touch to the path I've carved for myself."

"I see," I replied. I'd seen Lane struggle with his parents' wishes for him and wanting to follow his heart, so I understood a little bit, though I couldn't relate. Abuela had always supported my dream, encouraging me at times to challenge myself even more, and frequently saying that no dream was too big for me to accomplish if I set my mind to it.

"What would you like to do today?" Conner inquired.

I collected our plates and put them in the dishwasher, then added the two skillets after rinsing them off, using the time to think about what options we had. "I don't think we saw the whole house last night," I responded.

Conner laughed. "You're right. We saw very few parts of the house, but I did have a wonderful night."

The exact details of the whole evening were fuzzy. Together, we'd finished two bottles of wine. I blushed, remembering how we'd started the evening with sex before dinner and ended it hours later in the bedroom.

"I suppose a tour is in order then," I said eagerly.

"I have a movie theater," Conner said.

My eyes widened in surprise. "No way!"

"Yes, I do. Is there a movie you've been wanting to see? The studios often send me whatever is upcoming six months before it releases, hoping to get a flowery review. Typically I'm too busy to watch them," Conner explained.

I could barely contain my excitement. There had been a few movies this year I'd wanted to see, but I'd been too busy. Now Conner was saying he had his own personal movie theater. Though I knew we could be having a conversation and continuing to learn more about each other, snuggling up for a good movie was just as appealing.

"A movie would be great. Lead the way, sir," I said with a smile and a bow.

Chapter 33: Conner

Monday, November 18

The last week had gone by in a blur. I couldn't remember a time in my life when I had been this happy, ever. I sat at table for two in a small coffee shop waiting for Agatha and found that every time I tried to stop smiling, it just kept creeping back onto my face. I took a sip of my coffee and finally spotted Agatha as she opened the door.

"Sorry, traffic was terrible," Agatha apologized and took the seat across from me. She added sugar to her coffee and then took a sip, gazing at me over the rim. "You're different."

I shrugged. "Maybe."

"I'm being serious, Conner. You look happy," Agatha said. "I take it things are going well with Kelsey."

I nodded. "Yes, that's why I wanted to talk to you. I need advice."

Agatha laughed and almost spit her coffee out. It took a few moments before she got ahold of herself. "Sorry. I don't recall you ever admitting that you need advice. I know you give people advice all the time, but asking for it … that's a new development."

I wrinkled my nose. "You can tease me all you want. But I'm serious."

"Fine, fine. What kind of advice do you need?" Agatha asked.

"I'm certain now that I have a Fien bond with Kelsey," I said, keeping my voice low. "Cassiel warned me about waiting too long to explain things to her. But I'm not sure how to tell her."

"Oh, you're going to tell her you're immortal!" Agatha gasped.

"Hush," I growled. I didn't want anyone to overhear us and was starting to regret meeting at a coffee shop instead of at my house.

"Sorry," she apologized. "I would take her someplace private, so likely your house since you won't be overheard by anyone who shouldn't be listening. Then, tell her—or better yet, show her. If things are going as well between the two of you as you're saying, then she must feel some twinges from the Fien bond by now."

I sighed. She was right. "You don't think I'll scare her off?"

Agatha laughed. "No. Otherwise you wouldn't be sitting here telling me this. You've spent the past few weeks getting to know each other. She knows about your work and how much money you have—"

"At some point, the media is going to catch wind of our relationship too," I muttered.

"I think the most critical topic hanging over the two of you is your immortality, followed by the Fien bond. If she can accept those two things, the rest will be simple." Agatha paused. "I have a different idea, but you might need to pull some strings to make it work."

"What is your idea?" I demanded.

"Take her home," Agatha said.

"Which home?"

"To your country estate. Let her see who you are when you're in *your* element. She could also meet your family," Agatha suggested.

I sighed, trying to digest Agatha's suggestions. "Kelsey has made it clear that she doesn't want me to interfere with her fellowship. She traded the typical paid holidays to have a three-week break in September and doesn't have any paid time off to use for the duration of her fellowship." I was also worried about overloading Kelsey with too many things at once. *Though I suppose if she can accept that I'm an angel, the introductions to my family would be less complicated. We could be honest about who we are.*

"The good news is that I have a solution for that particular problem. The new fellow who is supposed to start December first has asked to start before Thanksgiving," Agatha replied.

"How do you know that?" I demanded.

"Fabio. Without him, I don't know where you would be. He is a godsend. I hope you tell him how much you appreciate him on a regular basis," Agatha replied.

I should have known Fabio would have given Agatha the information. Fabio wanted to see things work out between me and Kelsey *and* had access to the hospital computer system. "Okay, so the new fellow wants to start early. If I'm understanding correctly, you want me to take Kelsey to my country estate for Thanksgiving?"

Agatha nodded. "Yes! You already know she doesn't have Thanksgiving plans since she was slated to work that week. There is no reason to be concerned about ruining her family plans. It's just a matter of convincing her to go with you."

Without pissing her off about manipulating her schedule. I wondered if Fabio might have an idea about that too. *Perhaps her boss could give her the time off.* If the schedule change wasn't handed out by me directly, I could hopefully avoid Kelsey's anger.

"It could work. I'll have to think about it before I broach the topic with Kelsey," I said. Agatha did have a very important aspect going for her suggestions—taking Kelsey to my country estate meant we would be alone. If she got angry at me, then we could handle that in private. Or if she had lots of questions. A whole week to sort through everything.

"Now, assuming your week goes well," Agatha said. I made a face, but she kept going. "It would likely be helpful to consider your professional statuses and how you want to make that work at LACH. Keep it secret, have it out in the open ... what the pros and cons of each option are. Any negative effects will likely be felt by Kelsey and not *you.*"

I frowned. "I get your point, Agatha, but at this time it's hard to see past the week at my estate, *if* she says yes. Baby steps are all I can manage right now."

"Fair point," Agatha said, then her phone vibrated. She glanced at it. "I need to go. They bumped up the timeline for the shoot today, so I need to head back to the studio."

I stood up and we embraced. "Have fun," I said with a smile.

"I usually do," Agatha replied, then collected her purse and departed.

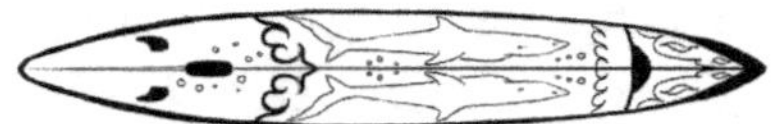

I was in the large conference room on the board of directors floor with Azinak going over final details for the new security system. Though the sun had been out this morning, the sky out of the large windows was full of dark gray clouds. So far it had only been drizzling, but I expected it to do more than that just in time for five o'clock traffic.

The end of the table we were standing at was actually a large screen that was under the glass of the table, but we were able to draw on it. Currently, we had the schematic of the main level on the screen. We had started at the bottom level, basement level three, and were working our way up. The main level was the only floor with exterior access doors.

"There will be security guards patrolling the exterior exits. As you know my original plan was to have them permanently stationed, but that will have to be added to the budget for next year. A patrol should be sufficient, definitely a major upgrade to what you currently have—subpar cameras and no guards except at the patient entrances," I said, pointing to the blue dots on the schematic that showed the guard patrol route and the larger blue circles for where the permanently stationed guards were. Green dots represented the security cameras and red dots, badge swipe stations. We had doubled the number of locations badges would have to be swiped to get through.

"Okay, so the Monday after Thanksgiving, the new cameras will go online, more badge swipe stations, and the additional security guards will start, correct?" Azinak asked, looking up at me.

I shook my head. "Almost. Each point where a new badge swipe will have to occur requires us to install the doors and partition. By that Monday, basement level three through level one will be installed and can be activated."

"That's not even twenty percent of the building," Azinak growled.

I stood up straight and met his gaze. "I am aware. I sent you a memo a week ago telling you that there was a delay at the supplier with the new doors. The plan was to replace the existing doors *and* add new ones. They are all bulletproof and custom."

"That's what magic is for," Azinak said harshly.

I clenched my fists and then released them. Yelling at Azinak was not going to accomplish anything. "You know very well that there are some things magic can't do. We also have humans who audit LACH. What would they say if we didn't have a way to account for the shiny new doors and security system?"

Azinak didn't reply; instead, he turned away and walked over to the windows. "I'm sorry. The whole board is breathing down my neck about the new security measures. They're scared after what happened in Dublin. Humans and immortals, everyone thinks they're next. It's not only our hospital, but also hospitals across the world. Probably why there are supply issues too."

His words were true. About half of the other hospitals I dealt with had placed orders to upgrade all of their existing doors and interior windows to bulletproof glass. The only difference was that I did not have a direct hand in those upgrades. I would have recommended them if they had asked, though.

"Apology accepted. Would you like to continue our review?" I asked, hoping Azinak had collected himself and would be willing to wrap this up. I was hoping to catch Kelsey on her next break in a few hours. She was halfway through the second day of back-to-back twenty-four-hour shifts.

Chapter 34: Kelsey

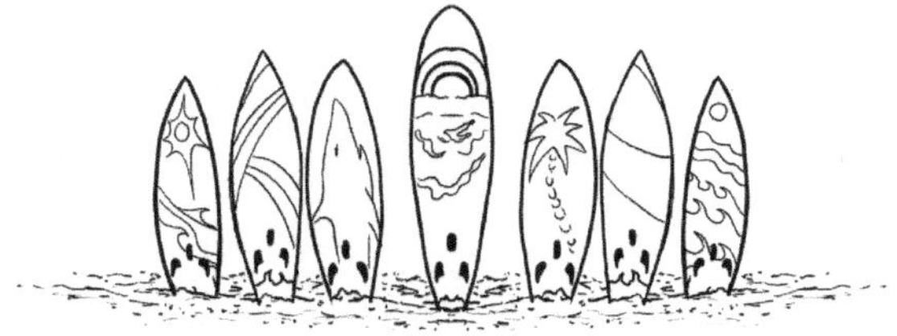

Thursday, November 21

I was just placing the last suture in a broken leg repair. We had had to place a titanium plate with three screws to hold the two pieces of bone together. One of the things I loved the most about LACH was all the surgeons I worked with were not only specialists in a particular type of medicine, but specifically in pediatrics. In orthopedics, the age of the patient made a significant difference to what options were feasible. A seventy-year-old man with a broken femur presented vastly different challenges than a six-year-old girl.

I snipped off the wire and gave Dr. Sinclair the thumbs-up. He nodded and examined my sutures, then declared our work done.

"Good work, Dr. Floras," he said.

"Thank you, Dr. Sinclair, for the opportunity," I said politely.

"If only all the fellows were like you," Dr. Sinclair said.

I gave him a confused look, but with my surgical mask still in place, I'm not sure he noticed. We walked out of the room, taking off our gowns and disposing of them.

"There are a few upcoming surgeries going into winter break on my schedule. I'd like you to assist on them. Tendon and ACL tears, one is a possible meniscus. All the high school students try to get scheduled over their winter break to miss as little school as possible," he explained.

"I'm available whenever you need me," I replied.

"Great! Have a good day," Dr. Sinclair said, then walked away.

Taking a deep breath, I headed to the staff room. I had an hour for lunch. *Not long enough to see Conner.* It amazed me that I had put Joel off, saying I wanted to wait until after my fellowship, but now that I was dating Conner, it didn't feel like I was too busy. He just *fit* into my life. It was weird. I had never expected to have anyone who didn't mind the crazy hours and actually understood why I did what I did, through the highs and the lows.

An envelope was taped to the outside of my locker. I recognized Conner's writing immediately. Curious, I pulled the envelope off and removed the note.

Come up to my office when you're on break. Promise I won't make you late. -C

I wondered how he expected me to get into his office when I didn't have clearance without his badge. I realized there was something else in the envelope. Sure, enough a visitor's badge was inside. I shook my head, wondering what Conner was up to. Shoving the badge into my pocket, I took a swig of water from the bottle in my locker and then locked it and headed to the elevator.

The first elevator was too full for me to fit, which suited me just fine. The next one was surprisingly empty, and no one else from our floor had shown up. I stepped inside and swiped the badge. The elevator closed; I could hear the pulleys working as it carried me up to the top floor. I was planning to talk to him tonight over dinner about my plans for next week. A new fellow had requested to start early, and Dr. Pierce had agreed and was giving me the whole week off. I had spent the morning debating and decided I wanted to see if Conner wanted to spend Thanksgiving in Santa Barbara and officially meet Abuela. We'd also be able to surf as much as we wanted to.

The elevator dinged and then opened. Today, there was a receptionist at the front desk. She gave me a polite wave and then returned her gaze to her computer. *Either she was expecting me or doesn't care who shows up.* The latter seemed strange given the floor was reserved for the board of directors. There was no doubt that I, in my purple scrubs, did not belong here.

Conner's office door was ajar, so I went in. He was sitting at his desk on the phone. My heart fluttered in my chest as I took him in. His short-cropped red hair with just a hint of gray at the temples, clean-shaven face, strong jaw. He was wearing a light gray suit and a black shirt with a black tie. I had discovered when he was working, he always wore tailored suits and a tie. *I suppose a man doesn't have many options for what is considered business formal. A woman could wear a suit or a dress.*

Butterflies fluttered in my stomach. I wanted to kiss him but was afraid to disrupt his phone call. Conner caught my gaze and hooked his finger. I went over to him, and he hung up the phone.

"How was your surgery?" he asked, gazing at me from his chair.

I moistened my lips with the tip of my tongue, finding myself lost in his eyes and at a loss for words.

Conner chuckled and pushed his chair back and stood up. He kissed me, and I melted into him, wanting more.

I lost track of time as we kissed. Eventually Conner stopped to catch his breath. "You only have a short break," he teased.

I frowned at the reminder. *Maybe we shouldn't have kissed. It usually leads to things I don't have time for right now.* Except with Conner I found it difficult to turn off the desire until it was satisfied.

"I got your note. Here I am," I said, moving over to the couch.

"Yes, here you are," Conner said with a smile.

"I'll let you go first, since you wrote the note," I offered.

"What would you think about going with me to England next week?" Conner asked.

I gasped in surprise. Of all the things I anticipated he would ask me up here to say—*or do*—traveling out of the country was not one of them.

Blurting out the first thing that came to mind, I said, "I don't have a passport."

Conner shrugged. "I have the paperwork on my desk and can have a passport for you in twenty-four hours."

"A *real* passport?" I asked, wondering how on earth he could get one that fast. The last time I'd investigated getting one, I was told eight to twelve weeks.

"Yes, a real passport. I assure you I have no interest in getting mixed up in illegal activities. Everything I do is aboveboard," Conner said matter-of-factly.

I felt bad. "Sorry. I am not used to things like that being fast." *Another thing I'll have to get used to if Conner and I continue dating.* The gala felt like ages ago even though it had been barely over three weeks. It was still hard to believe that a I was falling in love with a billionaire, who was turning out to be just a man. Even after confessing my feelings to Penny, it felt surreal.

"Don't worry about it," he said smoothly. "Now that we have the issue of a passport out of the way, what do you think about my idea?"

Taking Conner to visit Abuela in Santa Barbara—a two-hour drive—was entirely different from flying six thousand miles to his country estate. To a country I'd never been to, nor did I know anyone there.

"Will I meet your family?" I asked, not sure if his response would be a deciding factor or not. Though we'd spoken about them and I knew that his parents and sister primarily resided in England, meeting them had never come up.

Conner's eyes widened. "Do you want to meet my family?"

I smoothed the front of my shirt, considering his question. "I was going to ask if you wanted to spend Thanksgiving at Abuela's." I knew it wasn't a direct answer, but I hadn't considered meeting his parents—at least not in the short term. From our time together, I had gotten the feeling that he didn't get along with his father, he hardly ever mentioned his mother, and his sister was always busy.

"I would love to meet Abuela, but Santa Barbara is only two hours away. We could do that on any of your days off. England isn't great for a short trip, certainly not doable in a day. You'd said you don't have any other time off before your fellowship ends, so I thought next week would be a great time to go. It's up to you though. I'd be happy to go with you to Abuela's for Thanksgiving," Conner replied.

He had a valid point; even a direct flight to London would take at least ten hours, and that was one way. Since I hardly ever was home for the holidays, I hadn't considered asking Conner about anything holiday related. *I don't even know his religion.* Redirecting my thoughts to an important concern about the trip, it wasn't just a matter of me going to England. *Do I want to spend a week with Conner?*

With my heavy work schedule, the longest time we'd had together was thirty-six hours, unless you counted when we first met, but even that was not continuous. No matter how much time we spent with each other, I always felt like it wasn't enough. I had more to tell him. *More I want to do.* I blushed. The theme was the same. I wanted more time. Now, Conner was offering precisely what I'd been longing for: uninterrupted time together. *I guess if we can survive a week together, then maybe it really is meant to be.*

"Kelsey?" Conner prompted me.

"Hmm?" I murmured, then realized I must have been lost in my thoughts for more than a few moments. "Sorry, I was thinking."

Conner chuckled. "I noticed."

I shrugged. I didn't want to give him an answer that wasn't how I really felt. "Yes, I would love to go with you to England for the week."

"Perfect!" Conner said, grinning. He closed the gap and pulled me into his arms for a passionate kiss.

My phone buzzed. I had set an alarm to ensure I wouldn't be late returning for my shift. "I need to go."

Conner sighed and released me. "I'm sorry you didn't have time to eat."

I shrugged. It wasn't the first time I'd missed a chance to eat a full meal while working at a hospital. "I have a stash of protein bars for a reason. I'll be fine, promise." I headed to the door, then looked back at him. "When are we leaving?"

"Tomorrow at five p.m. We'll arrive in London around lunchtime. Ideally, we will eat dinner, sleep, and then eat brunch once we get to our destination. I've found it's the best way to quickly recover from jet lag," Conner explained.

I nodded and left as my phone buzzed again in warning. I dashed toward the elevator and impatiently waited for it. My shift ended tomorrow at two p.m. I was certain Conner knew that, but it still seemed like it was cutting it close to make a five p.m. international flight. Then it dawned on me. He had mentioned having a private jet before. I imagined the airport protocols for private flights were significantly different—*and less crowded*—than if we were flying through a main LAX terminal. I was certain I would be ready to go to sleep once we got on. I had a two-hour break from six to eight p.m., which is when Conner and I were getting dinner tonight, and then I would be working in the emergency room from eight p.m. until I got off tomorrow.

Conner drove us to the airport in his Audi SUV. I'd been expecting us to fly out of LAX and was surprised when we pulled up at a gated entrance to Santa Monica Airport instead.

"A regional airport can handle international flights?" I asked after Conner had identified himself to the gate guard.

Conner smiled. "Yes, or at least some of them can. We have a hangar here at Santa Monica Airport. We can store both private jets and the helicopter here. It's convenient to my house, LACH, and the building Hudson International bought last month in downtown."

I swallowed. His explanation made sense, but I was still trying to wrap my mind around how much money he actually had. *Not that we've compared bank accounts or anything.* But I wasn't stupid. I had ballpark ideas of how much a Malibu house cost and the fancy cars he drove. Yet he seemed almost indifferent at times, like it really wasn't that big of a deal. *Maybe it's not.*

"Are you okay?" he asked, giving my hand a reassuring squeeze as we pulled through the gate. He drove over to a hangar that had a gigantic sign saying *Hudson International* over the top of it. The smaller of two private jets was sitting on the tarmac outside of the open hangar doors.

"Yes," I squeaked. Then I blushed, knowing I didn't sound very convincing.

"You'll be fine, I promise. This is way smoother than the helicopter ride, and you handled that with grace," Conner replied. He put the car in park and gave me a quick kiss.

The trunk popped open, and Fabio walked over from a desk toward the back of the hangar and said cheerily, "Good evening!"

I hopped out of the car fully intending to take my suitcase from Fabio when Conner captured my hand and tucked it under his arm. I leaned into him as we gazed at the plane. Fabio wheeled my suitcase away and handed it off to someone at the top of the plane steps.

"I promise I won't let anything happen to you, Kelsey."

I peered up at him. "Thank you ... I ...." I snapped my mouth shut, realizing that I'd almost uttered "I love you." Terrified of what Conner would do if I said those three words right now, I hoped he hadn't noticed.

"Yes?" he prompted.

I wrinkled my nose. *Nothing gets past him.* "I ... can't wait to see the inside of the plane."

"Then what are you waiting for? Let's go check it out," Conner replied. Lowering his arm from my shoulders and taking my hand in his, he led me to the plane. We had to go single file, so he motioned for me to ascend the steps first.

Pressing my lips together, I made my way up the stairs, noting the Gulfstream G650ER label on the inside of the door. My legs were shaking, and I really hoped Conner wouldn't ask about it. Planes didn't make me nervous, so I had no idea why I was shaking. I stepped through the doorway and made it two more steps before I halted, jaw dropping in shock.

To my right were four pairs of black leather executive seats with the Hudson International logo embroidered on them in white and white contrast piping. There was a remote in each seat, though I didn't see any screens, so I wasn't sure what it was for. About halfway down the length of the plane was a padded leather wall divider with a walnut door in the middle of it.

A flight attendant with dark brown hair pulled back in a severe bun appeared from the left. "I'm Diane. Is there anything I can help you with?"

I shook my head and scooted out of Conner's way.

Diane gave Conner a warm smile. "Dinner is almost ready, I'll serve you after we're in the air. Is there anything you need until then?"

Conner shook his head. "No thanks. Is the suite prepared?"

"Of course," Diane replied.

Conner headed down the aisle toward me. "Is there a particular seat you want?"

"Is anyone else coming with us?" I asked.

"Nope, it's just us, Diane, and the two pilots. Diane is also a licensed pilot, as am I, if there was any reason we needed to swap," Conner replied.

I gazed at the identical eight executive chairs. "What's in this room?" I asked, unable to contain my curiosity any longer.

"You can open the door," Conner responded.

I turned around and opened the walnut door. The lights turned on as I stepped through, revealing a queen-size bed, a small chest of drawers, and a bathroom with a shower. "A regular-sized bed?"

Conner chuckled. "You said when we discussed the trip you'd be tired. When I fly back to London, I typically sleep on the way there too."

"But it's a real bed … in a plane," I repeated.

"Yes. Would you like to test it out?" Conner asked.

Our gazes locked. I took a step toward him, and then my stomach made the loudest noise ever. I burst out laughing, and Conner followed suit.

When he caught his breath, he said, "I'll take that as 'food first.'"

"Yes, but sleep would be great after food," I replied.

"It's a plan," Conner replied. Then, he sat in the seat closest to the bedroom on the window side.

I slid into the chair next to him. Just as I had expected, it was insanely comfortable, and the leather was buttery to the touch. The door we entered through shut with a loud thump, then a few moments later the plane started moving. Glancing out of Conner's window, I caught sight of the lights blinking on the runway. Then, the engines started revving.

"We can leave just like that?"

"The pilots have clearance from the tower. Another reason to fly out of this airport is it's not as busy and it's fairly quick to depart," Conner explained.

Less than twenty minutes later we were in the air and Diane was serving our dinner: petite filet mignon with parmesan asparagus and smashed sweet potatoes. She poured us both glasses of cabernet. Wanting to be polite, I finished my glass but declined a refill.

Yawning, I peered over my shoulder at the walnut door. "The bed is calling my name," I told Conner, trying and failing to stifle another yawn.

"Then let's heed its call," he replied.

I led the way to the bedroom. Once the door was shut and

locked, I stripped down to my bra and underwear and climbed into the bed. Conner folded my clothes and then removed his own except for his boxers and slid under the sheets. He wrapped his arms around me, and I fell asleep.

Chapter 35: Conner

Sunday, November 24

Pressing my foot on the accelerator of the bright blue Aston Martin Valkyrie AMR Pro, I blasted into the straight section of my track at a blistering two hundred miles per hour, tapping the brakes at the precise moment to ease into the first turn. I had woken up early, a combination of not needing much sleep and stressing out over the impending conversation with Kelsey about my real identity and the Fien bond. I also didn't want to prevent Kelsey from getting the rest she needed to quickly get onto the correct time schedule. I opted to go for a drive.

Driving the Valkyrie took extreme focus, which was why I had chosen it: to momentarily block out the thoughts that had been eating at me since we left Los Angeles. Particularly that the Fien bond was strengthening, and I was in love with Kelsey—and I was scared to tell her either thing.

Twenty laps later, I was ready to face Kelsey and whatever the day with her would bring. Pulling into the garage, I was certain I needed new tires, *again*. One of the trade-offs of owning such an extreme car that was rival only to a real F1 racecar was that every time I took it on the track, I'd go through a set of tires. Carefully extracting myself, which was a chore given how tight the space was in the Valkyrie, I glanced at the stack of new tires. *I'll need to order more*. There was only one set left. If I was home for a whole week alone, I would have been upset not having more tires, but with Kelsey here, I wasn't likely to take this car out on the track again. Too many things could go wrong, and until we'd had the conversation about my immortality, I didn't want her to stress about how dangerous this car was.

I planned to see if she wanted to go for a drive on the track—nothing like sharing a hobby I was passionate about with my girlfriend—but I was going to choose a much more comfortable car. Two options sat in the garage: a dark gray Aston Martin Vantage, and a bright red McLaren GTS.

My phone vibrated in my pocket. I pulled off the helmet and set it on the rack, then answered the phone. "Hello?"

"Kelsey is awake," Fabio announced. He'd arrived this morning, using his magic to travel to the estate.

"Good timing. I just got done," I replied.

"Yes, I am aware. I can see the track on the cameras, remember?" Fabio said.

"Right. The cameras. Is Kelsey hungry?" I asked, regretting my choice to come out here to drive and leaving my girlfriend in a strange house with people she didn't know.

"I have everything handled. Head over here when you're done," Fabio reassured me.

I sighed. "Thanks." The line went silent. I ran my hand over my face. Usually, I took a shower here before returning to the house, but I was reluctant to spend that much time here. *I'm not being a very good host.* Part of that, I had to admit, was due to not being used to having guests with me. Here, I was able to do whatever I pleased. *Kelsey wasn't the one who called*, I reminded myself, which meant she wasn't concerned about where I was. Fabio was just getting ahead of the situation.

I peeled off the tracksuit and dumped it in the laundry basket. My T-shirt and shorts clung damply to me. I wrinkled my nose in distaste and locked up the garage. Not wanting to waste any more time than necessary, I took off at a run toward the main house. The slight breeze helped alleviate the feeling of the damp clothes against my skin enough to make it bearable.

Fabio opened the door as I reached for it. "She's upstairs."

"Thanks," I said and took the stairs two at a time.

I could hear the shower running as I entered the bedroom.

"Hello!" I called.

"In here!" came a muffled reply.

Quickly removing my shoes, followed by my clothing, I went into the bathroom.

"Want company?" I asked.

"Of course," Kelsey said with a sly smile.

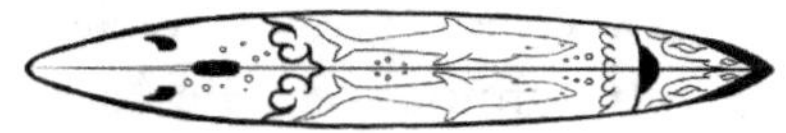

After our shower and two mugs of coffee, I was ready to go back outside. Kelsey and I were sitting at a large wooden table in the empty kitchen.

"Would you like to go on a tour?" I suggested.

"Sure," Kelsey responded, smiling. "I feel way more normal this morning than I did yesterday. You were right about how sleeping on the plane and having yesterday be 'normal' would help me adjust to the time difference."

"Excellent. I was thinking we would just walk. Is that okay? My hope is once I show you around, you'll be able to find your way without too much trouble. I know how much you love running in the mornings," I explained.

"Sounds great," Kelsey replied.

I collected our coffee mugs and stuck them in the sink. Then, I snagged two sweatshirts off the hook by the back door and stepped outside. I offered Kelsey the burgundy Cambridge University sweatshirt, and I pulled on the heather-gray Nike one. I wasn't cold, but it was good to keep up appearances—at least for the moment.

We headed out of the grounds immediately around the house,

through the wrought iron gate in the redbrick wall, then turned to the right. There was a winter garden and a spring garden, but neither had much to look at right now. The two gardens made way to the small fruit orchard. There was a field between the orchard and the woods.

Kelsey was quiet until we reached the woods, taking everything in. "This is all yours?"

I nodded. "Yes. I have forty acres. Most of it is woods."

"It's incredible!" Kelsey gasped.

I smiled, and we walked in silence, the sunlight filtering through the trees. On the track, I had promised myself I would talk to Kelsey today. *Now,* I ordered. Except it was far more difficult to convince myself to reveal my true nature to Kelsey than I anticipated. Glancing to the right, I saw a fallen tree that hadn't been cleared yet.

"There's something I want to talk to you about," I started. "You should sit."

Kelsey spotted the fallen tree and sat down, her face upturned toward me. Her hair was trying to fight its way out of the braid. I wanted to fix it, but knew it was a delaying tactic.

"What did you want to discuss?" Kelsey asked calmly.

"There is no simple way to tell you this," I began. I watched Kelsey's face change from happy to withdrawn, as though she were anticipating a breakup.

I took a deep breath. "The first thing I want to say is, I love you, Kelsey. No matter what you think of my next words, I want you to know that I love you."

"I love you too," Kelsey whispered. I could tell she wanted to get up but didn't.

Deciding the best way to explain to her would be to show her, I released the hold on my true form. I flexed my wings, making the feathers rustle.

Kelsey stood up. "Is this a trick?" she demanded.

I shook my head and took a step toward her. She stepped back, and her legs hit the log.

"No, it's not a trick. I am an angel—an immortal being."

"Angels aren't real," Kelsey said, her voice shaky.

"I assure you, I am very real. Feel free to come closer and touch my wings if you'd like," I replied. *She didn't run screaming*, I told myself, though she wasn't accepting my words yet either. I had hoped that she would be amenable to me.

"What does it mean to be an angel?" Kelsey asked.

I considered the question, debating how much to tell her now and what to hold back for another discussion. "I'm immortal and have some magic abilities. I can heal myself, I can use my wings like a shield, and I can fly."

Kelsey swallowed. "Say I believe you. If you can fly and essentially do whatever you want, why are you a billionaire who manages hospitals?"

"Because most of the hospitals that serve humans are run by demons, and my job is to ensure that they are managing the hospitals in an appropriate manner and not, for example, using the hospital as a feeding ground," I replied matter-of-factly.

"Feeding ground?" Kelsey squeaked, then shook her head when I opened my mouth. "No, please don't tell me. I don't actually want to know. Let me get this straight—you can't die and demons run the hospital I work for?"

I covered my mouth to stifle my chuckle. She was smart, I had to give her that. "Yes. You can ask me anything. I will answer your questions. I was being honest when I told you I love you, Kelsey."

Her lips pressed into a thin line, and she sat straddling the log. "I might have told you I love you in return, but right now I don't know what I think."

"I understand. I am not trying to pressure you into anything. If you want to leave, you can leave. The jet is fueled and ready at the airport, or if you want to fly on a commercial plane, Fabio has a ticket for tomorrow morning you can use," I said smoothly. The last thing I wanted was to force her, or make Kelsey feel compelled to stay in England if she was no longer comfortable being around me.

"Look, Conner, I might have questions, but right now I need to process what you told me. The best way for me to do that is to run, *alone*. Can you give me a few hours to myself?" Kelsey said.

"Of course. You can have as much time as you need." I took a deep breath and flapped my wings twice, lifting me off the ground about five feet, and then I used my magic to transport myself into the house.

Chapter 36: Kelsey

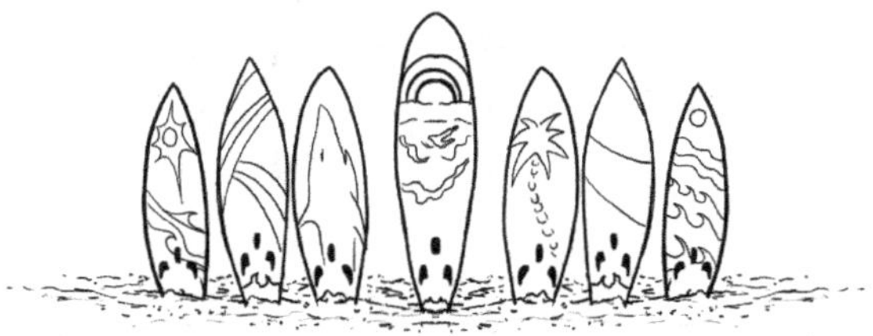

Sunday, November 24

As soon as Conner disappeared, I slid off the log so it was at my back and curled into a tight ball, hot tears streaming down my cheeks. Of all the possible things Conner could have told me on this trip, this truth had me reeling. *An immortal?* It was difficult not to believe him, especially after he demonstrated that he could fly and disappear. Except if he was immortal, then everything I'd ever believed was wrong, and that was what I was struggling with the most.

Angels and demons are real. If I ever tell anyone, they'll likely check me into an insane asylum, I realized. I pulled the sweatshirt hood up and wrapped my arms tightly around my legs. When Conner had started our so-called discussion by telling me he loved me, it had caught me off guard. However, him dumping me after he'd gone to all the trouble of acquiring a passport and bringing me to his estate didn't fit either. I ran his words over in my head. He mentioned he could shield. Closing my eyes, the last hole in my memory of the accident revealed itself.

The massive red dually was barreling toward us, and a few

seconds before impact, Conner wrapped his arms and shimmering white wings around both of us, creating a protective shell. When I came to, he was outside of the Prius shouting through the open window that help was on the way.

I opened my eyes, throat tight. *Conner saved my life.* Even though part of me was still angry with him for leaving after the accident, the knowledge that he had saved me, and likely risked that I would discover his secret when my memories returned, mostly left me with more questions. *Why did he leave after saving me? Did he know the person—or immortal—driving the truck?*

Wiping the tears from my face, I used the log to leverage myself to standing. Using running to think through things was exactly what I needed. Checking my shoelaces and confirming they were still double-knotted, I took off at a jog, weaving through the trees. The ground was not completely flat, and I welcomed the challenge.

Two hours later, I ran up the driveway to the front door. Conner opened it as though he'd been waiting. *Or watching?* A shiver rippled down my spine. My feelings were still mixed when it came to Conner, and the only way I would resolve that would be to ask him questions.

"Would you like to talk?" he asked, keeping his distance as I stepped through the door. I noted his wings were hidden again. He looked like the red-haired British billionaire I'd fallen in love with.

"Yes. I have questions," I confirmed, following him into the library with its worn green suede couch and endless shelves of books.

"As I stated earlier, I will answer any questions you have," Conner replied.

He gestured for me to sit and poured two glasses of scotch, setting them on the coffee table in front of the couch and chair. I sat on the couch and Conner sat on the chair, his expression solemn.

I almost felt bad for him, except he'd put himself in this position by telling me the truth. "I can ask anything?" Conner nodded. I blew out my breath, then spoke. "I got my last memory back from the accident. You shielded me with your wings moments before the truck ran into us."

"Yes, that is correct. I shielded you," Conner said, his voice soft.

"If you made the effort to save me, why did you leave?" I asked, my tone sharp.

Conner ran his hand over his face, then set it in his lap. "Because I was protecting you."

"By leaving?" I said incredulously.

"Yes. Let me explain, please," Conner replied. I picked up the scotch and took a sip, waiting for him to speak. "I've told you a few times that my father and I are not on the best terms. Earlier that day, if you recall, I had an unexpected visitor and had to step outside of the beach house. The visitor was my father's third-in-command, Octavio, ordering me to return to Los Angeles immediately. The order came with an implied threat that if I didn't comply there would be consequences. I did not leave immediately and had been on my way to the airport when I came across you at Toucan's. Octavio was driving the truck that hit us. Your accident was caused because I delayed my return."

I drained my entire glass, anger rising. *What kind of person is his father to punish Conner by nearly killing me?* "Let me guess, when you finally returned, you were told to stay away or they'd finish the job?"

Conner sighed. "Yes. That is the gist of it. Angels aren't allowed to kill humans unless it's in self-defense, and only if other resolutions have been attempted and failed. Octavio has found ways to bend the rules, which is why my father relies on him for tasks that require a more aggressive touch. I wanted to reach out to you, but I was terrified that you'd die because of me. I decided I would rather live without ever have known what might be between us than gamble with your life."

"I'm sorry. I don't know what it's like to grow up with a father, but none of the father figures who have ever been in my life would have treated their sons like that," I replied. Though one thing was bothering me about his explanation: If the threat was real, how were we together now? We'd been seeing each other since a few days after the Halloween gala.

"Why are we together if there is still a threat on my life?" I asked.

Conner blinked and then drained his glass and set it down with a thump on the table. "You know how the Halloween gala was also a birthday celebration for me?"

I shook my head. "I must have left before they announced it. I had an emergency call."

Conner ran his finger along the rim of his glass, then met my gaze. "Well, it was not my thirty-eighth birthday. It was actually my fifteen hundredth. When an angel turns fifteen hundred, they take part in the ascension ceremony. The ceremony bequeaths an angel with their full powers and titles. In my case, since my father is an archangel—the highest title an angel can hold—I am now an archangel too, and an equal to my father. As such, he cannot give me orders and require obedience. Unless I were to give Octavio a direct order to kill you, he is no longer allowed to do so, because you're under my protection. Breaching that would be a punishment far worse than death."

My boyfriend is fifteen hundred years old! I spied the scotch carafe on the shelf by the fireplace; I stood up and retrieved it, then filled my glass to the brim and poured half into Conner's. I took small sips until I'd finished half of the glass and was starting to feel slight effects of the alcohol. I wanted to talk to Penny, to bounce my thoughts off of someone else, but she'd never believe me. Even if I lied, most of what Conner had shared so far sounded more like a fantasy movie than real life. I felt marginally better after Conner said my life was no longer at risk—at least by any immortal threats.

"Are angels and humans allowed to be together?" I inquired.

Conner's Adam's apple bobbed, then he spoke. "No, it's against the rules. But ..." My grip tightened around the glass enough that it was almost painful. "There is an extremely rare situation when it is allowed. If two individuals experience a Fien bond, then any rules regarding cross-species mating are ignored."

"I would know if there was any sort of a bond between us," I blurted out, quickly realizing my mistake. Until three hours ago, I had had no idea immortals were real. How would a human like me know what a Fien bond would feel like?

Conner set his glass down, then reached over and pried my fingers off of mine, taking both of my hands in his. "Fien bonds can take a long time—months, years, or even centuries—to fully develop. I have felt the one between us forming since our first kiss. I didn't know what it was, though, until right before my birthday. As I said, they're extremely rare. A pair of individuals who share a Fien bond are highly regarded among the angels and demons, no matter their status prior to it forming."

Needing facts, I asked the next logical question. "What exactly does a Fien bond do?"

"That's where it gets tricky. Each Fien bond is different. There tends to be a heightened need to have a connection between them, either physical or magical. In some circumstances there is heightened fertility, additional magic abilities, or telepathic communication," Conner replied.

"Can you break a Fien bond?" I wondered aloud.

Conner shook his head. "No. The only thing that breaks a Fien bond is death, and both individuals die."

"Well, that answers my next question, about our differences in ages and the fact that you're immortal, fifteen hundred, and I am almost thirty and will likely die in the next sixty years," I said quietly. If what Conner said was true—that we had a Fien bond, even if I couldn't feel it—then no matter what I said or did, Conner was bound to me and would die when my human life ended. With everything I had learned today, I knew he valued my life over his own, and I was confident that if I decided to break things off with him, he would respect my decision and we'd go our separate ways.

The problem was, the longer we sat here, the more I found myself wanting to believe Conner and believe that there was a reason why, when I considered leaving and never seeing him again, I couldn't breathe. Penny had told me two weeks ago when I suggested I was in love with Conner that relationships happened that way. Except now I knew the Fien bond could very well be why. *The universe is telling me we're meant to be. Why not take a leap of faith?* I mused. Except I'd never been one to rely solely on faith. I wanted facts. Proof that we were together because we're madly, deeply in love with each other.

The answer I sought came to me. I released his hands, setting my own in my lap, then spoke. "I have a proposal for you."

"I'm listening," Conner said, leaning forward eagerly.

"You dumped a lot on me today. I was expecting a quiet week-long vacation at your estate and a chance to meet your family. I would like to continue with our plans and see how the rest of the trip goes. But I want you to know that I might want to break up at the end. Being with an immortal and its ramifications is not guaranteed to be the right fit," I said.

Conner smiled, his eyes sparkling. "Your proposal is fair. You're free to leave at any time, just say the word. That will never change. No matter what you decide."

"I'm glad you see it that way," I replied. I stood up and crossed over to his chair. Straddling his legs, I sat on his lap, tipping my head down and kissing him deeply.

Chapter 37: Conner

Monday, November 25

I was in my office reading through emails while Kelsey was out for a morning run. Charlie was coming over for lunch. I'd reached out to her after the deep conversation with Kelsey yesterday hoping that meeting Charlie before my parents would help reduce any nervousness Kelsey might feel meeting other immortals.

Kelsey and I had snuggled in bed, but she had made no moves to have sex. I wanted to respect her space, so I kept my hands to myself. The last thing I wanted was Kelsey to feel pressured to accept me or the Fien bond. *Except,* a small part of my mind nagged me, *sex might speed up the Fien bond and influence Kelsey's desire to stay.* I ignored those internal comments, knowing, from what Cassiel had said, Fien bond magic had no rhyme or reason.

I heard a loud knock on my office door. I shut my laptop and stood up. The door burst inward, and a lithe woman with auburn air, tan skin, and bright green eyes sashayed in. I rolled my eyes.

"Was that necessary?"

Charlie stuck her tongue out. "I was downstairs, but you didn't hear my polite knock, so I took matters into my own hands. Your fault, not mine."

"I was focused on work," I said dryly, walking around my desk over to my sister. I pulled her into a hug and then released her, stepping back.

"I'm surprised you can get any work done with Kelsey around here. She's H-O-T!" Charlie said, loud enough that I hoped Kelsey wasn't going to overhear things and take them the wrong way. "You, on the other hand, look like you need a really good fuck ... So again, why is she running the property when she could be riding you?"

I shook my head and brushed past my sister to yank the door shut. "What would Cassiel say if he heard you talk like that?" I asked.

"You wouldn't dare," Charlie hissed.

"Are you sure?" I replied and pulled out my phone, playing a recording of what she'd just said. "All I have to do is push send."

Lightning quick, Charlie threw a punch at my face. I ducked; her second punch landed on my shoulder. I scooted to the side, but she kept coming,

"Your form sucks," I told her as I easily blocked her punches with my forearms.

"How's this?" she asked and then changed how she was punching. I winced as her fist connected with my elbow.

"You made your point. I will delete the recording," I said and held the phone out as I deleted it so she could verify I had done so.

"Promise me when Kelsey comes back into the house that you're not going to tell her we need to go into the bedroom for a fuck," I told her seriously.

"Fine, fine. I promise. But it's really good advice," she said with a smirk.

"Why the sudden interest in my sex life?" I asked. Usually when I saw Charlie we talked about cars and she could care less about who I was dating.

"Father told me about the Fien bond," Charlie said.

I raised my eyebrows in surprise. "He did?"

"Yes. I was just as surprised as you are. Maybe he's realizing that we're both adults and should be treated as such," she replied.

"Are you going to tell him about your F1 racing then?" I inquired.

Charlie shook her head vigorously. "Not a chance in hell. He might respect your Fien bond, but he'll never understand or endorse the 'risks' I take by participating in human racing."

Before my birthday, I would have wholeheartedly agreed with her. Now I wasn't so sure what to think about Cassiel anymore. I heard the door downstairs open and close.

"She's here. Be nice," I reminded Charlie, then walked past her and out of the office, taking the steps two at a time.

Kelsey looked more relaxed than she'd been since our discussion yesterday. *Hopefully she is still relaxed after meeting Charlie.* "How was your run?" I asked her conversationally.

Kelsey flashed me a brilliant smile, and I felt weak at the knees. "Amazing. I can't believe you don't like running, even here where it's so peaceful."

I shrugged. "I prefer driving or working out in the gym. I wanted to introduce you to my sister, Charlotte."

Charlie shoved me out of the way and hugged Kelsey. "I'm Charlie. Nice to meet you, Kelsey!"

Kelsey smiled uncertainly. "Nice to meet you, Charlie."

Charlie hooked her arm through Kelsey's and guided her out of the foyer and down the hallway. *"Don't you dare follow us,"* Charlie warned me telepathically.

"Remember your promise," I replied, then headed back upstairs. I had no doubts in my mind that Charlie wouldn't say anything to Kelsey that would cause problems; she just wasn't like that.

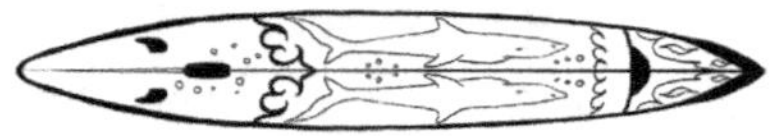

After lunch, Charlie talked me into driving a few laps on the track, wanting to give Kelsey a chance to see me in my element. They were in the viewing stand at the side of the track. Even though she hadn't said it directly, I knew that at times Kelsey got nervous in cars—an issue caused by the accident, not that I could blame her. She seemed content to watch, and she and Charlie had clearly hit it off.

I rounded the corner heading into the straight section of the track, foot on the accelerator of the Aston Martin Vantage. The lights on the console started flickering. *Odd.* I hit 120 miles per hour, and the car completely shut off and the brakes were unresponsive. Concern increasing, I kept my hands on the steering wheel to try to keep control of the car. Sparks flew and smoke billowed out of the hood.

Guessing it was an electrical malfunction and knowing time was running out, I decided to abandon the car. I teleported out to the side of the track and watched as the car hit the gravel and spun, flames licking out of the hood.

Kelsey and Charlie ran over, halting beside me as the car slammed into the wall and went up in flames. I studied Kelsey. Her face was pale and her lips were pressed together in a thin line, and she was visibly shaking.

I stepped around my sister and pulled my girlfriend into a hug. Her shoulders shook as she cried into my chest.

"Hush, I'm fine," I said soothingly.

"Are you sure?" Kelsey muttered. She tipped her head back, peering up at me.

"I promise. Remember how I told you I'm immortal?" I asked. Kelsey nodded. "Mmmhmm."

"This is one of those times where I was safe. It was a human-created car malfunctioning," I explained calmly.

"This is going to take getting used to," Kelsey replied.

"What happened?" Charlie demanded.

"Something electrical," I replied, shaking my head. "I really liked that car too."

"I'm sure you can get another," Charlie replied.

I was about to say something else when we heard a siren in the distance. As it came down the hill, a small fire engine became visible.

"Now what?" Kelsey asked uncertainly.

"They'll put the fire out, and then Fabio will arrange for what's left to be picked up and taken to a junkyard," I replied.

"Just to be safe, you should have Nate inspect it. I know you know cars, as do I, but it would make me feel better if you confirmed it was indeed a manmade problem," Charlie said.

Deep down, I knew she was right, especially after what happened at CM Hospital. "I'll call Nate. Just give me a sec." I moved away from Charlie and Kelsey, knowing that my sister could help Kelsey relax.

"Nate, it's Conner. Do you have a minute?" I said into Nate's mind. Though I could, I didn't feel like I should keep tabs on the whereabouts of my close friends.

"Sure. What's up?" Nate replied.

"Well, I was driving the Aston Martin Vantage on my track and the brakes went out," I explained.

"Wow, I hope everyone is okay," Nate replied.

"Luckily, I was the only one in the car, and I was able to keep it away from Charlie and Kelsey. But I think it would be a good idea if you inspect it to ensure there was no magic involved," I said.

"Of course. When would you like me to come by?" Nate asked.

I considered the question. I wanted to give Kelsey a chance to work through any emotions she was feeling when we got back to the house. *"Two hours? You'll still have enough daylight,"* I responded.

"Sure thing. I'll see you in two hours," Nate said. I could feel him pulling away and let go of the magic tying my thoughts to his.

Charlie and Kelsey were both gazing solemnly at the wreck while the fire engine's crew put out the fire. I closed the gap between us.

"Let's go back to the house so I can get cleaned up," I said, giving Kelsey a quick peck on the cheek.

Charlie shot me a look over Kelsey's head. *"She's shaken up. You should talk to her."* Then, she said aloud, "I'm going to head home.

I think Cassiel and Samara are coming over this evening, and then we'll have a family meal Friday before you fly home."

"I'll see you then," Kelsey replied, her voice soft.

Chapter 38: Kelsey

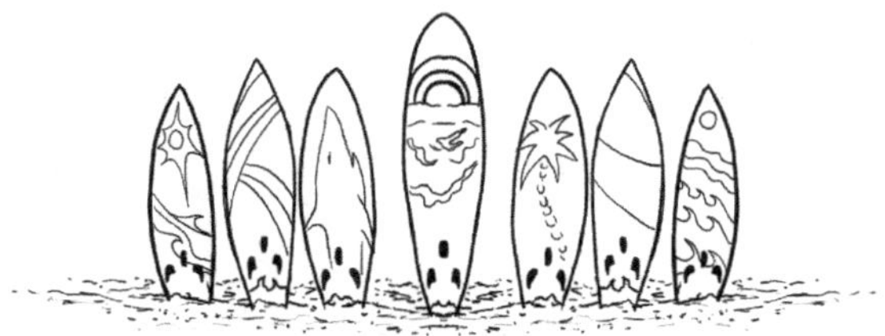

Monday, November 25

Watching Conner nearly crash had been terrifying and brought with it flashbacks of my own accident. Forcing me to think about my mortality and what would happen if Conner weren't immortal and had died in the car crash. That I'd never see him again. He'd simply be gone. The thought was unbearable. I knew now with certainty that this was where I belonged, with Conner. Even though I hadn't met his parents, after meeting his sister, I felt like I was part of his family. Charlie had treated me like a sister, telling me about her childhood with Conner and how he'd gotten her hooked on driving fast cars.

To date, Conner and I had had steered clear of discussing what our future might look like if we stayed together. Honestly, I didn't care about the details anymore, as long as we were together.

We were at the back of the house, and I pulled Conner to a halt, needing to voice my feelings now, before I lost the courage.

"I love you, Conner. Even though your world is new to me, I want to be a part of it. Your almost-accident just now made me realize how much you mean to me," I told him. I could feel tears welling in my eyes because of the intense emotions I was feeling.

Conner pulled me to him. His shirt was sweat-soaked, but I didn't care. I kissed him, desperately. As though we were running out of time, even though I knew we had all the time in the world.

"I love you too," he whispered. With his arms wrapped around me, I felt a slight tugging around my belly button, and then I peered around and saw we were no longer outside of the house but inside the bedroom.

"How did you do that?" I demanded.

"Magic," he replied and kissed me again.

I tugged at his clothes, needing to feel his skin against mine. Desire coiled through me. He took half a step back, giving me the room I needed to unbutton his pants and help them slide to the floor. I returned my attention to undressing myself, quickly yanking off my shirt, sports bra, and running shorts.

When I met Conner's gaze again, his eyes were molten with desire. He tugged on my panties and let them fall around my feet. I stepped out of them, and then he picked me up. I gasped in momentary surprise and then wrapped my legs around his waist. He adjusted my position so that I could feel his cock at the apex of my thighs.

Conner carried me over to the large oak dresser, the perfect height for him to set me on. He pulled my bottom just to the edge so I was barely on it and then dipped his head down to suckle on my breasts. I wiggled my hips, desperate to have his cock inside of me.

Thankfully, he obliged, plunging deep into my drenched core. As Conner moved inside of me, I knew that it was unlikely another man would ever make me feel this way. We fit as though we were made for each other. He returned his attention to my mouth, and my breasts tightened as his chest brushed against my sensitive nipples.

The edge of the dresser was biting into me; I shifted, hoping to adjust without interfering. Of course, Conner noticed.

"Are you okay?" he asked, immediately halting his thrusts.

I hissed, "Why'd you stop?" My whole body was throbbing with need, and the pause was more unbearable than the dresser digging into me.

He chuckled but didn't resume. "I want you to be comfortable."

I stuck my tongue out at him, and he gave the barest of thrusts with his hips, nearly sending me over the edge. "If you do that again, I won't be able to answer you," I muttered. "The dresser is digging into me."

Conner frowned, and then his eyes lit up in excitement. "I'm going to rearrange your legs, okay?"

"Anything, as long as you hurry up," I said in a strained voice.

To my dismay, he pulled all the way out before rearranging my legs. When he was done, my legs were propped on his shoulders. I felt rather ridiculous draped on his dresser in this position, but I was also curious what he was going to do next.

Nothing could have prepared me for the feel of his cock inside of me in this new position. It was electrifying. Both figuratively and literally. He eased in slowly about halfway before pulling almost all the way out. "Is this better?"

"Yes," I said in the barest of whispers.

With renewed energy, Conner slammed into me. I'd never felt like this when we'd had sex before. My whole body was tingling as he drove me closer to my orgasm. On the third stroke, an intense swell roared through me. I clutched the edge of the dresser and gasped, "Conner!" Wave after wave of pleasure assaulted me. I was glad that I was on the dresser because there was no way I could support my own weight right now.

I thought Conner had finished when I did, but I was wrong. His strokes were fast and hard, our eyes locked, and he gave me a wicked grin and then plunged his finger beside his cock and began tugging and teasing. My back arched and toes curled as another orgasm ripped through us simultaneously. Conner sagged against the dresser, then gently lowered my legs and pulled out.

"That was ..." he whispered, staring at me, awestruck.

"Intense?" I supplied, not sure it was the right word, but unsure of how else to describe it.

"I think the Fien bond is strengthening," Conner finally said.

I cautiously sat up and ran a hand through my hair, trying to figure out what to say. I settled on something simple. "Do you want a shower?"

"Sure," Conner said agreeably, then picked me up and carried me into the bathroom.

There was a knock on the door, which creaked open slightly, and a surprisingly loud Fabio called to us, "Nate is here. Shall I tell him you'll be down or let him inspect the car without you?"

I ran my hands through my hair, wondering what Fabio was talking about. "Who is Nate?" I asked.

Conner sighed and shut off the shower water. "You can send him out to the car. I'll be there shortly." Fabio tugged the door shut.

When it was closed, I looked at Conner. "What's going on?"

Conner ran his hand over his face, then reached outside of the shower for the two towels and offered me one. "Nate is my friend. Charlie thought it best to have Nate look the car over before I send it to the junkyard."

"Why Nate and not you?" I demanded, using the towel to dry off.

"Each angel has different kinds of magic, and his can detect things that mine can't. I doubt he's going to find anything, but he is here to humor Charlie," Conner explained.

"Sounds like a smart plan to me. Why would you not have him look it over?" I asked.

"Because though uncommon, electrical failures do happen, and there was nothing that the car did that led me to believe it was a magical issue. It would also be nearly impossible for another immortal to gain access to the car," Conner said.

I led the way into the bedroom, wanting to get dressed before I met Conner's friend Nate. I snagged my phone off the bed and was surprised to see that his parents would be arriving in just under an hour. I frowned and then peered at Conner. "I need time to get ready for your parents."

"Jeans and a T-shirt are fine," Conner replied.

I rolled my eyes. "Because that's what you wear all the time?" I'd never seen him wear jeans, even in Santa Barbara. With what I knew about Conner and his parents, I felt like his suggestion would make me far underdressed for the occasion.

"They'll love you no matter what you're wearing," he said and brushed his lips lightly on my forehead. "But if it's important to you, then I'll go down to see what Nate has to say and you can get ready."

"Thanks," I replied and gave him a quick kiss. I guided him out of the bedroom and locked the door.

Taking a deep breath, I considered how the day had shaped itself and the impact the Fien bond was having on any opportunity we were presented to have sex. *This is ridiculous*, I told myself. No matter if it was a magical connection I hadn't known could exist until yesterday, I doubted that it would exist to make our sole purpose to stay in bed. *We could have lots of children if that were the case*, I mused, then shook my head. That was another conversation we'd steered away from. Though I knew if things were going to work out between us, it was one we should have sooner rather than later.

Meeting his parents would be the first test of whether I could indeed turn off the sex drive aspect of the bond or not. It was embarrassing to ask Conner, and I wasn't sure if he even knew the answer.

I walked over to the closet and selected a tan blouse with long sheer sleeves that buttoned at the wrist, a hunter green, dark tan, and cream plaid skirt, and dark brown calf-high suede boots. Selection made, I returned to the bathroom to dry my hair and put it in a chignon and apply makeup.

Chapter 39: Conner

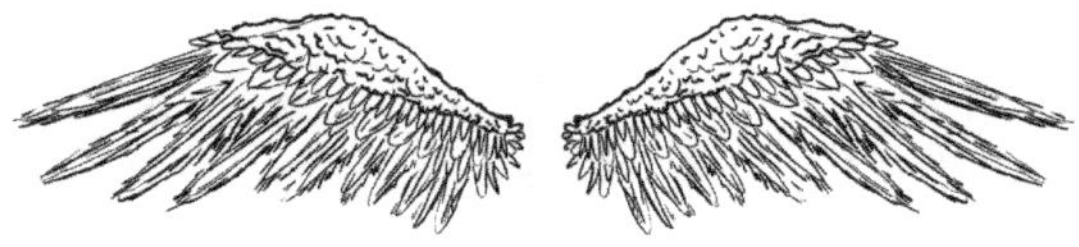

Monday, November 25

I assumed Nate's inspection would be fast. There wasn't much left of the Vantage to look at. Using my magic, I left the house and reappeared in the shop, where the crew had moved the pieces of the car. Nate was kneeling in front of what remained of the engine.

"Find anything?" I asked.

Nate glanced up at me and then stood. "You're not going to like what I found," he replied.

My throat went dry. "Please tell me," I said. My voice was scratchy.

"There is evidence of magic, though I can't tell yet any details on the kind of magic—only that it is there. Trace amounts around the engine and brakes. I need to take everything to my lab, then we can get the answers you seek," Nate explained.

I stared at the engine, thoughts churning. Before I ascended, I had been considered by most untouchable; clearly that had changed. The last thing I needed was to concern everyone at dinner tonight. *Nate and I can handle this*, I decided.

"How about you take the car back to your lab and let me know as soon as anything definitive comes up? We fly back to the States Saturday," I said.

"I probably won't have answers before you leave, then. One of the tests can take up to a week, but it's extremely accurate in identifying the individual who did the magic," Nate replied.

"Then it will be worth the weeklong wait," I said. *Knowing the exact immortal would mean instead of hunting aimlessly and wasting time on interrogating demons, I could catch the culprit and be certain.*

"Are you going to tell Cassiel?" Nate asked cautiously.

I shook my head and spoke firmly. "No. I can handle this incident myself." I glanced at my watch. "Cassiel and Samara are due any minute. Thanks for helping out, Nate."

Nate clapped me on the shoulder. "I'm glad you listened to your sister and called me. I'll see you in a week."

"See you in a week," I replied and with a pinch of magic transported myself to my closed bedroom door.

I raised my hand to knock but lowered it when the door opened, revealing Kelsey in a tan blouse and plaid skirt. Her long brown hair was pulled back in a chignon and held in place with a simple silver clip. Desire shot right through me, and I swallowed hard. *Dinner*, I reminded myself.

I flashed Kelsey a smile. "You look stunning."

She blushed and gave me a light kiss on the cheek. "Thanks. You look ... the same as usual," she said with a grin. I was wearing a royal blue tailored suit with a white shirt and a silver tie.

I shrugged. "What can I say ... the guest room closet only had suits."

"C'mon, why don't you introduce me to your parents?" she said encouragingly.

Arm in arm, I led Kelsey down the stairs to where my parents were waiting.

Chapter 40: Kelsey

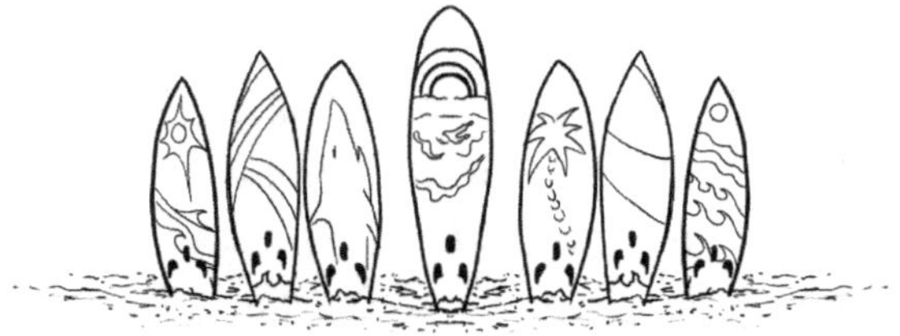

Monday, November 25

Butterflies fluttered in my stomach from nerves. I tried to keep my grip on Conner light, so as not to give away my feelings, but I was fairly certain when he kissed my forehead that he could tell how nervous I was. Thankfully, he didn't comment.

Cassiel and Samara stood side by side in the foyer, smiling as we approached. Cassiel had tan skin and vibrant blue eyes, and he wore a navy blue tailored suit with a gray-and-white striped shirt. He had wavy shoulder-length dark gray hair and seemed about the same height as Conner. I could see where Conner had gotten his build from. I focused on his mother, Samara. She had long natural red hair that fell in waves to her waist and the same warm brown eyes that Conner had. She was a head shorter than Cassiel though—still taller than me—and wearing a cream-colored long-sleeve blouse with a floor-length hunter green tweed skirt.

Conner cleared his throat and stepped within arm's reach of his parents. "Cassiel and Samara, I would like you to meet my girlfriend, Kelsey."

Cassiel stuck his hand out. I took it and we shook. His grip was firm but casual.

When he released me, I stuck my hand out for Samara but was surprised when she leaned toward me and kissed me on each cheek. I blinked, not sure how to respond, and Samara gave me a bright smile. "It's good to meet you, Kelsey."

"It's nice to meet you too," I said, hoping my voice sounded calmer than I felt. Charlie and Conner had given me two entirely different versions of their parents. I wasn't sure which one to believe. *Or perhaps the best option is to see for myself*, I mused, realizing that I had no way of knowing all the details of the interactions the siblings had with their parents.

"Let's go into the dining room. The food should be ready," Conner said smoothly, gesturing toward the formal dining room.

Cassiel led the way as though he'd been here many times before. *Which he likely has*, I reminded myself. Samara was behind me, and Conner brought up the rear. The gigantic sixteen-seat table was gone. In its place was an oversized square table made of birds-eye maple surrounded by four matching chairs. Each place was set; I noticed the plates had wildlife around the edges. Cassiel sat in the chair closest to the foyer, and Samara sat across from him, putting Conner and me facing each other.

Fabio came from the kitchen with a pitcher of water, filled our glasses, then departed. I took a sip of water and waited for someone to talk first. The silence was becoming awkward, though I would've sworn from the expression on Conner's face he was having a conversation.

Samara coughed and looked at me. "I'm sorry, Kelsey. Cassiel and Conner are being rude. I know Conner told you about us—immortals—so there is no reason to not tell you that angels can speak telepathically to one another. However, you are human and do not possess magic. What is it that you do at the children's hospital?"

I set my water glass down and focused on Samara, wishing Conner was close enough to kick for having a telepathic conversation.

"I am a pediatric surgical fellow with about seven months left till I complete the fellowship."

"I am not familiar with what a fellow does. Can you explain it?" Samara asked politely.

I nodded. "Of course. I completed medical school, a surgical residency, and the general surgery boards. The fellowship gives me the opportunity to further specialize so that I can work with children. I can take the pediatric surgery certification board exam once I complete the fellowship. Los Angeles Children's Hospital only treats pediatric patients. It was my top choice for a fellowship because I am being exposed to many different types of cases."

"I see," replied Samara. "When did you decide that this was the career you wanted?"

"My whole life," I said thoughtfully. "This has been my dream. Though there was a short period of time where I briefly considered becoming a professional surfer."

"You didn't tell me that," Conner said, breaking into our conversation.

I shrugged and felt my cheeks heating in embarrassment. "There were three years that I competed in local surfing competitions and even had a recruitment offer to join one of the high school state teams. But the rules and requirements for being on the team were very complicated, and ultimately I decided it was not worth the time and money we would have to invest. That was also the summer my best friend Penny broke her leg surfing, and I realized how uncertain that path would be. Versus a career as a surgeon. I had to commit to a crazy amount of schooling, but there was no risk that if I got injured, everything would disappear."

My throat went dry when I said that and realized how wrong I was. If the accident the weekend I met Conner had gone differently, I could have quite possibly lost my ability to operate, or even be dead. I hastily grabbed my glass and started drinking, hoping Conner would jump into the conversation while I recovered.

Instead, Cassiel asked me a question. "Has Conner taken you

sightseeing at all? I heard this is your first time abroad."

"No, we've been hanging out here at the estate. To be honest, this whole trip was quite spur of the moment. I didn't have a chance to brush up on what there is to do around here. Is there anywhere you'd recommend going?" I replied.

"London has many sights, and Conner has a condo there. It could be worth the trip. Though I would understand if you chose to stay at the estate. I imagine your work schedule is quite intense as a surgical fellow. Sometimes the best vacation is being able to simply relax and not be on a schedule," Cassiel said.

The words popped out of my mouth before I could stop them. "If we're close enough to London, then I'd love to go. I'm sure Abuela will yell at me if she finds out I didn't take the opportunity to see the city."

Samara chimed in, "There is no reason why you cannot make another trip if you don't make it into London this time. I'm sure your abuela is also aware of what type of work you do."

"Yes, she is," I replied. Opening my mouth to say more, I was interrupted by the arrival of our food. Fabio and a young man I hadn't met before entered the dining room, each carrying two plates. I sniffed the air and it smelled delicious, though I had no idea what it was.

Fabio set my plate in front of me. I identified an herb-encrusted chicken breast, potatoes, and an assortment of grilled vegetables. The conversation died as we settled into consuming the meal.

When the last plate had been cleared, Conner stood up. "Let's go into the library," he suggested. Conner came over to me and took my hand when I stood. "How was your food?"

"Amazing," I replied.

"Excellent. I've got scotch in the library. Do you want me to grab something else for you?" Conner asked.

"No, I'll pass. Thanks for asking though," I said.

We followed Cassiel and Samara into the library. With a full stomach and the events of the day, I was unsure how long I'd be able to stay awake. The scotch would have for sure made me fall asleep. I yawned.

Conner chuckled and paused before we reached the couch. "How about coffee?"

I mulled the offer over. "Yes, that would be good. With cream …"

"And sugar," Conner supplied. I blushed. "I know how you like your coffee."

His words wrapped around me, and I almost wished we could retire now. Except I didn't want to cut things short with his parents, not when this was my chance to get to know them. "Thank you," I replied.

Conner disappeared, and I sat on the loveseat. Cassiel and Samara had chosen the individual chairs instead of the couch that would have fit both of them. I was intrigued. *Maybe if they've been married for thousands of years, they don't need the close contact anymore.* I realized that it was possible since Conner and I shared a Fien bond that perhaps our relationship was different than his parents. *Do angels marry for love?* It would be an awkward question for me to ask them, though maybe if I remembered I could ask Charlie about it.

Conner returned and set a steaming cup of light brown coffee on the end table next to me. He then sat down so that our legs touched. "Samara, I know you and Kelsey were talking about what she does. Why don't you tell Kelsey what you do?"

Samara's forehead crinkled as she smiled. "It's not nearly as interesting as what you and Cassiel do. But I suppose I can." I took a cautious sip of my coffee, waiting for her to explain. "I keep track of who enters and exits the Ash Realm."

"What is the Ash Realm?" I asked, shooting a glance at Conner.

Samara and Cassiel exchanged a look of surprise. Then, Cassiel spoke. "You didn't tell her?"

Conner shook his head. "I was trying to not overwhelm Kelsey before she decided if she wanted to accept what I said and continue dating."

Cassiel cleared his throat. "The Ash Realm, or Ianialar, is where angels and at times other immortals reside."

"Do you mean like heaven?" I asked uncertainly.

Cassiel frowned. "In a way, I suppose it could be like what humans call heaven."

"Would I have to be dead to go there?" I asked.

"Humans are not allowed to go to Ianialar," Cassiel replied firmly.

I gave Conner a questioning look, not sure if there was a reason for me to be able to go to Ianialar or not. Conner gave my leg a reassuring squeeze. "Don't worry about it," he said softly.

Samara looked as though she was going to speak, then didn't. Instead, she picked up her glass of scotch and drained it. She set it down with a clank and stood. "It is time for us to go. We will see you Friday for dinner."

Confused at the turn of events, I rose from the couch, and we said goodbye to Cassiel and Samara. When they had left, I turned to Conner.

"That went well, right?" I asked.

He nodded, though his expression was distracted. "Yes. Now that you've had a whole cup of coffee, what would you like to do?"

I blushed. "An honest answer?"

"Of course," Conner responded.

I turned to face him, stepping close, and kissed him, catching him off guard. It took him a moment before he returned the kiss. I tipped my head back, gazing into his brown eyes. "Ever since you sat next to me on the couch ..."

Conner chuckled and pulled me tight against him. I was surprised when I felt his cock already hard. "You have been driving me wild," he whispered against my ear, sending shivers of desire down my spine.

"Then why don't we do something about it," I replied sweetly.

Conner swept me off my feet and into his arms, and I couldn't help but giggle as he carried me upstairs into the bedroom.

Chapter 41: Kelsey

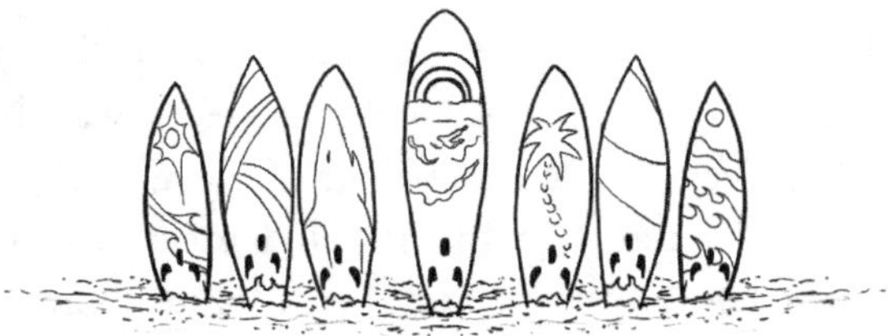

Wednesday, November 27

It felt strange that at home tomorrow was Thanksgiving. Since leaving for medical school, holidays had become a thing of the past. More of a marker of a year drawing to a close than anything else. Here in London, it was just another November day. After spending yesterday hanging out at the estate, I decided that I would like to at least spend a day in London before we flew home. Since we didn't have much use for a car in London, not with the subway system, Conner transported us to his condo using his magic.

We arrived in the middle of the living room facing the backside of a dark brown leather couch. Where some might have put a TV, there was a landscape painting of the sun rising over what I thought was likely the English Channel. Unlike the estate house, Conner's condo had minimal furniture.

"Do you come here often?" I wondered aloud, absently running my finger over the cuff of his leaf-green cardigan sweater.

Conner shook his head. "No. Though Hudson International has offices here as well as two hospitals I work for. I probably spend ... two months a year here."

"Wouldn't it make more sense to just do a short-term rental?" I asked.

Conner shrugged. "Perhaps, but there are two other factors. The first is I've owned this entire building for two hundred years, and the second is that money is not really an issue for me or my family."

I swallowed, trying to let Conner's words sink in that he'd owned this building for two hundred years. The inside of his condo looked updated. I would have never guessed it was that old.

"How many places do you call home?" I inquired.

Conner took my hand in his and led me around the condo. The kitchen had white cabinets with white granite countertops, though the columns throughout the condo were made of red brick. "Two—the country estate and the house in Malibu. Though I own over twenty different pieces of real estate around Europe."

My eyes widened at the thought of managing that many properties. Then, it dawned on me that likely Conner had a property manager and didn't handle those matters on his own. I had learned in the past month we'd been dating that though he was a billionaire, he worked as much or more than I did, and from where I was sitting, seemed to enjoy his career.

The condo, it turned out, had two bedroom suites—one at either end. "Was this always one unit?" I asked.

Conner smiled. "You're astute. No, this was originally two. When the tenant next door moved out about twenty years ago, I decided to knock down the wall between them and renovate. Do you need to use the bathroom or have something to drink before we head out?"

I shook my head. "No thanks. I'm ready when you are."

With Conner leading the way down the two flights of stairs, we emerged onto a quiet residential street with both sides sporting three-story redbrick buildings like the one Conner owned. The street was lined with cars, and I guessed that garages were not as common here as they were in the States.

The sky was gray, and I was grateful Conner had insisted I bring a coat to keep me warm in the chilly forty-degree morning. Conner's stride was confident as we walked down the street. When we rounded the corner, I was surprised to see that the next street was far busier, with a line of cars making their way through a stop-sign intersection.

Weaving our way through foot traffic, we barely slowed when we reached the subway station entrance and took the stairs underground. We passed by a large map showing the different subway lines and stops before halting for a brief moment while the train I assumed was ours ground to a halt.

"Perfect timing," Conner said.

I wondered if it was perfect or if Conner had been able to use his magic to get the information. Here in a crowded subway full of people was not a good place to ask such a question, so I filed it away for future use.

"Where are we going?" I asked as the train started moving.

"I thought we'd start at the British Museum. Then, we can decide from there what you'd like to see," Conner replied.

Museums had never been part of my wheelhouse, and I was fortunate that Conner was understanding. We went through most of the exhibits fairly quickly and at just under two hours were on our way out the gates.

"Since that wasn't your cup of tea," Conner said with a smile, "what about Westminster Abbey?"

"Sure," I replied. He knew far more than I did what landmarks were worth visiting.

We took the subway again. When we reached the street, I could see the abbey just ahead. I was in awe of its sheer size. I set my foot on the steps, intending to go up to the entrance, when Conner's phone started ringing.

"Give me a sec," he said and moved off a ways to answer it.

I pulled mine out. It was still too early to call or text Abuela, but I had some photos to send her as soon as it was a reasonable time back home.

Conner returned to me, his expression serious. "It pains me to say this, but I need to go to a meeting at Royal London Hospital."

"I can come with you. I don't mind," I offered.

Conner shook his head. "No, that's not fair to you. This is your vacation. I don't want to ruin it by having you accompany me to a hospital. I've called Charlie, and she will meet you here in about thirty minutes. Which gives you time to tour the abbey. I texted you a ticket for the tour."

I stepped close to Conner and kissed him. "I will be fine, promise. Thank you for asking Charlie to meet me. I'll see you later."

Conner kissed me back and reluctantly backed away. "See you soon."

I sighed and walked up the steps to the abbey, pulling out my phone. Sure enough, he had sent a picture of a ticket with a QR code. The guard at the doorway scanned it and shooed me inside.

I made it about ten feet before abruptly halting. The architecture was impressive, and the sheer scale and the age of the building made me wonder how they had accomplished this without the technology of today. Glancing over my shoulder, I realized a line had formed behind me. Blushing in embarrassment, I muttered, "Sorry!" and kept going deeper into the abbey.

I completed my tour of Westminster Abbey in thirty-six minutes, slightly longer than Conner had predicted. Charlie was waiting for me in almost the precise spot Conner had said goodbye from.

Her blond hair was pulled back in a ponytail and she had a bright red scarf tied around her neck with a black peacoat to stay warm. *Do angels get cold like humans?* Another question I'd have to ask when we had more privacy.

"Hey!" I said to Charlie. She waved and smiled.

"Good afternoon," she replied.

My stomach rumbled. I hadn't realized that much time had passed since breakfast at the estate.

"It sounds like you're hungry. I know just the place!" Charlie announced.

"Great, where to?" I inquired.

"You'll see. I don't want to spoil the surprise," Charlie replied, her eyes glittering in excitement. I followed Charlie down to the subway station that Conner and I had arrived from, except Charlie picked a different line for us to go on. After a quick ride, Charlie was dragging me through the crowd and up a spiraling staircase.

I was shocked when we stepped off the staircase and were inside of a building that was like a shopping mall. Charlie grinned at me and marched straight toward a small boutique store.

"I did a special order, and they told me it arrived. I hope you don't mind the detour. It was closer to come here first, then eat."

I adjusted my purse on my shoulder. "It's no problem."

"Then come on. I think you'll like the store," Charlie said and dashed inside.

I eyed the storefront. It had Victorian-style dresses, scarves, and lots of lace. I was fairly certain this was not a store I would go to on my own, but wanting to be polite, I trailed behind Charlie. I could hear her voice coming from the back.

In the middle, they had a magazine rack. I picked up the latest *Vanity Fair* and flipped through it. The skinny models were not terribly appealing to me, but usually near the middle the magazine would have a couple of lifestyle and travel articles that were easier to stomach.

I was on page fifty when I did a double take. I recognized Conner's estate immediately, and Conner was in a black suit, kissing a woman. I dropped the magazine in shock. Then, I peered around to make sure no one was paying attention. Hesitantly I picked it up and flipped back to the section I'd been on. Skimming the contents of the article, I saw the author wrote that Conner and Agatha were engaged. I studied each photo, and it was difficult to ignore the visible chemistry between Conner and this woman.

I bristled and snapped the magazine shut. *He's engaged to another woman.* My heart hammered in my chest as I realized the whole trip, everything I'd had with him, had been a lie. Shaking, I walked up to the counter and paid for the magazine. Then I walked out, clutching the magazine. I couldn't decide if I should get a taxi to the airport right now or give Conner a chance to explain.

Charlie came up beside me. "What's wrong?" she asked, eyeing me. Then, she glanced down to my hands. "I see ..."

I turned toward her, eyes narrowing, "You see? You knew about his engagement and didn't think it was worth mentioning that your brother is a liar?!"

Charlie held up her hands defensively. "The photo shoot is not what you think. If you'll give me a chance to explain ..."

It felt like the wind had been knocked out of me. My shoulders slumped forward, and I backed up a few steps so I could lean heavily against the store window. "Fine, explain," I said harshly.

"Back at the end of August or early September, my father and Agatha's father decided they wanted to force an arranged marriage on them. Except once Conner had his birthday, he would no longer be required to obey Cassiel's orders. Agatha got Conner to agree to do the photo shoot to provide proof that he was following along with what the fathers wanted," Charlie explained.

I inhaled deeply, my nostrils fluttering. It felt like I had a giant rock in my stomach. "If it was fake, then why didn't they pull the story from the magazine?"

Charlie twisted the end of her hair between her fingers before meeting my gaze. "Honestly, it had to do with the magazine. They got the spot because someone dropped out. By the time Conner wanted to pull the spreads, the magazine had been printed—past the point of no return. As to why he didn't explain this when you started dating, my best guess is he forgot all about the shoot."

I swiped at my eyes where I could feel tears starting to form. I had to admit that Charlie's explanation did make sense. Even her reasoning for why Conner hadn't said anything. It was just hard to stomach that the man I loved was now publicly "engaged" to this woman, Agatha.

"Who exactly is Agatha?" I asked, deciding that would be a good place to start.

Charlie smiled slightly. "Conner's best female friend. To answer your next question," she said with a knowing look, "they did try dating years ago, but Agatha prefers women and no amount of magic can change the fact that Conner has a penis."

My eyes widened at her bluntness, especially in a public place. "I see. It sounds like I need to talk to Conner about it. I do appreciate your candor, Charlie. Now ... how about the lunch you promised?" I was hungry. Though my anger was receding to the point where I didn't feel like I had to catch the next flight home, it was hard to let the whole photo shoot and kissing Agatha go as though it hadn't happened.

Charlie nodded. "Of course. I was going to take you to The Dapper Lamb."

I gave her a questioning look. "As long as there is food, I am game for anything."

"Good. Now ... follow me." Charlie had her bag in one hand and stuck her other arm through mine, then led me through a door marked *Employees Only* into an empty hallway. "Since you're hungry and ... still annoyed, I figured it would be better if we just travel with magic. I know Conner has done this with you."

I nodded. "Yes."

"Good," Charlie said.

I felt my arm tingling under her grip. Then there was a loud pop, and the hallway vanished and was replaced with the inside of a phone booth. The phone was digging into my back, and Charlie grimaced.

"Ugh, sorry." She squeezed past me and out the door. I followed her, catching a glimpse of a street sign that said Ely Court.

The street was lined in small shops with brightly colored awnings and an assortment of wares—antiques, dolls, and a bakery, to name a few. On the opposite side of the street from us was a dark gray stone building with black-trimmed windows. The sign swinging above the door said Ye Old Mitre. The name was vaguely familiar, and I thought perhaps I'd read about it in one of the magazines during my summer break.

On the right side of Ye Old Mitre was a plain black-painted door that Charlie was making a beeline for. "Are you sure this is the right place? That looks like an emergency exit."

Charlie nodded and replied mysteriously, "Yes, it's the correct door. I promise you'll understand once we're inside."

I opted to follow instead of asking more questions, and we entered through the door. Charlie kept going, but I hit a solid wall.

"Ow!" I yelped.

Charlie turned around to see what was going on. I could see her, but there was an invisible barrier blocking me from going any farther. Charlie slapped her forehead. "Shit. I forgot ... Give me a second!" Then, she disappeared. Not sure what was going on, but with nothing else to do, I settled to wait.

A few minutes later, Charlie returned with a person in what I assumed was a costume. He reminded me of a reptile with skin of dark blue iridescent scales and golden eyes with slit-like pupils.

"Mavin, I need you to let Kelsey in," Charlie said firmly.

The costumed person stared at me, and a long, dark red forked tongue flickered out of his mouth. I was beginning to wonder if it was a costume or ... *An immortal.*

"Perhaps, we should eat lunch somewhere else," I said.

Charlie gave me an unreadable look, then focused on Mavin. "Kelsey is Conner's girlfriend."

Mavin hissed, and then whatever was keeping me from moving closer to them disappeared, and I stumbled forward, barely catching myself before I ran into Mavin. "I will allow it this time as a favor to you, Charlotte. Next time, if Conniel wants his girlfriend to be here, he needs to be here too," Mavin said. His voice was raspy.

Charlie gave Mavin a curt nod and led the way inside. The restaurant felt like a classic British pub with dark wood paneling on the walls and heavy beams. Light from antique glass lamps filled the space with a warm cozy glow. On the far wall was a bar of polished black marble with burgundy leather stools, some with high backs and others with no back. An immortal who looked very similar to Mavin stood behind the bar. I had to glance back toward the door to confirm that it wasn't Mavin himself.

We found a vacant round high-top table and sat. I hung my purse on the back of the chair and couldn't help but stare at Charlie. Her eyes were such a vibrant green they were practically glowing. Large gold wings spread out behind her. There was a tattoo on her neck of a rose that hadn't been there before.

"What is this place?" I demanded.

"A safe space for immortals to be seen for who we really are, without judgment or fear. The barrier you couldn't pass through keeps humans from being able to come in," Charlie explained.

"Should I even be here?" I wondered aloud. Mavin had refused to let me in at first, and now I was wondering if he shouldn't have given in to Charlie. I was a human. What would these immortals think to have me invading their space?

"Conner is one of the highest-ranking immortals in existence. You share a Fien bond with him, which means you belong where he goes. The Dapper Lamb is one of the few places that Conner frequents to spend time with other immortals. So yes, to answer the question, you do belong here. If being here at this pub makes you uncomfortable, then you are going to have to come to terms with it, especially if you want to marry Conner. This is who he is," Charlie said.

My throat tightened at Charlie's casual mention of marriage, I opened my mouth to speak when another angel walked over. I recognized her immediately from the photo shoot. It was Agatha. She had olive skin and black hair in tight shoulder-length ringlets. Like Charlie, her golden eyes seemed to glow. Agatha's wings were cream colored, and her dress was the same precise shade too.

Agatha stood behind the chair, her gaze flicking to Charlie and then to me. "Good afternoon, Kelsey. It's nice to finally meet you," she said and extended an elegant hand toward me. I shook it lightly and then shoved my hand back in my lap.

"Hi," I managed to say. I wasn't sure I wanted to say it was nice to meet her when I was still angry at Conner over their photo shoot.

Agatha's gaze was focused on Charlie, and I would've sworn they were talking telepathically. When Agatha looked at me again, she pulled out a chair to join us. "It sounds like Conner made a mess of things. I'm not entirely surprised. Let me tell you this. The photo shoot was nothing more than a ruse for our parents. He is madly in love with you, Kelsey, Fien bond or not. I don't know if he told you this, but he desperately wanted to go back to Santa Barbara and see how you fared after the accident. But that was before his ascension. He doesn't have to obey Cassiel's orders anymore."

"I don't entirely understand," I replied.

"Cassiel and now Conner are the only two archangels alive. Prior to his ascension, Conner answered only to Cassiel. Now they are equals, which gives Conner the ability to make his own decisions that are the best for him. Not skewed by his father's opinion," Agatha explained. "Let's order food, and then we can talk more."

I sighed in relief, and a waiter came over. Although he looked like a human with short black hair, brown eyes, and coffee-colored skin, I assumed that was not actually the case since he was here in The Dapper Lamb. There seemed to be no menus. "Good afternoon, ladies. I am Oakel and will be serving you today. For lunch we have shepherd's pie or steak and kidney pie."

I waited for Oakel to list off the rest of the menu, but when he stayed silent, I realized it was only two options. "I'll take the shepherd's pie," I decided.

Charlie and Agatha declined to order food, simply asking for water all around. "Good choice," said Agatha. "Their shepherd's pie is the best in London."

The food was out within minutes. Unable to resist, I dug into the shepherd's pie ravenously. Charlie and Agatha talked about upcoming modeling gigs they both had, including one in Dubai where they would be at the same photo shoot, something that I gathered happened rarely.

Oakel returned and removed my empty plate, then refilled our waters. A few moments later, someone else headed our way. I recognized Conner's friend Nate; I'd glimpsed him through the window earlier in the week when he was out looking at the wrecked Aston Martin. He had pale gray wings, almost white blond hair, and blue eyes. He wore a plain black hoodie and white jeans with giant holes at the knees.

"Charlie, I wasn't expecting to see you here today," Nate said.

Charlie shrugged. "Conner had an emergency meeting and asked me to keep Kelsey company."

"Well, he's on his way," Nate replied.

Charlie's face paled. "He's coming here?"

"Of course ... or did you think he wouldn't find out you brought her here?" Nate inquired.

I frowned. "I can leave if my presence is a problem."

Nate turned toward me. "You're here. What's done is done. I'm sure Conner would have preferred to decide when he wanted to bring you here. The Dapper Lamb can be a lot to take in at once, and since you've known about immortals less than a week ..."

He had a valid point, but as he said, what's done is done. I knew that Charlie had only brought me here because she thought it would be fun for lunch, not out of malice. Meeting Agatha had certainly helped smooth things out from earlier too. Racking my thoughts for something else we could discuss, other than that I shouldn't be here, I asked the first thing that I could think of. "Do you live here in London, Nate?"

Nate flashed me a smile and took the last chair at the table. "Yes, I do. Unlike Conner, I tend to stay in London full-time. Not that I don't travel, but not on the scale he does. I believe he mentioned to you the other day that I have a lab. It's located here in London, about ten minutes from this pub."

"How did you meet?" I inquired.

Nate chuckled. "That is a story that is best saved for another time. With lots of alcohol."

"Oh?" I said, intrigued.

"Hello, everyone," Conner said, loud enough that all four of us turned toward where he was entering.

My heart stuttered in my chest as I caught sight of him. His luscious white wings, the feathers of which almost seemed to be limned with silver, were spread out behind him, and the leaf-green sweater and form-fitting dark-wash jeans looked exactly as they had this morning. The anger and frustration I'd felt earlier melted away as he walked toward me, his brown eyes locked with my green ones. Ignoring everyone else at the table, Conner swept me into his arms and kissed me. My lips parted, inviting his tongue in, and he deepened the kiss. Part of me was embarrassed that we were in a restaurant kissing like this in front of his friends; the other part didn't care one bit.

He ran his hand down my back, and I shivered, heat coiled at my core. I pulled back, "Holy shit," I whispered.

"Hello to you too," Conner whispered and captured my lips again. I lost myself in his touch. I had no idea how long he held me and found I no longer cared. His friends and family knew we shared a Fien bond, and I was happy to blame that for any inappropriate kissing we engaged in.

Agatha coughed, and Conner reluctantly unwrapped his arms from around me. "Are you going to say something, or should you take her back to the condo?" Agatha asked.

"Fuck, I'm sorry," Conner said, and I half expected Charlie to tell us that's what we were about to do.

"Is everything okay at the hospital?" Nate asked, and I was grateful he provided a distraction to the growing awkwardness at the table.

"It's fine now. The CEO called in sick, and the rest of the board was panicking that it was another assassination when they couldn't get ahold of him. He was sleeping and his work phone was off," Conner explained.

"Glad to hear it's only an illness," Agatha said. I nodded in agreement.

Conner kept his arm loosely draped over my shoulder; one could say it was possessive, though I didn't mind. "How exactly did all four of you come to be at The Dapper Lamb at the same time?"

"Coincidence," said Agatha at the same time as Nate.

Conner didn't look like he believed that, but his next comment did not pursue their answers. "I was hoping to introduce Kelsey to Agatha myself. It warms me to see that you're all getting along."

"Yes, we are … and I don't want to be rude, but I'm ready to go. My feet are tired from all the walking, and there are things that I want to talk to you about in private," I said quietly to Conner.

"Of course, it's your vacation. If you want to return to the condo to rest, then by all means we can do that," Conner replied and gave me a light kiss, a promise I hoped of more to come while we were resting.

I looked at Charlie. "Thank you for everything."

"Any time," Charlie said demurely.

I walked away from the table, and Conner wrapped his arm around my lower back.

"Are we using magic?" I asked as we headed toward the door.

"No, we're only two blocks from the condo. I figured it's close enough to walk," Conner replied.

"Sounds good," I responded.

Once we were outside and heading in what Conner said was the correct direction, I decided I should confront him about the photo shoot before I got distracted.

"Why didn't you tell me about the *Vanity Fair* article on you and Agatha?"

Conner met my gaze briefly, then wisely focused on where we were walking as he answered. "You distracted me. I know it's not a good excuse, but it's the truth. Hopefully, your impromptu lunch with Agatha gave you a chance to see that we truly are *just* friends. And if I'm being open right now, then she is why I invited you to the estate and took the risk of telling you about immortals and the Fien bond. She's been one of the few angels I can talk to about my relationship with my father who won't go running back to tell on me. Or my sister, who is the princess of the family and never sees Cassiel the same way I do."

"Thank you for explaining," I said and gave his arm a squeeze. "It sounds like Agatha is the type of friend I have in Penny. It's always nice to have someone in your corner."

Conner halted, and I immediately recognized the building where his condo was.

"Will you let me make it up to you?"

I pursed my lips in thought. "Perhaps."

Conner leaned down and kissed me thoroughly on the steps. The desire I'd felt spark in the restaurant was reignited.

"Let's go inside and find out," he said and escorted me to his condo.

Chapter 42: Conner

Friday, November 29

The five of us were sitting in the formal dining room at my country estate. Cassiel was regaling Kelsey with the humorous parts of raising Charlie and me. We were departing tomorrow, and as I peered around the table, it was hard to believe our trip was ending and that the outcome had exceeded my expectations. *Agatha was right. Everything worked out.*

I had had a few fleeting thoughts of proposing on this trip but decided against it. I knew Kelsey wanted me to meet Abuela, and I felt that I needed to respect her relationship with Abuela and wait until after that meeting. No matter what Kelsey said, I knew that she leaned on her grandmother more than she cared to admit. I wanted her abuela's approval, as much as Kelsey had wanted Cassiel's.

When Cassiel's story ended, Kelsey cleared her throat and asked, "Is it possible for us to have children?" She was looking directly at Cassiel when she asked the question. Clearly, she had picked up on the fact that Cassiel knew the most about Fien bonds out of our group. Though I was moderately surprised she felt comfortable enough with my parents to ask the question directly.

Cassiel laid his hands flat on the table, and I saw his jaw momentarily tighten, then relax. "I wish I had a useful answer for you,

Kelsey, but I don't. As I'm sure Conner told you, Fien bonds are extremely rare and have rules of their own. Since each pairing is unique and as far as I know there has never been one between an angel and a human, only time and your personal choice will tell us if you can have children. But it pleases me to know that you are thinking of your future with Conner, and I ... *we* would love nothing more than to see you have children together."

My father's voice entered my mind. *"You might want to make sure she knows that you physically cannot sire a child until you're married under our laws. That is one rule that a Fien bond can't disobey—at least not if an angel is part of the bond."*

"I will make sure we have that discussion," I replied.

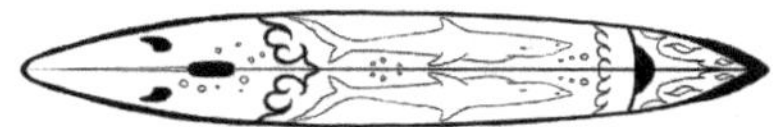

I lay awake in bed while Kelsey slept wrapped in my arms. My father's warning about marriage was in many ways a blessing. I doubted human contraceptives would prevent me from siring a child with Kelsey, even with her on birth control pills. The issue was going to be that an angel marriage ceremony was different than a human one, with a magical aspect. Traditionally, humans were not allowed to enter the Ash Realm, so I prayed that the Fien bond would nullify that requirement since our marriage ceremony would have to take place there.

The idea of having children with Kelsey filled me with a happiness I hadn't expected. I had resisted the idea of marriage to another angel for so long, I think I had also assumed I would never have children either.

I must have dozed off when Kelsey's alarm started buzzing. She had insisted on setting it to ensure she had plenty of time to pack her things before we were due at the airport.

"Good morning," I said and gave her a light kiss.

She smiled, then gave me a gentle push. "I need to pack. As much as I'd love to spend the morning in bed with you, *again*, I need a dose of reality ... I have work on Monday."

"You could always quit," I suggested playfully.

Kelsey smacked me a lot harder, this time on the arm. "I am not giving up my dream just so I can spend days at a time in bed. Besides, are you going to quit your job too?"

I stole another kiss and then shot out of bed before she could retaliate. "I wasn't planning on it. Though I think you've jump-started the morning with the conversation I wanted to have on the plane, my love. How about you finish packing, and I'll scrounge up some breakfast?"

"It's a deal," Kelsey replied.

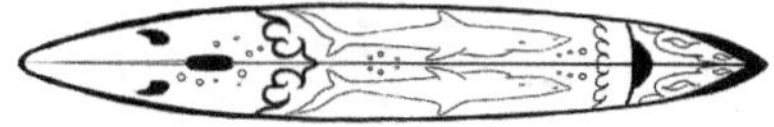

We settled into our seats on the plane. Kelsey had chosen to sit across from me, which I had to admit made it easier to have a conversation. Worry crept into my thoughts that we were not ready to have a conversation about the future. Maybe we should wait longer.

Diane brought us lemonade and then vanished up front.

Kelsey nudged me with her foot. "You said you wanted to talk when we got on the plane. Well, Conner, we are now on the plane. Are you going to wait until we get off to have the conversation?"

I blew out my breath. She was right. If we truly felt as we said about each other, then this was a natural progression of our relationship. "The topic came up a bit last night and this morning, but I wanted to discuss the future. Namely what your deepest desires are and how I fit into that."

Kelsey reached for her glass, then set her hand back in her lap, meeting my gaze. "I am happy to share my thoughts on those matters with you, as long as you also share yours. Perhaps we can alternate so we both answer the same question."

"We can do that. Why don't you choose the first question?" I suggested, hoping that letting Kelsey steer the discussion would help both of us relax.

Kelsey gave me a sweet smile. "Of course. I have always wanted children, as you might have guessed, since I asked Cassiel about it last night. It is a need that I have considered using a sperm donor or potentially adoption to fulfill once I complete my fellowship. I would love to have two if I had a partner to help raise them. I never had a sibling, and there are times I wished I did. Do you want children?"

I took a sip of my lemonade, staring into the glass and trying to collect my thoughts. Of all the questions Kelsey had to choose from, she chose the one I was least certain about. "I don't know if I want children. I've spent a good portion of my life waiting for my ascension and the ability to get out from under Cassiel's thumb. What I do know is that if it's important to you, I would be willing to try."

Kelsey made a face. "Try? Is that 'try to get pregnant' or 'try to be a father'? I seriously hope it's 'try to get pregnant,' because if we go down that road *together*, then you must be willing to be a father. Not just try and walk away if it's not the right fit for you."

I set the cup down and reached across the table to snag one of Kelsey's hands. "I'm sorry if you took it that way. I would never walk out on you or our child. But ... there is a key thing that could be a problem."

"Oh?" murmured Kelsey.

The engines of the plane revved. I retracted my hand and sat back in my chair, not wanting to be awkwardly over the top of the table when we took off in the next minute or two. It also gave me a chance to debate the best way to say it; then I decided there was no *best* way. "Angels cannot procreate until we are married."

The plane accelerated, and we barreled down the runway. Then, the nose of the plane rose, and we lifted into the air.

Kelsey shifted in her seat, then replied, "A built-in birth control. That's convenient."

"It's not that simple. Our laws require marriage to happen in the Ash Realm. Humans are forbidden to enter, and you're human. There is a possibility the Fien bond changes things and would allow you to enter. You certainly had no issues entering The Dapper Lamb," I explained.

"I don't understand," Kelsey responded.

"The Dapper Lamb is technically in the Ash Realm, not in the human world. Which is why there is a magical barrier preventing humans from entering. The fact that Mavin was able to open the barrier and you walked through leads me to believe that you are the exception," I said.

Kelsey took a sip of her lemonade as the plane leveled out. "I see. Let's speculate that I am not able to enter the Ash Realm, which would keep you sterile. Would you be open to the possibility of using a sperm donor or adopting a child?"

"Of course, but either way, I must point out that if we go down the path of becoming parents we will have to decide how we are handling my immortality. Not a topic for now, but as we said earlier, this is a chance for us to talk about the future. I don't want to mislead you, Kelsey, into what it means to stay with me," I said.

"Thank you," Kelsey replied. "On to the next question ... our careers. I will go first because I want to make sure you're perfectly clear. I am not giving up my dream. I want to be a pediatric surgeon, and I don't care how much money you have, I don't want to be a housewife to a billionaire."

I chuckled at her bluntness. I hadn't expected her to say anything else on this topic. "The offer will always stand that you don't have to work, but it's one of the things I love about you. The passion you have for becoming a pediatric surgeon is awe-inspiring. As far as my own work, the only hospital that currently needs a more hands-on approach is LACH. Typically, it takes about a year or so for me to get a hospital on the new track, and then I can have a much more hands-off approach. Due to the nature of my work—managing demons who run hospitals—it would be tricky to quit."

"Why would you quit?" Kelsey demanded.

I shrugged. "The fact you mentioned ... that I'm a billionaire.

I don't have to work to have money to sustain us, Kelsey. If you ever decided you wanted to disappear from the world for a while, technically I can make that happen."

Kelsey wrinkled her nose. "While I might enjoy a long vacation on occasion, I don't see ever wanting to disappear. My friends and family would worry."

Kelsey had brought up the two larger topics, but there were more finite details that had to be laid out. "Do you have any thoughts on timing?"

Kelsey studied me as though deciding if she knew what I meant or not. After several minutes of silence, she replied, "I never expected to fall head over heels for you while I was doing everything I could to stay focused on my fellowship. Assuming if by 'timing' you mean getting married, I am afraid that if we take that step before I complete the fellowship and the pediatric surgery boards, I will lose sight of my objective. Part of me worries that we're rushing things ... I don't know of anyone who talks about marriage after dating for less than a month. I also want to make sure that *I* am the reason I complete the fellowship and pass my boards. I don't want our relationship to influence it and have coworkers wonder if I got a free ride because of who you are."

I steepled my hands together. "I understand where you're coming from. I can only promise that I will not intentionally influence or interfere with your fellowship or board test. I was taking steps to ensure our relationship has been discreet when we're at the hospital. That will not change."

Diane appeared with a pitcher of lemonade to refill our cups and a charcuterie board. Kelsey selected piece of prosciutto and cheese to nibble on. Comfortable silence fell around us.

Chapter 43: Kelsey

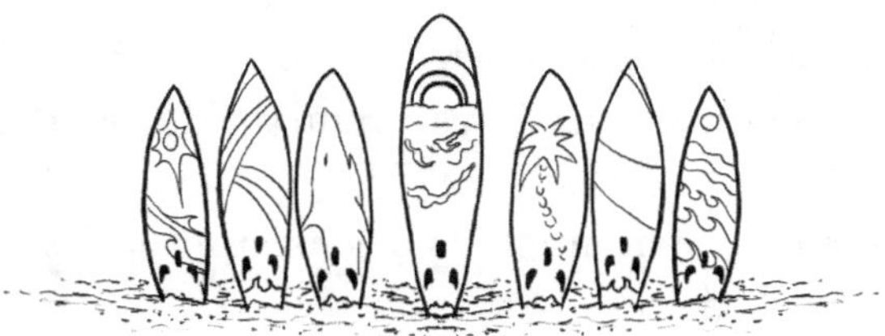

Monday, December 2

For an immortal, Conner knew a surprising amount of things about humans, including the best way to prevent one from suffering severe jet lag. Which was how I found myself at six a.m. Monday morning, bright-eyed and bushy-tailed, ready to take on three pre-operation appointments for Dr. Sinclair's high school students who had scheduled orthopedic surgeries over the next three weeks leading up to Christmas.

Conner was scheduled to be at the hospital all week over-seeing the security system upgrades. I had a fairly normal twelve-hour-a-day schedule for the next seven days, and Conner had agreed to stay at my apartment so we could spend the nights together and he wouldn't have to worry about his commute either.

I was sitting at a desk at the nurses' station reviewing my case notes when the lights flickered. I glanced over at Ronda, who was entering cases into the computer from the graveyard shift.

"Did they say anything about upgrading the power today too?" I asked.

Ronda shook her head. "Nope. Just the security system. Probably the power company. I'm sure we'll be fine."

I was halfway through the case notes for my second appointment when the power shut off and stayed off.

"The generators should kick on," Ronda said confidently.

We waited in silence. I glanced at the clock on the wall, which was analog and not tied to the power. It was 7:05 a.m.

"How long should we wait before investigating?" I asked. Ronda had worked here for years. I was certain she'd experienced power outages.

"It's been over five minutes. The generators are usually pretty fast," Ronda replied.

I debated if I should call Conner and ask him what was going on. I didn't want to have to go to him every time there was a small problem I had to deal with at work, not after telling him I truly wanted to be independent and hold my own job.

Ronda and I waited. A few nurses passed by, but they didn't give us any news. I was about to call Conner, since it was 7:20 a.m. and the power was still off, when my cell phone rang. Conner's number flashed on the screen.

"Hey!" I said, hoping he'd have an answer.

"I need you to meet me in supply room five," Conner replied.

"The one in basement level three?" I asked, confused. We'd never met in the basement before on purpose.

"Yes. The power is out, and I need to give you more details, but remember how we talked about getting you a secure phone?" he asked.

"Mmhmm," I replied.

"Well, we haven't done that yet, so I can't tell you what's going on. We need to meet in person," Conner explained.

"Okay. I will have to take the stairs. I should be able to be down there in five minutes," I responded.

"See you soon," Conner said, then hung up.

"I was asked to check the transformer in basement level three," I told Ronda, creating a half-truthful excuse to leave.

"Okay. Take the flashlight. The stairs get really dark!" Ronda said and handed me a flashlight that she kept in her desk drawer for emergencies.

I walked over to the door to the stairs and pulled it open. The door swung shut with a loud click behind me. I turned on the flashlight and descended the five flights of stairs to basement level three.

I emerged from the stairway into a pitch-black hallway. None of the basement levels had any windows, and apparently they didn't have any battery-powered lights either. Making my way slowly to the middle of the hallway, I checked each door sign until I reached supply room five. I pulled the door open and cautiously stepped inside, swinging my flashlight in an arc.

"Conner?" I called.

A shadow reared up out of the darkness, and then blackness swallowed me.

Chapter 44: Conner

Monday, December 2

The power went out when we were in the middle of testing the third door we'd installed on level one. We moved on to the next door. I knew the generators would kick on, and none of the door installs required power to complete. We only needed it to test the badge readers.

When the installation for the fourth door was completed, I checked my watch. It was seven thirty a.m., and the generators had not kicked in. I had a two-person installation team with me at this end of the floor, and there were three other crews, one in each of the wings.

"I am going to see what is going on with the generators," I informed Sam. He was the head of the construction team I'd hired to install the doors and perform any other structural updates to the building that would be needed in the next six months.

"We will continue here, Dr. Hudson," Sam replied.

I departed and headed for the stairwell. The generators were on the roof. Opening the stairwell door, I confirmed that no one else was present, and I transported myself using magic to the top of the stairwell at the door that led to the roof. I tried the doorknob and it seemed stuck. I slammed my shoulder against it, and it still would not budge. Frowning, I placed my hand around the doorknob and pushed my magic into the door. The door blasted outward and skidded across the concrete roof about fifteen feet before clattering to a halt. I stepped through the destroyed doorway and turned around. There were wide metal straps on the frame that I assumed had been used by someone to prevent anyone from coming through the door. *Who would do such a thing?*

Then, it dawned on me. The attack at CM Hospital had been an immortal. We'd never found the culprit, and presumably he or she was still out there. *Or here.* I rushed around the corner from the door to where the generators were, except they were gone, as though they'd never been there at all. While a human might be able to attach metal straps to the door, the generators had both been the size of a medium car. A human couldn't easily remove those undetected, but there were quite a few immortals who could make an object vanish into thin air.

I took a deep breath. I knew what I had to do: warn my father.

"LACH is currently under attack," I said. I wasn't entirely sure where he was going to be this week. He'd made a few offhand comments about meetings in Boston and in Dubai, but I had been unclear if they were in person or remote.

"You're an archangel now. I'm sure you can handle whatever is going on without my assistance," Cassiel responded. Then, the connection between us was cut off. I sighed, knowing he was likely right, but at least now he had a warning. Pulling out my phone, I called Kelsey. Her phone went straight to voicemail. I left her a brief message and then called Azinak.

"Conner, do you know what's going on with the generators?" Azinak asked.

"Yes, I'm up on the roof. They're gone," I replied.

"Gone?" Azinak questioned.

"Yes, as though they were never there. A human wouldn't be able to move them, not without help, and someone would have noticed. Which means that there is an immortal behind this," I said calmly.

"I will notify the board and have everyone who is here in the hospital move to the safe room. Do you need help looking for the immortal?" Azinak asked.

I frowned. I knew his offer was genuine, but it was quite possible he was the target, and helping me would not keep him safe. "I'm fine for now. I'll let you know if that changes."

"As you wish," replied Azinak, then ended the call.

I decided I would make my way through the hospital looking for the attacker and continuing to try to reach Kelsey. Deep down, I knew it was quite possible she had been in the middle of a surgery when the power went out and was now scrambling in the dark.

I made my way methodically, checking every room, level by level. Twice I tried Kelsey's cell phone with no luck. The more time that passed without finding evidence of the immortal or getting a response from Kelsey, the more I felt my magic pushing against me, wanting an outlet. With iron control, I kept the magic in check and searched.

Even moving fast, it took two hours before I reached the nurses' station for the pediatric surgery floor. I heard Ronda Fitzpatrick's authoritative voice coming from the break room and headed there. The formidable woman was a gold mine of information.

"Ms. Fitzpatrick?" I called as I pushed open the door to the break room.

Ronda turned toward me in surprise. "Dr. Hudson! What are you doing down here?"

"Trying to resolve the power outage issue. Have you by any chance seen Dr. Floras? Dr. Malcom was trying to reach her about a critical matter and asked me to pass the word on."

Ronda shook her head. "I'm sorry, Dr. Hudson. I haven't seen Dr. Floras since she went down to the basement to check on the transformer. In fact," she said, checking her watch, "that was over three hours ago. She should have returned by now."

Schooling my face into an expression of neutrality, I replied as calmly as I could. "Thank you, Ms. Fitzpatrick. I will head down there now and see if she needs any assistance."

"We appreciate your concern, Dr. Hudson. Most of the board members are not like you. They don't care about us folk down here," Ronda said.

I forced a smile on my face. "You're welcome. Now let me see what I can do about getting the power back on!"

Walking out of the break room calmly took all of my self-control. I could not afford to reveal my true self to the humans, which meant I had to behave as they expected. Even though it only took a few minutes to get to the staircase, it felt like more hours had passed. Kelsey had gone to the basement three hours ago and hadn't returned. All my instincts screamed that something had happened to her.

The darkness in the staircase might hinder human eyesight, but I could see perfectly. I ran down the stairs, taking them three or four at a time. Without knowing what I was heading into, I was reluctant to use my magic to transport myself down there and go in completely blind. I stopped my breakneck speed when I was at the bottom of the stairwell, facing the door to basement level three.

I created a shield around myself with my magic, then cautiously opened the door. The hallway was silent, and my footsteps echoed. I frowned. So much for surprising whoever was down here.

I checked the room with the transformer first. It was at the end of the hallway closest to me and a logical place to start. But no one was in there. However, the cables had been severed, making it the source of the power outage. I debated my next move. The hospital needed power to operate. Lives were at risk every minute we were without it. I pulled out my phone and called Azinak, keeping my voice quiet.

"The cables to the transformer have been cut. Give me thirty minutes, and then send someone down here to take care of it," I ordered.

"I can send someone now," Azinak offered.

"No," I growled. "Too risky." I hung up on him and silenced my phone, praying he would follow my instructions.

Returning to the hallway, I checked each room but came up empty-handed time and again. I was about halfway down the hallway. The door to storage room 3B was a few paces away. I set my hand on the handle when something plowed straight into me, launching me into the air. I hit my head on the low ceiling and fell to the ground, not quick enough to get my feet under me.

The hallway was glowing with magic. Calling my glaive, I found comfort as its oak shaft filled my hand. I rose and was shocked to see Octavio facing me in the hallway, a large broadsword in his hand. Octavio's black wings were spread wide behind him, his bright gold eyes were wild with emotion, and his mouth was in an angry scowl. He was wearing doctor's scrubs, which explained how he'd gotten into the hospital undetected.

"What are you doing?" I asked, raising the glaive to block Octavio's vicious strike.

The hallway gave us precious little room to maneuver. I backed up a step as I worked on a strategy to neutralize Octavio.

Instead of answering my question, Octavio charged, sword aiming for my stomach. I scooted to the side and he rushed past me. I shot a bolt of magic at his back and sent him sprawling. The sword slipped from his hand and spun out of reach. Octavio flipped over and flung threads of black magic toward me.

Holding the glaive in front of me, I spun it like a baton, pushing magic into it. The black threads hit the glaive and bounced back toward Octavio, then fizzled out.

Suddenly, Octavio fell forward onto his knees. My eyes widened as the power turned back on and the hallway regained its lighting. Cassiel, face red from anger, had a black boot firmly planted in Octavio's back. Cassiel's pure white magic wrapped around Octavio, and Octavio's wings disappeared from view as his human appearance fell back into place.

With a flick of his wrist, Cassiel had Octavio on his knees, hands bound behind his back. Keeping one eye on the hallway and one on my father, I waited to see what he was going to do.

"Octavio, you are found guilty of attacking a hospital with the intention of causing harm to humans. What do you have to say for yourself?" Cassiel said harshly.

Octavio spit at Cassiel's feet. "You have never treated me as was my due. You call me third-in-command yet I'm nothing more than an errand boy allowing you to keep your wings clean."

Cassiel's jaw tightened, but he did not respond. I decided to take matters into my own hands.

"Where's Kelsey?" I snarled. Only Cassiel's presence kept me from pummeling Octavio.

"Your little bitch is not harmed ... too much," Octavio said and laughed.

Confident my father had Octavio under control, I sprinted down the hallway toward the storage room I had been about to enter when Octavio attacked me.

I could feel traces of Octavio's magic around the door that had been hidden previously. With a bit of magic, I burst the door open. Kelsey was sitting between two shelves tied to a chair with a gag in her mouth, head lolling to the side.

"Kelsey!" I shouted, falling to my knees in front of her.

Her eyes opened. They were bloodshot, and dried tears stained her face. I gently removed the gag from her mouth and untied her.

"Is it over?" she whispered.

I gathered her in my arms. "Yes. It's over. Cassiel has Octavio in custody."

"You called me and told me to come down here, except you weren't here. Octavio was," Kelsey said as she shook in my arms. I wanted to take her to my house and comfort her, but I had responsibilities to the hospital.

Kelsey and I exited the storage room. Cassiel was waiting for us in the hallway. There was no sign of Octavio or our fight.

"I'm glad you're okay, Kelsey," Cassiel said roughly.

"Me too," she said softly.

"Conner, why don't you take her home. I'll help Azinak sort things out here," Cassiel offered.

I couldn't hide my surprise, especially after my initial call for help when he told me to handle everything on my own. "Okay, but we should talk later."

"Of course," Cassiel said in dismissal.

Not needing another suggestion to leave, I wrapped my arms around Kelsey and, using my magic, transported us to my Malibu house.

Chapter 45: Kelsey

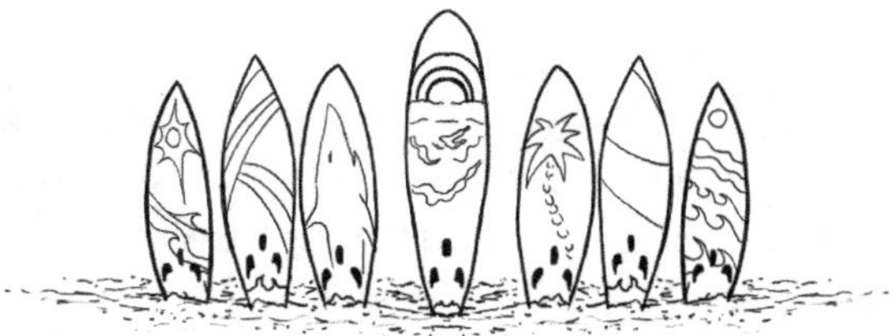

Tuesday, December 24

I was standing in Conner's garage at his Malibu house staring at his assortment of cars. After some negotiation, Conner had agreed we could drive to Santa Barbara to visit Abuela for Christmas as long as we took his car. Except now we were discussing cars again—which one to take.

"The Revuelto is the most fun to drive," Conner said candidly.

I shook my head. "I thought we were still trying to stay under the radar. Your Revuelto practically screams who you are anywhere you go. Is there something wrong with your SUV?"

Conner sighed. "No. It's just not as fun to drive. But you're right; it does blend in much better than anything else in here. The Audi it is." He snagged the keys off the hook and pushed the button to make the trunk pop open. I slid my purple suitcase in the back, then opened the passenger door and climbed in.

Conner slid into the driver's seat and started the SUV. Turning onto the Pacific Coast Highway, we headed north toward Santa Barbara. I leaned back in the seat, thinking of the past three and a half weeks since the attack on the hospital and my short stint as a hostage. I was still jumpy, thinking every time I turned a corner someone was going to grab me. The only time I found I could let the fear go was when I was working with a patient, in surgery, or with Conner.

One of the hardest things about the whole hostage ordeal was that we had to lie to my coworkers. No one could know I was held hostage. The story we came up with was I'd found the cut cables and had called Dr. Malcom and was given instructions to wait down in the basement for the electrician to arrive to do the repairs. Thankfully, no one had questioned the story.

"You're very quiet," Conner said, glancing at me.

"I'm fine. I'm looking forward to this year being over," I replied.

Conner raised my hand to his lips and kissed it. "I'm sure three days of surfing and visiting your Abuela will help."

I gave him a slight smile, knowing he was right. Surfing solved everything, and I was looking forward to finally introducing him to Abuela.

The drive was beautiful. The highway hugged the ocean, though the view was occasionally blocked by cliffs. It was far more enjoyable than driving through the valley.

When we were within the Santa Barbara city limits, Conner had the GPS provide directions to Abuela's house. Now that we were mere minutes away, I found I was getting nervous. Butterflies filled my stomach. I rubbed my arms, reminding myself that Abuela had been just as excited as I was for her to meet Conner.

Conner parked next to Abuela's burgundy Packard, and we got out. I used my key to go inside. I assumed Abuela was working on lunch since I'd told her we'd be there around lunchtime.

"Hello!" I called, leading the way down the hallway toward the front of the house.

"Hola!" Abuela replied. We emerged from the hallway and saw her setting a platter of tamales on the table, which was already set.

As soon as her hands were free, I rushed forward and hugged her fiercely. She returned the embrace, then stepped back, keeping her arms on mine and gazing at me.

"I missed you, Nieta."

"I missed you too, Abuela," I replied and hugged her again.

Conner coughed behind me. I blushed, remembering my manners and withdrew from Abuela's embrace. "Abuela, this is my boyfriend, Conner Hudson. Conner, this is my abuela."

To my surprise, Conner bowed formally and spoke, "Es un honor conocerte, Abuela."

I gasped as he greeted Abuela in Spanish, a language I had not been aware he knew. Abuela beamed and replied, "¿Tienes hambre?"

"Yes! We're starving," I replied. I had no idea how much Spanish Conner knew, but my stomach let out a loud, embarrassing rumble, causing Abuela to give me a knowing look.

"Sit, eat. Then we can talk," Abuela said.

"Thank you," replied Conner, then proceeded to pull a chair out for Abuela and then me before seating himself.

Companionable silence filled the room as we ate the tamales. I could tell from the way Abuela was glancing at Conner that there was much she wished to talk about. Which was why I was glad we had decided to stay for two nights. As an apology for the hostage situation, Dr. Malcom—whom I had recently learned was actually a demon named Azinak—had given me Christmas and the two days before off.

As soon as Conner finished eating, Abuela declared herself full too and peppered him with questions, mostly asking about his work and family. I knew she was trying to get a sense of who he was without my opinion coloring things. I polished off my third tamale and stood up. I collected the plates and silverware and retreated to the kitchen. I couldn't help but smile when whatever they were talking about made Abuela laugh.

When I finished washing the dishes and putting them in the cupboard, Abuela came into the kitchen and set her hand on my arm. "You did good, Nieta. I can tell he loves you very much."

"I love him too," I replied.

She smiled at me. "Then make sure he knows it. Your parents had love like this. I am glad you have found it too."

"I love you, Abuela," I replied and hugged her.

She waved me off. "Now go surfing, silly girl."

I kissed her cheek. "Yes, we will go surfing. We'll be back in time for dinner, I promise."

Abuela shooed me out of the kitchen instead of responding.

I went into my bedroom and shut the door behind me. Conner had set our suitcase on the bed. I chose one of the two swimsuits I'd packed and put it on, then pulled on a pair of blue board shorts and slid my feet into flip-flops that were in the closet. There was a light tap on the door.

"Come in!" I called and turned toward it.

Conner walked through. He was wearing black swim shorts with a royal blue stripe across the thigh and a white button-up linen shirt. "The surfboards are loaded up. I'm ready if you're ready."

"Then let's go!"

Conner didn't enter an address into the GPS, and at first I thought he was going to one of the beaches we'd surfed at last time we were in Santa Barbara together, but he drove past the turnoff.

"Are you lost?" I asked. I had a pretty good idea of where we were, but I had no idea where he was trying to take us.

"No, Abuela suggested a different surfing spot. One you haven't used in years," Conner responded.

Intrigued, I stayed silent, mulling over what surfing spot we could be going to and drawing a blank. Conner pulled into a small parking lot that was on top of a cliff.

"We're here," he announced.

My eyes widened as I recognized where we were. When Penny and I were twelve, Abuela had found us here and forbidden us to come back. The hike down to the beach was precarious, especially if you were packing a surfboard. I was surprised Abuela had recommended coming here.

"I'll carry the surfboards," Conner informed me.

"Okay. I'll carry the towels," I replied, not wanting to make Conner carry everything on our hike down.

He unstrapped the surfboards and hiked them over his shoulder. I tucked the towels into a beach bag from the trunk, and we began our trek down the trail. It was much steeper and rockier than I remembered. Conner was ahead of me and seemed oblivious to it. I, on the other hand, was feeling every step through my burning calves. He rounded the bend and disappeared out of sight. Instead of rushing after him, I kept my pace even.

The trail leveled out, and I knew I was close to the beach as the gravel gave way to cream-colored sand. I passed through two large gray rock formations standing like sentinels guarding the way up the treacherous path.

I froze in my tracks as I saw a trail of red rose petals meandering across the sand toward the water. Clutching the towels, I followed the rose petals, heart hammering in my chest, my hands clammy. At the bottom of the small sand dune, Conner was waiting for me, standing in the surf. As I closed the distance between us, I could feel tingles along my skin that I had come to recognize as part of the Fien bond's magic. When I was a few feet away, red rose petals in the shape of a heart appeared in the damp sand around us.

Conner dropped to one knee in front of me, holding up a ring. My breath caught in my throat as I realized what was happening.

"Kelsey, from the moment we first met, I knew there was something special about you. When we are together, I feel complete, as though you are the missing piece that I've spent my entire life searching for. I love you, Kelsey, and would be honored if you will be my wife," Conner said, his voice full of emotion, his eyes locked with mine.

I dropped to my knees in front of him. "Yes!" I kissed him, knowing deep down that this was also what I had been waiting for, even if I had never known it.

When we stopped for air, Conner took my left hand in his and slipped the ring on my finger. A huge heart-shaped blue stone was in the center, framed by smaller gems that I was confident were diamonds. The edge of the band was engraved with ocean waves.

"It's beautiful," I said, then added, "Not very practical for a surgeon."

Conner chuckled. "I have a solution for that." He pulled another ring out of his pocket and laid it on the palm of his hand. It was a simple band of white gold engraved with waves.

Warmth filled me. "I love you."

"I love you too," Conner replied.

I lost track of time as we sat there on the sand gazing at each other. Eventually, I came to my senses. "Are we still surfing?"

"Of course," Conner said with a smile.

Side by side, we carried our surfboards out into the ocean.

About the author

E.R. Jensen was born and raised in Los Angeles, California. She has lived in Oregon and Idaho, and currently resides in Atlanta, GA with her husband and three sons. A Swell to Remember is her 6th adult book to be published and first paranormal romance.

When not writing E.R. can be found enjoying her horses, traveling, and spending time with her family.

Also by

<u>Twisted Talent Series:</u>
Hoodwinked in Hotlanta
Spellbound in Spud City
<u>The Lost Fae Queen Trilogy"</u>
Throne of Dusk
Heir of Blood
Crown of Emeralds